The Blackout

MANY DEATHS IN THE MULTIVERSE BOOK ONE

Christopher Zammit

For Karen,
Whose love, support and encouragement made
such a daunting task possible.
This layer of the Multiverse and all those that
surround it, are for you.

Table of Contents

Prologue
A drop in temperature

Over the Mojave Desert, Utah

5.43am - Monday, December 28th, 2048

Kyle Ferine stared into the darkness of the aircraft's cargo hold as it bumped and shook its way across the sky. The sound of wind and snow striking the airframe woke him from his dreams of death, destruction and the imminent end of the world. All around him, the floor was littered with the bodies of sleeping men. The repetitive bass hum of the engines and the proximity of many warm bodies had lulled most onboard into a restless, disturbed sleep. From one end of the cargo hold to the other, soldiers lay on the grease-stained deck in full body armour with warm weather clothing and insulation jackets shoved under their heads as pillows.

The few men who were unable to sleep busied themselves with routine tasks of checking gear, weapons, and ammunition. A few whispered to their mates about their kids, their wives, their dogs or reminisced about the last drinking session they had shared. Like Ferine, others sat and stared at nothing with faraway looks as they contemplated their fates, their futures and the loved ones that waited for them in the new world.

Looking around and seeing everything was as it should be, Ferine let his mind wander once again to the global disaster and the chain of events that had made this mission necessary. He'd gone over it a million times in the weeks since the Blackout... and the announcement. He knew the answer as well as anybody, probably better. He knew the inside story because he was there at the beginning when the whole thing kicked off. He was a key player in the end of the world, and he hadn't even realised until after it had happened.

Deciding his time could be better spent. Captain Kyle Ferine climbed to his feet and made his way through the dimly lit cargo hold towards the aircraft's tail. There were sixty Australian and New Zealand troops aboard for the rescue mission; one platoon of thirty men from each nation. At the completion of the task, they would become the first combined ANZAC force to initiate hostilities for over one hundred years. Those who knew of the mission – and there were very few who did – felt a surge of pride at the old ANZAC spirit being revived by this new generation of men. Tears filled the eyes of many hardened military leaders on seeing the rising sun badge pinned to a traditional slouch hat for the first time. This icon from the past had been transposed into the present to stand as a symbol of hope, strength, freedom, and for some, revenge. The fact that it was perched atop a modern uniform of resin coated body armour and twenty-first-century military attire did little to detract from the effect. There was no mistaking that the spirit of the ANZAC which had been born in the trenches of World War One had lasted through the years. The legend that spoke of brotherhood, bravery, and sacrifice was about to be reborn. A surge of nationalistic pride was predicted from the occupants of both countries when - and if - the mission was ever announced.

"Can I have your attention, please?" Ferine called. There was a stir of activity as the men in the cargo hold shook their sleeping comrades awake and began to rise to their feet. When everyone was standing, when he had everyone's attention, Ferine began.

"You men know better than anyone why we are about to do this. Australia and New Zealand have always been peaceful nations that have had little or no interest in global power struggles and world domination. For decades the world watched while the corporations of the US systematically bullied, bribed and invaded other countries into joining its self-proclaimed Empire. The world held its breath as an impotent U.N. stood by and watched nation after nation be taken over by a self-serving conglomerate of corporations that had little respect for human lives, let alone human rights." Ferine paused for a moment to observe the heads of his soldiers nodding in agreement.

"Australia and New Zealand stood by passively and did nothing because we were supposed to be their friends. Well, we soon learned that that didn't count for anything when the Imperial military, the good old U.S of A, our so-called allies, decided to invade us and level Sydney to the ground." Disgusted headshakes and a few choice profanities floated from the troops.

Ferine decided to turn it up a notch. With his voice raised, he began to speak again. "They attacked us and killed innocent people who had no other interest than to move their families to safety before the coming disaster could bring them to harm." Ferine paced back and forth as he spoke.

"They will pay for the damage they caused us at the battle of Sydney." He called over the troops cheering.

"We gave as good as we got on that day and we'll give them back, even more, this time." Ferine paused to give the new ANZACS a moment to express their feelings.

"But, we're not like them. Our disagreement is not with the American people. We won't bomb civilians as they do; we won't hurt the innocent as they do. We will go out of our way to ensure that anybody who is not wearing a military uniform goes unharmed. We are at war with the Imperial government, not with their people. We represent the ANZAC spirit, so we won't sink to their level of violence, and we won't walk away while they hold our friends, and our families captive!"

The flashing of the warning light caught Ferine's attention. Instantly he knew that they had reached their destination and it was nearly time to leave the transport.

"Alright, team!" Ferine called out.

"We now have less than five minutes to get in position. Grab your gear, find your place and do a quick - and I do mean quick - inspection of your buddies kit. There's no time left now for farting about. Just remember what we practised, and it will all go to plan. Hop to it; you know what to do."

Around him, men clambered to their feet while others dropped to pick up equipment or redress themselves in their bulkier layers of cold weather clothing. An air of anticipation bordering on excitement had arisen. Satisfied that things were going to plan,

Ferine turned and spoke to Captain Austin who stood waiting beside him.

"Make sure the point guys are weighed down with enough supplies and ammo to give them a good head start. I want that mustering area in place before the rest of us hit, OK?"

"Will do. It's a shame you're not dropping in with the point group. You're gonna miss a lot of the action." Austin replied.

Ferine shook his head and smiled. "Trust me; I've seen enough action over the last few weeks to last me a lifetime."

Austin smiled in return and gave a knowing nod. He had seen what Ferine and the ANZAR initiative had gone through on TV. As he watched the Captain leave, he marvelled at how he had come to be working with the man whose recent actions had saved billions of lives.

"Point team, this is the flight commander." Ferine heard through his headset as he stepped beside the rear door of the aircraft. "You are go for point team drop on my mark."

With that, a large opening in the side of the jet slid aside in an explosion of wind and ice. The temperature inside the plane dropped considerably as a strong, icy breeze, began to whip through the cabin. Almost as if they'd forgotten it was cold outside, the men zipped up their jackets as far as they would go and turned on the heating in their thermal underwear. For the first few seconds, the frigid air came as a welcome change from the stifling heat that the team had endured for much of the flight. The freshness of it cleared away the last of the sleep that fogged their minds. Friends turned to each other and swapped sheepish grins as the concept of what they were about to do became a reality.

Huddled around the door like kids at an ice-cream truck, the point team was soon lost in a veil of snow and condensation; loose equipment flapped around in the breeze and was quickly crusted with fine flakes of ice.

"Point team, you are go for egress, good luck." The Commander finished in his formal businesslike tone that all military personnel seemed to use when giving orders over a radio.

Within seconds the six men on point had disappeared out the door. It happened so fast you could almost wonder if they had ever been there at all. Snow billowed through the empty door more fiercely without the natural barrier of the soldier's bodies in the way.

"Get that door closed," Ferine called to no one in particular. A stout looking soldier of Japanese ancestry gave a quick nod, stepped forward and hit the switch to close the hatch. Once again, they were enveloped in a peaceful silence, the last they would experience for a while.

It was time for the rest of the team to do what they came for, and hopefully, go to their new homes once it was done. For the troops, the mission details were as simple as they needed to be, they were to land outside the walls of a research base located approximately 50 miles east of Las Vegas. The location of their target made the whole process all the more bizarre as far as Ferine was concerned. Not just because of his previous close ties with the United States but because this would be the first time since the Helium-3 wars that America had been invaded, and by no less than two platoons of troops from supposedly allied countries.

The facility - as these places were inevitably referred to – was located in open ground that, until recently, had been the Mojave Desert. Now it was set in a landscape that had more in common with Alaska. As was the case with much of the Earth in recent weeks, everything as far as the eye could see was powdered in a heavy covering of snow. What had once been a vista of rich ochres, yellows, and vibrant earth tones was now weather-worn into a muted monochromatic white.

As it was just before sunrise the ANZACS would be difficult to spot on their way to the ground. Anyone who happened to look up would be hard pressed to see the sixty men free falling towards them through the clouds and drifting snow. If things went well, they'd have no time to sound the alarm and get their troops into position before Ferine's men could overrun the base.

But this wasn't to be a regular drop.

The idea was for all the men come down in the same area. Once on the ground, the ANZACS were instructed to lie still, recover and wait. Within a few moments of impact, the signal to attack would be given. At Ferine's command, everyone would stand up and take the base. That was the plan anyway.

The remaining troops fought to keep their balance as the aircraft banked steeply on its way back towards the drop zone. Men grabbed at overhead support straps, the walls, and each other in the effort to keep their feet. Groups of soldiers huddled together with their arms around each other's shoulders in what looked more like an act of emotional, rather than physical support.

Ferine could make out the deep rumble of muffled explosions from outside the aircraft as the plane shook and bounced from the shockwave of each near miss. It quickly became apparent to him that the Americans had had a decent lookout on duty that morning. Evidently, the ANZAC point men had been spotted, the alarm had been sounded, and the defence of the base had begun. Anti-aircraft artillery shells exploded around the transport plane as the ground troops attempted to shoot down a target they could hear but not see. The explosions started softly at first and rose in volume and ferocity as the gunners on the ground came progressively closer to hitting the plane. Many inside the transport lost their footing and fell to the deck as the aircraft rocked and swayed more violently. The men who fell immediately began struggling against the weight of their gear and the motion of the floor as they tried to get back on their feet. Every few seconds another shockwave hit the shell of the plane, causing it to sway and vibrate loudly. The erratic movement made it impossible for many of the men to stand. Some gave up trying and opted for the simple alternative of bracing themselves as best they could on the floor.

Another sound joined the cacophony of noise outside, just as loud but more welcoming. Amongst the explosions and gunfire, the familiar high-pitched reverberation of the RAAF's newest fighter aircraft rose in volume as they pulled alongside. What was officially top-secret craft up until their life-saving debut at the battle of Sydney, the Black Diamonds were wholly Australian designed and built machines. With armoured hulls of engineered diamond and magnetic shields, they were all but impervious to any form of attack. They had boldly just come through the barrage behind the transport and were in no doubt getting ready to take out the heavy guns on the ground. All Ferine's transport needed from them was a little time to drop off the men, turn around and set a new course for home.

With the distraction of the explosions around the transport, nobody inside heard the Flight Commander's countdown or noticed the jump light when it turned green. All the men knew, was that one second they were standing safely in the dark of the cargo hold, the next, they were outside the plane, free-falling amidst a significant air battle. The floor hadn't opened up or slid aside; it had just disappeared.

As one, the men gave surprised gasps as the temperature dropped by eighty degrees. In less than a second, they had gone from the warm inside of the plane's cabin to the freezing high-altitude air. For most, it was a graceless tumbling exit without any form or style. They found themselves hurtling towards the ground as flack and anti-aircraft fire popped and exploded around them. With his little protective bubble of warmth and safety gone, Ferine felt as if he had been dumped into the world and left alone to fend for himself. For him, it was akin to being born again.

The roar of the wind as they rushed towards the frozen Mojave Desert was littered with the sounds of everything from far-away ground explosions to anti-aircraft gunfire. The screams of fighter jets and helicopters faded in and out of hearing as the aircraft flew above, below and around them.

Ferine spied the faint shapes of the buildings where the Australian scientists were being held. Tipping his body forward, he increased his rate of descent, eager to get down to the ground and free the innocent captives.

It would be a quick journey. As none of Ferine's team was wearing parachutes, they would hit the ground in record time.

Travelling at terminal velocity, they would slam into the frozen sands of the Mojave Desert in little over a minute.

As he fell, Ferine's mind briefly reflected on everything that had happened to bring him to this time, to this place, to this situation. His mind wandered back to the events that had started at Gate 23, to the people that had been lost, to the scientist's search for them, and to the snowballing events that had pulled him into its madness and had made him a key player in the abandonment of the Earth.

1

Outside Gate 23

Sir Kingsford Smith Spaceport – Sydney.

7.00am - Monday, July 27th, 2048

A tear ran down Craig's cheek as he stared at the embracing couple. Like an island in a sea of people, they stood oblivious to the crowd of travellers which parted and flowed around them. Both seemed lost in the moment, neither willing to let the other go as they whispered their goodbyes, as they enjoyed the feel of each other in their arms. Sooner than they had hoped, a computerised voice announced the final boarding call for gate twenty-three. Knowing that there was no more time to waste, the woman reluctantly stepped away from her partner and looked sadly into his eyes. She held her arm outstretched, her hand still holding his, reluctant to let go, unwilling to break contact. With a sad smile, she slowly slid her hand from his and turned towards the boarding gate. With a final wave and a sorrowful look at her lover, she wheeled her bag past the smiling stewards and disappeared from view.

Their farewell tauntingly re-enacted a scene from Craig's past; a scene which he wished had never been played.

His chest heaved, and a weak sob escaped his throat as he rose to his feet to stop the woman from leaving. He wanted more than anything to be able to cross the tiled floor, to grab the woman by the shoulders, to shake her, to tell her not to go, to force her to stay here with her family. Craig lifted his foot and took a step forward before eventually coming to his senses. Before anyone could notice, he lowered himself onto the plastic airport seat and grabbed one of the three coffee cups that sat empty on the table beside him. He raised it to his lips with shaking hands and sipped the dregs of the now cold liquid.

That woman wasn't my mother, he thought as his gaze returned to the now empty spot where the couple had stood. In their place, his mind's eye replayed the moment in which the lives of everyone he knew had turned upside-down. Craig could see his younger self-standing with his father, uncle, and cousin outside this very gate as they had said goodbye to the women who had boarded the ill-fated flight. His mother and aunt were only supposed to be visiting America for a few days, but due to some wrong information and an overzealous Homeland Security Chief, they had never returned.

Craig's eyes continued to water as he remembered their rushed farewell on that open expanse of tile, none of them knowing that it would be for the last time. As he played the scene over in his head, he wished that he had said more to his mother in their final moments together. Thinking back, he couldn't even be sure if he had told her that he loved her before she had walked away. He had a vague memory of her bending down to kiss him on the forehead. He could recall glancing at her briefly, almost dismissively, as he continued to discuss the latest *Star Wars* film with his cousin Luke. A frown crossed Craig's brow as he tried to remember the details of that wasted opportunity to tell her how much he cared. He would give anything to have that moment back again, to be able to look her in the eye, to give her all his attention and tell her that she was loved and appreciated, as she deserved. The more he turned that moment over in his mind, the muddier the memories became. Craig *thought* he had told her he loved her, at least, he *hoped* he had. But there was no way to be sure. After all, he was only nine when it had happened.

Struggling to fight off the wave of depression that inevitably arose when he thought about the loss of his mother, Craig tried to think of the coming weeks that would finally put an end to the pain and suffering of the past. If their next experiment bore fruit and everything went to plan, the stain that her loss had left on his life would be removed; cleansed, erased, almost as if it had never happened.

Almost.

A small smile crossed his lips at the thought of seeing his mother again.

The opening stanza of a news report blared from one of the many monitors in the terminal. Craig reluctantly turned his attention away from gate twenty-three. His mind, still filled with memories of loss, struggled to make sense of the jumbled images and information on the screen. As the ABC news cut from the protests in New Zealand to the viral epidemic in Zaire, Craig looked back at gate twenty-three, down at the floor, then at nowhere in particular. With nothing left to do but wait, he took another sip of his cold coffee, raised his left arm, glanced at his watch and then dropped it into his lap with a deep, troubled sigh.

Seven am. She's late, he thought.

Despite the time, Terminal 3 of Sydney's Kingsford Smith Airport was already awash with human traffic. All around him, a dense crowd of people hurried on their way to and from various cities around the world. Suited businesspeople, elderly vacationers, and youthful backpackers struggled to get past exhausted parents who wheeled oversized suitcases and pulled overexcited children through the terminal. Craig watched as a bedraggled looking mum struggled to get two screaming kids past the ice-cream stands and confectionary stores that lined the concourse. The two young boys pulled at their mother's hands and stared longingly at the brightly lit displays of treats that they were being forced to pass by. The grief on their faces mirrored his own as Craig watched them disappear into the crowd.

The TV news once again caught Craig's attention. On screen, the Australian and New Zealand Prime Ministers stood side by side on a podium. With the flags of both nations waving patriotically behind them, they pledged to stand by each other in the face of the recent military threats from the American Empire. What had begun as a trade disagreement over the sharing of technology had steadily deteriorated into a state of mutual distrust after the seizure of an Australian research vessel by the Imperial Navy. The HMS *Gillard* had been in transit between Sydney and Auckland when an American battle group had intercepted it. For reasons still unknown, the lone ship was boarded, the crew detained, and the vessel pillaged. The handful of Australian researchers who had been aboard at the time were currently being held as guests of the American Empire in an - as yet - undisclosed location.

With the New Zealand Prime Minister by her side, the Australian Prime Minister, Kathryn Mundawoy, stood at the podium and spoke harsh words and made firm promises about the future of American – Antipodean relations. Unable to hear everything they were saying, Craig caught enough of the tone to figure that both countries were intending to make a political stand against the old U.S.

Craig's attention was pulled away from the television broadcast by a synthesised female voice which seductively announced that the next QANTAS flight to Newton Station was still due to depart from gate sixteen in just under an hour. In a voice that somehow managed to sound both monotonous and sexy, the Inter-Orbital terminal's notification system wished everyone a good day and fell silent.

With his attention drawn away from the ABC newscast, Craig did another slow scan of the terminal. As if on cue, he spotted Karen as she exited the security area. He smiled to see her dressed in her usual outfit of tight black trousers, V-neck t-shirt, and her favourite black, all-weather, Vinyl Jacket. On seeing her again, it occurred to Craig that she rarely wore anything that varied from this basic style. She had found a look that suited her and, to her credit, had stuck with it. As far as he was concerned, she looked good in whatever she wore. As he watched her draw nearer, Craig couldn't help but admire the cute little bounce in her step. No matter how much he watched her, no matter how familiar he had become with every quirk and nuance of her character, he had never been able to figure out what it was about her walk that made her body move the way it did. She had an endearing and seductive way of bopping along wherever she went. To him, she looked as if she didn't have a care in the world. He couldn't help but envy that.

"Sorry I'm late, babe," Karen said as she drew closer. "The flight was delayed because of this trouble with the Americans.

You wouldn't believe the security checks I had to go through." She greeted him with a brief hug and a quick peck on the lips.

"Don't worry about it." Craig smiled. "You're here now. That's all that matters. How was your week at home with your folks?"

They had both taken two weeks away from the Station to have their first holiday together. They had spent the first week in a small resort in Fiji where they had sat on the beach, drank cocktails and tried hard not to think about work. Neither of them had wanted the time to end, but other obligations had forced them to spend the second week of their vacation apart. Karen had travelled to Perth to visit her ageing parents while Craig had returned to tidy his all but abandoned family home on the outskirts of Sydney in preparation for his family's return.

"It was fine," Karen began. "It was a bit dull after our week away together. I would much rather have spent the extra time with you at that resort."

She transformed her face with a smile as she sat down beside him. It was something he loved to watch every time she did it. When her lips parted, and her mouth stretched back into her patented grin, her eyes lit up, and her face shone, she was transformed into the most beautiful thing he had ever seen.

"But, still. It was good to see mum and dad again," she continued.

A frown crossed Karen's face as she took a moment to study Craig's. After all the time they had spent together, she had become very good at reading his emotions. Just by looking at him she could tell there was something wrong.

"Been thinking about your mum again, haven't you?" she asked as she reached over and took Craig's hand in hers. As she waited for him to respond, she glanced towards the entrance to gate twenty-three and wondered why he would want to put himself through the torture of waiting for her here instead of somewhere else in the terminal.

Craig gave a nervous giggle. With only her touch and her concern, she had managed to lift the dark mood that had so nearly overtaken him.

"C'mon babe, we'd better go find Professor Turp," Craig said in an attempt to change the subject. He rose to his feet and poked his thumb at an especially large duty-free store behind them. "He went into the liquor shop about twenty minutes ago; we better get over there before he empties the place of all their Myer's rum. Knowing him, he'll probably try and carry aboard double the allowed limit for Inter-Orbital flights."

Craig lifted her bag and placed it on his trolley as she fished out her passport and boarding pass.

"I see you're still referring to your Dad as Professor Turp. It'd be nice if you dropped his title once in a while." This was a discussion they had had more than once during their time away from the labs. "I know, I know. It's just a force of habit, babe. I'm required to call him that around the lab, so I guess it sort of stuck."

"I know," she replied as she stood to take his hand once again. "I just worry about the way you two always talk about work and never seem to do any of the other things that a father and son should do."

"Like what? Play soccer on the lawn and go on picnics? We live on a space station remember?" he retorted with an intentional smirk to show that he didn't mean any offence. "I guess I just grew up differently than most kids, but I'm happy with the way things are at the moment. I never miss that Father and son stuff anyway."

No, not now you don't. But you will when he's gone, she thought. "Did he give you a message for me from my boys?" she enquired after Jamie and Timothy, the two precocious and complicated toddlers whom she was employed to care for at the labs. They could be a handful at times, but as much as she enjoyed her time away from work, she found herself missing the children more than she could imagine. She hoped they hadn't fretted over her as much as she had for them while she was away.

"Yeah, Dad said that they were nagging him about a present, a book or something. He said it was to do with dinosaurs."

"Typical, isn't it? I've been worried sick that they'd be traumatised by my going away, but all they care about is if I've gotten them a present." She smiled at the thought of seeing them again.

"I don't think you have to worry about them not missing you, Karen. You did call them every day while we were away." Craig reminded her as they began to walk away from gate twenty-three.

"So, I suppose your dad has been talking your head off with news about how the research went while you were away?" Karen asked as they turned the corner into the main terminal used for all orbital flights. The long walkway was lined with even more duty-free shops, newsagents and food stalls that stood testament to how commonplace space travel had become. The fact that passengers could casually buy a morning paper, skim milk latte and a bran muffin before shooting into orbit demonstrated how for many, it was just another way to commute to the other side of the world. Albeit, a much quicker and more expensive way to get there.

After negotiating their way around a crowd of chatting tourists who were busily debating the difference between red and blue vodka, Craig finally replied to Karen's question.

"Not as such, he did seem a bit excited about it though. Naturally, I asked him how it all went as soon as I met him this morning, but I didn't get much of an answer. He just smiled and said we'd talk about it when we were back on the station."

"Well, what do you make of that then? Do you think he got the results he wanted?" Karen asked.

"It's hard to say, babe. The Professor... Dad has never been one to show his emotions too much, so I don't know how to take what he said. I mean, he did seem excited... for him. So, if I had to say one way or the other based on his research on the Conduit, I'd say the probes must be close to locating the address we're after. I have a lot of faith in my father's ability to get this to work."

"You see, that's nice to hear. It wasn't so hard, was it?" Karen congratulated him.

"What do you mean? I always said I had faith in my father; he's probably the greatest quantum physicist alive today."

"That's not what I meant, silly. That's twice in a row now you've referred to him as your father and not Professor Turp. I think I'm actually getting through to you." Laughing, Karen leant over and took Craig's arm. In one fluid movement, she pulled herself towards him and snuggled into his shoulder.

What they both understood was that they had not only been lovers in for the past two years but were also each other's best friends. Their relationship was made up of a spattering of romance when they could find the time, with a healthy dose of respectful mockery thrown in to stop them taking each other's quirks and faults too seriously.

"C'mon you, the docs in there." Craig pointed to the sales counter of the nearest duty-free store where Professor Turp was in the process of having a large box of alcohol sealed for the flight.

"He's really stocking up on the rum, isn't he?"

Craig stopped and stared at his father. "It doesn't look like Rum," he said to Karen. "That's wine he's buying." Craig turned to Karen with a smile on his face. "That's mum's favourite brand. Things must have gone better than I thought."

The Professor had finished filling the packing crate with a dozen bottles of Shiraz and was waiting for the cashier to complete the transaction. Professor John Turp had a certain air about him that didn't make him instantly recognisable as a scientist and an intellectual. As for most men of his age who had reached their mid-seventies, he insisted on wearing the style of clothing that was common in his youth. It was a small rebellion against the rapidly changing world and a living demonstration of the generation gap. At the age of forty, he had refused to adopt the styles of the day which had become more and more bizarre in his eyes. He thought the new combinations of colours and fabrics weren't meant for his generation; they were intended for the younger members of society to parade around in. So, he - and others of his age - had settled on a style of fashion that was more familiar. For his generation, the era of denim jeans, canvas sneakers and logo emblazoned t-shirts were the norm. With all the new artificial fabrics available today, nothing – in the

Professor's opinion – could beat a simple cotton T-shirt for comfort and practicality. On a sunny day, he would still proudly sport a baseball cap turned backwards to keep the sun off the top of his balding head.

"C'mon, let's go over," Karen said as she ran ahead to greet the Professor, leaving Craig to wheel the baggage trolley between the precariously stacked displays.

When Craig arrived at the sales counter, the Professor and Karen were greeting each other with a warm embrace. They had both become quite fond of each other in the two years that she and Craig had begun seeing each other.

"Hi Dad," Craig said as he greeted his father in their traditional way, with the shaking of hands. The Professor raised his eyebrows at the greeting and flicked his head in Karen's direction.

"I see she's been on at you about the Professor thing again, huh Craig?" he smiled and shot a wink at Karen. "Now how about giving me a hand here by putting this stuff on the trolley?" Professor Turp indicated the boxes and then made an exaggerated show of rubbing his back. "I'm getting a bit too old to go lugging this sort of stuff around the place."

"Oh, come on, John. Who are you trying to kid? Seventy- five is the new sixty-five, isn't it?" Karen playfully mocked the Professor.

"Actually," Craig joined in. "I think they updated that, I heard seventy-five is now the new fifty-five. So, you're twenty years ahead of where you should be. See, you've gone back in time already."

Professor Turp winced at Craig's remark "Not here Craig, please. We can talk when we're back on the station, Okay?"

"Sure, sorry, no problem dad," he shrugged his shoulders at Karen. "I didn't mean anything by it. Are you all set to go?"

"I know you didn't. I've just been a bit anxious the last few weeks, what with having my star researcher away on holidays. But, I'm glad to see you're back now. Come on you two, let's get on that plane and go home."

Craig, Karen and the Professor left the store and turned right as they made their way to departure gate sixteen and their flight back home to Newton Space Station.

Karen idly observed the displays of duty-free goods as they walked along. She didn't see Craig and the Professor turn their heads and stare at the entrance to gate twenty-three as they passed.

She didn't see the looks on their faces that revealed a combination of sorrow, regret and strangely... hope.

2
Leaving the Earth

Sir Kingsford Smith Spaceport – Sydney.

7.56am - Monday, July 27th, 2048

The roar of the twin ramjet engines increased in pitch as the pilot pushed forward on the throttle. With a slight adjustment, the co-pilot tightened the radius of the exhaust cowlings and gave the Captain a nod.

With the brake disengaged, a jolt travelled through the passenger cabin as two concentrated jets of flame pushed the aircraft up to speed. Terminal buildings, emergency crews and other aircraft passed by in a blur as Qantas Orbital Flight Q3876 strained to free itself from the ground.

Inside the cabin, the passengers endured a rapid, but not unpleasant, vibration as they were gently pressed into their seats by the space plane's increasing momentum. Many looked out of the windows in amazement at how fast they were moving, others simply slept or read the morning paper, blasé to everything that was happening around them. In the cockpit, the pilot moved the control stick back and pulled the plane into the sky. With further adjustments to the exhaust nozzles, the Qantas jet was set on a course that would take them beyond the Earth's atmosphere. Onboard, two hundred and thirty-six passengers and six crew members headed towards orbit and a rendezvous with Newton Station's International transfer terminal.

As the Qantas flight neared the end of the runway, Craig felt the vibration in his seat disappear as the wheels of the aircraft left the ground. As a senior staff member of the Australian and New Zealand Aeronautical Research Corporation, or ANZAR as it was commonly known, Craig was given many opportunities to travel back and forth from Newton Station to attend meetings with investors, technology companies and the assigned ANZAR representative who dealt with the re-supply of the science sector of the station. No matter how many times he came and went from Newton, Craig always got a kick out of the take-offs.

The airline industry had gone through its own renaissance when the introduction of inter-orbital flights cut travel times from London to Sydney from twenty-one hours to just under two. The method was simple, and the theory had been in existence for decades before it was eventually deemed economically viable to implement. With the collapse, then privatisation, of the US space program after the Helium-3 wars, the ability to travel into space became available to the public for the first time. Gone was NASA's near monopoly on spaceflight. With the decision that near-Earth orbit work was too costly an endeavour for the government to support, the US Congress had cancelled the program and shortsightedly sold NASA's technology to whichever tech companies would pay the most. The world's airlines had scrambled to get their hands on over one hundred years' worth of space research and flight data. Rocket parts, fuel formulas, and even a second-generation shuttle turned up on online auction sites where they were sold for a fraction of what they had originally cost to develop.

This sharing of information and technology saw a new space race develop between the world's privately-owned airlines. Learning from NASA's past successes and failures, plus the benefit of substantially larger budgets, the private sector continued to work on new spacecraft that went beyond anything that had come before. Qantas, Virgin, British Airways and Emirates airlines rapidly spent millions of dollars in an attempt to be the first into space with a new generation transport system. Within a few years of NASA closing down, eighty percent of the world's airlines had either developed or purchased space-going capabilities that revolutionised the transportation of passengers and cargo in this new age of astronautics.

To make the new Inter-Orbital Airline system practical as well as cost-efficient, each major destination was run as a ferry service with a single airline servicing each country. Passengers travelled from nation to nation by joining an Inter-Orbital flight that departed from their nearest airport. Flights to and from Australia were flown solely by the national carrier, Qantas. Whereas flights from London heading to and from Newton station were handled by the national airline, British Airways. The aircraft (or space planes as they were more commonly referred) would take off, head into low Earth orbit and rendezvous with either the Australian operated Newton Station or the nearly identical, New Zealand owned, Kaupeka Station which circled the Earth on opposite sides of the globe. Once arriving at either space station, the passengers simply had to wait for the relevant connection with their destination countries airline and jump onboard a regularly scheduled return flight.

The need to rendezvous with a space station held great appeal for both airlines and political regimes the world over. As a result of this system, security worries were greatly reduced as the only aircraft that could take off and land in any given country were those that had originated from that country. This eased the minds of the more security conscious nations as they no longer had aircraft from 'undesirable' regions frequenting their airspace. As an added bonus, the ferry system offered the benefit of reduced air traffic, reduced atmospheric and noise pollution and most importantly of all, it solved the previously insurmountable fuel to weight ratio problem. An original concern about Inter-Orbital transport was the amount of fuel required to lift a load into space and return it safely to Earth. The heavier the load, the more fuel would be required to complete the round-trip. This became a catch-22 situation, as more fuel meant more weight. The problem was solved by ANZAR research staff who proposed breaking flights into two stages. Each space plane would dock with Newton Station, offload its outgoing passengers and cargos, be refuelled by ANZAR and then reload with incoming passengers for the return trip. This method cut the fuel loads (and weight) by half, as aircraft no longer needed to carry enough fuel for the round trip. Aircraft only needed to carry enough Helium-3 on take-off to get it into orbit where it would be refuelled via an ingenious and secretive method devised by ANZAR scientists. Speculation was rife amongst the world's governments and media about how and where the fuel for the return trips came from. When questioned, ANZAR always answered with the stock-standard response; it's a trade secret.

The Qantas flight rose into the sky over Botany Bay. It banked sharply to the right as it turned onto the designated flight path that would carry it out over the Tasman Sea. Due to the excessive noise created by running two ramjet engines at full throttle, Inter-Orbital burn maneuvers banned anywhere near populated areas. Only once the space plane was clear of the mainland could the pilot initiate the Orbital Burn maneuver which would lift it out of the atmosphere.

The airlines knew that the act of travelling into space, for many tourists, held as much appeal as arriving at their final destination. As a means to humour the spirit of adventure in their passengers as well as giving a respectful nod to tradition, the orbital engine burn was preceded by a ten-second countdown. Although to some, this old NASA tradition may have seemed a little contrived, it always managed to drive home the significance of the occasion to those on board. Everyone was made well aware that they were about to join an exclusive club which had been founded almost one hundred years earlier by the original pioneers of spaceflight. They were about to become part of the ever-growing percentage of the global population to leave the Earth and travel into the vacuum of space.

The passengers counted along with the digital display in the centre aisle. It seemed as if every one of the two hundred plus, men women, and children aboard had joined in the ritual. The space plane slowly lifted itself onto its tail and pointed its nose towards the waiting stars as all onboard sank back into their seats. The sense of anticipation grew as each second passed. When the timer reached zero, a cry of "Ignition!" filled the cabin. The thrust of the engines built into a deep rumbling vibration that shook everything within the large craft. A sense of weight overcame everyone as the plane shot forward, and their bodies grew heavier. The space plane bored through the atmosphere towards orbit; the engines roared loudly as the aircraft attempted to free itself from the pull of the Earth's gravity.

Seated by the starboard side window, Craig smiled as the vibrations of the aircraft shook his body. He wanted to share this moment. He wanted the contact of another human being to make this seem more real, so he turned to look at Karen who was seated beside him. She was doing what most others on board were doing right now. She was grinning from ear to ear, enjoying the thrill of the ride. Tearing through the atmosphere, experiencing the dual rush of the aircraft and his adrenalin, this was the most content Craig had felt in months. He was on his way back to the place where he felt most comfortable; travelling with the two people he cared for most in the world. He was glad to be leaving the Earth and going home.

The vibrations slowly faded into an expectant silence as the aircraft left the atmosphere behind. Craig watched as those around him slowly raised their heads from their seatbacks and stared at their fellow travellers in amazement and joy. Many faces showed expressions of exhilaration at the experience they had just enjoyed; others showed discomfort and fear at what they considered to have been a brush with death which they were lucky to have survived. Still high on the adrenalin rush that accompanied the launch; many passengers looked around the cabin with rapid bird-like flicks of their heads as if trying to commit everything to memory, as if trying to take in everything at once. Others stared at nothing with a profound look of awe on their faces. For some, the act of leaving the Earth had helped them realise an emotional connection with it. To see one's home from so far above, in all its complexity and beauty, was a humbling and inspirational experience that many found life-changing.

To help relax the passengers and clear their systems of adrenalin, soft music began to play throughout the cabin. Violins, flutes and a softly caressed piano added the soundtrack for the next part of the journey. As flight Q3876 arrived at the edge of space, the slow, soothing classical tunes were eventually drowned out by the passenger's ooh's and ahh's on seeing a slow stream of ping-pong balls emblazoned with the Qantas logo float out of the ceiling. Hands and arms rose above the seatbacks as those on board made a game of swatting the balls around the cabin. The sounds of laughter grew louder as seatbelts were un-clicked and the more adventurous attempted to float down the aisle. A few passengers discovered that controlling yourself in a weightless environment was trickier than they had imagined. A few first- time flyers found themselves trapped between and even under the seats, in a variety of awkward looking positions.

On the other side of the aisle, Craig looked over in time to see an elderly woman somehow get herself wedged between her husband and the seat in front when she made a particularly aggressive lunge in an attempt to snare one of the balls as a souvenir. With no way of stopping herself, she ended up with her legs in the air, her face near the carpet and her false teeth floating somewhere in-between. A male steward made a weak attempt at getting her dislodged while struggling not to join in the laughter of the passengers around him. With a few tugs on her ankle and a shove from her deeply unimpressed husband, the woman came loose and was positioned gently back in her seat. She was red faced but otherwise unharmed.

Outside his window, Craig glimpsed the coast of Western Australia as it disappeared far below and behind the plane. He was amazed at the distance they had covered in the space of no more than a few minutes, in a short time they had made the four thousand kilometre journey across the Australian continent and had passed beyond its western borders. Towards the nose of the aircraft, Craig could make out the East coast of Southern Africa as it crept over the horizon of the turning globe. As they flew westwards into night, he watched as the clouds were slowly painted in shades of red, orange and yellow by his second sunrise of the day.

"It's beautiful up here isn't it?" Karen whispered as she leaned over his shoulder to sneak a look out of the window.

"And Peaceful," Craig agreed. "From up here you would never know that everyone on the surface was busily trying to destroy the planet and wipe each other out, would you?"

As per usual, on his return to Newton Station, he felt overcome with a sense of awe inspired by the view below. When he was able to view the globe en-masse this way, he felt a strong connection with the Earth and its people. With its political borders rendered invisible, he found it hard to understand why the people of Earth had become so disjointed and divided over the centuries. From Low Earth Orbit, everything he could see seemed unified and coherent, everything seemed to live and move with an acute sense of harmony, the only renegade to this balance of nature was his own species who refused to co-operate with their environment, choosing instead to fight and damage it in the selfish pursuit of their individual secular needs.

"I know what you mean," Karen began. "If only everyone could get the chance to come up here and see what we see now. If they could look out the window and see all of humanity at a single glance living on that big blue ball below us, they might appreciate the unity of everything. They might even understand that the concept of them and us is wrong, there is only us."

"Whoa, that's pretty deep baby." It was Craig's turn to give her a cheeky grin. "You should either become a philosopher or go into politics with that line. Man, I'd vote for you."

"And so would I, my dear girl," Professor Turp agreed as he floated back to his seat after retrieving his glasses from the overhead locker. "The world needs more empathetic minds like yours, Karen. It's Suffice to say that if everyone thought the way you did the world would be a much better place."

"With this crisis between Australia and the American Empire that's going on at the moment, I can hardly see that happening anytime soon, Doctor Turp." Karen sighed. "It still amazes me that it's the middle of the twenty-first century and we still haven't matured as a species or learned anything from the violence we caused in the last century."

"I know what you mean," Craig agreed. "I'm getting to hate coming down to the surface and being confronted with all the political bullshit that's messing everything up. We've got three wars in the Baltic region, multiple famines in Africa and high levels of homelessness the world over. And then the rest of us that are lucky enough to have been born in a 'developed' country have to work crazy hours and not get to see our families to afford the basics such as food and shelter. We've lost sight of what's important. We're so stuck in our patterns of violence and greed that it would take something like a global disaster, an alien invasion, or the imminent threat of extinction to get us to grow up. Until some external influence arises to make us see ourselves as a single, global species and change our way of thinking, then we're just going to carry on the way we always have. And if a global event ever does arrive, it will probably come upon us so unexpectedly that we won't have time to deal with it before we've wiped ourselves out and the Earth along with us."

Doctor Turp looked at them both thoughtfully; he wanted so much to tell them of what was going to happen in the next few weeks, but they would have to face what was to come without any foreknowledge. The two young people before him had such significant parts to play in the encroaching drama - of which he could tell them nothing - that he couldn't help but feel guilty at his inability to forewarn them. He knew that both Craig and Karen possessed the qualities that would be needed to get the world through the coming transition. They were both smart, considerate and fair people who would act as both examples and beacons for people around the globe. Most importantly, they cared for their fellow man and the world around them. The last thing the world needed now were people who did not care. To the professor, indifference was the worst of all the negative human traits that existed. From indifference, the seeds of other major character defects stemmed. If a man did not care about something, he could not show it compassion, mercy, or love. Worst of all, someone who is indifferent will stand aside and allow crimes against man and nature be committed and do nothing to stop them. He had raised Craig to be aware of the world he lived in and to understand the global perspective of every action that humankind undertook. He had tried to teach him about the unity of life and the planet and how humans could easily disturb the balance that nature had created. He was glad to see that what he had taught Craig had made him aware and concerned about his surroundings, the exact opposite of indifference.

That trait would prove essential.

"We have a general meeting scheduled for when we arrive at the station," the Professor stated almost robotically as he returned from his thoughts. "I think you two will find what's going to be announced interesting. As a result, you may even get to see your Earth changing scenario come about after all, Craig."

3
Through the debris

8.36am - Monday, July 27th, 2048

"Good morning, ladies and gentlemen." A curvaceous flight attendant in a skin-tight red mini-skirt floated into the centre of the aisle and began the in-flight audio tour in a cheery, sultry, female voice.

"On behalf of Qantas Trans-Orbital Airways, I would like to welcome you to Low Earth Orbit as we circle the globe en-route to the Newton Station Transfers Terminal. Or, the NSTT as we call it." The stewardess dutifully inserted the recommended laugh at the corporations approved moment. Having heard this speech hundreds of times before, Craig turned to Karen and pretended to laugh along in time with the steward.

"And you're supposed to be one of the world's leading quantum computing specialists?" Karen asked in mock indignation. She held her face rigid as she tried not to laugh at Craig's antics.

Craig smiled at Karen and shrugged his shoulders before turning to look back out the window.

"We will be arriving in approximately fifteen minutes at transfer gate D where we will begin disembarkation into the gravity regulated sections of the station," the steward continued. "Once onboard please make your way to your relevant connection point where you will be given a boarding pass for your re-entry phase of the flight. If you would like to explore the station or try your hand at the Levitorium in the zero-G visitor's wing a timetable with scheduled departure times for your destination city will be made available. Your airline ticket includes a one-day pass that allows unlimited use of all station facilities for up to eight hours. Please be aware that all passengers from this flight must join a connecting ferry by no later than six pm this evening or a compulsory extended stay visa will have to be purchased. As we approach the station, I'd like to give you a little background information on Newton. A common misconception is that the station was named after the famous Australian television presenter Bert Newton. As much as we all love Bert, that simply isn't correct. As you may or may not be aware, Newton is the world's first space station to have artificial gravity installed. From that, you can appreciate that the name was actually inspired by the man who first discovered gravity, Sir Isaac Newton. That part has always confused me though." The steward looked at her disinterested passengers with a broad, goofy grin on her face. "I mean, how can you discover gravity...really?"

The hostess' scripted banter and inane laughter went unheard by Craig as he soaked in the view of the Earth that slowly slid below the wing. Clouds and continents fell out of sight as the space plane begun the rolling maneuver that would clear the debris field and bring Newton Station into sight. This part of the launch was the most fraught with danger. It took a skilful pilot aided by a knowledgeable ground controller to navigate the layers of debris that encircled much of the globe. Many passengers sat with their faces pressed to the windows as they watched the calming vista of the Earth being slowly replaced with something that resembled the remains of a science fiction battlefield.

In what was primarily a short-sighted cost-saving measure, NASA had decided it would be more economical to manufacture new equipment for every mission than to waste the increasingly expensive (and scarce) fuel reserves they had amassed by carting unnecessary weight home. As a result, discarded equipment, tools, packaging and waste products tumbled and turned in an artificial asteroid belt that stood as a testament to man's skewed priorities. The major conflicts of the three-year-long Helium-3 wars had succeeded in adding even larger pieces to the debris field: abandoned ore transporters, military defence craft and the ruptured hulls of hundreds of privately-owned military subcontract vehicles littered the sky about the Earth in a graveyard of metal, glass, and plastic.

"Well, it's good to see this eyesore is slowly getting smaller," Craig mentioned to Karen as she leaned over him to take a look at what floated outside.

This was Karen's fourth return trip to Newton station since she had begun working in ANZAR's research wing. The sheer amount of waste amazed her every time she passed through the debris field. The remnants of war and the discarded relics of man's visits to space drifted around the spaceplane as abandoned as the polluters regard for the environment and the once proud history of the space program.

"Yeah, if it wasn't for Greenpeace this thing would be getting bigger rather than smaller." Karen pointed at a large white object amongst the debris. "At least ANZAR can claim that Newton and Kaupeka are run as green facilities that aren't tarnishing the environment and their reputations like NASA once did."

Deep within the debris field a second-generation shuttle painted in faded rainbow stripes floated amongst the waste looking as if it too were an abandoned piece of wreckage. Time and the unfiltered rays of the sun had dulled the hull from white to grey. Dents, scratches, and scrapes marked every surface where the shuttle had repeatedly been nudged, bumped and scraped by the floating detritus. The fact that the cockpit was lit from within, and that movement could be seen within its open bay doors, were the only signs that *The Rainbow Warrior Six* was still in use. A long metallic arm stretched far out into the debris field pulling a lightweight metallic cage full of garbage back to the ship. Eight space suited volunteers hovered around the cage like a swarm of flies buzzing around a garbage skip. They reached out with their pudgy, pressure-suit inflated arms to grab at whatever last pieces of debris they could snare on their way back to the shuttle. Regardless of size, they made an attempt to retrieve every piece within their reach before it had a chance to fall out of orbit and pollute the Earth below. As in past decades on Earth, Greenpeace felt that it was man's duty to keep the world clean and free of pollutants. They believed that everything on, in and around the Earth was interconnected, so it was beneficial to all nations that this literally global pollutant be removed.

With space travel never being cheap, Greenpeace had found a novel way to fund this initiative by selling the more interesting pieces of space junk on their own online auction site. Within just a few years, this form of income had replaced charitable donations as Greenpeace's primary source of funding. ANZAR's generous donation of free fuel to help with the operation also went a long way in keeping costs down.

After a few minutes wait, the Ground Control Guidance Officer supplied the Qantas pilot the coordinates of a hole in the debris field that the ground radar had predicted would be large enough and remain stable long enough, for them to pass through. With meticulous care and many bangs and pops from the spaceplane's control thrusters, the pilot managed to safely maneuver them through the large gap in the debris field as it slid past their position.

As the last of the garbage fell away behind them, a small bright spot appeared on the horizon. Newton Station had risen above the curve of the Earth and was heading towards the shuttle at a deceptively slow looking twenty-eight thousand kilometres an hour. At this rate, those onboard the station made one orbit of the earth and got to see a new sunrise, every ninety-three minutes. With the station moving towards him at such a high speed, the Qantas pilot had to carefully hold his current course and bring his vehicle up to the same velocity in order to make a successful dock. If he timed this maneuver correctly, the faster moving space station would catch them up at precisely the same time as the spaceplane matched its speed.

The passengers craned their necks to follow the Earth as it crept towards the rear of the spaceplane and disappeared from view. Those seated on the starboard side momentarily sighed in disappointment as they lost sight of their homeworld. They were soon placated by the jaw-dropping view of an unending vista of stars. Twenty seconds later, with the pilot's one hundred and eighty-degree turn complete, the passengers seated on the port side giggled in delight as the Earth curved into view, presenting them with an unimpeded view of North America.

With their tail now pointed directly at Newton, both ramjet engines on Qantas Flight Q3876 ignited. A sense of pressure slowly registered with the passengers as the engines gave a long steady burst of power to get the spaceplane moving in the same direction as the incoming station. As the craft's momentum increased, the constant pressure pushed the passengers deeper into their seats. The illusion of gravity and weight made it feel as if they were lying on their backs with the aircraft standing on its tail.

What first appeared as a small sized moon with numerous bumps and protrusions soon grew in detail to resemble a large metallic sphere with dozens of shiny skyscraper-like cylinders attached to the outside. Looking more like a giant world war two sea mine than a space station, Newton blocked out the stars as the spaceplane passed underneath its massive frame and slowly made its way towards the cylinder which housed the QANTAS arrivals terminal.

Almost identical, both the Kaupeka and Newton space stations were administered by ANZAR – The Australian and New Zealand Aeronautical Research Corporation, which was founded fifteen years earlier as a combined Antipodeans research company. Following NASA's collapse and the birth of the new Inter-Orbital Flight system, the privately owned ANZAR pioneered a means to monopolise a key segment of global travel. Their largest competitor and the first Inter-Orbital airline, Virgin Galactic, was still five years away from completing a space-based docking station which was yet to be designed and would be needed to be built from scratch. ANZAR realised that they had a distinct advantage and immediately set about converting its two existing research stations into Low Earth Orbit docking platforms. With the addition of an extra module to each station, they succeeded in creating temporary docking facilities that were the equivalent of any airport terminal found on Earth. Once the system was operational ANZAR had created itself a little cash cow that raked in almost a billion dollars in the first year of operation. The terminals were little more than viewing platforms where transiting passengers could float, have a coffee and watch the Earth turn below them as they awaited their destination city's connecting ferry service. ANZAR soon discovered that many travellers were using the service to primarily visit the space stations themselves, to get a taste of what the old space age was like. Many passengers were disappointed to find that these space stations had a weak form of artificial gravity and apart from the view, were just like being back on Earth. With this short test phase into Inter-Orbital travel, ANZAR realised that visitors to space wanted a more authentic and traditional space travel experience, so they set about creating a family resort in space.

Using the profits from their Inter-Orbital monopoly, Newton station was then commissioned and built over the space of six years. With a central sphere shaped public area that measured over five kilometres across, the newly built station had all the features of an Earth-based resort with a selection of cafe's, restaurants, cinemas, gaming facilities and other forms of entertainment. To gain the best of both worlds, the station was designed in such a way as to allow visitors to experience the thrill of both zero gravity and artificial gravity environments. The design of the station itself was conceived as a means of creating a sense of awe in those who visited. With all internal buildings constructed and fixed along the inside curve of the main sphere, visitors could stand at any point in the open public area of the station and look in any direction to see the inverted horizon curve around and above them. As hoped, the station's interior proved to be a disconcerting phenomenon for visitors and soon become a must-see for every global traveller.

The alien view of being on a world effectively turned inside out, where you could look up and see the roofs of buildings on the opposite side of the sphere, caused a few panic attacks in early visitors. This problem was partly removed with the addition of the Levitorium, a zero-gravity recreation facility in the centre of the orbs open-air space that was decorated to resemble the insides of the old twentieth Century space stations. Visitors could choose to stopover in the Mir Hotel or the International

Space Station Stop-and-Rest. It was an instant hit with the public and became the station's main tourist attraction. Ironically, the space tourists had found the experience they were looking for - a traditional space experience within the confines of an entirely artificial environment. Visitors could float around the padded areas or try a variety of games and tasks including human ping pong or the zero-g mazes known as Tubular Hells. Considered as much an intellectual challenge as it was a physical one, the prize of a free return trip back to the station lured people in to try and break the maze record. Many found the challenge addictive and returned to the maze repeatedly to beat their personal best times. It had even featured as a demonstration sport in the recent 2048 Olympics in Tehran.

With their financial future assured from fuel sales and the tourist dollars they raked in, the scientists at ANZAR could sit back in their own wing of the station and concentrate on their true vocation, scientific research.

With one last maneuver and a final vibrating thud, the pilot slid the space plane between the station's spires and made a successful docking with the QANTAS arrivals terminal.

After a few minutes wait, a slight change in pressure and the accompanied smells of bottled oxygen - with a hint of Helium-3 - told Craig that the door had opened.

He was home.

4
ANZAR and the Empire

ANZAR Labs – Newton Station.
2.15pm - Monday, July 27th, 2048

Nestled between the research labs in the ANZAR wing of Newton Station, the Common Room filled the multiple roles of a lunchroom, study hall and community gathering place for anyone who needed a time-out from the labs. Primarily designed as an area for the staff's fortnightly general meetings, it looked like any meeting room found on Earth. It was long, rectangular and had four walls that surrounded a sizeable laminated table and twenty plastic chairs. No real concern was shown for its decoration, charts and posters covered much of its wall space. Film stills and glossy nature scenes competed with large graphs and scientific charts for attention. An enormous periodic table covered much of the back wall by the small kitchenette where the steam from an ancient tea and coffee urn had slowly discoloured and curled one edge.

In its monotony, the meeting room was unremarkable. The dominating feature that distinguished it from all others was the large, room length window that framed one of the best views of the Earth on Newton Station. The light reflecting off the oceans and atmosphere of the nearby world bathed the room in a soft, dreamlike blue glow that imbued the space with a feeling of calm and contentment.

Eighteen of the twenty seats around the big table was currently filled with an assortment of men and women whose names read like a list of Nobel laureates. The best scientists in the world in the areas of Physics, Chemistry, Biology, Astronomy, Engineering, Quantum Computing, Quantum Mechanics, Medicine and Nuclear Physics talked amongst themselves as they waited for the meeting to begin. These gatherings were always a casual affair. None of the attending professors had attempted to dress up or make an effort to instil a sense of ritual to the proceedings. Many were dressed in their day to day garb of jeans and t-shirts with the occasional lab coat thrown over the top.

Behind the seated department heads stood a group of younger men and women dressed in the unofficial, yet traditional, uniform of the white lab coat. The lab assistants usually only attended the fortnightly meetings if their department heads required their assistance with a presentation. But for this meeting, everyone within the ANZAR scientific team was in attendance. Today, ANZAR's founding members, Professors Turp and Weekes, would announce whether they were ready to put the last fifteen years' worth of research into effect. Whatever the announcement, everyone wanted to hear it firsthand.

Craig sat at the table with his father and swapped stories of what each had been up to while Craig had been away on leave. A few minutes into their conversation, Luke Weekes stepped into the room and immediately walked up to Craig and patted him on the back.

"Hey mate. It's good to see you back!" Luke smiled.

Craig rose to his feet and gave his friend a quick hug. Being the sons of the two founding members of ANZAR, Craig and Luke had known each other since birth. Although not related, the two men shared a bond that went deeper than friendship and made them more akin to brothers.

"It's good to be back," Craig laughed. "How were things around here while I was gone?" he asked.

Luke smiled and took an empty seat beside Craig. He gave Professor Turp a nod before continuing.

"It's been amazing, mate," Luke beamed at Craig. "You wouldn't believe the responses we got back from the probes. Apart from losing contact with one of them, the tests came back better than we could have hoped."

"We lost a probe?" Craig asked. "How did that happen?"

Luke shrugged and gave a lopsided grin as if to say who knows?

"We sent out over a hundred of the damn things in total, so it only makes sense that at least one of them would have a malfunction and not make it back." Luke leant forward in his chair and pointed at Craig. "Statistically, we should have lost more. It was plain bad luck that the one we lost was one of your advanced models."

"We lost one of my smart probes?" Craig sounded a little shocked. He had spent months working on a new range of robotic probes that were designed to be self-motivating and free-thinking. Traditionally, the small, white spheres were inherently mobile cameras jam packed full of sensors and scientific equipment. What Craig had done with the smart probes was to fit them with a quantum computer of his design that elevated their intelligence to near-sentient levels. Although they fell short of what could be described as true artificial intelligence, the dozen units he had created were advanced enough to understand what they were, their place in the environment and complete assigned tasks as well as create new ones as they identified a phenomenon that warranted extra attention. They were so close to thinking like a human that the written reports that accompanied the probe's data were detailed enough to pass as being written by a human.

The loss of one of them was to Craig, was like losing a sentient, aware creature. They were more than just machines to him.

Luke patted Craig on the back and grinned as he affectionately made fun of his friend. "Maybe you made those things so smart that one of them decided not to come back," he laughed.

"Which one was it?" Craig asked.

Luke looked at the ceiling for a moment as he tried to recall the specifics. "Twelve I think. Yeah, that last one you built. Probe 12."

"12," Craig sighed and shook his head.

Around the table, other researchers turned towards Luke at the mention of the research. Seeing that the guts of the meeting were about to be spilled ahead of time, Professor Turp gently interrupted the excited and impetuous young scientist.

"That's enough of that for the moment," Professor Turp said softly. "I think all that can wait a few minutes until your father arrives, Luke."

Unfazed, Luke smiled and nodded his ascent and deftly changed the subject.

"Hey, did your Dad tell you that he finally named the VAPERs?" Luke continued.

Craig turned to his father with an excited look on his face, the loss of probe 12 all but forgotten with this next piece of news. "No, he didn't." He looked at both men in turn as he waited for one of them to continue.

Before Craig left to go on holidays, there had been much debate amongst the senior ANZAR staff over what their two newly completed experimental vehicles should be named. The Vacuum and Atmospheric Personal Experimental Rovers, or VAPER for short, were designed using innovative technology that the ANZAR team had spent the better part of a decade developing. Their ingenious hull design and revolutionary method of propulsion were expected to make them the benchmark for all future modes of space and earthbound transport. The two vehicles were designed to act as small spacecraft it seemed only fitting to the ANZAR scientists that they should both have names.

"Well, what did you call them?" Craig blurted at his father after a short pause.

Professor Turp shook his head and pointed at Luke. "This really should have waited for the meeting as well," he admonished the youth.

Luke shrugged and waved his hand as if to say big deal. "It's just the names of the ships, Uncle John. It's not exactly top secret."

With another shake of his head, Professor Turp gave a long sigh and continued. "We named VAPER 1 after Professor *Feynman* and VAPER 2 after *Hawking*. I was going to go with Schrodinger, but it didn't roll off the tongue as nicely."

From across the table, an aged engineer of Vietnamese ancestry smiled. As the builder of the VAPERs, Henry Tran had earned himself a position of respect amongst the ANZAR science team and most likely his next Nobel Prize when the vehicles are unveiled.

"Both are very respectable names for two distinguished ships." Henry smiled at Craig, Luke and Professor Turp. "If I do say so myself," Henry finished.

"You did a great job with those, Henry." Professor Turp smiled back at his colleague. "You can't begin to imagine how much the *Feynman* and the *Hawking* are going to change things around here."

Henry smiled once again and leant forward in his chair. "Oh, I can, John. I, more than anyone can fully appreciate how important those two crafts are."

Before the conversation could continue, Luke's father and Professor Turp's long-term business partner, Professor Weekes, stepped into the room. He walked with a spring in his step and a smile on his face. Displaying good posture, clear skin and graceful movements that made him appear thirty years younger than his actual age of eighty-two years.

Professor Weekes stepped up to the head of the table and looked around the room at the group gathered before him. When his eyes met those of Professor Turp, he exchanged a look of concern with his friend and colleague. Both men knew what he was about to announce and neither man was looking forward to the response. Choosing to stand, the Professor placed a small tablet device on the desk and began to speak.

"Good afternoon to you all," Professor Weekes began in a crisp, clear, loud voice.

All twenty chairs around the meeting table were filled. With another glance at those seated before him, the Professor noted that everyone who needed to be here for this meeting was indeed present. The faces of his senior professors watched him with a look of expectation. They all knew he had something important to announce, but none of them had any idea what it could be.

"Does anyone have anything urgent to bring up before we begin?" Professor Brian Weekes asked the room.

No one attempted to reply. Everyone remained silent.

"Very well," he continued. "I'll get straight to the point then."

Professor Weekes took another quick glance around the room before continuing.

43

"Professor Turp and I have received word from Conrad Stephens in our head office down in Sydney that the Americans have somehow gotten wind of what we're doing up here." The Professor shrugged to show that he had no idea how that could have happened. "As a result, I think we should bring the launch date forward for Project Reunion... to tomorrow."

Gasps and sighs burst from those in the room as they heard the news.

"Why?" Craig asked.

"The military actions which have been reported to the United Nations over the last few months have made me very uncomfortable about our current deadline. Not to mention this attack on the Australian research vessel recently. It only goes to show that Australia is no longer safe from the Empire's military."

"Oh Brian, you can't just drop the whole timetable because the American Empire is rattling their sabres again," Doctor Anderson, the Chief Medical Researcher and Head Biologist interrupted.

"No, actually that's not it, Peter," Professor Weekes replied. "The U.S. isn't just flexing its muscles this time. Over the last two months, they've forced the closure of an alarming number of research labs around the globe due to the alleged manufacture of illegal chemical and biological weapons. I can name three labs of which we deal with that have inexplicably shut down. Conrad's spent days on the phone and net trying to get in touch with anyone who used to work at them, but he's had no luck. Ro-Conn, Exertech, Valmeers labs. We can't seem to find any of their staff or their families. People are disappearing." Professor Weekes began to grow agitated and distressed.

"There have been unconfirmed reports that each shutdown has been watched over by a unit of American soldiers that storms the buildings, places everyone under arrest and confiscates all their research. I don't know why, but the Empire seems to be making a grab for technology."

"And if they know what we have up here then we can be pretty sure that we're on their list," Professor Turp agreed.

"Exactly, John!" Professor Weekes nodded. "If they know the contents of our research they'd be up here in a heartbeat to shut us down and take everything we've worked so hard for."

"They wouldn't dare!" Henry Tran barked. "Everyone knows that both Newton and Kaupeka are neutral territories in which troops from all nations are banned. I can't believe that they would blatantly ignore that, Brian."

Professor Weekes sighed and shook his head. "If it were anyone else I'd agree, but their egos won't stand for the Australian and New Zealand governments benefiting from such a major technological advantage as what we will soon be providing. The balance of world power would turn overnight with all non-Imperial nations coming out on top."

"How much do the Americans know, Uncle Brian?" Craig asked.

"They've only got a vague idea of what's going on at the moment. They have some wild ideas about what we're up to. Some of which are accurate, most are total fantasy. They're saying we've invented everything from a new kind of nuclear warhead to the capability to kill soldiers and civilians with the power of thought. Naturally, their thinking centres around violence and are assuming that most of what we work on up here is intended for military use. Their war on terror has been going on for so long that they've become pessimistic and suspicious of everything. Hell, I can't even be sure if they really believe that or if it's just spin for their eventual takeover. Naturally, they're using the usual smear campaign that we're all just a bunch of terrorists and are plotting to destroy the American way of life. Blah, blah, blah, etcetera, etcetera, etcetera."

"This is nuts! Everything we make up here is designed to prolong human life or improve the quality of it. We're not in the weapons business, and the only military benefit to our work will save lives, not take them," Luke spoke up from his place from further down the table. The look on his face and the anger in his voice demonstrated his feelings to everyone present. He was not alone in his dislike for the new American Empire. Many of the

Professors shared his fears on what the birth of a new global power would do to the world.

"The way things are going they can shut us down anytime without justification or proof that we're doing anything wrong. What's the good of us knowing that ANZAR has always been committed to solving the planets climate and medical problems if the rest of the world believes we're up to something covert?" Craig added.

"Naturally I expect that our governments will see that this misunderstanding is cleared up before somebody gets hurt, Craig." Doctor Turp turned back towards his business partner who waited patiently. "Well, at least I'd like to think that they would," he added.

With a deep sigh, Professor Weekes interjected. "That's the problem. We're not supposed to know anything about this. Our governments are in enough trouble with the Americans over this trade embargo rubbish. If they broach the subject, they'll give away the fact that we have effectively been spying on the U.S. and it will only make us look guiltier of doing something clandestine."

The level of tension was beginning to rise amongst those present at the meeting. The anger being felt by those in the room was an echo of what had been brewing within many of the world's citizens who thought that the American Empire was taking too many liberties with the rest of the world's rights and freedoms. Since the war on terror had begun nearly fifty years earlier, the US had taken it upon themselves to act as judge and jury in the affairs of the International community. Since the day that a handful of independent extremists flew aeroplanes into American buildings, the rest of the world had been paying the price for their crime. With that one excuse to act, the U.S.A. had set itself on a misguided course towards the domination and regulation of all the worlds' people and resources. All the death and terror that was to follow was performed - ironically - in the name of freedom.

"It's not all false information."

All eyes turned towards Professor Weekes.

46

"Somehow they've learnt about our medical ModChips. It seems that this is the item on the list that's most caught their attention. With their little Empire based on military might, it's only natural that they'd fear a device that could potentially render all their weapons useless."

Professor Weekes rubbed at his forehead and looked at the table in front of him. He didn't look up when he next spoke.

"We all knew our research would one day change the world. But I didn't think it would be this soon. All the evidence points to the likelihood that the Americans are planning to come up here and clean us out. We must make preparations for a military takeover of this station."

The meeting erupted in a subdued roar of questions. Everyone wanted to know what they could do to avoid this situation. What they could do to save their research and preserve the vast store of knowledge they had amassed.

"The idea is absurd, Brian. We're their friends. Why would they invade a coalition research station and risk threatening the good relationship between Australia and the Empire?" The station Astronomer Glen Hanson looked as confused and bewildered as everyone else in the room felt.

"For the exact reason you just mentioned Glen, they are no longer the country we supported in multiple military campaigns over the last century. As you just put it, they are now an Imperial force. Empires don't have allies. They have minions who do what they say without question or face their wrath. That is the position we now find ourselves in."

Henry Tran was a polite, quietly spoken man who had never been heard to raise his voice in anger. He came pretty close now. "Well, what should we do, Brian? Do we just abandon everything and go into hiding? If that's the plan, it won't work. I can easily hide the VAPERs from the Americans, but I guarantee that some of the work done by the people around the table isn't as portable, like the station itself for example."

"I know what you mean Henry, but that's not the plan." Professor Weekes gave a slight smile as he looked around the room. His smooth, soft hands slowly rolled a ballpoint pen backwards and forwards across the desk as he waited for those gathered to settle. Back and forth the pen went in a slow rhythmic movement that soon had the entire room watching it expectantly. Only after total silence was achieved did the pen stop and Professor Weekes speak again.

"It seems quite obvious to me that the easiest way to deny any group or government the chance of possessing a monopoly on something is to make it freely available to everybody. That's why I propose we launch Mission Reunion tomorrow. We do what we have to get done, then we pack this place up and hand everything over to the Australian and New Zealand governments. We need to publish papers on every piece of research we have so that everybody has access to it and everyone here gets the proper credit for it. We can't run the risk of one group having a monopoly on what we've created up here. That would just be plain irresponsible."

"But, that would mean also giving it to the Empire as well." Craig turned to his father to gauge his reaction to the news. He expected him to be thinking along the same lines of thought as he was.

"I refuse to let them have any of my work after what they've done to us," Luke almost snarled. "Dad, they killed our mothers." Luke gestured at Craig and himself. "They murdered yours and Uncle John's wives on a mere suspicion. We can't allow them to benefit from anything we do. It would just be plain wrong." Luke finished. He stared at his father with a look of rage and sorrow on his face.

Professor Weekes stared back at his son with a look of sympathy and sadness for a few moments before he responded.

"If everything goes to plan tomorrow, that will all be set right. It will be like it never happened," Professor Weekes tried to reassure his son without really feeling too sure himself.

Tears rolled down Luke's cheeks as he rose to his feet and headed for the door. "How can you say that after what losing her did to both of us? Whether we get her back or not, it won't change the fact that we've spent the last fourteen years without her. No matter what happens tomorrow, I still had to live most of my life without her in it. As far as I'm concerned, it still happened," he snarled at his father as he made his way out of the room.

Craig felt like following his friend to comfort him. Knowing Luke, Craig understood that at times like this, he would rather be left alone. When he was ready, Luke would come to him, and they could talk it over. After all, they both lost their mothers in the same disastrous incident. Nobody understood how Luke felt as well as Craig did.

At the front of the room, Professor Weekes sat down heavily in the last empty plastic seat. He rubbed at his eyes with a handkerchief for a moment before continuing.

"I suggest we all begin to get our research filed and sorted," he began softly, his voice thick with emotion. "We'll need to pack all hard copies and prototypes for removal. I suggest you transfer any work you have to do for tomorrow's test onto your tablets so you can do it remotely. We don't want to leave anything behind on the station's computers that we can't take with us. If we do, you can guarantee that the Americans will find it when they come."

Adam Fehrenbach, the head of ANZAR's version of mission control and who was also the lead flight controller for the station, interrupted Brian with a comment that stopped everyone in their tracks. "Knowing our luck, they'll probably turn up right when we're in the middle of taking the *Feynman* out tomorrow."

Professor Weekes gave a heartbroken smile and responded in a soft voice that was aimed at not only his friend but the whole room.

"Oh, I believe we may still have as much as a few weeks before we have to leave. Everyone here knows how important this is to Professor Turp and I. We've spent more than twelve years working up to this moment. After all the years of research on the Conduit, there's no way we're going to let anything stop us. But still, whatever happens, happens."

The room fell silent for a moment as everyone's thoughts turned to what they had to do.

"Well, that's about all we need to discuss on that matter at the moment," Professor Weekes piped up once more. "Due to the looming disruption to our schedules, we'll hold off the rest of the meeting until next time. I'm sure the progress reports and demonstrations can wait until then. If there are no further questions, then we may as well adjourn." The Professor shifted his weight in the seat as a precursor to standing up. He gathered his coat around himself and with his arms supporting his weight on the table; he began to rise to his feet.

"I have one last question, Professor," Craig said from the back of the room where the crowd around him had already begun to slowly move towards the door. "How did the Americans find out what we were doing? Do you think somebody told them?" Everyone stopped and looked at Craig with a look of surprise. Now that it had been verbalised they were shocked that the idea had not occurred to anyone else in the room.

Professor Weekes' mouth turned up at the sides, making what appeared to those who did not know him to be a macabre grin. He was, in fact, smiling at the perceptiveness of the young man standing at the other end of the table.

"That's actually two questions Craig," he replied. "Sadly, I don't know the answer to either of them."

Even though none of the ANZAR researchers would ever admit to believing that one of their own could be capable of leaking information to the Empire, Professor Weekes spotted a few furtive and suspicious glances being exchanged between his colleagues as everyone slowly shuffled their way towards the door and out of the room.

5
Sweet dreams

Accommodation wing – Newton Station 8.27pm -

Monday, July 27th, 2048

Karen lay lengthways across the worn and beaten sofa with a giant, dark brown teddy bear wedged under her head as a pillow. Ten feet above, a ceiling full of artificial stars glowed softly. Their pale green light shone down to give a hint of what this corner of the crèche contained. Cars, trucks, trains and soft toys vied for space on a long shelf above the two single beds where, Karen hoped, the boys were now finally asleep. In the dim light, she turned her head to look at each of the children in turn. With their bodies hidden beneath layers of cotton and silk, she could almost imagine that they were as normal as any other four-year-old boys on the planet.

With only the sound of the children's breathing to keep her company, her mind wandered back to the strange circumstances that had brought them into her care. They had been found three years ago in the abandoned lab of an American biotech firm which had abruptly ended its contract on the station. Their experiments complete, the researchers had packed up and gone home, leaving the then one-year-old infants locked away in the empty laboratory to fend for themselves. Whether it was out of fear of being prosecuted for illegal research or a simple lack of moral values, the American researchers had been unwilling to take responsibility for the lives they had created. They were unwilling to ensure that the boys were taken care of... one way or the other. Luckily for the children, that was a hectic time for ANZAR. The particular lab which they had occupied was in high demand and had been booked by a different firm under another contract. Karen had often wondered what it would have been like for the boys if the maintenance crews hadn't arrived the very next day to clean the rooms for the new tenants.

At first sight, it is evident that the two young boys were not entirely normal. On meeting them, Professors Weekes and Turp immediately decided that the children would have to remain with them on the station. Sending them to Earth was not an option in their eyes. The two children would either end up locked away in an orphanage or worse, end up in the hands of a researcher as morally ambiguous as those who had created them in the first place. Ironically, the Professors gave the boys a home within their labs to keep them from becoming test subjects in someone else's.

All this happened before her time and Karen was thankful that men like Doctor Turp and Professor Weekes were in charge to ensure the children were looked after. Everything began well until a horrible mistake was made in the choice of carer for the boys. Sister Clarence was a pleasant looking elderly nun who, on the surface, oozed compassion for the children. In public, Sister Clarence acted like the perfect carer. She doted after the kids and behaved like a loving grandmother. In private, it was later found that she had been abusing the boys both mentally and physically. She had been with them for just over a year, in which time she had managed to cause extensive emotional and psychological damage. Under her care, they had been forced to endure daily beatings while she screamed and cursed and swore at them. Sister Clarence told them they were freaks and taught them that they were evil. She made them feel that they were a mistake of nature and an abomination of God. From the safety of their sound-proofed rooms, she screamed at them until they began to cry. She made them believe that they were totally unnatural and unworthy of love.

A tear ran down Karen's cheek as she stared at her sleeping boys and tried to imagine what it must have been like for them to begin their life that way. As much as she tried, she couldn't comprehend what it would have been like for them to be struck and yelled at, to have so much hate directed at them from the moment they woke until the time they went to sleep. Karen cringed as she remembered one of the boys telling her what Sister Clarence used to say to them every night before they went to sleep.

"Sleep well you evil bastards," she would glower at them from beside the door. "For if God is truly gracious, then tomorrow he will give me the strength to rid the world of you two horrid abominations." That was the closest thing to a bedtime story they would ever know during their time with her.

Luckily Doctor Turp suspected something was amiss and had arranged surveillance of the crèche where the truth was finally discovered. Sister Clarence was immediately removed from her position and reported to the police where she was charged with multiple counts of abuse. Her ravings about God and the evil nature of the boys resulted in her committal to a mental hospital where it was later revealed that she, in turn, was being mistreated by her carers.

Maybe there is a God after all, Karen thought.

Karen had started work with the boys the following week. She spent hours every day trying to build up their confidence and teaching them to speak. They both proved to be exceptionally bright children. With love and encouragement, they began to utter their first words. Within days, entire sentences were being spoken by the boys. Once they had started to talk, the extent of Sister Clarence's hatred became clear. Karen was shocked when the boys first managed to tell her that their names were Judas and Lucifer. The religious meaning was not lost on her, and she understood what the names implied. How the nun could find any similarities between two of Christianity's most hated characters and the beautiful children she had come to know was a mystery to Karen. Appalled that nobody else had caught on to this obvious clue to the nun's instability, she began to set about giving the boys a fresh start, with new identities.

Judas, on being read a list of popular names from a book had decided what he wanted to be called. After much thought, he smiled up at Karen and said. "Jamie, I want to be Jamie. I like that name," he told her. "It sounds like a happy name."

Lucifer, on the other hand, was more resistant to change, but eventually decided that Timothy was an acceptable substitute. He felt comfortable with the three syllables in his name for a reason known only to him. As a result, he would only answer to his full name, Timothy. *Never* Tim.

Within a year, Jamie and Timothy had begun to grow and transform into happy children. The only apparent side effects visible from their year of abuse were the regular night terrors that affected their sleep. In their dreams, they still saw Sister Clarence. She still had command of this one last part of their lives.

After raising the boys in an environment of love for the past two years, Karen was happy with their emotional and psychological development. The only area in which she believed they were lacking was in the development of social relationships with other children. Karen wished the day would come when she could take them away from the brightly decorated prison that circumstance had created for them. She believed that the kids were indirectly being punished for the sins of their creators. They had been locked away from the world to hide the fact of their existence. She was eager to take them out into the real world which floated out of reach outside the crèche's window. On more than one occasion she had entered the room to find the boys staring down at the Earth as if deep in thought, wondering what was down there and what they were missing.

They belong outside like other kids, she thought. *They deserve the chance to be able to play in a park and to feel the sun on their faces with a breeze ruffling their hair.*

She looked down at the boys once again. She loved them. If she never had children of her own, Karen felt she could live content that she had helped nurture and raise these amazing little men.

And if I do have children later in life, she thought. *Then I will always think of Jamie and Timothy as being my first little boys.*

A stirring from the bunk to her right returned her from the daydream. Timothy had begun to sit up and was looking at her with glazed eyes. "Is that you mummy?" he slurred. "Is it morning already?"

Karen smiled and went over to the half-asleep child and kissed him on the forehead. "No baby, it's still dark. You lay back and go to sleep, OK?"

With a slow nod, Timothy eased himself back onto the mattress where Karen covered him with his blanket. A hand came out from under the covers to gently hold hers as Timothy smiled sleepily up at her. "I love you, mummy."

She couldn't help but smile back. "I know you do baby. And I love you." She realised that her eyes had begun to water. The boys were so kind and loving even after all they'd been through. The thought of the cruelty these two children had suffered nearly broke her heart. "I'm so proud of you and your brother. I couldn't wish for better boys. Now you go back to sleep baby, OK? We've got a busy day tomorrow."

As Timothy rolled onto his side, he looked around the head of his bed as if searching for something.

"Where's my silky, mum?" he asked. "I need my silky."

Out of the two boys, he was the one who appeared the most affected by their earlier ordeal. Although much improvement had been made, Timothy still felt in need of something to cling to. He had found comfort in an old silk pillowcase that Karen had left in their room after one of her regular sleepovers.

Karen pulled the dishevelled piece of material from its hiding place under his pillow and placed it by his head. Timothy immediately began to slowly rub it against his cheek as he took in its scent and enjoyed its silky texture against his skin.

A soft knock at the door alerted Karen to the fact that Craig's meeting was finally over. With one last kiss on each of the boys' cheeks, Karen turned towards the door. Before leaving, she whispered her nightly farewell that she repeated to the boys before they went to sleep. Even though both children were well under, she repeated it anyway, as much to comfort and reassure the boys as well as her. "Sleep tight, my boys. I wish you both happiness and want you to know you are loved. You are both the most special and beautiful little men in the world. Sweet dreams until we wake tomorrow for another day of laughter and fun. I love you."

Slowly she turned and silently slid out of the room. Her heart was heavy as it always was at this time. Memories of how the boys used to be sent to sleep tormented her mind. She hoped and believed, that if she repeated it often enough, her nightly message of love would drive Sister Clarence's legacy of hate from their minds.

6
Project Reunion

Accommodation wing – Newton Station.

8.45pm - Monday, July 27th, 2048

Karen padded out of the darkened room and gently pulled the door closed behind her.

"Thank god they're both finally asleep," Karen whispered as she clipped a child monitor to her belt and smiled up at Craig. She had spent every moment with the boys since their return to the station that morning. Looking after Jamie and Timothy had become more than a job to Karen; the two boys had become the most important thing in her life. Not only had the children grown to think of her and Craig as their real parents, but she had also begun to feel protective and possessive of them as a real parent would.

"You can't blame them." Craig smiled and rubbed Karen's arm. "They haven't seen you for two weeks, so it's understandable they'd be excited and not want to settle. Two weeks in toddler time is like six months to us."

Karen nodded as they quietly stepped away from the boy's door and walked along the corridor that led back towards the labs in the ANZAR wing. She couldn't help but look back as Craig led her down the hallway.

"So, what do you reckon?" Craig asked as he threw an arm around her. "Should we hit the mess and grab some lukewarm food and terrible coffee?"

Karen smiled once again and hugged him back as they turned the corner at the end of the hall. They saw very few people. At this time of night, most of the research staff were either relaxing in their cabins or still going hard at it in the labs. The few people they did see smiled or waved a quick greeting as they walked past.

"Seems pretty quiet around here tonight doesn't it?" Karen said. "It feels like something is going on."

Craig shook his head at her perceptiveness. "Yeah, you're right. There is."

Karen looked at him. "Well? Are you going to tell me or what?" she jibed him.

"Yes. But let's get something to eat first." Craig rubbed his stomach. "I'm starving."

By this time, they had reached the long rectangular mess hall. It was all but deserted apart from a few lab-coated ANZAR staff who were scattered amongst the rows of laminated tables that filled one side of the room. Craig nodded to each of them as they passed. All but one gave a grunt of response and carried on eating.

"They're not exactly a sociable bunch, are they?" Karen whispered as they walked past.

"Nah, they're alright," Craig smiled. "They're a few of Professor Tran's engineers. He's pretty much a perfectionist and works them pretty hard. Those guys will probably be up most of the night testing and retesting the VAPER's systems to get ready for the project launch tomorrow."

"So, something is happening. What's the project launch?" Karen asked.

As Craig thought over how to begin, they both grabbed a tray and walked up to the serving area and stared down at the dishes of food.

"I forgot how bad the food up here is," Karen sighed as she bent down to scoop some mashed potato and a few dried sausages onto her plate.

As he waited, Craig began to fill her in on the next day's activities.

"You know how my father and I work in Quantum Physics right?" he began.

"Yeah, not that I get what that really involves. But, yeah," Karen answered as she spooned peas onto her plate.

"Well, for nearly ten years now, we've actually been working on a way to manipulate matter and travel through space and time using microscopically sized wormholes that occur naturally within nature."

"What?" Karen stopped what she was doing as she spun to face him. "Like a time machine?"

"No... well, yes. Well, sort of," Craig replied as he bent over and began to fill his own plate. His voice echoed slightly off the hard surfaces of the serving area as he spoke. "I guess I better start at the beginning," he sighed.

Turning to face her, Craig picked up his tray, and they both made their way to an empty table, far from anyone else.

"Remember I told you how my father and Professor Weekes have been working together since before I was born?" Craig said as he sat down.

Karen nodded in response.

"How they both lived in the Campbelltown area, they both taught at the University of Western Sydney, and they both built careers as successful physicists by working in the same labs and working on the same projects," Craig continued.

"Yeah, sure. I remember. You called them the Abbot and Costello of the physics world." Karen smiled from around a mouthful of food. "They were always together."

"They were inseparable. Because of their devotion to their work they didn't have much contact with anyone outside their labs. Both sort of became reliant on each other for professional and social company. They were both obsessed with their line of research. They talked of little else. They became single-minded in their goals..."

Karen interrupted Craig. "And what were those?" she asked.

"What was what?" Craig looked confused.

"What were the goals that they became so obsessed with?" Karen shook her head and smiled.

Craig waved his hand as if shooing away a fly. "Oh, feeding the world, erasing poverty, eradicating diseases. You know, the usual lofty goals of well-meaning scientists the world over. But they've pretty much abandoned that line of research. The technology they were developing is still being worked on by Henry's people and a few other departments, but to the professors, that stuff no longer really matters to them..."

Karen frowned. "Really? What could be more important than curing disease and saving lives?"

"The deaths of their wives," Craig said matter-of-factly. Karen blinked.

"You see, both men gave their lives to their work. Like I said, they never went out, they never socialised." Craig looked at Karen. "They never dated until Jean and Lynda came along. They were two female Physicists who were as talented as the men were obsessive. John and Brian were both besotted with them as soon as they showed up in the labs. By that time, Dad was in his early forties, and Uncle Brian was over fifty. You could say both of them found love late in life."

"Better than not finding it at all." Although she had heard a brief account of these events before, Karen nevertheless smiled in return as she continued to listen and eat her meal.

"Well, the fact that they had gone so long without it made both men fall in love faster and harder. Dad and Lynda hit it off while Professor Weekes and Jean began to spend more and more of their time together." Craig sighed and gave Karen a weak smile before continuing. "Anyway, so by 2024, they had all gotten married and had begun to start a family. I was born a year later, and Luke followed in 2026."

Craig shrugged. "All in all, they had ten years of happy family life before it all came to an end when both women were killed as a result of the 2034 terrorist attacks on America."

Craig looked down at the table as his emotions got the better of him. Karen reached over and took one of his hands in hers as she waited for him to continue.

"I was nine when she died." Craig looked up with tears in his eyes. "I can still remember the last time I saw her at Sydney airport before she boarded her flight. Both mum and Auntie Jean looked happy and excited to be travelling abroad for the first time since having us kids. Dad and Professor Weekes would have gone with them, but they chose to stay and do some work and spend some time with Luke and me. Like you, mum used to nag my father to try and spend more time with me. You know, to form a bond. In the end, I think that backfired. Although he loves me, I'm sure a small part of him blames me for the fact that he wasn't there with her when she died. He's been a little stand-offish ever since."

Karen gasped and looked Craig in the eyes. "You can't seriously believe that?" she asked. "Don't forget, I've known your father for a couple of years now, and I don't think he would ever blame you for that."

Craig looked back down at the table and shook his head slowly from side to side. "Either way. My mother's death messed both of us up. She didn't deserve to die like that."

His voice grew thick as he struggled not to cry. "People say it was just a case of bad luck. You know, wrong place wrong time." Craig smiled sarcastically to show absurd it sounded. "It was just a bad coincidence that their flight was approaching the American coast as the terrorists struck."

Craig poked at the table top with his index finger and hissed what he had to say next through clenched teeth. "Their plane was shot down and over two hundred people killed on a hunch. All because the U.S. military suspected there might have been terrorists onboard. We never even got the bodies back. We ended up burying empty coffins."

Craig rubbed his face with the palms of his hands as he took deep breaths and struggled to compose himself. Karen rose to her feet, stepped around the table and sat in the seat beside him. She wrapped one arm around his shoulder and began to rub his back.

After a few moments, he looked up, and she gave him a light kiss on the cheek.

"Sorry." Craig tried to smile. "It's been fourteen years. You'd think I'd be over it by now."

"Don't be so hard on yourself, babe," Karen tried to reassure him. "Losing somebody like that must be very hard. I'm sure your father still probably feels the same."

"He does," Craig nodded. "That one incident has become the single defining moment of both of the Professors' lives. Both men broke down when they got the news. I can remember seeing my father collapse onto the living room floor when the airline reps came and told him what had happened."

Karen continued to rub Craig's back as she listened to the story which she had only heard bits and pieces of previously. "It must have been a terrible time for everyone involved," she sympathised.

"It was." Craig rubbed his eyes. "It was the worst. Both Professors fell into a deep depression and soon lost interest in work. The company they had worked so hard and long to create had become irrelevant to them. They became bitter and angry for the loss of Lynda and Jean. After a few months, neither man could function, and they eventually hid away from the world and each other. They didn't have a falling out as such; they just drifted apart and gradually lost contact. I guess seeing each other brought back too many memories."

"And what about you? What were you doing while all this was going on?" Karen asked.

"Luke and I were still with our fathers. We got ourselves dressed, took ourselves to school and came home to watch TV each day. I know it was hard for dad to lose his wife like that... but I lost my mother, and I was only a kid. We both used to cry ourselves to sleep each night, alone in our separate rooms. My dad still looked after me, but he remained cold and distant for a long time." Craig shrugged.

Having never heard the story of this part of Craig's life before, she was genuinely interested. "What changed that?" Karen asked.

Craig smiled at the memory of which he was about to tell. Karen could see that the story had passed its darkest point and had made a turn for the better.

"Well, one day dad was lying on the couch in his pyjamas when a knock came at the door. He got up to answer it, and there was Professor Weekes with a large cardboard box full of what looked like files and data-cubes."

Craig turned to Karen, growing serious once more. "The part that sticks with me the most was the Professor's face. He was smiling from ear to ear. From that moment on I knew things were somehow going to get better for all of us. I never really saw exactly what was in the box; I was more excited to see Luke again. While both of us kids ran off to play, our dads apparently decided to snap themselves out of their depression and go back to work together."

Craig shook his head in amazement as he thought back. "I wish I knew what was in that box," he sighed. "Whatever it was, it gave both men their lives back and gave them a goal to work towards. One that they thought was not only achievable but one that would fix everything that had gone so wrong recently."

Craig paused, lost in his own thoughts. Karen waited for him to continue but in the end, had to ask.

"Well? What was it?" What was this new goal of theirs?"

Craig looked her in the eye and placed a hand on her cheek and gestured at the room around them with a twitch of his head. "All this. Newton Station, ANZAR, all of our research, all of our staff. Everything we do up here is designed for one purpose."

Craig paused and held Karen's gaze.

"All of this is so that the Professors can go back and stop their wives from getting on that plane."

Karen didn't know what to say. She knew that Craig and his father were both gifted physicists, but she had no idea that they were working towards such an ambitious and seemingly impossible goal.

"Can they do it?" was all she could ask.

Craig smiled and nodded. "It wasn't going to happen for at least another month, maybe two. But with the Americans planning on shutting us down, we've had to move the schedule forward."

"To tomorrow?" Karen asked. Her mind was reeling with the shock of what Craig and her father were preparing. She didn't know whether to feel excited or to fear for their sanity. "Just think, babe," Craig smiled. "This time tomorrow I'll

be able to introduce you to my mother."

With that, Craig leant over and hugged her. She could feel the beat of his racing heart as he pulled her close.

My God, they're really going to try this, she thought.

7
Taking leave

Professor Weekes' office – Newton Station.

11.15pm - Monday, July 27th, 2048

Brian Weekes sat hunched over the desk with his face pressed against the glass of his computer screen. Calculations and Conduit addresses filled his head as he tried to make sense of what the new data could mean. In their last round of tests, he and Professor Turp had successfully launched twelve probes into different sectors of the Multiverse to gauge the characteristics of each. Eleven of the probes had returned filled with images and data, number twelve failed to return at all. Although this would have little to no effect on his and Professor Turp's mission the next day, the ramifications for future research had the potential to be enormous.

With a deep sigh, Professor Weekes looked up at his friend sitting opposite him in the darkness.

"Probe twelve does have me a little concerned, John," he began. "But... not enough to stop me getting my Jean back."

Professor Turp gave a sympathetic nod of his head and took another sip of rum from the tumbler he had been nursing.

"I know what you mean," he replied. "Since we took our first steps into the Multiverse, we've always known that there would be alternate versions of our own reality which we would have to contend with..."

"But how do we know we've got the right one?" Professor Weekes smacked the table in frustration. "How can we be sure that we aren't going to kidnap our own wives from some other reality in which their plane didn't get shot down?"

Professor Weekes looked back at the computer screen with tears in his eyes as he struggled with the problem. "Remember what losing them did to us?" he asked his friend slowly and softly. "Do you really want to inflict that kind of hurt on someone else if we get it wrong? Even if it is a different version of us... and our boys?"

John Turp leaned forward in his seat until the glow from Professor Weekes' monitor painted his face a deep blue. He was filled with both anger and compassion for the man in whose office he now sat.

"Listen, Brian. I am as sure of this as I have been about everything else we've done for the last fourteen years." He began to tap on the desk with the index finger of his right hand while he nursed the near-empty glass of rum in the other. "I know that we have found the right Conduit address this time. I know we have found the right version of reality in which it is still 2034, and our wives are about to step on that plane and fly off to their deaths. After all this time, we have the means to go back and stop them from getting on that flight. I won't walk away and leave my Lynda to die all over again because you're worried about upsetting some alternate reality versions of ourselves."

Professor Turp rose to his feet and slammed his glass down on the desk. "What about us, huh? What about Craig and Luke? We've all suffered long enough over the deaths of Lynda and Jean. We deserve to have them back and if some Parallel universe versions of ourselves get hurt, then... then too bad for them!" John Turp fiddled with his pockets and looked around the room as his eyes blinked away tears. He wiped at his face with the palm of his hand then looked down at his friend who sat crying silently before him.

"Look Brian. I'm sorry, but we need to do this," he began compassionately. "This thing has dominated our lives for too long. We need to get it done and move on."

Professor Weekes tapered off, not knowing what else to say.

A knock on the door startled both Professors from their thoughts of wormholes, parallel universes and a past that they feared to meddle with. After a moment's pause, Professor Weekes rubbed his eyes and spoke aloud.

"Come in," he called out.

The door slid open to reveal the station's resident Astronomer, Glen Hanson. He entered the room almost warily with his hands buried deep in his pockets. His demeanour, combined with the nervous look on his face, made him look like a schoolboy who had just been summoned to the headmaster's office. His age added to the impression he gave off of being a troubled youth. At only thirty-four he stood out from the other scientists at Newton as he was the youngest Professor by more than ten years. The fact that he was blessed with youthful good looks and unblemished skin only helped to accentuate the age gap between his peers and himself. What he lacked in age, he more than made up for in experience. With over a decade of solid research behind him, Glen had become the head of his discipline and had pioneered the burgeoning field of Quanta-Astronomy. Brian Weekes saw him for the brilliant asset he was and knew that the group's program of research on board Newton Station would not have progressed as far as it had without his considerable input. Like all of his scientists, Brian knew that Glen had eccentricities. His main one is that he was extremely shy and found it difficult to communicate with people he wasn't familiar with. The fact that he looked so ill at ease as he walked into the room told the Professor that Glen was deeply troubled.

"So, what are you looking so worried about there, Glen? I hope I didn't put the fear into you too much with all that talk of the Americans at the meeting, did I?" Brian asked.

Like always, Glen looked a little taken aback by how well the Professor could read him. "No, not at all." He looked from Professor Weekes to Professor Turp who just stood in the middle of the room and stared at the floor. The Astronomer could tell something was wrong but had no idea what it was.

"Sorry if I'm interrupting," he began. "I can come back later if you like."

"No, no. That's fine," Professor Weekes replied. "What can we do for you?"

"Well, it's just that... I wanted to clear up with you whether it would be safe for me to still take that couple of weeks off to go see my father for his birthday. I mean, I'll still be here to help out and see you and Professor Turp off on Project Reunion. I wasn't planning on leaving until the six o'clock shuttle to London tomorrow evening. You know, with everything that's going on I understand if you think it's not possible for me to..."

The Professor cut Glen off and reassured him in a sympathetic tone. "Of course, of course. Like I said in the meeting, I don't believe anything will happen due to the Americans for a few weeks yet. I know how much your mother wants you home for your father's seventieth and I wouldn't dream of letting you disappoint her. So, go, go." The Professor made a playful act of shooing him out of the room. "You have worked long enough and hard enough to warrant some time off. That's why I insist you go and don't make any more fuss about it. "

Glen still didn't look convinced. "Well, I'll get my team onto the packing up and securing of all data and files before I go so that won't take too long. I'll make sure that we're prepared for an inspection just in case."

Brian Weekes attempted a smile but could only nod. "Fine, fine. Just go and have some fun, will you? And wish your old man a happy birthday from me, Okay?" With a polite but dismissive wave, he sent Glen on his way out of the room.

After taking two steps towards the door, Glen turned to the Professor once more. "As long as you're sure nothing's going to happen while I'm gone."

"Trust me, my dear boy," the Professor sighed. "The Americans won't make their move while you're away. They need time to prepare and find out what we're doing before they risk interfering."

With one last smile and a final look that said that he still wasn't convinced. Glen turned and left the room.

Professor Weekes turned to John Turp and exchanged a knowing look. "That's what we've been told at least."

8
Farewell

ANZAR Labs Engineering Bay – Newton Station.

9.12am - Tuesday, July 28th, 2048

Professor Weekes stepped into the engineering lab and paused just inside the door. The brightly-lit room was filled with at least a dozen white-coated ANZAR staff that were busy making last-minute preparations for the launch. After a quick scan of the room, he spotted who he was looking for; the top half of Professor Turp was visible over the domed cockpit of one of the VAPERs.

Professor Weekes chuckled as he began to make his way towards his old friend. The sight of the two experimental vehicles docked within the engineering bay had always struck him as slightly comical. With only the tops of their transparent diamond hulls visible, the *Feynman* and the *Hawking* resembled miniature icebergs that floated in the centre of the room. The fact that most of their bulk lay hidden in made-to-measure airlocks beneath the floor only added to the illusion.

The Professor had to duck and weave around the engineers and their equipment as he made his way across the ample open space. As he grew nearer the *Feynman*, he could see that Professor Turp was deeply involved in a serious discussion with someone hidden beneath the floor. Stepping over one last box and positioning himself beside his friend, Professor Weekes looked down into the floor and spotted Henry Tran in the pilot's seat of the *Feynman*.

"Good morning, Brian," John Turp said as he pushed himself away from the *Feynman*'s cockpit canopy and turned towards his business partner. "We pretty much have this thing ready to go."

Professor Weekes nodded thoughtfully and smiled down at Doctor Tran who sat five feet below them testing the *Feynman*'s controls. "How goes it, Henry?" the Professor called out.

ANZAR's Chief Engineer looked up from his work and gave a reassuring smile. "Good morning Professor Weekes." He balanced the tablet computer he had been using on the armrest of the pilot's seat and climbed to his feet. Henry offered his hand in greeting, and Professor Weekes shook it. With Henry standing on the pilot's chair both men's faces were less than a foot apart.

"I have a few more tests on the flight controls to run, but the engines and the reactor are both working beautifully," Henry beamed.

"And get this." Professor Turp smiled and patted Brian on the shoulder. "Henry's even worked out that bug with the hatch that gave us so much hell on the test flight." Both doctors smiled at the memory of being trapped inside the airtight vehicle for over thirty-six hours before an embarrassed Doctor Tran managed to get the hatch open.

"Well, that's a relief," Brian laughed.

"Are the guys in the control room ready for us?" Professor Turp asked.

Brian nodded. "Adam's got the Conduit address for our destination point keyed in and ready to go. He can have a few dozen wormholes located and opened for us as soon as we're ready."

The door to the engineering bay slid open. Craig and Luke entered the room accompanied by the station's medical researcher, Doctor Anderson. The two boys carried a small duffle bag each while the doctor brought a briefcase. Both Professors watched as the trio made their way towards them.

"Hi Dad," Luke began. "We've brought along a few things we thought you might need. You know, for when you pick mum up." He smiled nervously as he handed his father the bag.

"What's in them?" Professor Turp asked as he turned to face Craig. His son's face showed the depth of emotion that the boy was feeling. It looked to the Professor that his son had most probably been crying.

Craig looked at his father and gave a shy shrug. "We both thought it would make sense to pack some of our mother's clothes in case they should need a change before they get back."

"Yeah," Luke agreed sombrely. "I've also made up a photo file and placed it on a small display that you can show them. You know, just in case you have a problem convincing them of what's going on and where you're from."

The two Professors looked at each other.

"Photo file?" Professor Turp asked, "What's on it?"

"It's just a collection of photos of the four of us from between the plane crash and now. Sort of a montage of what they've missed." It was Luke's turn to shrug. "We thought it might help them get their heads around the time that has passed..."

"And prepare them for seeing us as adults." Craig indicated Luke and himself.

"That's a good idea, boys." Professor Weekes nodded and made a weak attempt at a smile. A wave of emotion coursed through his body for the thousandth time since they had dreamt up this 'rescue mission'. He could feel tears brimming in the corners of his eyes once again as he struggled to keep himself calm.

Thank God this will all be over with today... one way or the other, he thought.

John Turp opened the bag that Craig had handed him and took a peek inside. He reached in with one hand and pulled out part of an item of clothing. It was a thick red bundle of wool that he recognised immediately.

"That's your mum's favourite jumper," the Professor sighed. "She used to love this thing," he said thickly.

"I know," Craig nodded. "When I think back to her, when I see her in my mind, she's always wearing that." Craig blinked away tears as he struggled to continue.

Professor Weekes watched as John leant forward, grabbed his son and pulled him close. Feeling overcome with emotion himself, he closed his eyes to regain his composure.

On opening his eyes, he could see that Professor Turp and Craig were still hugging. Both men appeared to be crying softly into each other's shoulders. Fifteen years of loss washed over the Professor in a wave as he realised that in many ways, he had also lost his son the day he lost his wife. With all the time they had spent working on a way to get their wives back, he had somehow managed to miss precious time with the only family he had left. In a wave of emotion, Professor Weekes grabbed Luke and pulled him close in a firm embrace. Luke went rigid with surprise as his father wrapped his arms around him. After a moment, his body relaxed, and he hugged his father back.

The two families held each other and softly wept. The outburst of emotion was bittersweet. They cried both in sadness for what they had lost and in anticipation of what they hoped to regain.

Out of respect, none of the engineering staff commented or attempted to approach the group. They all knew what this mission was about and was well aware of its intensely personal nature. Doctor Anderson, who had entered the room with the boys, subtly moved a few feet away and looked inside the cockpit of the nearby *Feynman*. Henry Tran was back in the pilot's seat and gave the doctor an awkward grin. Both men waited silently as they gave the Professors and their sons a minute to themselves.

A few moments passed before someone behind the doctor finally spoke.

"Uhm, Doctor Anderson," Professor Turp said as he coughed and cleared his throat. "I assume that you have the ModChips for our wives in that briefcase there?"

Doctor Anderson turned to face the Professor. All four men were now standing around and looking at him. After their emotional moment, they seemed to be all business again. "Yes. Yes, they are." The doctor handed the briefcase over to the Professor. "If you would like me to go over the

application procedure again I'd be more than happy to."

"No. No, thank you." Professor Turp gave a strained smile and placed the case at his feet. "I think I can manage it."

"Well." Professor Weekes burst out suddenly as he clapped his hands together. "Shall we get aboard and get ready to depart." He slapped Professor Turp on the back.

John knew Brian well enough to understand that this was his friend's way of trying to shake off the emotion from a few minutes before. He envied his apparent resilience.

Henry climbed out of the *Feynman*'s cockpit and made space for the Professors to enter.

With one last hug, Craig and Luke said goodbye and made their way towards the door.

As he left the room, Craig turned back in time to see the top of his father's head as it disappeared into the *Feynman*.

That was the last time Craig saw his father in this world.

9
Wakeup call

Accommodation wing – Newton Station. 3.02am -

Thursday, August 13th, 2048

Dreams of air disasters, images of death and memories of his father's departure floated through Craig's mind. Pained and tortured faces flickered into view long enough to scream an unheard message before fading back into the darkness only to be replaced by another. Tossing and turning and covered in sweat; this is how Craig had slept since his father's disappearance.

In his mind's eye, Craig saw the *Feynman* fade out of existence with both his father and Professor Weekes aboard. The mission to rescue his mother had started off well; everything had gone perfectly. There was no sign of trouble until the designated return time came.

And went.

The Professors were scheduled to return in exactly one hour. Slightly concerned but not overly alarmed, the ANZAR team in the control room had exchanged a few puzzled glances and continued to wait. It wasn't until the Professors were three hours overdue that someone voiced a concern. Options were discussed; courses of action were considered and discarded. At the twelve-hour mark, Craig argued for taking the second VAPER, the *Hawking*, out to look for them. All agreed that this would be a dangerous move that would likely result in the loss of both vehicles. Not to mention leaving both the Professors and those who went after them with no hope of rescue. Besides, Adam Fehrenbach pointed out; they had been given strict instructions to wait if the Professors return was delayed.

The hours turned into days as everyone within the ANZAR wing waited for the *Feynman* to return. Craig and Luke grew sombre and quiet. Both boys began to believe that they had been over-ambitious in their plan to retrieve their mothers and as a result, had lost their fathers in the process. Neither of them wanted to leave the control room. Both men ate little and slept even less. They dozed amongst the rows of computers and control stations as they waited and worried over their fathers' return. After three days, with hopes of the Professors' return fading, Karen managed to talk them into allowing other station staff to keep watch. Begrudgingly, Luke and Craig began to once again sleep in their beds and take time away for meals.

Craig lay tossing and turning in bed while Karen slept soundly beside him. It had been ten days since the Professors had disappeared and his dreams had grown more disturbed, more erratic. As the memory of saying goodbye to his father played through his mind in slow motion, an incessant buzzing noise began to invade his dream. The steady thrum rose in pitch and volume until it became impossible to hear what his father was saying. In his sleep, Craig could only see his father's lips moving. All sound was buried beneath the unbearable, irritating buzz that he now found impossible to ignore.

He awoke to discover that it was the middle of the night. The noise that had disturbed his dream was the ringing of the phone. With a mind still half filled with memories and sleep, he ordered his hand to move and pick up the receiver.

"Yeah?"

Luke's voice bellowed down the phone in reply. "Mate, great news. The conduit has just come back online, and it's gone into warm-up mode." There was no mistaking the excitement in his voice. "We're receiving a return signal. Once the warm-up is complete, we should have the *Feynman* back in about thirty minutes."

"Just like that, huh?" Craig mumbled. Even with the exciting news, he was still slow in coming fully awake.

Everyone on the station had put in a lot of overtime to try and figure out what had happened to the Professors. Many of the ANZAR group were feeling the strain of the long hours and stress beginning to take its toll.

"I know. It's weird, isn't it? They vanish for ten days with no contact and all of a sudden it looks like they're coming back. The mystery deepens as they say." A slight pause followed as both men explored their thoughts and concerns for a moment.

"Well, anyway. I just thought I'd let you know so you can be here when they get back in. I'll see you in the control room in five, OK?"

"Hey, Luke," Craig called down the phone before his friend could hang up. "Any idea how many are onboard," he asked hopefully.

"Not yet, mate," Luke sighed. "At this point, I'd be happy with just getting our Dads back. We can always try again for our mums later on."

There was a slight pause on the line.

"But hey, who knows huh? They've been gone long enough. Maybe the dirty old buggers decided to whisk their wives away to somewhere secluded to catch up first... if you know what I mean." Luke laughed.

"You're disgusting, man." Craig laughed in return. The prospect of getting their fathers back had put both men in a good mood.

The line went dead, and Craig hung up. He sat motionless on the edge of the bed as a wave of relief washed over him. He tried not to get too excited, the fact of their return was great news, but he wasn't about to begin celebrating until they were safely back home.

Craig slowly rose to his feet and gave a quick stretch then turned to check on Karen. She was curled up on her side of the single bed with her forehead pressed against the wall. Soft breathing sounds floated up from her in time with the rise and fall of her chest. She looked peaceful where she was, and he debated whether or not to wake her. Since the start of the emergency, she had effectively been doing double shifts. After spending most of the day babysitting the kids in the nursery, her nights were occupied consoling and reassuring Craig as he slowly sank deeper and deeper into depression. Although not physical, the combination would have been emotionally draining for her.

Craig appreciated that she needed her rest as much as anyone on the station.

As he stood and watched, Karen slowly stirred in her sleep and rolled over in the bed. Craig decided that she was also concerned for his father's wellbeing, and it would be selfish of him not to tell her after everything she had done. He placed one knee on the bed and gently pulled the covers away from her face. He took a moment to smile down at her before giving her a quick peck on the cheek. Her eyes fluttered open, and she looked up at him.

"Is it morning already?" she yawned.

"Not quite," Craig smiled. "I just had a call from Luke. It looks like the professors are on the way back."

Karen raised herself up onto one elbow as the news brought her fully awake.

"Oh my God, that's great news," she smiled in return. "When will they get here?"

Craig turned and sat on the bed as he began to pull a pair of socks on.

"Not long. Less than half an hour." He turned to look at her. "You want to come watch?"

Due to their busy schedules and circumstance, Karen had never been into the control room where many of ANZAR's major experiments were controlled. Her duties within the crèche caring for Jamie and Timothy kept her too busy to visit that part of the station. With the boys safely asleep and the imminent return of the Professors, she had ample reason to visit the control room tonight.

"Do you know if it worked?" she asked Craig as she slid out of bed and began to dress.

Craig looked at her for a moment as he considered the question. "Do you mean worked as in did they get my mother back?"

"Yeah," she nodded.

Craig shook his head and pulled a t-shirt over his chest. "We won't know that one until they get back."

10

Decontamination

Accommodation wing – Newton Station. 3.10am -

Thursday, August 13th, 2048

With their twelve department heads and extended support staff, the ANZAR team was the most extensive research group on Newton. Although their facilities occupied nearly half of the labs, they were by no means alone on the research wing. Six-month leases were auctioned off once a year to private companies and research groups who paid handsomely for lab space that was not only far from prying eyes but free from the political and legal constraints that hindered research back on Earth. Space was neutral territory. What was illegal on Earth was merely morally questionable in Low Earth Orbit.

Even though it was just after three in the morning, the corridors were still brightly lit. The station was in operation around the clock as scientists from a broad cross-section of nationalities worked and kept time with their own countries time-zones. It was realised early on that a set twenty-four- hour day was impossible to adhere to as the international community onboard needed to be able to work and converse with their earthbound counterparts during their local business hours. With ANZAR's head office being in Sydney, all ANZAR staff worked hours that corresponded to local Sydney time. With this system, the station was never empty or quiet, and it was not uncommon to see and hear people passing in the corridors at all hours.

Craig and Karen turned right into the main access corridor for their wing of the accommodation module. Around them, a light flow of human traffic came and went as station staff headed in both directions. They passed dozens of cabins in this corridor alone and greeted many scientists who were either on their way to or from work. Many of the people he saw were unknown to him as they were under the employ of private companies who had little or no association with ANZAR. At the time, there were nine corporations currently enjoying the freedom associated with renting lab space on the station. All corporations were strictly segregated and allowed to work on their projects in privacy and relative anonymity to that which was available on Earth. The accommodation area was a hive of social activity and one of only two places in the research wing where teams from different groups could come into contact outside of their separate labs.

After a few minutes walk, they arrived at the main airlock junction which acted as a security screen and decontamination point between the accommodation area and the labs. They both took turns in placing their faces in front of one of the many surveillance sensors that dotted the station. Nicknamed the Nerve, the security systems near invisible lens stared impassively down the corridor as it recorded the actions of everyone who came and went. The system was designed and built by the ANZAR group and encompassed a web of sensors that scanned and identified the faces of everyone who passed. Many of the station staff resented the idea of having their whereabouts constantly monitored and considered it a gross invasion of privacy. As a result, the system soon became known as the Perve.

With their faces identified, Karen and Craig both reached out and placed their right hands on a glass identification pad located in the middle of the wall. As they waited, Craig took the opportunity to slip his left arm around Karen and kiss her on the top of the head. With a slight smile, she leant sideways and nuzzled into his chest, oblivious to anyone who might wander past and see.

As their prints were scanned and DNA tested, Craig looked into the eye of the Nerve sensor and wondered if Luke was watching. Between experiments, his friend enjoyed taking time out to observe the comings and goings of everyone on the station via the security system. Over time, it had become his chief form of entertainment that he likened to having his own private reality show. A smile came to Craig's face as he imagined Luke sitting at a desk in the control room urging them to get a move on.

Karen looked up at his face and asked what was funny. "Nothing." Craig shook his head and continued to smile.

"I'm just relieved that this whole mess might be over soon."

With a low buzz, the Nerve signalled approval for entry. A loud click echoed around the end of the corridor as the large vault-like door slowly swung open. To avoid a backlog of foot traffic between the accommodation wing and the ANZAR labs, the decontamination booth was designed to hold and process up to halve a dozen people at once. As a result, Karen and Craig were able to enter the airlock side by side. The room was the size of an average elevator and was as featureless as the corridor outside.

As Karen slipped her hand into Craig's, the door thudded shut behind them. Its echo quickly faded into total silence. Having been through the process numerous times in the last two years, they both knew what to expect. Still, that didn't stop the sharp and sudden hiss of inrushing air from the decontamination system from making them both jump. As the air pressure rose, they stood still, faced forwards and closed their eyes, ready for the decontamination routine to begin.

A feeling of warmth washed over, and through them, as low levels of radiation cleansed their bodies of germs and bacteria. Craig found the combined effects of the heat and rushing air from the decontamination process to be quite pleasant. As the breeze tousled his hair and the radiation warmed his skin, he felt a wave of calm and peace wash over him. The sensation brought back memories of a trip he had taken to Towradgi beach with his father when they were both much younger. With his eyes closed, he could easily believe he was basking in the sun on that summer's day with both of his parents by his side once again. The intake and outtake vents co-operated with the memory to create the illusion that he could hear the soft hiss of the surf as he and his parents stood and watched the sea. He found it reassuring that the simple memories of building a sandcastle and swimming in the ocean with his dad held more emotional value for him since his father had disappeared. Before the experiment had gone wrong and his father appeared lost, he would have said that these simple pleasures were trivial and less important than the work they had performed in the labs. Their research time was still vital to him. He was glad that he had had the opportunity to be involved in that side of his father's life. As good as those times were, they paled next to the memories of his dad being a father, not a Professor.

With a soft beep and a sudden stillness, everything shut down as the decontamination unit finished its job. Craig's daydream ended with the heat and the breeze as Craig was forced back into the real world. The air conditioning and the cool hard lighting of the station made him realise that the warmth he had felt in the presence of his father may have left him for good.

The inner door to the ANZAR holistic research facility slid open. With the way cleared, he and Karen stepped over the threshold to find out what, if anything had happened to his father.

11

The return

Karen and Craig stepped out of the decontamination unit with their hair tousled and their bodies warm. After the comforting warmth of the radiation, the air-conditioned environment of the ANZAR labs felt almost chilly by comparison. Without pausing, they walked along the main corridor that ran the length of the research wing. From within the labs, sporadic snatches of muffled conversations mixed with the hum of technology floated through the closed doors as they passed. Under the circumstances, Craig was only mildly surprised that a few research departments were working later than usual. With the impending arrival of the American armed forces now being measured in days rather than weeks, time was short. The need to get the labs secured and their research stored off-site had become urgent.

At the end of the corridor, they stopped at the last door where the Nerve system once again checked their identification. After yet another security scan, the door slid aside and allowed access to the main ANZAR control centre where the most impressive sight on the station greeted them.

A full-length window much like the one in the meeting room covered the entirety of the centre's longest wall and framed a fantastic view of the planet below. The Earth dominated the left side of the panorama as it slowly turned on its daily cycle. Like the meeting room, the control room was bathed in a vibrant cyan glow from the soft blue earthlight which poured through the window. To the right of the Earth, a vast region of open space was visible. Countless stars shone in a variety of colours which were invisible from the surface of the Earth. They filled out the vista, displaying an impressive example of what could only be described as a busy emptiness. Of all the sights on Newton, this was the one that made Craig appreciate the enormity of where he was and the importance what they were doing. Nowhere else was it possible to obtain such a clear and open view of the Earth as it turned on the edge of the void.

The control centre measured thirty metres by fifteen and was full of observation screens and equipment. Its function would have been apparent to anyone who had worked in the space industry during the last one hundred years. Its design was borrowed from - as well as a homage to - the mission control rooms from the early days of the NASA flight missions. Rows of workstations spanned the dimly lit room, illuminating the forms of the few ANZAR staff who were on late duty awaiting the Professors' return. On the right of the room, a one-hundred-inch H-OLED screen displayed a crystal-clear image of two satellites that floated closely together just a few kilometres away from the station. They had sat in the same spot for the last ten days like shadows against the background of stars as they patiently awaited the return of the *Feynman*. With the Professors' imminent arrival, the satellites had become active and displayed a sequence of flashing lights that demonstrated they were ready to accept the return of the long overdue craft.

The Conduit's colour wheel filled a smaller display on the wall alongside the main screen. It was comprised of a three-dimensional circle of light that for all effects looked like a rainbow turned into a ring. The spectrum was plainly visible as the colours gradually faded from one to the next. Violet blurred into magenta, then to pink and red to orange and yellow then green and teal which led into cyan and blue before finally completing the circle back at violet. The colour wheel was devised as a visual means of representing what was primarily an abstract mathematical concept. The regions of space and time which the VAPER was capable of moving within were found to be more readily understood and controlled with this method. Each block of colour represented a shift of millions of degrees in space. Each one of those degrees was, in turn, its own separate universe with its own individual attributes and conditions. Each colour shift was perceived as a means of mentally grouping large areas of the Multiverse that displayed similar characteristics. Test probes sent out in previous weeks were intended to identify the underlying conditions of each of the colour shifts. The data returned proved to be both perplexing and exciting at the same time. The prime concern amongst those involved was whether they had misunderstood that information and had allowed the Professors to travel into conditions in which they were unprepared. Wherever they had gone, everyone expected the men to come back with some amazing stories.

"It's about time you two got here," Luke said as he turned from a control desk at the rear of the room to greet Craig and Karen as they entered. "You could have been here a lot sooner if you hadn't stopped for a snog in front of the decontamination unit." Luke smiled.

Craig shook his head and laughed. "I knew you were watching."

"Hey, you know me." Luke shrugged and resumed his seat in front of three large monitors that displayed an assortment of data as well as a smaller image of the two satellites on the room's main screen. The desk was strewn with food packaging and rubbish which suggested that Luke had pulled another long shift keeping watch for his father.

"Has the Conduit become active?" Craig asked hopefully as he pulled a chair up and sat beside his friend.

"No, but it should do at any minute. The system has cycled up to ninety percent, so we should see some action soon."

Doctor Tran moved over to the control desk from where he was standing nearby. His demeanour showed how tired and forlorn he felt. As the most senior ANZAR representative on the station with the two Professors missing, he had found himself in the unenviable position of filling in for both men until their return. Judging by the look on his face, it couldn't be soon enough.

"Hi, Doc. How are things?" Craig asked the ageing man. A slight nod and a half-hearted smile was the only response he got as the Engineer lowered himself into a seat near the console. Karen took the Engineer's lead and dragged the last available seat closer to Craig.

"So, has Luke got you up to speed on all this stuff Henry? I know the conduit wasn't really in your field of expertise."

"Not really." The Engineer seemed to come awake and slowly turned to face the younger man. "Your father showed me a couple of things when I was installing the conduit control systems in the *Feynman* and the *Hawking*, but I wasn't really listening to all the theory behind it. I was concentrating more on getting his machine to work with mine. Knowing specifically what it does or how it does it was unimportant to me at the time." A slight shake of his head showed his frustration. "But it seems pretty important now. I'm an engineer, that Quantum stuff always went in one ear and out the other with me." A nervous smile flashed across his lips at his own ignorance of the subject. The Doctor was a great Engineer, but his attention span was short when it came to the research of others. His mind constantly wandered back to his own work as it tried to solve whatever problems were present at the time.

"I know what you mean. I get like that with the medical stuff a lot of the time," Craig empathised. "I don't even know for sure how the ModChips I built work on the human body, anatomically I mean. The technical side I know like the back of my hand, but I'll be buggered if I know in which order the tissue's regenerate or how it affects the body as a whole. I left that part up to Doctor Anderson to figure out."

The sounding of a soft alarm caused those in the control room to hurry back to their stations. A voice over the room's intercom announced that the conduit had reached full activity.

"What does that mean?" Karen asked no one in particular. "It means that the gate is actively searching out wormholes for the Professors to travel through. Once it's found enough, we'll see the VAPER begin to return," Luke answered as he pointed his finger at the larger display. "See? You see that light there between the satellites?" With the alarm signalling his father's impending arrival his mood changed immediately.

"That blue star you mean?" Karen asked.

"That's not a star, babe," Craig joined in. "That's the Conduit. That light is coming from the energy release that a rip in space-time creates. What you're looking at are hundreds of tiny wormholes which the *Feynman* and the professors will soon pass through."

Luke turned to face his friend with a look of relief and elation. "The sensors are registering life signs on the other side of the wormholes. Somebody alive is definitely coming back through."

The room had become a hive of activity as other station staff rushed in to take up positions at the remaining consoles. Soon the control centre was filled with the voices of over twenty specialists who were eagerly calling out instructions and technical readings across the room. The excitement was palpable as the light from the conduit grew brighter. As it expanded, it appeared to divide until it was no longer visible as a single point of light but seemed to resemble a tight cluster of tiny stars. The process was amazing to see, and all eyes in the room watched as it neared full size.

Karen looked slightly confused. "Why do you need hundreds of wormholes? Why can't they pass through just one like in the movies?"

"This one I can answer," Henry Tran piped up from the back of the group. "You see, wormholes are tiny. We're talking about something that is microscopic in size. These things exist naturally, but only at the most minute scales, we can measure. Plus, they only appear for a fraction of a second. At that size, it's impossible to pass anything physical through them. The only thing we can send is information in the form of data encoded lasers."

The alarm was getting louder as the time to the VAPER's return drew nearer.

"So, is that why you need to scan the VAPER and its occupants?" Karen remembered this point from a previous conversation with Craig.

"Exactly," Henry Tran replied. "That's why everything that goes through has to be fitted with one of Craig's ModChips. For this to work, both the passengers and the vehicle itself have to have them. What they do is reduce everything down to pure encoded information that is capable of travelling through that tiny space at high speed." Henry paused to see if she was following. With a nod of Karen's head, he continued. "With so much information needed to deconstruct and reconstruct the human body, as well as the details of every aspect of the vehicle, there is no way we can get all that through one hole in the short time that they stay open. We need to use hundreds, sometimes thousands at a time. It's kind of like BitTorrent. Millions of tiny chunks of information arrive via slightly different paths and are seamlessly combined to create the package."

Craig turned from the monitors and faced Karen. "On the surface, it all sounds really complicated, but the simple way to put is that basically, the VAPER and its entire contents are scanned by the ModChips. That information is then temporarily stored on the *Feynman*'s computers while wormholes to the correct time and place are found. The computer can scan at the Planck level at a billion times a second to find the holes that lead to where you want to go. Once enough are found, the system begins to decode the vehicle and its occupants into small packages of information. These are then shot individually into the wormholes at the speed of light using Doctor Tran's advanced laser messaging system."

Henry gave Karen a shy modest shrug. "That was easy. It was Craig's breakthrough with the ModChips that finally made the entire process possible," Henry added. "You see, they are in charge of breaking down the ship and its occupants at the start of the transit as well as reconstructing them again at the other end. So, they have to be last to leave and first to arrive. They take a separate route through a slightly different wormhole that allows them to arrive at the destination point a few seconds before everything else. At the other end of the wormhole, the mod-chips reconstruct themselves in time to receive the rest of the data through these conduits and decode the information as it's received."

Craig gave a quick snorting laugh. "Yeah. That was a pain in the arse. It took me a year to simplify the chips so that they could be compressed into a single message burst under 80 Terabytes."

Karen looked from Craig to Henry and back again. "Sorry guys. I still don't get it." She smiled awkwardly. "How does something so small squish a human being and a spaceship through a tiny hole? I mean, where does the original go?"

"Okay, let's try a different approach," Craig replied, eager to talk about his invention. His excitement caused him to talk swiftly. "The two primary roles of the ModChips are to store data and manipulate matter. I designed them as a miniature quantum computer which has enough memory to store 64 Yottabytes of information. That's enough data space required to store the location and composition of every atom in the human body. And that's exactly what it does. We place the chips in everything that travels in the VAPERS. Every item has one installed either on or in them just like the crew has them placed under the skin at the backs of their necks." Craig pointed to the base of his skull." They need to go right up in here, near the brain so..." He paused and seemed to reconsider what he was about to say. "Well, they need to go up high for other reasons that aren't relevant right now. Anyway, the chips know where every atom in a body or object is and in what order they need to be placed to recreate that person or object on the other side of the wormhole. They do that by adjusting the vibrations of superstrings present in atoms in the air or gases in space. To recreate the ship or person, they grab atoms from the destination point and change their properties, so they become whatever is needed. They literally tell the strings in an atom to stop vibrating as say... oxygen or CO_2 and get it to vibrate and behave as carbon or water or whatever element is needed. These altered atoms are then combined in the right order to recreate the stored object. It's pretty amazing how it works."

It was Henry's turn to ask a question. "So, how on Earth do you manage to handle all that data? I'm no biologist, but I know that the human body must be made up of billions of atoms. I can't see how a small chip could handle all that in anything close to a practical time."

"True! The human body is complex, but when you get down to the minute sizes we're dealing with, everything sort of simplifies." Craig thought for a moment. He always enjoyed the chance to explain his work. These kinds of deep, scientific conversations always made him feel alive and vibrant. Karen and Henry were also providing him with a handy distraction as they waited for the Professors to return.

"Okay, everything in the world is made up of atoms. Atoms, in turn, are made up of protons and neutrons and electrons etcetera, right?"

Karen and the Engineer nodded.

"Well, all the protons, neutrons and electrons are really the same thing. They're all strings, little packets of energy that oscillate at different frequencies. The type of particle they become depends on how fast or slow they oscillate or vibrate. So basically, if a string vibrates at say 1000 MHz, it takes on the properties of an electron, if it vibrates at 4200 MHz it becomes a proton and so on. So essentially, the data of the human body or anything solid is just a combination of the same thing; Strings which vibrate at different rates to appear to be different things. All we're doing is altering the vibration rates of one type of thing but on a massive scale. This simplifies everything greatly so that the chip only needs one piece of software to do this. Hell, there was even room left over on the chip to add a few extra features in the newer versions, for example, the chip can..."

The primary monitor on the control room wall suddenly lit up with a soft blue glow. "Enough of the lecture now, mate," Luke interrupted. "It's starting."

Luke enlarged his view on the monitor which until recently had been displaying the empty space between the conduit's satellites. As he zoomed in, the blue glow rushed forward to fill the screen. Its details became sharper and more readily visible. Thousands of tiny points of light flashed in, and out of existence as the wormholes repeatedly opened and closed. The effect was not unlike watching a firework display through a thin cover of cloud. Though in this display, all the fireworks were blue.

Over a loudspeaker in the control room, one of Henry Tran's engineers made an announcement. "36 out of the 40 ModChips from the *Feynman* have made transit and are now on our side of the wormholes. All are currently receiving data and preparing to begin reconstruction."

"Where are they?" Karen asked. "I can't see them."

"No. You won't be able to from this distance," Luke said as he scrolled through the incoming data that ran down the left of the screen. "The ModChips are only a bit more than an inch long and about as wide as those vitamin tablets the doc keeps prescribing."

As this was the final stage of the first live test of the technology, many ANZAR staff had not witnessed the sight of an active Conduit appearing before them. The control room alarm kept ringing as those not busy at work fixed their eyes on the large monitor to watch the progress of the *Feynman*'s return.

The last message before the return came over the speakers. "First components coming through in 3...2...1..."

Seemingly from out of nowhere a large transparent shape began to take form. Pieces of the VAPER seemed to appear on the ship as if they'd been shot out of the Conduit from a gun. Within a second the main hull of the craft was complete and floated in space looking like a frozen teardrop. Earthlight and sunlight combined to paint its clear diamond hull in shades of blue and orange. The VAPERS shell was primarily made up of one sealed unit which was rapidly being filled with components and equipment as those on the station watched. The wormhole rapidly ejected sparks of data which flew at the craft and fastened themselves both inside and out. As the flashes of light struck the ship, they became solid, transforming into wires, engine parts and fuel rods.

"My God, it's going so fast," Karen sighed.

"No way." Luke looked around. "We set the reconstruction rate at two percent so that we could film it for later study. In reality, the entire process should only take around two seconds. It's almost instantaneous."

With the return process begun, the alarm was switched off to allow for easier communication between the station staff. Another message came over the speaker system that chilled Karen's blood.

"Technical reconstruction is nearing completion. The first body parts are now coming through."

"Body parts? No! Shit, what happened to them?" Karen asked in shock.

"Nothing, babe." Craig reassured her, "It's normal. Like the VAPER, its occupants come through one piece at a time."

In the control room, they stared at the transparent ship as its pilot seat slowly began to fill. First, a spinal column and ribs occupied the seat, patiently waiting for the rest of the parts that would complete its form. Bones appeared around the body in brilliant flashes of orange light. Almost immediately, organs filled the chest and abdomen. The heart, lungs and intestine shone briefly in the sunlight as they were interwoven with veins and arteries to reintroduce blood flow. Muscles bloomed over the body, spreading outwards from the legs to the chest; they arrived just in time to prevent the newly reconstructed internal organs from slipping out onto the floor. Just before the body was enveloped in a protective layer of skin, the screen showed one last amazing site. As the chest muscles closed over the heart, those in the control room witnessed it take its first new beats.

"OK. That's one. Where's the other one?" Luke said in agitation. "They should have both come through at the same time. Shit! One of them didn't come back." Jumping to his feet, he was about to make his way to the control desks to see what had happened. His agitation was visible as he tried to hold back tears at the knowledge that his father had probably not returned.

The reconstruction now complete, the VAPER floated peacefully outside the control room window. Evidently, no one else was coming back. Only one of the men had survived the journey.

As Luke passed Craig on his way to the main control area, a hand was gently placed on his shoulder, stopping his advance.

With teary eyes, Luke looked up into the face of his friend and saw his own grief mirrored there.

"Calm down Luke. Look at the monitor." Craig indicated the large screen with a nod of his head. "You've got nothing to worry about. Your dad's sitting right there in the pilot's seat."

Luke turned to see his father's body slumped in the *Feynman*'s pilot seat. His jaw was slack as his head lay against his shoulder, unconscious. If not for the movement of his chest from his steady breathing, Luke would have thought he was dead.

"Oh... thank god. I thought I'd lost him." The realisation hit him as he spoke the words. Turning back to Craig, his anxiety returned as he asked the question he already knew the answer to. "So, where's John then? What happened to your father, Craig?"

With a sigh, he answered the only way he knew how. "It looks like he didn't make it."

12

Followed

ANZAR control room – Newton Station. 3.42am -

Thursday, August 13th, 2048

"What do you mean you can't close it?" Craig yelled across the room to the mission controller. "Just shut the bloody power off."

The situation had gone from bad to worse since the VAPER appeared. With the realisation that one of the Professors had not returned and the other was seemingly unconscious, the control room had fallen into a stunned silence. Everyone stood motionless as they stared at the display screen which showed the near lifeless image of Professor Weekes slouched in the pilot's seat. Everyone was dismayed at how a simple one-hour transit could have gone so drastically wrong. Minutes passed before anyone noticed the fact that the Conduit through which the one surviving Professor had travelled had not closed.

"We have. We turned the power off already!" Adam Fehrenbach screamed back. He had to yell for his reply to be heard over the sound of the alarms, and the frenzied conversations in the room as Tran's Engineers tried to solve the problem. "The satellites are dead! Whatever is keeping that thing open, it's got nothing to do with us. Personally, I can't even see how it's possible. These wormholes are so unstable that they immediately collapse after use." Craig could see that the controller was alarmed by the situation. The man was starting to ramble, telling him information that he already knew. "You know... that's why we use so many at a time. These damned things never stay open this long. They can't."

Luke slipped behind a group of engineers who had removed the front panel from a computer console and were busily ripping out wires in an attempt to shut the system down. As he passed, he could hear the engineers swearing as they tried unsuccessfully to get the unresponsive Conduit to deactivate. The ANZAR staff were not yet in a state of panic, but as Craig looked around the control room, he could see a few individuals who were teetering on edge. For the most part, a sense of extreme urgency had enveloped the room.

Luke stood beside Craig and Adam, before he could speak the computer issued an automated verbal warning over the intercom.

"Objects now returning through the Conduit. Expected arrival in twenty seconds," the sultry female voice of the station's computer announced.

"Hear that?" Adam barked. "It must be a technical fault. The computers just announced the Professors return nearly ten minutes after he made it back. It has to be a bad sensor that's failed to recognise his passage through."

Luke joined the conversation. "That doesn't explain why the Conduit is still open, though."

Adam was looking more relaxed now as he had a real reason as to the cause of the problem. "Actually, it does. The computer doesn't know the VAPER came back, so it's holding the Conduit open." He almost began to laugh at the thought. "I mean, it's amazing. Professor Turp built that safety mechanism into the system so it wouldn't shut down halfway through a transit, but we had no idea that it could keep so many wormholes open as long as it has. It's unbelievable."

Craig was about to respond when he was interrupted by another announcement. The constant interruptions from the computer system were making conversation difficult.

"Objects now arriving through the Conduit. Repeat, two objects now arriving through the Conduit," the computer stated in an impassive monotone.

"God that sensors screwed, isn't it?" Craig sighed. This would give them a lot of repair work to do in the coming days. With the inevitable inquiry into the total screw-up this transit had become, the last thing he wanted was more work piled upon him.

"Correction," the computer continued. "Total of six objects arriving through the Conduit. Conduit pathways are now expanding. Transit expected in fourteen seconds."

What now, Craig thought. *The system seems to be getting more confused by the second.*

Craig heard his name called from somewhere behind him. He turned to see Karen standing near the computer terminal where he had left her. He waved her over. As Karen neared, Craig put out his hands; with an awkward smile, she held them. He could tell just by looking at her that she was becoming more than a little concerned at the noise and activity around them.

Before he could speak, a brightening of the light from the monitor caused everyone to look up.

On the screen, something unexpected happened. The millions of points of light that had once been a multitude of tiny wormholes had disappeared. In its place was what appeared to Craig to be a blue hole in space. The stars behind the conduit seemed to wither and fade against the brightness; the distant suns could not compete with the size and proximity of this new light source. As they watched, those in the station realised that they were seeing a section of blue sky floating above the Earth. Through this strange new window, soft clouds drifted by in an unseen breeze; their outlines made visible as rays of sunlight backlighted them.

"Technical!" Adam yelled across the room to a young technician seated at a workstation nearby. "What happened to the Conduit?"

The technician looked at his instruments in dumb amazement before answering. "It says here that the system has shut down 99.99% of wormhole activity. I don't get it," he said almost to himself. "According to this, we've just gone from 32,356 active wormholes to one." He looked up at Adam and shrugged his shoulders knowing that what he had reported didn't make sense.

"That's impossible," Craig stated. "Look at the monitor it's too large to be just one wormhole. We don't have the energy or ability to create something that size."

"Well then mate," Luke turned to his friend with a look of concern. "If we didn't make it, who did?"

As they watched, a bright, white sphere of light suddenly burst through the opening. It cleared the Conduit at high speed and turned in a sweeping arc towards the station. Everyone in the control room stared in shock as it rapidly drew nearer. Thinking that an impact was imminent, many in the dimly lit room dropped to the ground or uttered an involuntary gasp as the glowing orb turned away at the last second.

"What the hell was that thing?" Adam yelled as he rubbed his eyes to clear his vision. He tried in vain to look out the viewing window to see where the thing had gone, but his eyes weren't cooperating. The passing sphere had been so bright that its outline had been burned into his retinas, hiding everything he looked at behind a lingering after-image of the bright white sphere. "Damn it; I can't see." He was beginning to get concerned. Thoughts about the end of his career came into his head; he started to worry about what would happen to his family if he were unable to work as a consequence of losing his sight. Concern began to turn to panic.

"Can anybody see?" he called to the people he knew were around him. "My eyes are shot. Craig? Luke? How are you guys? You OK?"

"Yeah. A little dazed, but its clearing now. Luckily it doesn't seem to have done any permanent damage. Man, looking at that thing was like staring into the sun," Craig answered. "Whatever that light was, it was moving bloody fast. We'd better call ground control and let them know we have a problem. Warn them that we have incoming...things ...coming out of the Conduit."

Craig felt an arm wrap around his waist and suddenly remembered Karen was in the room. He turned in her direction, his vision clearing enough to see that her face was awash with tears. She looked into his eyes for a moment; a tangle of emotions contorted her features to reveal that she was unsure whether to feel embarrassed or angry that he had seen her emotionally exposed like this. Feeling uncomfortable, she looked away and returned her gaze to the viewport; her eyes widened in surprise at what she saw.

More spheres of light came out of the oversized wormhole at high speed. The fact that the Conduit was now an actual opening in space became apparent as the new objects travelled through. His vision all but cleared, Craig observed them moving through the small patch of dislocated sky in an ordered procession. From what he could see from the control room's viewing angle, a line of spheres appeared to stretch back into the Conduit for eternity. The scene reminded him of a night parade he had seen as a boy – literally a lifetime ago – where clowns and acrobats had carried lights and torches down a city street, illuminating the smiling faces of onlookers as they passed. Now, the scene was reversed. Night had become day as the small suns marched from one world to another, illuminating faces filled with fear rather than joy. A high-pitched whine could be heard through the hull as the glowing spheres passed over, under and around the station, pursuing whatever purpose they had come for. Through the confusion, many slipped away from Newton and headed towards the Earth at incredible speeds.

"My God, Craig. What are they?" Karen whispered by Craig's side. "There must be thousands of them."

"I don't know babe. But I get the feeling that this is somehow connected to whatever happened to my father. I think they didn't exactly go where they were supposed to on that test. It looks like the Professors somehow ended up wherever these guys are coming from."

"You mean they lead them here?" Luke interjected. A look of shock and a dawning understanding crossed his face. He turned on the spot and headed over to the mission controller. "Adam...Adam!" With his eyesight now back to normal, the controller waved him away as he busily barked orders to the other staff in the room that was going mostly unheard and ignored in the confusion.

"There's no time." Luke interrupted anyway. The urgency of the moment was forcing him to act. "We need to contact ground control and inform them that these things may be hostile."

Adam turned to face him. "That's a hell of an assumption, isn't it? You're not suggesting that we get the military involved, are you?"

"No, not at all. We need to be prepared for the possibility if they make a move on us. The fact that the *Feynman* came through that wormhole with my father unconscious and John Turp missing suggests that we should at least be a little cautious about the situation. I think we should let head office know what's going on, just in case."

"We don't need to tell them. They already know," Adam replied." Conrad and the ground team are watching the whole thing live through the station cameras. He wants us to wait and see what happens. Besides, there's not much we can do either way." With that, he turned back to his work.

The control room flickered with the light of the passing spheres that had begun to travel as close as a few feet from the station. While the majority of the spheres sped off towards the Earth at high speed, the ones surrounding the station travelled at a more languid pace. They slowly flew past the windows of the station on a more leisurely mission that required less haste than that of the others. With their speed decreased, their movements took on a dreamlike quality which those who observed the phenomenon found strangely calming. Their slow, fluid movements were beautiful to watch, the onrushing assault of light from a few moments before had been replaced by a slow-motion ballet of light in which the stars themselves appeared to participate. For some, the change in pace helped calm their nerves, and for others, it left a disconcerting impression of being circled by a group of predators. The spheres illuminated the station like high powered searchlights, their radiance moved over every surface of Newton, revealing its usually unseen external components, alcoves and plating. A few were even reported to pause momentarily at the station's windows as sneaking a look inside.

"They seem pretty interested in the *Feynman*," Craig called to Luke who turned his attention to the small craft that still contained his father.

A group of twenty spheres had moved into position around the *Feynman*, their near stationary positions gave the impression that they were involved in a detailed study of the craft. The attention they were giving the VAPER as they slowly moved around the small ship leant credibility to the idea that it was the *Feynman* itself that had led them here. They moved over every surface of the vehicle, their lights shining deep within its diamond hull to illuminate its contents. A gap in the crowd allowed Luke to catch a quick glimpse of his father on the monitor. He didn't appear to be in any danger at the moment. Disturbingly, he still seemed to be unconscious. The distance and the blinding light made it impossible to see what the spheres were doing in any detail. The monitor was still locked on the VAPER but showed only what looked like a cluster of extremely small stars. It was as if they had stumbled across something vastly attractive to them and were merely just exercising their curiosity.

If the VAPER had crossed over to their time, or world, or wherever the hell they're from, Craig surmised. *I hope it is just their curiosity they exercise over here.*

"Sir!" another controller called out to Adam. "The computer has counted 386,475 spheres which have come through the Conduit so far. It's working on a possible theory on what they're up to, but there's nothing yet."

"That doesn't look like nearly 400,000 things out there. Where are they all?"

"The computer is registering approximately two thousand spheres in our location," the controller continued as he read the information on his screen. "Apparently most have positioned themselves in a stationary orbit around the Earth. They seem to have spaced themselves evenly around the globe at a distance of approximately fifty kilometres apart. Apart from taking up these positions, they don't appear to be doing anything at the moment." He turned back to Adam, Craig and Luke.

Craig didn't voice what many in the room would be thinking. After the technician's report, the natural assumption was that the spheres could only be waiting for one thing. Orders. He hoped it was not the order to attack or simply destroy the planet.

Hundreds of years' worth of Science Fiction stories had made the possibility all the more real to the people in the control room. They'd seen the Earth destroyed hundreds of times over in the movies and found the sight of the spheres surrounding the planet to be uncomfortably familiar. The thought of coming into contact with aliens from distant civilisations was something that was regularly joked about in the earlier days of Newton. With no strange sightings and no reports of UFO's of any kind, the idea slipped from everyone's minds as they settled in and became accustomed to working and living far above the Earth. The jokes didn't seem so funny anymore, nor did the idea of making first contact with people from another world feel as exciting or as uplifting as he imagined. Craig felt a little wave of fear wash over him as he realised that these things could just as likely deliver the death of the human race, rather than its rebirth.

Outside the window, the spheres had stopped moving and now hung motionless in space. They surrounded the Earth in a gridwork pattern of lights that would be clearly visible from the surface. Craig wondered what those on the ground below were making of the whole thing. Until now, he had liked to think that humanity would act maturely and not panic in this type of situation. His own fear and worries over what was going to happen next made him certain that it would be bedlam on the Earth below. He dared not imagine how many people were already dead or dying in the ensuing panic.

"Sir, we've got a power spike in the Conduit," the technician reported. "We've got a fresh opening. It looks like a signal of some sort is being transmitted through."

There was a pause as those in the room took the time to look at each other for reassurance. The moment dragged on as they took the time to study the people around them that they had lived and worked with for the past few years.

"I don't know what it is, but it's extremely powerful and appears to be directed towards the spheres," the tech finished.

There was an air of expectancy amongst the ANZAR staff. As one they all came to the understanding that something significant was about to occur. Their senses warned them of impending danger, but they had no clue as to what it could be. As they looked from the spheres to each other, nobody said anything. No-one said goodbye, to do so would be to give in to irrational fears and admit to giving up hope.

No-one said goodbye, but many thought it.

Craig pulled Karen close as they waited to see what would happen. He turned and gave her a quick smile which she could not find the will to return. Using a single finger, he gently turned her face toward his, so he could look into her hazel eyes. Even though her features were tear-streaked and etched with worry, he realised that she looked more beautiful at that moment than he had ever seen her before. Her very fear revealed a level of warmth and depth that he had never seen. She rarely showed such emotions to anyone, especially to him for some reason. Seeing her in this new light, he fell in love with her all over again. He felt glad that she had come to the control room tonight. For if this turned out to be as bad as he thought it would be, he was glad to have her here with him at the end.

As he leant down and kissed her softly on the mouth, the room filled with a light brighter than anyone had ever seen. They closed their eyes to the visual assault and clung to each other as they waited for it to end.

They didn't have to wait long.

They collapsed in each other's arms. Their bodies separated and came to rest in a tangled heap on the control room floor. The light had gone out for them…and everyone else on the station.

13
The last moments of peace

Cheam, South West London.

6.56pm - Wednesday, August 12th, 2048 (GMT)

Glen Hanson sank deeper into the lounge that occupied almost half the floor space in his parents' living room. It wasn't that the lounge was exceptionally large, rather that the room was exceptionally small. The two-storey terrace house was a tiny place located in South West London that he and his family had called home for all his life. The downstairs space was simply designed and consisted of only four rooms including the lounge room in which Glen currently sat. Even by British standards, the two-and-a-half-bedroom home was small. Opposite the hallway was the largest room in the house in which a dining table and two-seat sofa barely fit with bare inches to spare. At the rear, a kitchen that wasn't big enough to swing a cat in (Glen tried when he was ten) was jammed in between the back door and the bathroom. The latter allowed for just enough space for a bath, toilet and a basin on which users could rest an elbow while taking care of business. As Glen's mother and father had occupied the house in Cheam since their wedding day over forty years earlier, it was safe to say that they found the accommodations to be cozy and comfortable. They had always been happy in their little house. They had no desires to leave. With simple pleasures and their only son to keep them company, they had turned what some of the POSHER relatives called *The Rabbit Warren*, into a home.

Glen tossed the newspaper to the other end of the lounge and grabbed his cup of tea from the side table. Apart from the ticking of an old-fashioned clock that sat on the mantelpiece above the gas fire, the room was silent. As he slowly sipped the now tepid brew, Glen realised that the last two weeks had gone faster than he could have imagined. In just a few more days he would be required to return to Newton Station and the pile of work that waited for him in orbit around the Earth. Although his lab equipment and research data had been safely stored away off-site, he still needed to return to the station to supervise the disassembling of the three telescopes his team used to study the skies. If the political situation proved to be as bad as the Professors had predicted, Glen knew that within a matter of days he could find himself back on this couch drinking tea and reading the paper once again. Strangely, he didn't mind that possibility. The short time he had spent with his parents had helped him appreciate how much he missed living on Earth, and how happy and comfortable he felt to be back in his old home. The knowledge that his parents were always here, awaiting his return to the familiar surroundings made him feel almost eager to return. With a sudden pang of guilt that he was not making the most of his time with them, he threw the newspaper aside, grabbed his mug of tea and made his way into the garden to join them.

Outside, the afternoon was bright and warm. With summer coming to an end, the Met Office had made the daring prediction that the warm weather would continue well into the following month, stretching summer well beyond the usual two-week period it seemed to occupy. Despite the warmth of the sun, both of Glen's parents sat huddled in the stuffy conservatory that had grown oppressively hot in the afternoon sun. Glen was surprised to see that both parents were also wearing cardigans.

"Alright?" his mum greeted him as he stepped into the conservatory.

His guilt over sitting indoors while he read the paper abated slightly when he noticed that both his parents were also doing the same thing. He was glad to see that the old Hanson family tradition of being in each other's company while reading the paper still passed as social interaction. They had each made themselves comfortable in their favourite armchairs and were busily discovering what the rest of the world was up to as the day prepared to turn to dusk.

"Geez, it's hot in here," Glen sighed as he walked to the open conservatory door and looked out into the garden.

"You two must be sweating buckets sitting in here." He turned to them and pointed at their cardigans. "Isn't it a bit hot for those?" he asked.

"The weather said it was going to get a bit breezy this afternoon," his father replied without looking up from his copy of the Daily Mail.

"But its thirty-five degrees," Glen replied.

"You can never be too sure, dear. Can I get you another cup of tea? I was going to get myself one anyway," his mother asked as she placed the paper aside and began to rise.

Glen's father looked at his watch. "Don't be ridiculous, Margaret. It's only a quarter to. There are still fifteen minutes to go. You know we always have our afternoon cup at five."

With that, he returned to his paper.

"Like I said," Glen's mother continued. "I *was* going to have another one."

The discussion over, she sat back down and continued reading her paper.

Trying not to smile, Glen placed himself in the chair next to the clothes dryer that was also enjoying a rare break due to the milder weather. He looked at his parents seated opposite and realised that he would miss their small peculiarities once he was gone. They were a couple of characters who always managed to liven up his home life with their unique conversations. They had a peculiar kind of relationship and at times would argue about the most mundane things without even being aware they were doing it. He remembered a time when they had gotten into a heated debate over the name of a character on an old TV show. The 'disagreement', as his mother called them, lasted for nearly three days before the local newsagent informed them that they were both wrong. Naturally, when confronted with this news, neither of them would accept it and promptly told the bemused newsagent that he was being ridiculous.

"Charles," his mother practically yelled to his father. "Charles, did you say it was quarter to five dear?" A look of concern came over her face. "Bloody hell, it's Wednesday, and I haven't even put the pork chops in the oven yet." She was immediately on her feet and headed into the kitchen that resembled a short corridor with benches. "They need a good four hours if they are to be done right."

Ah yes. Glen thought. *Wednesday; pork chop day.* As long as he could remember, his parents had settled into a set menu of meals which they had assigned to a particular day of the week. Pork chops were always on a Wednesday, Sausage and mash on a Thursday and the inevitable chicken or beef roast on a Sunday. For lunch, not dinner, mind.

All three members of the Hanson family were set in their ways when it came to most aspects of their daily routines. There was a time and a place for everything as far as his parents were concerned.

Life was more predictable when one knew what was coming. His father would say. Glen was only now beginning to see those traits in himself and was a little alarmed by this glimpse of the future he got whenever he observed his parents. As much as he disliked the idea, he knew for a fact that when he reached their age, he would be just like them. Part of him was concerned by the idea, as much as he loved his mother and father, he didn't want to grow into being a mirror image of them. On the other hand, the foresight into what he would be like in fifty years appealed to his sense of familiarity and stability. It was strangely comforting to have some idea of what to expect in the years ahead. He felt it was better to travel through life with an inkling of what was to come rather than go through it blind. His parents would have approved of this philosophy.

His ruminations complete, he turned his attention back to the *Daily Mail* which was spread out on his lap. The paper had enjoyed a recent boost in circulation when it decided to break from the norm and go the more traditional route of printing the news on paper rather than just relying on online distribution. The idea was such a success that many believed it would herald the rebirth of a new printing era as some sectors of society yearned for the simpler times of the past and enjoyed the tacit feel of something solid in their hands.

A fresh political scandal covered the front page, yet another MP was involved in a drunken indiscretion with a minor. No change there. Articles devoted to the debate over whether the climate disaster the world had been expecting had been averted or not took up a few pages each day. Many believed that the work of the last few decades had succeeded in halting global warming, while others argued that there still wasn't enough being done. Glen was getting sick of hearing about the global warming issue that had been an ever-present drone in the background of his life. With little interest in politics and hypothetical debates, he skipped over those pages, reading further into the science section where the discussion on US jurisdiction over international research was heating up.

The American Empire was attempting to filter all future scientific ventures through the one organisation. Their stated goal was to have all advances in science, medicine and technology monitored by a single scientific group which would ensure all research was registered, tested and rated on its value to humanity, before being distributed evenly to all loyal societies on the planet.

The proposal met with a mixed response from the international community. The most contentious point was the stipulation that only nations which willingly integrated themselves into the American Empire would be granted full and free access to the oncoming advances in science. The debate raged between developed and undeveloped countries over whether or not to entertain the concept. The entire continent of Africa had jumped at the opportunity to become a part of the newly expanding American Empire. Tired of struggling in poor living conditions while being lorded over by petty dictators, six African nations had erupted into revolt as the people had their say. The self-appointed leaders of Africa's longest-running dictatorships were either arrested or killed. It was estimated that over twenty thousand people died in the ensuing violence as the region exploded into a state of anarchy and revolt that had lasted more than a month. During the same period, another half a dozen African nations decided to make a move to join the Empire using less violent methods. Votes were taken, and the people of those countries chose to assimilate their culture with that of the U.S. With little industry and scientific research facilities of their own, the more impoverished nations had little to lose and everything to gain from becoming a province of the United States. With this new foothold on the African continent, the US had placed themselves in an advantageous position in which it was now capable of surrounding and coercing the remaining African nations to join. Unlike other regions, America had managed to increase its Empire across Africa without the use of the military. With a dozen new provinces to control and nearly a quarter of a billion new citizens, the President felt that it was going to be a good year.

Emboldened by their success, the Americans continually appealed to the rest of the International community to hand over their research data and equipment to the Empire. They praised the foresight and wisdom displayed by the nations which had cooperated thus far. They spoke of how they wanted to bring an end to the division between the rich and poor countries of the world and bridge the gap between first and third world countries. The American President promised a future in which all the world would have access to the best of everything through an advanced allocation scheme coordinated by his government. With US control over technology, medicine and all other scientific avenues deemed beneficial to humankind, the American President guaranteed that any country that joined with his Empire and handed political control over to it would be rewarded with a helping hand into the twenty-first century.

Unlike the third world, first world countries were less inclined to participate. With more to lose than their poorer cousins, the world's developed nations were uneasy about handing this administrative power over to a single group, especially a nation that was seen to be as domineering as America. This bold push was perceived as the next step in the Empire's ongoing plans to transform itself into a world governing power. With the ability to control what technology was distributed to which parts of the globe, the Empire was seen to be attempting to place itself in the position where it held total control over the world's resources and industry. The planet would become dependent on the Empire's approval of all future construction, expansion and development that would require additional resources. The world would lose control over their local industry as many believed that the contracts and patents for all future technologies would automatically go to US corporations. America would grow stronger and more prosperous while the rest of the world was pillaged of its talent and resources. Finance experts the world over spoke of implications that would be disastrous for the International economy if the scheme went ahead. Worldwide recession and depressions would become the norm as the globe spiralled down into poverty and eventually war. Many believed that the discussions would soon move outside the realm of debate and would become more violent and physical sooner than expected.

Until recently, Glen was not particularly alarmed by this development. Professor Weekes' news about US interest in Newton Station had awoken him to the possibility that his work could be stolen from him. Although no ANZAR research team would ever willingly hand over their research, the possibility that it could be forcibly taken from them became a scenario that everyone on the station was beginning to prepare. He could at least console himself that he had removed all of his research data from the station before he came home. Copies had been made and hidden inside his parent's home as well as ANZAR's Sydney and Auckland offices. If the worst did happen and everything on the station was lost, he could still carry on elsewhere with a minimum of fuss. Providing the Empire let him.

Glen read on.

On the other side of the small conservatory, his father mumbled to himself as he usually did when he read the paper. His lips moved incoherently as he quietly discussed his opinion with himself regarding something that he either approved or disapproved of. Charles used to be an outspoken man. In his younger days, his views on life and politics were shared with anyone who would listen. Like much of his generation, he fancied that he could do a better job than the monkeys in charge. For a while, he even considered going into politics himself until he realised how much work it would be. Glen never knew why, but as he aged, his father became quieter and quieter when it came to political matters. He still voiced his opinions in private, although he no longer shared his views publicly.

His mother could be heard in the kitchen just behind him singing a Duran Duran song which had been popular seven decades earlier. Glen could see her reflection in the kitchen window sway to the music as she prepared dinner. Like his father, she had also mellowed in her later years. A smile came to his face when he thought of how effervescent she had been when he was younger, she had…

Something odd was happening. As Glen watched, his mother's reflection slowly disappeared. Around him, everything seemed to grow brighter. Turning to face the garden, he found it necessary to squint into the glare that now filled the yard. Instead of slowly becoming darker as the day headed towards sunset, the sky had begun to do the exact opposite and had started to grow brighter. The levels of light outside continued to increase as the shadows in the garden retreated and grew bolder under the intensifying light.

"What the hell?" Glen said as he got to his feet.

14
Yours or mine?

Cheam, South West London.

7.10pm - Tuesday, August 12th, 2048 (GMT)

Glen stared into the empty yard through the scuffed glass of the conservatory. Behind him, the sound of his father throwing his newspaper to the floor and rising to his feet seemed loud and invasive amongst the silence that had filled the neighbourhood. After a moment, his father stood alongside him, and they stared out into the yard together. The only sound either of them could hear was the old Duran Duran tune that was being shrieked from the kitchen. Apparently, Glen's mother had not noticed the strange change in light.

"Hey, Carole! Carole, come out here and look at this," someone called from a few houses up. Both Glen and his father turned their heads to stare at their boundary fence from behind which the voice came.

"My God! What's happened to the sky?" came the reply.

As they listened, startled exclamations echoed around the neighbourhood. To them, it sounded as if everyone in the street was outside and commenting on something that Glen and his father had not yet seen.

"Something's going on out there," Charles Hanson exclaimed as he made his way towards the conservatory door. "I don't think it's a good idea to go out there, Dad," Glen said as he followed his father towards the door. As curious as he was, he had a strange feeling that going outside would be a bad idea.

A gust of wind arose as they stepped out of the conservatory and onto the garden lawn. The towering pines that flanked the yard swayed and shook in the breeze, their movements fierce and strong. A cacophony of whistles and shrieks caused them both to look up to the sky where they noticed a flock of birds that had been caught in the maelstrom. Their tiny bodies flew and tumbled every which way as they were blown back and forth by the wind. Those that could grabbed at the trees, and hung on with their feet as they were swept into the fiercely swaying branches. As Glen and his father watched, a new sound grew in volume and rose above the howling of the wind. Through the occasional silences that punctuated each gust, Glen realised he could hear what he could only assume were the howls of dogs and the screams of terrified cats.

"I don't like this, Glen. I don't like this one bit. Something bad must be on the way to get the animals this bothered." Charles stared at the sky that shone so bright as to be white rather than blue. "Animals can sense atmospheric disturbances," he continued. "They can tell when a storm is coming; it's like they can smell the danger."

"Can you see that?" Glen yelled above the wind and pointed high into the sky overhead. "Can you see those lights up there, Dad?"

Charles Hanson looked straight up and stared at where his son was pointing. High in the upper atmosphere, thousands of points of light slowly came into view and spread out across the afternoon sky. As they watched, the lights danced above their heads like a cloud of fireflies before slowly coming to rest in a grid-work pattern that stretched as far as they could see in every direction. There was no doubt in either man's mind that this was not a natural phenomenon of any kind. Whatever the lights were, they were definitely artificial.

After staring for a moment, Charles asked a question that made Glen feel even more uncomfortable than he already was.

"So, do you think they are yours or mine?" he asked without looking away from the sky.

Glen didn't have to ask what his father meant by that. For years both men had nurtured a friendly rivalry between them that, for the most part, was a light-hearted debate between Glen's love of science and Charles' deep-seeded Catholic beliefs. The two men would regularly argue the merit of both science and religion, each eager to convince the other that they were right. Charles dearly wanted his son to embrace God and come back to the church that they had attended together when he was a boy. Glen on the other hand, simply wanted his father to have a more open-minded view of the world.

Knowing that this was neither the time nor the place to reignite the debate, Glen gave a non-committal answer in response

"I don't know, Dad. Angels or aliens, either way, it looks like trouble," he replied.

As they both stared at the sky above, a steady rumble began in the ground below. They felt it in their feet as a dull vibration that slowly increased in intensity until the whole Earth seemed to shake.

"What the hell?" Glen muttered as he watched everything move and shake around him. "Is it an earthquake?" he asked as he reached out and grabbed his father's arm for support.

As he swayed on his feet, Charles attempted a response which was drowned out by a deep roar which steadily rose in volume. The noise was immense and covered a vast tonal range. The bass rumble of some unidentified machine was overlaid with a high-pitched whine that was eerily familiar. As one, Glen and Charles realised where the sound was coming from and looked back towards the sky.

"Oh no," the elder man said aloud, although no one could hear him over the noise.

Out of the glare of the atmosphere, an object appeared and rapidly grew in size. It was descending towards the ground at an extreme rate of speed. Despite its predicament, its movement was graceful as it irrevocably plummeted towards the Earth. They both recognised the object for what it was while it was still a few thousand feet above them. The Union Jack emblazoned on the airliner's tail identified it as one of the larger British Airways models that operated domestic non-orbital flights within Europe. The shock of seeing a full-sized aircraft carrying five hundred passengers hurtling towards the ground caused them to miss one important detail. It was heading towards them.

A loud crash and explosion from the street thundered its way over the house and into the yard. The impact of a motor collision outside their home startled both men from the trance they were in and caused them to realise that they were not safe outdoors. They turned as one to rush back into the house in what Glen thought was probably a useless attempt to find shelter. His instincts inspired him to hide while his mind understood that if a 500-tonne aircraft landed on the house, it would make no difference if he were inside it or in the yard. The result would be the same.

With a quick glance at the sky above, Glen noticed that the British Airways plane was not alone. His eyes registered at least six of the great machines as they fell towards the Earth. They spun and twisted as they descended towards the ground, their brightly coloured fuselages were reminiscent of a ticker-tape parade for giants in which the aircraft played the role of confetti. Some planes flipped end over end while others casually flew towards the ground at impossible angles that ruled out the possibility that they were under any control. Whatever was happening, Glen was sure that there was nobody conscious or alive at the controls of these planes. The scene caused him to realise that something immense was occurring and that others in the city would be in the same predicament as him, running scared and confused from a threat they didn't understand. He gave one last glance into the sky to see where his piece of confetti would fall. His spirits rose as he noticed that the BA jet appeared to have moved to the south, slightly. The main fuselage would most likely miss his home though he was not sure what kind of damage the explosion would cause. With the hope of survival rekindled, he ran for the house.

For a moment Glen thought his death had arrived, a thunderous crash shook the ground and caused him to stagger the last few steps to the back door. A column of flame arose in the distance, not more than a few blocks away another stricken jet had hit the ground. With his parents' home lying beneath one of the many flight paths around Heathrow, Cheam had suddenly become a dangerous place to live. With his heart pounding and grateful to be alive, he turned to enter the back door.

The British Airways flight continued its fall.

Glen's senses were assaulted. As the initial explosion settled, the deafening sound of the still approaching jet engine vibrated his skull while the overpowering smell of fuel and fire filled his nostrils. It was like hell had come to his backyard. The heat, noise and fumes made every one of his senses scream. His eyes stung, his ears hurt, and his lungs ached. He could even taste jet fuel that had dispersed itself in the air from the first plane's crash.

Glen grabbed the door jamb for support as he stepped onto the back step. Feeling no safer for having a roof over his head, he took one last glance at the sky in time to see the airliner disappear over the neighbour's house.

The image of the doomed aircraft was frozen in his mind. For the split second he saw it, his mind managed to take in and record a considerable amount of detail. The airframe appeared undamaged as far as he could see. There was no fire onboard and judging by the noise the engines were still running. It passed so close that he could clearly read the aircrafts serial number and see the outlines of a few passengers who were slumped against the windows.

Amazingly, they looked as if they were sleeping through the last few seconds of their lives. The aircraft slammed into the ground travelling at a speed faster than anything he had ever seen before. The immense Impact shook the neighbourhood as a concussion wave of sound, heat and air travelled out from the crash site, causing damage as it went. The very air itself seemed to compress and slap him in the chest, flinging his body to the floor. The windows in the conservatory exploded inwards in a shower of glass that sprayed over Glen's crumpled form. Still conscious, he threw his hands to his ears in a failed attempt to block out the noise of the explosion.

Burning jet fuel rained on the garden. The pines and bushes in the yard caught alight and were engulfed in flames.

Delirious, he imagined he could hear his father yelling. He could feel hands moving over his body before they settled under his arms and feet where they struggled to gain purchase. Opening his eyes, he looked up to see his father gazing down at him with a look of concern. His parents half carried, half dragged him into the house where they would be relatively safe… for the moment.

"You okay?" his father yelled.

"What were you doing out there gawping at that thing? You silly boy," his mother began to cry. "We nearly lost you."

Glen tried to sit up but was unable. His head throbbed with pain causing spots of light to appear behind his eyes. He didn't remember hitting his head as he fell, but he was sure he was showing symptoms of a concussion. He laid back and looked at his parents. He closed his eyes for a moment to try and ease the pain in his head.

He lay that way for no more than a minute before the sense of panic in his mother's voice brought him around.

"Charles. Charles, I feel strange. My head's cold. I feel as if I'm going to pass out," she moaned.

Glen opened his eyes to see his mother leaning against the sofa for support, her face was stricken with fear. Her body was leaning to one side; her back arched forward as if trying to support a massive weight. His father was beside her but doing nothing to help. He looked as if he were in a daze as his body slumped and he slowly slid down the wall.

Whatever was going on was happening to both of them. Whatever it was, they didn't want it to happen and were fighting it.

"Mum? Dad? What's wrong?" Glen muttered as he made another attempt to raise himself from the floor.

"I can't fight it, Margaret. There's something in my head. I don't want it there." Charles forced himself to speak through gritted teeth.

As Glen rose, he became aware of a coldness filling his head. It felt like an icy finger had been pushed into his brain and was poking around. The feeling was not painful as much as unpleasant.

The last thing he saw and heard was his mother's shrill voice as she screamed "Get out of my head!" before falling unconscious to the floor. The last thing he realised before he joined them in oblivion was that someone or something was inside his head as well. He could feel them in there, poking and prodding around. What they were looking for or what they were doing, he had no idea, whatever it was had terrified him more than anything he had ever experienced before.

The darkness, when it came, was a blessed release.

15
The Blackout

Earth. Simultaneous global occurrences at 7.10pm GMT

Wednesday, August 12th, 2048

Bargo, NSW Australia - 4.10am

Sam Kidrie unrolled the fire hoses and glanced over his shoulder to check on the progress of the rest of his team. He was surprised to see that in the last few minutes they had been pushed back to within one hundred metres of the road. What had started as a simple winter back burning operation had turned into a major firestorm that had already destroyed three properties and threatened at least a dozen more. Behind Sam, a line of police cars and other emergency vehicles had been hastily parked across Remembrance Drive as a makeshift barricade to keep traffic and sightseers out of the area. For the time being, the road between Tahmoor and Bargo was off limits until the fire crews could manage to get the situation under control.

Sam was busy connecting a new hose to the tanker when the first lights appeared high above him. With their attention focused on the fire and the burning scrubland, none of the fifty-six firemen present took any notice as the stars began to dance across the horizon and the dark sky began to shine.

With the new hose connected, Sam waved over two of his men, and the three of them lined up to form a hose team in preparation for their attack on the blaze. Before they had a chance to pick up the hose, a strange feeling overcame everyone at the scene. A cold sensation filled Sam's head and began to move around inside his brain. At first, due to the heat of the fire, Sam found it almost cooling and pleasant, until he detected something unnatural and strangely sentient behind it. Around him, his men threw off their helmets and clutched at their heads in confusion. Out of the corner of his eye, Sam saw the men in the field drop their hoses and fall to the ground with their hands pressed to their heads. A few rubbed viciously at their scalps in the vain hope that friction would warm them up and drive the coldness away. All around him people fell to the ground, writhing and screaming in panic and fear. With their hoses discarded and their task forgotten, the fire front moved forward unhindered.

As Sam fell to the hot surface of the road and slowly slipped into unconsciousness his panicked mind dimly registered the screams of his men and the smell of charred flesh as the fire caught up with them, and they began to burn.

Approaching Cochin – Southern India 11.40pm
Ravish sat atop the train with his arms and legs wrapped around his little boy Binjee. The six-year-old felt grown up and proud to be travelling on the roof rather than in the passenger cabin like his mother and baby sister, Shruti. As they moved along the tracks at a rapid eighty kilometres an hour, the summer winds that blew past them due to the train's speed were both warm and soothing. Around them, other men sat and stared at the scenery that passed in the night. Many of the men had huddled together into small groups which sat back to back making it possible for them to sleep sitting up. Their dozing bodies swayed back and forth in dream-like trances on the warm roof of the train.

Binjee looked up at his father and gave a big smile to show how excited he was. Ravish tousled his little boy's hair and kissed the top of his head. Smiling, father and son turned to watch the lights of a sleeping village as it silently slid past in the dark.

As the train rounded a bend, Binjee squealed and pointed into the sky. As Ravish looked towards where his son was pointing, thousands of tiny lights began to flow across the heavens. Around them, the men on the train slowly rose to their feet to gain a better view of the sight before them. Binjee wanted to stand up for a better look as well, but his father held him firmly and informed him that it was much too dangerous to stand on the roof of a moving train.

As they watched from between the legs of the men standing around them, Ravish and Binjee saw the lights in the sky cease moving and simultaneously grow brighter. As they did, Ravish became aware of a cold sensation in his head that felt strange and unpleasant. Binjee wiggled and squirmed in his arms as he tried to get free of his father's grip and run from whatever it was that had invaded his mind. Despite his discomfort, Ravish managed to hold on to his struggling son. He knew that if he let go, his frightened boy would run straight off the edge of the train and fall to his death.

Just as he thought he would be unable to hold him any longer, Binjee fell silent and still in Ravish's arms. Around him, the men who had risen for a better look at the lights in the sky began to fall over one by one. Those near the middle of the carriages collapsed onto the roof with a loud thud. Those unfortunate enough to be travelling near the edge tumbled and fell over the side of the fast-moving train.

Ravish screamed for whatever was in his head to go away and leave him alone before falling unconscious on the train roof with his arms still wrapped around his son Binjee.

With everyone onboard out cold, the train sped on into the night with no one at the controls and the end of the line in Cochin just a few miles away.

Tuvalu Island – South Pacific 6.10am

More than half the village turned out to watch the United Nations rescue vessel dock. Men, women and children stood on the beach and waved at the massive container vessel filled with Earth and gravel as drew alongside the pier that stretched far out into the Pacific Ocean. With their nation island slowly sinking into the sea, the Tuvaluan government had spent the better part of fifty years crying out for help. As the world debated the existence of global warming and the possibility of rising sea levels, the Tuvaluans suffered and starved through regular floods and increasing ground salinity that sterilised the soil and made growing food impossible. Just months earlier, the international community had finally begun the slow process of lifting the small coral atoll one metre higher out of the sea with regular shipments of rocks, sand and Earth.

As the ship neared the dock, many of the villagers crowded forward and waded into the calm, warm sea to get a closer look. Fathers carried children on their broad dark shoulders while their wives nursed sleeping babies. It was a bright, sunny morning and everyone was in good spirits. There was much waving and cheering as the next stage in their island's revival slowly began.

Due to the early morning sun, no-one on the island of Tuvalu noticed the sky grow a shade brighter. As one, many of the celebrating Tuvaluans began to sway in confusion. The children, who had been running and swimming in the warm, shallow water, came to a sudden stop and started to cry. Feeling the same thing, their parents struggled to shake off their confusion and discomfort as they took panicked, lunging steps to grab their offspring and get out of the water.

Along the beach, the container vessel crashed into the pier with a deafeningly loud crash. The recently built timber and concrete pier sliced through the hull of the ship, tearing metal and spilling its cargo into the sea. The sound of twisting steel and exploding fuel drums echoed across the water in a rolling cacophony of sound that saved the lives of many Tuvaluans. Nearing unconsciousness, a lucky few were shocked back to reality by the sudden noise and resulting wave of adrenalin. Grabbing for the limbs of anyone within reach, they lunged for the shore dragging the bodies of their neighbours and loved ones behind them. For every Tuvaluan that made it ashore, half a dozen more lay floating face-down in the warm sea. Their bodies floated in the gentle surf as they slowly drowned in the waters that they had both loved and feared.

Santa Monica Freeway - Los Angeles 11.10am
A mixture of cars, buses and heavy movers sped along the highway between San Francisco and Los Angeles in a stream of traffic that was lighter than average for that time on a Thursday Morning. Being the tail end of summer, the weather was still

reasonably warm. A low bank of cloud cover over the two cities hid the sky and everything in it from those on the ground.

Robin Powers was speeding along the motorway in his favourite Porsche, weaving in and out of the traffic as he made his way to the studio to film the next episode in his hit TV series CSI: Death Squad. Something loud, fast and large swooped down through the clouds to his right, drawing his attention from the road. He turned his head just in time to see a massive passenger plane crash into a housing estate just a few miles from the motorway. As he slowed his 911 to get a closer look, another jet passed low overhead and slammed on top of the traffic just under a mile in front of him. In a panic, Robin hit the brakes and was promptly rear-ended by an SUV whose driver was too busy watching a third jet slam into the nearby beach to notice the traffic.

As he stepped from his vehicle, Robin saw the tail of the crashed jetliner poking into the air amidst a wall of flames and the twisted debris of crushed cars. A section of the elevated motorway had slammed onto the roof of a shopping mall that lay nestled beneath it, the other end sat broken and tilted into the sky like a poorly erected concrete barrier. A thick plume of smoke covered the area as the shops and office buildings under and around the motorway began to burn.

Robin breathed in ragged, short breaths as he struggled to pull his phone from his tight jeans pocket. Horrific screams floated out from the wall of flame that had spread to cover the entire width of the raised carriageway. He cringed on hearing what he knew to be the sounds of people in pain, people dying. After a short struggle, he freed the phone and lifted it to his ear. As he dialled 911, a spattering of survivors from further up the motorway ran past him on foot, eager to get away from the fire and devastation. As he watched them pass, his mind dimly registered the fact that the emergency line was jammed; his call to 911 went unanswered. Through the screams of the fleeing crowd, he could barely make out the sound of the busy tone.

Screams echoed all around him as the people on the freeway abandoned their cars to run from the wall of fire that had begun to proceed along the elevated section of motorway. Realising the danger, Robin turned and ran with the others. He saw a husband and wife trying to carry and drag three small children out of danger. Beside them, a businessman in a two-thousand-dollar suit clutched a briefcase to his chest as he ran, oblivious to everyone else around him. To his left, Robin spotted an elderly man as he hobbled along pushing an even older woman in a wheelchair. The one thing in common with each of these people were the masks of terror that they wore as they ran for their lives.

A searing heat hit Robin in the back as the wall of flame caught him up. Out of the corner of his eye, he saw the old man shove the wheelchair forward as the fire engulfed him. He screamed as his wife lunged forwards, his last act a desperate, yet futile attempt to save the woman he loved. A moment later, the fire caught her too.

Robin screamed as his shirt started to burn, then melt and then fuse to his skin. The air was sucked from his lungs as the fire and heat reached deep down inside his chest to char his flesh both inside and out. In stark contrast to the heat, Robin found the inside of his head growing immensely cold. As his life flickered out, he became aware of a presence inside his mind. His last thought was to wish it out more than he did the flames.

Ahead, in a desperate attempt to escape burning to death, dozens of men, women and children decided to take their chances with gravity by jumping from the freeway overpass to the ground far below.

Houston - Texas 1.10pm

The skydivers fell towards the Earth at terminal velocity. The fabric of their brightly coloured jumpsuits flapped in the wind that buffeted their bodies in a futile effort to sabotage their world-record attempt. Three hundred and fifty jumpers fell in the shape of a rainbow-hued snowflake two hundred metres wide. From the ground, they were a fantastic sight as they made their third and final attempt for the day. They would have to get all jumpers into position and hold the pattern for the allotted time before Guinness would allow them into their book.

Scattered across the plain of open ground far below, the families and friends of the jumpers stood staring at the sky along with hundreds of other locals from the surrounding towns. Parents ate popcorn and kids sipped colas as they watched the divers fall into position. Just as it looked as if the jumpers had completed the shape, it all fell apart.

A shocked cry echoed through the crowd as they registered that something was going terribly wrong. Specks of colour that represented the bodies of their loved ones began to tumble and turn through the sky. Where a moment ago all jumpers had been falling in a clean, controlled descent, they now spun and twirled in a jumbled disarray of tangled limbs.

The crowd began to moan and scream as a grim certainty fell over them. Many were crying before the first body hit the ground. Like the fall of coloured rain, human bodies slammed into the targeted area where they were supposed to have gently touched down. Splashes of red rose into the air as each body hit, bursting like raindrops on the hard soil.

Those watching in the crowd wept and turned the faces of their children away from the sight. As the last body struck, the members of the crowd gave an audible moan of discomfort and as one, reached up to clasp their heads in their hands. In small groups and clusters, they fell to their knees, screaming of a coldness in their heads, moaning of a finger in their brains.

Mere seconds after it had started, everyone lay unmoving on the ground. Just like the skydivers who had just broken the world record for the most deaths in a single jump.

Paris - France 8.10pm
Maria pushed the twin stroller through the rain in a hurry to get back to her apartment before the downpour became too heavy. Tourists and late-night diners strolled along the streets of Paris making her journey slower and more frustrating than she would have liked. On reaching the intersection outside the Gar du Nord station, a red light stopped her progress. She paused at the crossing and grimaced at the people in their dry, warm cars as they sped past. The two babies in the pram began to cry on the

cessation of motion. Maria rocked them back and forth as she waited for the crossing lights to turn green. After what felt like an eternity, the lights finally changed, and she stepped out into the street.

In the middle of the intersection, the babies began to cry. Maria thrust a hand up to her head and whimpered in discomfort. She felt herself growing faint and looked towards the line of traffic that waited beside her at the lights. She dimly registered looks of discomfort on the driver's faces as they too grabbed their heads. Falling to her knees, Maria pushed the pram across the intersection and up onto the opposite curb. With one final scream, the infants fell silent.

Maria collapsed into a puddle in the middle of the road, the coldness of the rain felt as warm as a bath compared to the coldness that filled her head. As darkness enveloped her, Maria became dimly aware of the wheels of the truck which had been waiting at the intersection. With the driver of the vehicle unconscious, the truck had begun to move. She could only stare and greet the darkness as the wheels slowly rolled towards and over her head.

16

Modern-day Rapunzel

ANZAR control room – Newton Station. 4.56am -

Thursday, August 13th, 2048

Craig floated through the blackness not knowing if he was asleep or awake. Everywhere around him was total darkness. As he stirred, unidentifiable images faded from his mind. He could recollect that he had been dreaming about something, but he no longer had any idea of what it could have been. Both their substance and meaning were becoming lost to him. His subconscious screamed that it was important that he remember what he had just seen.

Before he could make a conscious effort to remember them, they had faded and gone.

Craig yawned and was rewarded with a sharp pain deep within his skull. He raised his arms and rubbed his head. At the moment, all he wanted to do was roll over and go back to sleep. Through squinted eyes, the darkness in his cabin suggested that he had awoken early. The lights were programmed to come on automatically at 7 am every morning, ready for him to rise and start a new day.

Good, he thought. *More sleep.*

He attempted to roll over and noticed that for some reason he could not feel the bed beneath him. Coming fully awake, he was met with an aerial view of one of the instrument panels from the main control room. As he struggled to make sense of what he saw, a dark flowing shape passed in front of his view, startling him. It was a body. The long flowing hair of the female communications officer floated just below his chest.

"What the hell?" he muttered to himself. His voice carried far in the silence. His ears rang with it.

The station is never this quiet, he thought.

The constant and ever-present sound was a distinct characteristic of Newton Station. Air conditioning vents, whirring computers, cooling and heating fans, as well as human traffic, merged to create a perpetual soundtrack that all aboard the station quickly grew accustomed. The first thing that everyone commented on when waking after their first night's sleep aboard Newton was the constant sound, the continual auditory stimulation.

But now, it was missing. Craig found the silence to be more intrusive and unsettling than the constant noise. Silence meant that things weren't working as they should. Silence meant that the air conditioning vents weren't distributing air. It meant that the computers weren't turned on. It meant that there was no power. Worst of all it meant that there was nobody else around him. The thought of being alone on the station scared him more than he would have imagined.

"What happened?" he asked himself again. Craig spoke this thought aloud as much to exercise his curiosity as to create a reassuring sound that would break the silence.

He remembered the lights from the Conduit.

The last thing he could recall was standing in the control room with at least twenty other people, many of whom he considered friends. Now, he had no idea where they were.

They had all stood motionless while they watched the lights explore the station. They had felt helpless as they observed the spheres surround the planet below. He remembered the fear that arose in him as the strange lights formed that unusual grid pattern around the Earth.

He relived the moment when he knew things were going to turn bad.

He shuddered at the memory of the icy finger in his brain. Finally, he remembered Karen.

The thought of anything happening to her gave him the inspiration to move. He kicked his legs in the stagnant air in a vain attempt to reach the ground. As he kicked and waved his arms about like a drowning man, he called her name.

"Karen! Karen! Are you in here?" He struggled to look around the control room for her. He hoped that she and the others were still here somewhere, alive, but unconscious as he had been. The lack of light and gravity made it impossible for him to see more than a few feet in any direction. After a few more moments of calling he was rewarded with a response.

"Craig, that you?" a groggy voice spoke out of the darkness. He could tell by the tone of voice that the speaker was nearby and male. Not Karen then, but somebody at least.

"Yeah," Craig answered as he tried to turn himself in the direction he thought the voice came from. "Luke, is that you?"

"No, it's Adam. I've got Luke here beside me though. He's unconscious but breathing."

There was a momentary pause before Adam spoke again. "Gravity's gone. It looks like the powers out."

"Can you see anyone else around you?" Craig asked. "Can you see Karen there?"

"I don't know mate. It's pretty dark over here. I can just make out a couple of people floating nearby, but I can't tell who they are in this light."

The fact that he was no longer alone reassured Craig. He felt confident that Karen was still in the room somewhere, invisible but alive in the blackness. "We're going to have to get the power back on before we either suffocate or freeze to death. Can you reach the master panel on your side?"

Sounds of deep breathing and grunting came to Craig from out of the darkness. He could imagine Adam struggling to turn himself around to examine his surroundings in zero gravity.

"I can see the master panel below me," he eventually replied. "The standby light is flashing, so that means the reactors are still online at least. I can't reach it though. I'm floating too far above it. I'm pretty much stuck here." Muffled curses floated across the room to Craig. "Shit. Those sphere things must have really screwed with our system. The whole station must be offline. I bet the tourists over in the resort wing are freaking out."

Craig imagined the chaos that would ensue if everyone on the station was in the same predicament as they were. With at least ten thousand people aboard Newton station at any one time, he would be surprised if there weren't at least a few fatalities from this.

The communication officer's hair brushed against his hand, startling him out of his thoughts. With the stress of the moment, he had forgotten that she was there. He looked down at the still form that floated below him. It was hard to tell in the dim lighting, but he was pretty confident that the unconscious woman that floated beneath him was Suzanne. She was one of those rare women that were both highly intelligent and highly attractive, a rare girly-girl in the scientific community. She prided herself on both her mind and her appearance, and her long hair trailed behind her like a testament to her femininity. Her long, blonde hair brushed Craig's face once again, giving him an idea. If he could bring her back to consciousness again, she could use the control stations to pull herself across the room to the master panel and restore power to the entire station. The gravity would return, and they could then locate and treat anyone else in the room.

Craig called her name in an attempt to rouse her with no response. She was out cold. He was too high to be able to reach her physically otherwise he would have tried to wake her with a light slap on the check or even shake her back to consciousness. The only part of her within his reach was her hair. He gave an exploratory tug, no response. He waited a moment and grabbed a handful of hair and pulled even harder, hard enough that if she were awake, she would probably have screamed out in pain. The only change he saw was the movement of her body as she rocked back and forth in zero gravity. Something about it caught his attention. The bottom half of her body remained stationary, while her arms head and torso swayed around like a ragdoll. Understanding that her legs were hooked under the desk, he gave another experimental tug on her hair and found himself slowly moving past her to the floor.

Like Rapunzel in reverse, he climbed down her golden locks to reach the safety rails that lined the control room's consoles.

"We're in luck!" he called to Adam. "I've found a way to the floor."

"How'd you manage that?" he replied.

"I'm using Suzanne as a rope. Her legs are pinned under the desk, so I used her to climb my way down."

"Where are you now?"

"I'm just beside the communications console. I've got a hold of the guardrail here, so I'll make my way over to you."

"Okay, the Master control panel is in the next row back from where you are now. Come along until you're level with me, then you'll have to somehow jump across to the next aisle," Adam advised.

Craig pulled himself hand over hand along the steel rail. His legs floated behind him as he made progress across the room. Shapes appeared to him from out of the darkness. Limbs, hands and feet of those he worked with moved past in a macabre parade. The darkness leant a sinister atmosphere to the scene that, on a conscious level, he knew held nothing to fear. The shapes were only his friends who were not dead, just comatose.

The rail came to an end as Craig reached the last control station.

"I'm here," he said and was surprised to hear Adam respond so closely.

"Okay, the next aisle is about nine feet behind you." His friend's voice came from nearly directly overhead. "The safest bet is to make a dive for the next rail but aim low. It's better to hit the floor than to go flying off towards the ceiling again."

Craig understood the logic. If he missed and travelled too high over the next aisle, he would end up across the room near the ceiling and be trapped in the weightless environment once again.

He saw the room in his mind's eye and pictured where he was and what he had to do. With the image set, he placed his feet against the bar and aimed himself in the direction he needed to go.

With a nudge, he leapt.

Craig didn't want to overdo it, so he didn't put too much force into the leap. The trip across the gap took a few seconds. Just when he thought he had misjudged and missed, his outstretched fingers made contact with something solid. He grasped for a handhold as his body caught up with his flailing hands, all he could feel was a flat, steel surface.

"Mate, reach higher," he heard Adam call from above him. "I can hear you banging the shit out of the partition wall. Slide your hand up it and grab the railing at the top."

Craig did as Adam suggested and was rewarded with the feel of a cold aluminium bar. He grabbed on with both hands to steady his motion and made his way along to where he could see the master control panel lit up before him.

"Alright, I'm here now," he puffed. "What do I do?"

"The whole system's automated, so you don't have to do much. See the yellow button on the top left of the console?" Adam asked.

"The one that keeps flashing?"

"That's the one, push it in and hold it for a few seconds."

Craig tightened his grip on the railing. As he released one hand to reach across to the button, his legs floated out above him, putting him in a vertical position. From his perspective, it felt as though he was working on a ceiling mounted control panel above his head with Adam giving instructions from below.

Craig pushed and held the button.

A screen lit up before him showing a list of menu options. "Hit the emergency reset button, top right," Adam guided.

Another menu appeared that asked if he wanted to restart with original settings or reconfigure.

"Do we want original settings or reconfigure?" Craig asked. "Start with original settings, mate. We can reconfigure later if need be."

"Alright, we have a list of options here as to what we can turn on first. Is there any particular order we need to do this in?" Craig looked down past his feet to where Adam floated unseen in the darkness above him.

After a moment's thought, Adam replied. "Usually the startup order wouldn't matter, but under these circumstances, I think we should turn on the lights first, so we can see what's going on around us. I'd hate to turn on the gravity first to find that someone was floating in a way that would cause them injury when they came down.

"Okay, makes sense. The lights it is."

The room was filled with a dazzling brightness that forced them to squint their eyes against the glare.

"Jesus," Adam moaned. "Woah!" Craig whispered.

The control room looked intact. Whatever the spheres had done to them, the station at least appeared to be undamaged. On looking around the room, the only thing that seemed out of place was the array of ANZAR staff that were still suspended in the air.

"Everyone looks alright," Craig said as he looked around the room to find Karen. He spotted her floating near the door that led to the rest of the station. She had somehow ended up upside down with her head pointed towards the floor. As Craig pondered how to stop her breaking her neck when the gravity was re-activated, she began to stir. The sounds of groaning and confused exclamations started to arise around the room as those still unconscious began to awaken as one.

"It must be the lights that are waking them up. At least we know they're OK." Adam pointed to the controls in front of Craig. "You can turn the gravity on to one-sixth and set it for an incremental increase. That way the others should float to the floor and not come down too fast."

Craig looked up, or down to him as he was still inverted, to see Adam floating a few feet above him with one of Luke's legs held tight in his hand. Luke too had begun to waken and was starting to move his head from side to side and wonder what the hell was going on.

"I want to give it a ten-second delay. I need to get over to Karen and turn her the right way up, or she'll break her neck if she comes down like that."

Before Adam could respond, Craig had set the timer and was bringing his feet down onto the handrail that he still gripped. The display below him counted down the ten seconds he had requested. At five seconds, he had managed to place his feet on the bar between his hands. He alternately glanced back and forth between at his girlfriend and the display to mark the time.

When the clock read two seconds to go, he pushed off the rail as hard as he could. He flew across the room with his arms outstretched, ready to grab the woman he loved before she could hit the floor.

As he approached, he could see her body slowly start its descent. The gravity was on. He slammed into her with the entire momentum of his one-hundred-kilogram frame, knocking them both towards the back wall of the room. As they dropped together towards the ground, he grabbed her waist and twisted her around into a vertical position, completing the turn just as his feet touched the floor. Karen fell against him in a daze. She was awake but groggy.

"What happened?" she asked as she made contact with Craig. "I had the strangest dream; I can remember things…. things that…" A look of confusion came over her and Craig could tell that she had probably experienced the similar dream images that he had forgotten on waking.

He kissed her gently and affectionately on the lips. "It's okay, babe. Whatever happened, it's over now," he tried to reassure her.

Behind them, the rest of the team began to mumble and talk over their experience, or lack thereof. A single voice broke through the chatter and caught Craig's attention.

"Craig, get over here. You've gotta see this," Luke called.

Taking Karen's hand in his, he led her over to the main control panel which Adam and Luke now stood in front of, rather than above it. On the small monitor on the desk, a view of the Earth below was showing some strange discolouration.

"What the hell's that?" Craig asked as he stared at the image in denial of what he knew it to be. He looked to the main window for a better look but noticed that the view was blocked by the titanium safety shield that slid into place when the power had begun to fail.

Adam noticed where his attention now lay and reached across the controls to deactivate the shield so that they could get a look outside.

As the metal rolled out of the way, the blue light of the Earth began to fill the room; its warmth was reassuring, although the vision that greeted them wasn't. Scattered around the parts of the globe they could see, patches of orange light stood out in stark contrast from the blue of the atmosphere. The spots flickered and danced as they watched. Their minds struggled to comprehend what they were seeing.

"Oh my God," Karen gasped. "They look like fires."

"They can't be. They'd have to cover dozens of square kilometres to be visible from up here. They must be something else, they're way too bright," Adam disagreed.

Luke was busy punching keys on the control panel in front of him, after a moment he turned to the others with a dazed look. "They're fires alright. According to this, every nuclear power plant on the planet has suffered a meltdown and exploded."

As those in the room watched, the Earth continued to turn, presenting them with its night side. The fires were even more visible now. With the glow of the cities extinguished, they stood out as the only light on the planet's surface.

MEDITERRANEAN SEALED OFF!

Alan Oldman reporting from Gibraltar

I'm standing here at what used to be the old passenger terminal in the Gibraltar docks. As you can see from the destruction wrought by yesterday's events, the city of Gibraltar and its surrounds have been hit hard. Behind me, the small province is still in flames due to the destruction caused by two aircraft that crashed into 'the rock' within minutes of each other. As we've seen in other cities, the pilots of the stricken craft are believed to have been amongst the first of the world's population to experience unconsciousness. There is an unconfirmed theory within the scientific community that altitude played a factor in the order of which people were affected. Whatever the reason, the two aircraft inevitably pitched into the rock, bathing the town below in a cocktail of burning airline fuel that has all but utterly destroyed the city.

Across Spain alone, we have reports of aircraft impacts in most of the major cities including Vigo, Madrid and Barcelona.

This tragedy was not limited to those in the air and on land. If you look into the straits of Gibraltar ahead of where I'm standing, you can see the extraordinary sight of three merchant vessels that ran afoul. With the entire crew of these ships rendered unconscious by 'The Blackout' as it is now being called, they drifted together and collided in the worst place imaginable. The three partially submerged wrecks have claimed the lives of nearly fifty people and have effectively blocked access to the Mediterranean from the Atlantic, barring any future sea travel until they can be removed. Officials expect that that may take as long as two weeks.

As reported earlier, the scene here is one that can only be compared to a war zone. The estimated dead here at Gibraltar stands at around sixteen thousand, many of whom were visiting tourists. We aren't able to gain access to the city due to health reasons as we understand that there are still many bodies littering the area. Sadly, this is a scene that we have seen echoed around the world in the last twenty-four hours.

MILLIONS DIE NEAR CHINESE REACTORS

Hayden Gee reporting from Beijing

The government of China has always regarded its independence and privacy as one of their greatest assets. Now, we find that in this time of need they are ready to accept aid from the west for the first time in recent memory. Sadly, it may be the case that none will be forthcoming as the rest of the world begins to lick its wounds after 'The Blackout'. With uncertainty still existing over the cause of this global catastrophe, many believe that it is still unsafe to fly, leaving the world's populations grounded and stranded, with no way to supply international aid or help.

If any country in this crisis is in need of aid, it is China. The death toll here probably won't be fully realised for months or even years due to the scale of destruction. The most spectacular event was in the Zhejiang province where the AP1000 Sanmen reactor exploded, bathing a fifty-kilometre area with a deadly dose of radiation. Grave concerns are held for the six million occupants of this area. Scientists estimate that nearly twenty percent of the country has been left uninhabitable, leaving millions displaced in what is still the world's most populous nation. China's population may have turned out to have been its downfall, with its increasing reliance on nuclear fission to supply its growing power needs the country may have unwittingly sealed its fate. We know from satellite imagery that no less than sixteen reactors have suffered meltdowns, we can only assume that the remaining facilities have either done the same or been shut down. Whatever the case, with millions left homeless by this immense tragedy, there are millions more who still have their homes but no power. As with the rest of the world, we can be sure that China is hoping that the cause of these events is over and there will be no further repeat of yesterday's 'Blackout'.

CSIRO INVESTIGATES MISSING HOURS

Andrew Price reporting

The world awoke this morning to news of utter devastation. It is now known that the incidents experienced across Australia overnight were not a local phenomenon. Reports are coming in of mass unconsciousness in all parts of the globe. It is still early days, but it seems that no part of the international community was spared from this wave of destruction.

CSIRO scientists have begun what they promise will be an exhaustive study into the effects of the four-hour blackout experienced by the world's population. They, as are we all, are eager to discover what effects, if any, this incident will have on the physical well-being of the populace. I am joined now by CSIRO representative Bryce Farr.

"Good morning Andrew."

"Good morning and welcome to the show Bryce. I know you've barely begun to research this, but do you have any theories about what happened yesterday?"

"Well, like you said it is still early days, but we have begun our research by examining ourselves and our staff extensively. For legal reasons, you understand?"

"Of course."

"Uhm, what we found was that in each case we looked at, the person involved seems to have suffered a change in blood pressure to the brain, causing unconsciousness."

"What could cause a change in blood pressure like this?" "Oh, many factors can contribute. Diet, exercise or a

person's health. But because it is such a widespread phenomenon, we have to look outside the individuals and look at an external factor that would account for the numbers of affected we have seen thus far."

"And does the CSIRO have any theories at this stage?" "Yes, but they're just theories at this stage."

"And what are they?"

"Well, we think that there was a change in air pressure at the time of the Blackout. Minor ear damage in some of our test cases demonstrates this. A sudden change in air pressure, combined with a sudden drop in blood pressure which is also evident, if drastic enough, can induce a faint."

"What about the symptom of what has been called, 'the icy finger' that many report experiencing just before unconsciousness? Many well-respected people in the community, including doctors and high-ranking politicians, swear that they felt as if their minds were being invaded by another presence. Is that a natural symptom of this sort of thing?"

"Andrew, we take the reports of this ice finger as you call it with a grain of salt. It was probably a real pain that people felt, a pain that is only attributable to a severe cluster headache associated with the change in pressure. We see no reason at this stage to attribute any sinister motives to it."

"Well I felt it, and it scared the hell out of me. Didn't you notice it?"

"...Yes."

"And did it frighten you?"

"Andrew, it scared the shit out of me."

17
The Aftermath

Sunday, August 16th, 2048

Three days had passed since the incident the media labelled 'The Blackout' had occurred. Nobody on Earth had any idea where the perpetrators of the world's worst disaster had come. Theories abounded in the media; some networks claimed that the spheres seen in the skies around Earth were a natural phenomenon, while other experts came forward to claim that they were a new series of attacks aimed at the west by a revived faction of ISIS. The fact that lives had been lost in all the world's countries including those occupied by Moslems did little to dampen the growing enthusiasm for the theory. Racial slurs were thrown back and forth in what many worried would result in the rekindling of the religious-based war that was covertly fought in the early twenty-first century. Muslim people the world over began to fear another age of persecution at the hands of the non-Muslim members of the population who drew insane and ignorant comparisons with airliners crashing into cities and the spate of terrorist attacks that had occurred fifty years earlier.

The constant speculation into what 'The Blackout' had been created an air of instability around the world. The human race as a whole had taken a significant blow to its morale and infrastructure. The world looked for someone to blame and to punish. Apart from the ignorant racists who inevitably existed in all societies, everyone who looked at the situation analytically and logically came to the same conclusion. This was not done by any citizens of the Earth. No nation or human being, in general, could be responsible for the devastation that had been wrought upon the world. No country was suspect, as no country was left unscathed. The only answer to the question of whom or what caused this would not be found on the Earth, but somewhere beyond it.

The idea of an intelligently led attack by an alien race was ridiculed... at first. The understanding that the threat was external provided more weight to the theory. Still, the world debated. Why would another form of intelligent life wish to travel millions of miles and kill millions of people just to disappear without taking over the planet? To many, it didn't make sense.

On Earth, the world was in confusion as to what had happened.

On Newton Station, however, they had more information to go on.

18
The update

ANZAR meeting room – Newton Station.

4.15pm - Sunday, August 16th, 2048

Craig stood by the large viewing window in the ANZAR meeting room. He stared at the view of the Earth as his thoughts turned to where his father was and if he was alright. So much had happened in the last few days, not only to him but the world.

The scene below still looked much as it had done before the Blackout. The Earth was still blue with softer undertones of greens and oranges spread across the land masses. The only signs that something out of the ordinary had happened were the new brown spots that dotted the globe from fires that had raged unchecked for more than a day. The Earth looked as though it had been used as an ashtray at the galaxy's biggest party, where everyone who attended took turns in stubbing their cigarettes out on its surface. Craig observed the positioning of the burns and became disheartened every time he discovered one that was positioned where he knew a city should have been. The knowledge that the ANZAR team, including himself, were most likely responsible for the devastation made him wish that they had never gotten involved in the Conduit project.

A voice spoke from behind him. "Hey. I just heard that Glen's just arrived back on the station from London. Apparently, he has some news about what's going on."

Craig turned to see Luke stepping away from a knot of ANZAR staff that was waiting for the meeting with head office to commence. He saw now that the room was full of lab-coated scientists who stood around making idle chatter as they waited for Sydney to come into view so that the conference could begin.

"Somehow, I get the feeling that it won't be good news," Craig replied in a subdued tone. "How is he anyway? I heard his parents place narrowly missed being taken out by a BA jet."

"Yeah, he and his parents are fine. Many of their neighbours weren't so lucky, though." Luke turned to look out the window as if to study the damage first hand.

"Well, whatever he has to tell us must be pretty important for him to leave his parents under those conditions. I can't imagine what it would be that would get me to leave my dad in a war zone like that."

The murmur of conversation in the room died down as the buzz of white noise filled the air. After a few seconds, the sound was replaced by the voice of Conrad Stephens, ANZAR's man on the ground that ran the company's financial side of the business from their head office in Sydney. Without him, Professors Weekes and Turp would have never have been able to get the Australian and New Zealand Aeronautical Research corporation off the ground. A heavy-set man in his fifties, Conrad appeared on a large monitor suspended from the ceiling. All eyes in the meeting room now turned towards him.

Conrad meant business in a dark suit with a holographic tie on which the Australian flag floated up and down its length like an old-fashioned screensaver. Certificates, awards and photos of Australian Prime Ministers from the last few decades filled the office wall behind him.

"Good morning, everyone. I hope all is well and that you all fared better up there than we have down here."

The room filled with mumbled responses and answers ranging from "yeah, fine" to noncommittal grunts. As with the people 200 kilometres below them on Earth, the staff on Newton shared their uncertainty and insecurities after the events of the Blackout. More so they felt something that the average citizen on Earth didn't, a slight twinge of guilt that they may be somehow responsible.

Turning to Doctor Anderson who sat in the first row directly in front of the monitor, Conrad began his questioning. "Firstly, how is everyone feeling up there at the moment, Peter?"

"Well, if you mean physically, then no-one on staff has suffered any long-term injuries or complications over the bought of unconsciousness. The only injury as such occurred to our communications officer in the act of reactivating the power and gravity."

"Oh, Suzanne you mean? What's the nature of her injuries?" Conrad asked.

"Lifting of the scalp sir," the Doctor replied. "A necessary, but unavoidable consequence which allowed young Craig to reach the master panel and access the gravity controls."

A soft murmur of giggles broke out across the room as faces turned to Craig to mock him good-naturedly. Luckily, he could see the humour in the situation. While many in the room laughed at the fact that Suzanne had been internally de-scalped, he understood that they all knew the circumstances and respected what he had done. It would only have been a matter of hours until the carbon dioxide levels would have risen high enough to have become harmful to human health. His actions were recognised as having saved many lives onboard the station.

"My scalps still pretty sore, at least the feeling to the top part of my head has returned." Suzanne made a playful gesture of rubbing her head and staring at Craig who looked more than a little embarrassed by the remark.

Conrad smiled to himself for a moment to say he got the joke then continued in a more sombre tone. "And what of Professor Weekes? Is he still catatonic?"

Once again Doctor Anderson responded. "Yes, he's still under. The Blackout came at the worst time as far as the Professor is concerned. The delay we experienced in getting him medical help may have aggravated his condition further. We took the second VAPER out to pick him up as soon as we regained consciousness after the Blackout, but he was still left alone out there for nearly two hours by the time we got to him. He's still flaked out in the medical wing in a coma of some sort. We do have the idea I emailed you about that will revive him, but we are sure that it will cause him to lose all knowledge of what happened to him since before he and Doctor Turp left in the VAPER."

Conrad agreed. "No, no. Don't do anything like that yet, we need to find out what happened to him and Professor Turp in the ten days that they were missing. We'll give him a chance to come 'round on his own before we do anything as severe as what you recommended."

Doctor Anderson nodded his head in agreement. "Time is the only factor in his recovery now."

"Agreed, we really can't risk that information. Many down here believe the test brought those spheres through to the Earth. We've even received a report from one of our sources that the Americans watched the whole thing from the ground and are about to reveal to the world that ANZAR is responsible for this whole mess."

"What! That's bullshit, Conrad," Luke yelled at the screen causing many in the room to jump at his outburst. "They only want to use this as an excuse to steal our research." He turned to the others in the room, some of whom were nodding their heads in agreement. Doctor Henry Tran stared at him from the front of the room with a look that Luke had trouble deciphering.

"Be that as it may, we still need to find out what happened before the news is announced to the world," Conrad said. "We must not allow them to make ANZAR or the Australian government the scapegoats for their own financial and political benefit, whether they are right or wrong about us being the cause of the Blackout."

Craig had spent the last three days researching the Professor's activities during the test by accessing the *Feynman*'s computers. Confident that he could now say what had happened, he spoke up from his place by the window.

"What we have learnt so far is that we are, in some ways, responsible for what happened three days ago. With the return of Professor Weekes, I've been able to access the *Feynman*'s computers and discovered that the Professors didn't stick to the original plan."

Craig looked around the room to gauge the reactions of the others. Just as he had expected, they seemed to have already known, or at least guessed that that was the case. Craig reached into his Jacket pocket and pulled out a folded piece of paper and glanced at it before continuing.

"It took a little digging around in the *Feynman*'s computers, but I did manage to find out where they went during the ten days they were gone," Craig began.

"Why did you need to dig for that information?" Conrad frowned at him from the screen on the wall. "I thought the VAPER's computer systems were supposed to record everything and spit out an itemised report at the end of each transit."

Craig nodded as he spoke. "Usually, they do," he began. "But it appears that in this case the information was intentionally erased. It's only because I helped design the software that I was able to locate the information in a backup cache file. Otherwise, we'd have no idea what happened at all."

"Well, come on man," Luke said impatiently from beside him. "What happened? Where did they go?"

Craig looked at his friend then back at Conrad on the screen. "The file system was a bit of a mess, but I've managed to pull six Conduit addresses from the computer. Everything was all jumbled up in there, so I have no idea what order they visited them, how long they were at each destination, or even whether one or both of the Professors were at each one."

"I don't believe that," Conrad interjected. "Brian and John were both well organised and disciplined scientists. I don't believe that they would go off on a whim like this without informing the rest of us about it first."

Craig looked at the man on the monitor whom he believed knew his father almost as well as he did himself. "I didn't believe it either at first Conrad, but the evidence is there. They were only supposed to go to the coordinates at 1486.23.08.2034 in the blue sector, but the computer shows that they went to six completely different locations, mostly in the red sector which we never had any plans of visiting anytime soon. Hell, one of their transits was even way out in the green sector of the wheel."

"The green sector?" Conrad gasped. "We weren't even going to touch that for at least a few more years yet. Brian and John knew that travel in any other areas except the blue sector is still unapproved. We don't know enough about it yet; it's too dangerous."

"You're right. When I compared the data from the *Feynman* to that of the gates themselves, I found that the area of the Multiverse that the spheres crossed over from is in the green sector... and it was one of the six transit locations that the VAPER visited."

"So ANZAR is responsible then. If not directly, they at least led those things here where they killed one hundred million people." Conrad sighed. "They probably did it as a warning to us not to go back to their universe." With the Professors seemingly reckless actions in mind, Conrad looked down at his hands and seemed to have spoken to himself. "My God, what have they done?"

The meeting room became deathly silent as everyone stared at the figure on the screen and awaited his advice. The confirmation that the Conduit research had resulted in the most substantial loss of life in the history of the planet came as a blow to the team. The possibility that they may have achieved first contact with an alien species did nothing to improve their moods. The Conduit worked better than they had dreamed, but many began to wonder, at what cost?

Conrad finally seemed to come to a decision and looked up at the waiting group. "Whatever happened, I believe that your fathers would not have changed the test schedule on a whim. I'm certain that they would have had a very good reason to do this. For now, we must accept the evidence provided to us at face value and work on figuring out what our best course of action is."

Luke looked up at Conrad. "You're right, I agree. As soon as Dad regains consciousness, we can just ask him what happened. In the meantime, we should figure out what to do about the spheres." He turned to Craig with a look of sympathy on his face. "And what we can do for Professor Turp."

"There's no doubt about it; this situation is a mess. I can't approve any more Conduit transits at this point. Not with the U.S. Empire breathing down our necks like it is. We need to keep a low profile and go into damage control."

Conrad seemed to look around the room to make eye contact with each of the scientists in turn. Just as he'd nearly finished looking at each of the staff, the door to the control room opened, and Glen Hanson walked into the room. It is evident by the look on his face that he wasn't bringing good news.

19
From bad to worse

ANZAR meeting room – Newton Station. 4.32pm -

Sunday, August 16th, 2048

With a hesitant look around at those gathered, Glen strode directly to the centre of the room where he placed a battered briefcase on the desk.

On the screen, Conrad looked visibly relieved that Glen had arrived. "Uhh, Glen," he sighed. "How was the trip up? I bet it was a bit awkward getting on a flight with all that's happened. I'm sure a teleconference would have sufficed for you to tell us whatever it is that was so urgent."

Glen looked at the screen and tried to put on a pleasant countenance, but to all present, it was apparent that he was not in a good mood. "Well, once you hear what I have to say, you'll see why I had to come up in person." He turned to face the scientists in the room.

"The rest of the world is going to catch on to this sooner or later, but I didn't want us to be associated with this news in any way. What with the U.S. blaming ANZAR and the Australian governments for this whole disaster, we need to distance ourselves from it as far as we can for the time being."

"You mean publicly, don't you?" Craig asked.

"Of course," Glen replied. "We still need to research this thing to find out what happened to the Professors as well as figure out a way to avoid this new mess we're in. We just have to do it low key at the moment. We don't want to become the central figures in this drama when the full realisation of what has happened becomes public."

By his manner and tone of voice, Craig could tell that Glen had discovered something monumental before his return to Newton, something that must be worse than what had already happened.

A sense of dread overcame him as he found that he didn't want to hear what it was that Glen had to say. After all, what could be worse than the death of one hundred million people?

"After the Blackout, I took my telescope out into the backyard of my parent's place to see if I could spot any of those spheres that appeared just before the event. With it being dark when I awoke, the stars were out and seemed a little brighter than usual. I looked through the telescope at the sky and began to hunt for any signs of the balls of light. As we now know, they left pretty much straight away, so there was nothing to see as far as that was concerned."

Glen looked around the room and drew in a deep breath before he continued.

"What I did notice, however, was that something about the stars themselves seemed odd. I've been working in Astronomy for most of my adult life and have looked at the sky through a telescope nearly every night for the last twenty years. At first glance, when I looked up, everything seemed as it should be, but as I scanned the sky, I realised that everything had shifted."

Glen waved his arms around and began to pace the room as his excitement grew.

"I won't bore you with the details, but I took some measurements as best I could before I contacted some colleagues of mine at both the Greenwich Observatory and the National Observatory in Canberra. I got them to double check what I had seen, and they confirmed my theory with a 99.5% probability."

The room was silent once again as they awaited the punch line to Glen's story.

"Well, what did you find out?" someone up the back of the room blurted out.

"The stars appear to have shifted position. But as we all know, that's impossible. We think, sorry, we now know what happened when the spheres surrounded the Earth. The radiation, the unconsciousness and the millions of deaths were merely a side effect to what the spheres were really doing."

"So, are you saying they didn't intend to kill all those people?" Conrad asked hopefully. His visage stared back at Glen from the surface of the Earth with a look that showed that he was seriously grasping at straws with that comment and he knew it.

Glen turned to face Conrad's image on the screen for a moment.

"Technically, no." Glen looked at the floor in thought. "At least, not straight away. You see, what they did was form themselves up in a grid pattern around the Earth, and then they somehow moved it." He shrugged his shoulders as if to say *Hey, go figure.*

A murmur of confused vocalisations filled the room. People turned to those beside them to check that they had heard correctly and were not imagining what Glen had said.

"So, you're saying they moved the entire planet?" As much as Craig respected Glen's work, he was still a little sceptical. It beggared belief; his mind was feverishly trying to comprehend the enormity of the task. "How... how far? Where did they move it to?"

Glen sighed and looked down at a sheet of paper he had laid on the table beside him.

"Not far, but far enough. We're still working on the exact figures, but we think it's in the area of around a hundred thousand kilometres." He stopped for a moment to let this sink in.

A few of the more senior Professors in the room gasped as they understood the implications immediately.

After a moment's pause, Glen continued. "The worst part is that it's not a straight-line move. It's more like a shift in orbit. What they've done is expanded our course around the sun by 2 degrees. This orbital shift of just two degrees is enough to send the Earth out of our sweet spot as far as temperature is concerned. What they've done is nudged us out of the 'Goldilocks Zone'. With this minor course correction, the Earth will drop in temperature as our new orbit slowly moves us further from the sun. The Earth will cool, and the drop in temperature will kill everyone and everything on the planet within three or four months."

The room gasped collectively.

"So, the answer to your earlier question Conrad is, no. The spheres didn't intend to kill those people at that time with what they did. They're thinking bigger than that. They're trying to freeze to death every living thing on the surface of the Earth."

The ANZAR staff all reacted differently to the news. Some responded in shock and denial, saying that they must have gotten it wrong, that no-one could move an entire planet. A few of the younger staff began to cry at the news at what effectively amounted to a death sentence for everyone on the Earth.

Most stood silently. Many stared at their feet while others gazed out the window at the world below them that was now destined to travel a new course around the sun, alone and dead.

No one was watching the screen.

No one noticed that Conrad had been joined on screen by a young man in the military uniform of the SAS. A silent, but animated conversation passed between the two men as Conrad was handed a sheet of paper. With a sense of urgency, the young soldier departed, leaving Conrad to get the attention of the staff on Newton.

"Everyone...can I have your attention please."

Those still arguing over the most recent news fell silent as Conrad began to speak.

"We have another problem. Apparently, the news about ANZAR's alleged involvement in the Blackout is already all over the internet. The US President has jumped in saying that ANZAR and the Australian government are at fault and that they intend to shut you down immediately. According to the President, everyone will be contained on the station, and all of your research and equipment is to be confiscated. The arrogant fool's acting like he's just saved the world from a group of global terrorists."

Conrad paused for a moment to let the news sink in.

"This is not much more than we were previously expecting, so it's good we are already prepared. We just have to stick to the plan and get everything of value that we can into one of the VAPERS and move it down here to a secure location before anyone arrives. I can have a hangar emptied at the Holsworthy Army base in short order, so keeping your work safe shouldn't pose a problem. We need you all to go through your systems and delete everything of value. We can't give them anything to pillage from us."

On the monitor, Conrad seemed to look around the room as if searching for someone. He stopped when his eyes met Craig's. "Craig, we need you load up the *Feynman* with every piece of research and prototype you can cram into it, and get out of there as soon as it's loaded. It's imperative that you be gone before the troops arrive, or the Empire will end up possessing every piece of our technology and research. That's what they really want. If they get there before you're ready to go they'll never let you leave; they'll seal off the research wing, so you won't be able to go *anywhere* in the VAPER."

Craig locked eyes with Conrad and felt sure that his father's friend was trying to direct him in some way. The look he was getting said all he needed to know. The emphasis Conrad put on the words 'go anywhere in the VAPER', confirmed to Craig what he was being asked to do.

"How long do you think we have?" Doctor Tran spoke up from the front of the room for the first time.

Conrad broke eye contact with Craig and looked at someone off-screen. After a quick exchange, he turned back to the waiting scientists and answered. "Our source at the Cape says that they're loading up a military inter-orbital jet as we speak. From what he can tell, there are going to be at least twenty Imperial cavalry troops on your doorstep in around two hours."

PRESIDENT FINDS BLACKOUT TERRORISTS

Transcript of the President of the American Empires speech on
16/08/48

"My fellow Americans. I come before you to bring the news that we have discovered the perpetrators of the vilest attack on American soil since September 11. Just a few days ago the Blackout that was thrust upon the people of our fair country caused us a significant loss of life as well as damage to our infrastructure and cities. Rest assured that those responsible for the deaths of two million of our citizens in the homeland will not go unpunished. We also pray for the lives of the nearly forty million souls lost in our provinces and states around the world. Our hearts go out to the families of our brethren in Iran, Iraq, Mozambique, Mexico, Chile, Canada and the rest who suffered almost as much as we did."

"As is the American way, we will bring the full force of the law down upon them. The scientists responsible will be detained and held for questioning pending charges. We will get to the bottom of why these monsters did what they did, and we will ensure that they are punished. My only regret is that these men and women cannot be tried under the Imperial legal system, and so, cannot be put to death.

Nevertheless, rest assured that they will live out the rest of their days in a federal prison…working for the benefit of the Empire of these United States."

20

Here comes the Cavalry

En-route to Newton Station.

5.39pm - Sunday, August 16th, 2048

The radio from the cockpit blared sharp bursts of static as the pilots aimed the U.S. Air Force transport towards space. Unlike the comparative silence of commercial flights, the troops onboard the military jet were bombarded with audio information concerning the crafts pitch, yaw, trajectory and altitude. Information that was vaguely interesting at best and utterly useless at worst.

"Control, we are powering up the boosters to eighty percent thrust and are now at an altitude of fifty-five thousand feet," the pilot's voice crackled throughout the ship. "We are about to commence roll maneuver for orbital insertion."

Blah, blah, blah, blah de blah, Kyle Ferine thought as he stared at the gun-metal grey ceiling of the military plane, wondering how he had gotten here.

Fate had led him in a cruel and unusual direction when he had joined the Australian Army ten years ago. Ferine had signed up as a bright, twenty-one-year-old recruit ready to fight for his country and to defend his home and family. The Australian military had risen in popularity and enjoyed a recruitment boost with the realisation that the war on terror had settled down into being more of an abstract idea than a physical event. With Australia no longer occupying foreign countries or engaged in active combat duties, the youth of the day once again saw enlisting as a valid career move rather than a means of committing suicide.

With a young wife and plans for a baby, the military was the best career choice available to Ferine at that time. The trips to foreign lands and the time away from his family was a part of the job that he had grown to accept and deal with. The possibility of being placed on loan to the American Empire as a combat specialist and training officer had never entered his mind.

The Imperial government practically forced his superiors to sign over his services to them under the guise of a five-year exchange program. From what he'd heard, his old unit was still awaiting his replacement from the U.S. The move and transfer to America had all but ended his already struggling relationship with his wife, Marie, who resented the time he was forced to be away from her and their twin boys. Like many military wives, Marie found the idea of her husband travelling to America and returning home just a few weeks a year unacceptable. She saw no sense in being married to someone who couldn't be there for the family and fulfil the role as the father figure in her children's lives. She had packed up the kids and had moved back to her mother's house, where as far as Kyle knew, she still lived.

Ten years after beginning a career with one nation's military, in which the protection of Australia was their primary objective, he found himself a prematurely aged man in his thirties working as an Imperial Manipulation Specialist on his way to detain Australian citizens, all in the name of a foreign and corrupt regime.

Still, he thought. *Orders are orders. Only one more month to go and I'm out.*

He'd done enough morally suspect things in his time with the US Cavalry to have a clear and disturbing, understanding of what would happen to the occupants of the space station when they arrived.

He looked around the cargo bay of the aircraft. A row of benches lined the outer walls in which were seated twenty of the most apathetic soldiers he had ever worked with. Mission after mission, he was amazed by the callous nature in which they performed the duties assigned to them. With no respect for human life, they killed indiscriminately and, in some cases, for pleasure. Imperial Manipulation Specialists were not known for taking prisoners. Unless an enemy combatant was explicitly stated as being designated for capture, they killed whomever they came across. Through them, Kyle had learnt too well how the power of position could corrupt the soul. He didn't count himself as one of them; he couldn't bring himself to associate his duties with their actions. In his eyes, he was paid to keep the members of C-Unit under some semblance of control. The knowledge that he would be leading these men against unarmed researchers from his own country filled him with a sense of disgust that made him ashamed to call himself Australian. He made a mental note to address the situation ASAP.

Out of the twenty men under his command, Ferine only held out hope for the long-term careers of two of them. Although blindly and obsessively devoted to serving the Empire, Ferine's second in command, Sergeant Jackson, shared Ferine's views that cruelty and violence were not always the first and best response to any given situation. He was a good soldier that had something that most of the team lacked, common-sense and compassion. The other exception to the rule within C-Unit was a young recruit named Brendan Dockrill. At nineteen, the Private was still pretty much only a kid. Fresh off his parent's farm, he was joining this mission as his initiation into C-unit. Ferine wondered how long it would take the rest of the group to turn this fresh, innocent young mind into a warped, murderous drone with no sense of morals or compassion. Ferine dearly hoped that if he took the kid under his wing and gave him enough time and attention that could be avoided.

The cabin speaker burst into life, interrupting Ferine's thoughts. "Control, we are clear of the atmosphere and are now in orbit heading 080-567, over."

The cargo bay fell silent once more, for a moment.

The pilot's voice was transmitted into the cargo bay once again, this time through the communicator on Ferine's forearm. "Flight Commander to Captain."

Ferine raised his arm to his chin. "Go ahead."

"We've cleared the debris field and are heading towards the station. From what we can see on our long-range scanners, it looks like somebody told them we were coming'. There's a lot of traffic around the terminals so we might be a little while before we can dock. Either way, we've got about a ten-minute wait while we adjust our speed and trajectory before we get there. The fasten seatbelts light is now off."

Eager to have some free time in weightlessness, the men around him heard this news and began to reach for their seat restraints.

"Hold on a second, guys." Kyle had something to say first. He unclipped his belt and floated towards the ceiling, putting himself in an excellent position to make eye contact with all the men.

"Before we get too carried away on this one, I want to remind you all that this is a simple seizure operation. The President himself ordered and organised this mission. He wants as many people on this Station to be taken alive as possible. They have no military ties or weapons that we know of. Therefore they have been classified as non-hostile. We are not here to fight, just contain."

"Awww, shit! We never get to have no fun, Cap!" one of the men yelled good-naturedly.

A few of the other members of C-Unit laughed at this remark.

Ferine looked around at the men below him. He knew they would try and follow his orders as best they could. The problem with these guys though, was that they had their own interpretations of what fight and non-hostile meant.

"The ground rules are as follows. Safety first, no shots are to be fired unless you are fired at first. Even then, you shoot to maim, not kill." He looked around the room. "Understood?"

"Acknowledged, Sir!" they all answered as one.

"Good." That was the best Ferine could do for the moment. With this group, he knew fatalities would be unavoidable; he could only hope that his speech would limit them to a small enough number as to be acceptable to the men in charge on the ground.

"Right. This should be simple enough. As I said, we're not expecting any resistance, so we'll keep this one civilised by walking straight in the front door." Captain Ferine decided he may as well do a quick revision of the mission brief while he still had everyone's attention.

Ferine kicked off against the wall and floated over the heads of his troops on his way to the opposite end of the bay. He stopped his motion by grabbing a handhold on an overhead bar before reaching down to a control panel set into the wall. With the touch of a few buttons, a touch screen descended through the ceiling, displaying a three-dimensional schematic of what appeared to be an oversized sea mine.

"This is Newton Station." Ferine pointed at the display. "I'm sure most of you have passed through here at one time or another while you've been on leave. As you know, it's based on a spherical central area which consists of bars, shopping centres, the theme park, basically all the main public areas." Ferine pointed at the central sphere of the station as he spoke.

"The arms, spires, or whatever you want to call these long cylindrical looking things coming off it are the privately- owned wings of the station. These contain anything and everything from hotels, to airline terminals, offices as well as the research and habitation modules which we're interested in."

On the screen, the image of Newton rotated and zoomed in to give a closer look at one particular section of the station.

The arms of the private wings increased in detail as the image enlarged.

"This wing here, labelled in red, is the one we're after. It's occupied by the privately owened but partially government-funded Australian and New Zealand Aeronautical Research Corporation, or ANZAR for short."

A brief laugh issued form one of Ferine's men who was just bright enough to see the irony in the situation, but still nowhere near smart enough to keep his mouth shut. "Holy shit, Cap. They've got you chasing after your own guys," the private laughed to himself as he looked around the room at his comrades. "We better be careful up there guys, or we might shoot the Cap's daddy."

"Well if you want to do that, Jim," Ferine replied. "You better make sure you get your mum out from under him first."

Ferine knew better than to take this jibe personally. Imperial manipulation troops were an entity unto themselves who readily pointed out each other's differences at every available opportunity. Their ignorance distanced them from society and made them easier to control. The system appeared to be working for the Empire, so far.

He let them have their laugh before continuing. "Now, basically we are only interested in this one wing of the station here."

Ferine pointed at the screen in which one of the large tubular sections of the station flashed red.

"As I said," he repeated as he glowered at the soldier who had interrupted. "This is the ANZAR wing. The whole section is a large cylinder that locks into the main spherical hub. All this red area on the map is private property, only the station staff with the proper I.D. can have access to this high-security area. The base of the construction is filled with the research staff's living quarters; it's a long corridor with private cabins coming off it. We will need to search this area one room at a time and bring anyone we find to muster area A – which will be their main meeting room - where we can watch them. Above the accommodation wing are the labs; which are leased out to private corporations. This area is of less importance to us as we are mainly concerned with tracking down and apprehending everyone associated with the ANZAR group. For security reasons, we will need to round up anyone in this area and move them to the cafeteria, muster area B."

Ferine turned to his men to accentuate the point.

"It is vital that we keep these two groups of people separate. Anyone found in the rented labs is to be taken to muster area B where they will be identified and most likely released. Anyone from the accommodation wing or the ANZAR labs themselves must be taken to muster area A for identification and processing. Got it?"

"Acknowledged, Sir!" the group replied as one.

"Good. The last and most important area we need to look at is the ANZAR lab area itself. According to the schematic we have a series of a dozen rooms that will need to be searched and cleared ASAP. Once all staff have been moved out, we'll give the all-clear, and the Imperial science division will move in to bag and tag everything within these rooms. Anything that isn't screwed to the floor we take. Got it?"

"Acknowledged, Sir!"

"You all know the routine we practised in the simulations. Just do this one by the book, and you'll all be rewarded for your efforts with two weeks R&R. I'm sure you'd all like a bit of time at home to check on your families."

A chorus of cheers and whoops rose around the cargo bay as Kyle Ferine made his way over to his second in command, Sergeant Jackson.

"Want to come up front and check this place out from the outside before we head in?" Ferine asked the shorter dark-haired youth who was in the process of unclipping himself.

"Sure Cap. Be right with you."

As Ferine turned and pulled himself along the short corridor to the cockpit, he wondered once again how he had come to be in such an unfavourable position. This mission was so crucial to his supervisors, and therefore his chances of getting transferred home, that he hoped the bribe of two weeks paid leave would inspire the men to follow the rules just this once.

As the door slid shut behind the departing Captain and his Sergeant, the men released themselves from their restraints and began to float around the room, the conversation amongst the troops invariably turned to the following mission.

But not in any way that would reassure Ferine.

"So, what's the kitty on this one, boys?" one of the men asked as he rubbed his hands together in excitement.

They all turned to look at a mean looking trooper with the shaven head and scarred face who was busy thumbing through a small black book. His face was marked with two rows of poorly healed jagged flesh that ran the length of his head from forehead to chin. He claimed that it was from a hand to hand fight he had nearly lost with a lion while on tour in Africa. Those with access to his personnel files, such as Ferine and Jackson, knew that they were a gruesome souvenir from his wedding in which the disapproving father of the bride had slashed Wilkes' face with a Jim Beam bottle.

Tony 'Scarface' Wilkes was as scarred and ugly on the inside as he was on the outside. At six feet three inches tall, his body was a testament to the amount of spare time these men had on their hands. Spare time in which he spent much of it exercising. He was huge, with a 41-inch chest, 27-inch waist and 14-inch arms; he looked more like a Mister Universe contestant than a career soldier until you looked at his head. With his size, his looks and his demeanour, he was the archetypal battle-scarred soldier from Hell. He knew that his size was intimidating, in fact, he counted on it. It was his first line of defence when it came to dealing with the usual jibes he received about his looks. If that didn't deter any would-be-haranguers, his penchant for violence would quickly settle the matter

Scarface looked up at the men with a sadistic grin. With a slight nod of his head, he announced the amount of cash up for grabs. "Nine hundred and fifty dollars. It's gone up a bit."

"Nice," someone exclaimed.

"That'll come in handy on vacation, won't it?" another drawled.

"So everyone's clear about the rules," Scarface spoke conspiratorially. "Whoever scores the most kills on this mission, gets the dough. As you know, each kill has to look like an accident or an act of self-defence. Subtlety is the key. If the Cap or Jackson get in the least bit suspicious, or questions you at length about the details of any one of your kills, you're out of the game."

Scarface looked around the room before covering one last point.

"As usual, men are ten points, women twenty and anyone under the age of sixteen or over the age of sixty is fifty points. From what I gather, there won't be many kids or old people up here, so it should be mainly ten and twenty-point jobs."

The group was silent.

"One word of advice, if you do see any children up there, I suggest you bag 'em before I do."

The troops burst into fits of laughter. They were looking forward to the mission. It was going to be fun.

RIOTS AND LOOTING CAUSE HAVOC

We now cross live to Alan Oldman reporting from outside the white house in Washington.

"I wish I could say good morning David, but it is far from it. As you can see by the crowds behind me, the trouble we saw last night is showing no signs of abating. Downtown Washington was largely spared major damage from the Blackout of a few days ago, but all that has changed now. Our once great capital has been left in near ruin by a mob of its own citizens who have gathered here in their thousands to demand a better response to the devastation. As best we can tell, many in the crowd here hail from the worst hit areas in the Blackout, such as New York, Chicago, Denver and San Francisco. With their homes destroyed and nowhere else to go, this wave of refugees has inevitably sought aid at the home of authority. With the influx of refugees, riots have broken out all over the city, resulting in millions of dollars' worth of property damage. As is to be expected, a large portion of these rabble raisers are believed to be your standard anti-social criminals who are out to exploit the situation. That doesn't mean that the group, on the whole, doesn't have an agenda of some sort. A spokesperson for the mob this morning stepped forward to demand the President's resignation over what he claims is and I quote: 'a long list of past failings, which has accumulated in this heinous attack on American sovereignty."

"At this point, I'd like to remind our viewers that this internet news service does not agree with or condone these views."

"So, Alan, it appears that the people are blaming the President for the Blackout."

"No, not at all, David. Their main gripe with the President seems to be that he has not acted swiftly enough to ensure the safety of the American people and their allies. Many think that if the Empire had been more forceful in its acquisition of foreign research and technologies, then this whole situation could have been averted. Blame still lies squarely with the Australians, and their renegade scientific group turned terrorists, ANZAR."

"Hopefully, we will see an end to the violence once the issue is resolved, as we expect it to be by this afternoon."

"That's true, David. As I've promised in previous webcasts, I'm on my way to Newton Station shortly to cover the arrest of the renegade Australian terrorists. I'll bring you more as the situation develops."

21

Evacuating Newton

ANZAR meeting room – Newton Station. 5.45pm -

Sunday, August 16th, 2048

Craig shoved as much clothing into his rucksack as would fit. He ran his eyes around his cabin, weighing up the potential usefulness of every item to be sure that he hadn't left anything of scientific value behind. He hoped to eventually be able to come back and remove the personal items such as family photographs and tacky souvenirs he had bought on his travels around the world. The urgency of the moment forced him to disregard the things he could live without during this crisis. With a few changes of clothes and some bathroom products safely packed away, he turned to leave the room. As he reached for the door handle, he remembered the engagement ring. After a moment of internal debate, he turned and retrieved it from the top drawer.

Craig opened the silk-lined velvet box and looked at it with a sigh; the symbol of his love for Karen lay dormant and unused. With his father's disappearance, the right moment for him to present it to her had never arisen and with them now going their separate ways in the evacuation. It may not arrive at all. Being the eternal optimist that he was, he placed the ring in the bag with the rest of his possessions in the hope that he may still have that chance.

The corridors of the accommodation wing were busy with staff who were madly trying to get themselves packed and away from the station before the Imperial military could arrive. Everyone knew that the finger of blame was pointed at ANZAR and what likely ramifications there would be as a result.

Craig headed along the corridor at a fast walk, eager to get to the main research bay and airlock where the ANZAR senior researchers were organising equipment for the evacuation.

Being in such a hurry, the decontamination process and security scan seemed to take an age. As he bathed in the heat of the radiation and the wind ruffled his hair, his mind was filled with a thousand thoughts of what was needed to be done. After what seemed like fifteen minutes, but was still the regular two, Craig was granted access to the main corridor of the ANZAR labs.

Standing there waiting for him was the last person he expected to see.

Karen rushed forward and grabbed him by the shoulders. He could see that her face was tear-streaked.

"Craig, they want me to evacuate on the commercial flights with the others and leave the boys behind. You have to talk to them," she pleaded. "If we leave them behind, they'll die."

Craig placed his arms around her and attempted to draw her close. Karen gently pushed him away and stared him in the face. She was not in the mood to be comforted.

"Don't worry. It's alright. They're not abandoning the kids," Craig soothed. "They just can't go down on the commercial flights with everybody else. They'll cause too much attention. Conrad's looking at the options now, but I promise you we will not leave them behind."

Karen began to calm down with this news. She fell into his arms and allowed herself to be held. Briefly.

"Have you packed the kid's things?" Craig asked Karen as she stepped away and wiped tears from her face.

"Yeah, almost done," she sighed. "They're in their now trying to decide which toys to bring." Karen gave an awkward smile that revealed how deeply she cared for the two children. "Okay, look I have to get to the main engineering dock and prep one of the VAPERS to leave. As soon as you're ready, grab the kids and bring them along," Craig said as he slowly began to back away down the corridor. "Be as quick as you can. We've probably got less than an hour before the military gets here."

Craig turned to hurry away but stopped when Karen spoke again.

"We're coming with you?" she asked. "You're going to take us down to the surface yourself?"

"That's the plan," he smiled. "You and the boys are the closest thing I have to a family now that Dad's gone." Craig looked like he was about to be overcome with emotion himself. He pretended to examine something on the floor for a moment while he regained his composure.

Karen was about to reach out to him when he suddenly looked up. "Just be quick about getting down there okay?"

With that, he rushed along the corridor and disappeared around the corner.

It wasn't in the original plan to take Karen and the kids with him, but under the circumstances, he saw no other choice. She was right about the boys being in danger if they stayed. Regardless of what would happen to Jamie and Timothy if they fell into the wrong hands, there was no way either Craig or Karen could merely abandon them. Although taking them with him was a simple solution to one problem, it held the potential to create myriad others. Craig knew that he would have to work with what the situation gave him.

The ANZAR labs area was arranged over all three floors of the cylinder, after a few turns through the corridors he came to an elevator shaft and hit the down button. Commonly used areas such as the meeting room and control centre occupied the central floor on which Craig lived, most of the labs were situated on the floors above and below, out of the way of the main traffic areas. As the engineering department dealt with equipment that used outside the station in the vacuum of space, it had been built on the bottom floor with access to the only privately-owned hangar bay on the station.

As soon as the elevator doors opened, Craig stepped in and hit the down button. It was a short walk to Doctor Tran's engineering lab, and Craig found himself there in less than a minute.

The doors slid aside to reveal a large open spaced area that occupied most of the lower floor of the wing. Benches filled with machine parts, rolled wire and racks of tools surrounded the outer wall of the room. A crane and pulley system moved across the ceiling carrying a large steel box in its claw. The last of the ANZAR staff remaining on the station were either busy packing containers into the VAPER or throwing items into the nearby airlock for disposal.

"How's everything going?" Craig asked as he stepped into the room.

Adam Fehrenbach came over from a computer terminal beside the door where he and Luke had been monitoring the progress of the Imperial Military transport.

"Not bad. We should have about forty-five minutes before the Cavalry can get aboard. We should have plenty of time to see you off and make it through the maintenance tunnel before they get here. The Docs over there are just supervising the last of the stores now."

Adam pointed to the group of scientists who stood talking amongst themselves. They were squeezed between the transparent domes of the *Feynman* and the *Hawking* as they supervised the loading of the station's research data and prototypes into the *Feynman*.

"Once you've got the VAPER prepped, you should be ready to leave," Adam finished.

"No problem." Craig looked from the *Feynman* to Adam. "How full would you say the VAPER is?"

"Why do you ask?" Adam eyed Craig suspiciously.

"I was kind of hoping to take a few passengers," Craig replied.

"The kids, huh?"

Craig nodded. "And Karen… and Glen."

Adam looked surprised. "The Astronomer? What do you want to take him for?"

"Just in case I get lost." Adam stared at Craig.

"It will be handy to have someone who can find their way around space," Craig argued.

Adam continued to stare.

"Besides, he's the one that figured out about the orbital shift, so the Americans will probably be pretty keen to get their hands on him. He'll be safer where I'm going."

The conversation ended when the group of scientists who had been loading the VAPER made their way over to Adam and Craig to present them with a handwritten list.

Adam took the piece of paper and gave it a cursory glance. "Is this everything?" he asked Doctor Tran.

"Yes, that is a complete list of everything we have placed aboard the VAPER." The engineer answered. "One of each prototype has been stowed onboard. Any older equipment or superseded inventions have been placed in the airlock to be jettisoned into space if the need arises."

"Great, we not only have to lose equipment and research, but we're forced to add more shit to the debris field as well." Luke didn't even try to hide the sarcasm in his voice as he continued to work on the computer.

Adam handed the list to Craig who gave it a quick eye over. Most of it made little or no sense to him at all. He recognised the codenames of the half dozen items he had worked on or helped test, apart from those few, the list looked like a column of technobabble.

Adam noticed Glen standing at the back of the group looking like he'd rather be somewhere else. He figured now was as good a time as ever to tell him he would be leaving the station sooner than he thought.

"Glen!" Adam called to the Englishman. "How do you fancy hitching a ride back with Craig?"

Glen looked over his shoulder at the VAPER; a hint of a smile crossed his lips.

"You mean in that thing?" he said, shrugging one shoulder. "Sure, why not?"

"Good, get your things aboard. You're leaving as soon as everyone's ready," Adam said.

The other scientists in the group looked a little curious at this exchange but said nothing.

Adam turned his attention back to Craig.

"We've labelled the storage containers with serial numbers that match those on the list." Adam tapped the back of the piece of paper as he spoke. "If you need anything on here, just look up the name and match the serial number on the list to the one on the crates."

"What do you mean, need anything?" Doctor Tran snapped. "It's only a short flight. He's just taking the VAPER down to the surface where he can hide our work from the Imperials. He won't need any of it."

With his eyes locked on Craig's, Adam answered Doctor Tran without looking at him.

"Just in case something unforeseen happens. Who knows, he may need to access the weapons on board, or the Icarus packs, or simply want a bite to eat from the food processor we've supplied. It's always best to prepare for unforeseen eventualities isn't it Craig?"

Now he was sure. Craig felt better about the actions he was about to take. His confidence increased with the knowledge that others on the station understood the situation they were in and were trying to help.

Doctor Tran appeared more concerned by the second as he looked back and forth between the two men. "What are you two doing? It's not in anyone's best interests for him to travel anywhere other than back to the surface," the Engineer stammered. "I can't, and I won't allow it. Besides, it's impossible and hazardous for him to travel in the VAPER without a support crew. With the station evacuated there will be nobody here to guide him back."

"We'll be here Doc," Adam said. "My team and I will set up his first transit before we sneak off to return to the surface. We're a skeleton crew, but we'll get him away safely."

"You can't do this," Tran almost snarled. "How dare you play with other people's lives like this? Can't you see that what you are doing is a waste of time? If you stay here, you will be handing yourselves over to the Imperial troops. You'll be arrested, and Craig will be left…" Doctor Tran threw his hands in the air in disgust. "He'll be left with no-one to help him should he get into trouble."

Adam looked surer of the situation than Craig felt he should. The usually reserved technician seemed confident that what they were doing was not only the right thing but that it would succeed.

"All arguments are now mute anyway, Doc. There isn't another Qantas flight scheduled to depart for at least another hour, so we may as well stay and help. Everyone else has gotten away safely. The only people left in the ANZAR wing are those of us in this room."

"What about us?" a female voice called from the doorway.

The group turned to see Karen and the kids squeeze their way into the room. Jamie and Timothy each carried a large suitcase covered with stickers depicting their favourite cartoon characters in different poses. Toy trucks, cars and planes poked out of their pockets as they crawled into the room.

Once clear of the doorway, the two boys stood up to their full height and banged their heads on the nine-foot-high ceiling.

"What the fuck are they?" Someone yelled.

PRIME MINISTER LABELS IMPERIAL PLANS TO DETAIN ANZAR "A HOSTILE MOVE"

Sharon Goldsmith, reporting from Canberra.

"Good morning, Tom. News just in, the Australian Prime Minister's press office has just released a statement in which they formally condemn the move by the U.S. Empire to detain members of the Australian and New Zealand Aeronautical Research corporation. In the statement, the Prime Minister has requested proof of wrongdoing from the Imperial President before she will sanction the use of the military against any Australian citizens."

"Has the Imperial President made any response as yet? Or given any reasons for his suspicions?"

"No, not at all, Tom. Nothing has been heard from him since his announcement yesterday that he found the actions of the ANZAR group to be wholly responsible for the events leading up to and causing the worldwide 'Blackout'. A major bone of contention for the Prime Minister is the fact that the President has approved this type of action against Australian citizens without permission from, or notification to, the Australian or New Zealand governments. This type of contempt for foreign powers comes as no surprise to those who have followed America's history of growth from fledgling nation to domineering Empire. Their past is littered with similar instances of disregarding diplomacy."

"And what of the news of the ANZAR staff themselves, have they been apprehended as yet?"

"No, that's the strangest part. We have reports that a small team of Imperial Cavalry troops have arrived onboard Newton Station and are in the process of making their way over to the ANZAR wing. What with the announcement of this procedure being made over two hours ago, along with all the news coverage this event has attracted, I'd be amazed if the troops find anyone there when they finally arrive. The odd way in which this action was announced ahead of time draws suspicions to whether it is the researchers from ANZAR that the Imperials really want. As the Prime Minister suggests in his statement and I quote "one hopes that the voracious accumulation of foreign scientific research and data has not affected the President's sense of judgement. We can all but hope that he has not mistaken the difference between justice and opportunity. Sadly, given the Empire's history, I am not entirely confident that this action is being performed for the benefit of all humankind as he states."

22
Political Free Zone

Newton Station – Main sphere. 5.55pm -

Sunday, August 16th, 2048

Kyle Ferine marched his men through the crowded docking terminal in the Imperial wing of Newton station. Used as the arrival and departure point for all air traffic to and from the mainland United States, the terminal was filled with hundreds of travellers who had either just arrived on the station or were waiting to leave on a return United Airlines flight to the surface. As they walked along the concourse, Ferine and C- Unit found themselves surrounded by the familiar American landmarks of McDonalds, KFC, Toys R Us and Krispy Kreme which fought for the limited retail space between the boarding gates. As in the great Imperial tradition, the great American franchises had spread to all corners of the globe, including above it.

The crowds parted before the men as they made their way towards the spherical hub of the station. For the Imperial citizens of the United States of America, the sight of fully armed troops roaming public areas was a familiar one. Common sense and experience dictated that it was prudent to give soldiers a wide berth, the ongoing war on terror had demonstrated that they were not as skilled at differentiating between terrorists and innocent bystanders as the public would have liked.

After a few minutes' walk, the number of shops and food stores around Ferine and his men reduced in number as they made their way towards the exit of the terminal. The ambling pace of the duty-free area was left behind as C-Unit entered a sea of travellers who were making their way towards the central sphere of Newton Station. The milling shoppers transformed into a surge of people as C-Unit was swept up in a wave of new arrivals that grew thicker with each step they took.

As they walked, Ferine recognised a few hostile glances from those within the crowd. As terrible as the Blackout had been, he was surprised to see that many of the travellers around them appeared resentful of their presence on the station. In Newton's ten-year history, C-Unit held the dubious honour of being the first military force to set foot on the station in combat uniform. Military units passed through Newton all the time, but they usually did so unarmed and in civilian clothing.

Ferine angled his men over to one side of the crowd where they walked in single file against the wall. A bottleneck of people up ahead informed him that they were approaching the gravity transition zone where the architecture of the station allowed for more freedom of movement. As they walked along, the walls of the main corridor began to bulge and then curve outwards until Ferine's men found themselves marching through a large cylindrical tube. With the walls, floor and ceiling merged into one single curved surface; Ferine led his group out of the crowd and into a relatively clear space by walking up what had been, a moment ago, the wall of the corridor. With the gravity readjusted, the issue of space for this section of the station was solved by making it possible for all of the corridor's surfaces usable to foot traffic.

Newly arrived tourists burdened with luggage trolleys, strollers and children, made use of the extra space by spreading themselves around the inner surface of the walkway. Some, eager to beat the crowds to the security checkpoints, dashed the 'ceiling' of the cylindrical corridor where the crowd was thinnest.

The unfamiliar sight of tourists walking along the roof of the tunnel filled Ferine with a sense of respect for the skills of those who had made this feat possible. The feeling was short-lived when he realised that they were most likely the people he had come to arrest. He didn't know what was more depressing: that the same minds could create something as impressive as this station and also be responsible for the deaths of tens of millions of people in the Blackout, or, that his government was short-sighted enough to blame these people in a knee-jerk reaction for their own political benefit. Either way, it didn't sit well with Kyle.

The foot traffic slowed to a crawl as the tourists lined up ten deep to suffer the age-old rite of passage through customs. A dozen counters manned by Imperial border security and customs troops arced their way around the inner circumference of the tubular passage. This final barrier separated the incoming travellers from the freedom of the station itself.

Over the heads of the waiting travellers, Ferine could see the curved walls of the Political Free Zone, the tops of buildings passed above, below and to both sides of the exit, giving him the impression that he was looking down at the ground from above. With respect to the sanity of all involved, families with small children were ushered to the front of the queue to avoid the tantrums of over-tired toddlers. Ferine followed the families through the crowd with the screams of the children acting as makeshift sirens to clear the way. They were halted at the security gates by an Imperial officer who, on examining their ID cards, ushered them through the checkpoint. With barely a word spoken between them, they passed beyond the borders that constituted American soil and became the first military unit to enter the neutral territory of Newton Station's Political Free Zone.

Ferine turned to his men as he continued to walk. "No funny business in here. We've got a job to do, and I want all your minds on it. There are to be no interactions of any kind with the civilians while we cross the Political Free Zone." He looked each of them in the eye. "Got that?"

They all nodded their ascent before continuing on the journey.

This being Ferine's first visit to the station, he was amazed by what he saw ahead of him. He had been informed of the strange ways in which gravity had been artificially altered to allow for more living space in the cramped confines of the station. What he wasn't prepared for, was the physical reality that these odd configurations would present to his senses. Beyond the exit of the tunnel, the multi-storied buildings of the Political Free Zone rose up towards the centre of the sphere. Although his sense of orientation was adamant he was moving along a level surface, the visual input his brain was receiving insisted that he was walking up the inside of a vertical tunnel located below ground level. As he walked along the inside of the tubular walkway towards the street level above, Ferine was forced to close his eyes. The contradiction he was experiencing between his sight and other senses was beginning to make him ill.

The tubular tunnel slowly curved outwards like the end of a trumpet as the troops walked the last few metres out of the tube. Perspective played one final trick on their eyes as momentarily; they appeared to be stepping out of a corridor in the wall of the station, rather than a hole in the floor. Ferine stood on the edge of the precipice and looked out at the scene before him.

The political free zone clung to the insides of the station's central sphere, acting as the hub of Newton station itself. Hotels, bars and entertainment venues curved away in all directions, giving the impression to new arrivals that they had stepped into a world turned inside out. Artificial gravity acted evenly along the internal surface of the sphere, forcing everyone and everything within it to adhere to the curved surface. Streets full of tourists curved away in all directions, lending the scene a surreal atmosphere akin to being in a lucid dream.

Ferine found that if he looked straight ahead and stared past the walls of the buildings that towered ahead of him, he could see the rooftops of the structures that clung to the opposite side of the sphere. The nearest thing he could compare it to was lying on his back in the middle of a city street as he looked up at the buildings rising in front of him while a giant mirror suspended over the city gave him a reflected view of the rooftops below.

Tubular tunnels identical to the one in which Ferine and his group now stood were dotted across the landscape. Passengers could be seen moving in and out of the openings as they made their way to and from the aircraft terminals of their destination countries.

A series of flashing lights high above his head drew Ferine's attention to a complex series of transparent tubes that seemed to hover silently in the centre of the sphere. As he looked, he became aware of small shapes that floated through the tubing at various speeds. As each one turned a corner, they released a coloured flash of light that propelled them even faster through the maze of pipes. After watching for a few moments, Ferine realised that he was looking at the anti-gravity section of the station. The small shapes travelling through the tubing were people attempting to complete the zero-gravity maze known as Tubular Hell.

Above the maze of twisting pipes, Ferine could see the zero-gravity accommodation for the station that housed themed hotel rooms fashioned after the original designs of early space stations and vehicles. Visitors could stay in anything from a replica of the space shuttle to a copy of the accommodation area of the old MIR or International space stations.

With gravity still pulling him one way while he stepped in another, Ferine led his men up the curving exit of the Imperial Transit Wing and onto a footpath at the corner of a busy street. Now that they were on the inside of the sphere, it felt like they were on the ground in any normal city found on Earth, albeit one that curved slightly uphill in all directions.

The sights, sounds and smells of a hundred different countries and cultures greeted their senses as they began to make their way along a paved footway lined with stores and restaurants.

As in the terminal, the crowds in the street stepped out of the way to allow them to pass. C-Unit drew a lot of attention. Everything from anxious glances to cheers of support to openly hostile stares followed the armed group as they walked the few blocks to their destination. Ferine could tell that everyone knew who he and his men were and what they were here to do.

A small crowd greeted them as they turned into the street that housed the entrance to the ANZAR wing of the station. Men and women lined the streets to jeer and harass his men as they slowly walked the last fifty metres to their destination. Boos, hisses and a range of insults were spat at the members of C-Unit as they stoically continued their march, seemingly unfazed by the hostile reception they were receiving. Emboldened by the troops' lack of reaction to their taunts, one member of the crowd got a little too close for his good. In a fit of rage, a small blonde-haired man in his thirties stepped in front of Private Dockrill and began to scream abuse into the young soldier's face. To Dockrill's credit, he did not respond or react. He just kept on walking in time with the rest of C-Unit.

After a few moments of screaming, the lone protestor stepped aside and grinned at his bravado for having stared down an armed Imperial soldier, even if it was the smallest one in the line. Feeling proud of his accomplishment, he turned to face the crowd of protestors where he was met with cheers of support.

Emboldened by the support of the crowd, the young protestor turned back to the line of troops to repeat the move and was greeted with a contemptuous scowl from Scarface who happened to be the next in line. After a moment's hesitation, the protestor opened his mouth to begin his rant and immediately had it filled with the butt of Scarface's rifle before he could utter a single word.

The man's head flew back in a spray of blood and teeth as his body collapsed onto the hard surface of the road. A few of his fellow protestors warily ran forward to offer assistance with mixed looks of anger, disgust and fear on their faces. They looked up at Scarface who turned his head just enough to scowl at them. Seeing that he was not someone to be messed with, the crowd stepped back but continued to yell and scream at the passing soldiers in a cowardly, but determined, show of defiance.

With the protestor lying in the road bleeding from the hole where his teeth used to be, the members of C-Unit continued to walk on unfazed. Ferine didn't even look back. He could tell what had happened by the sounds of the crowd. As usual, there was always one person who overstepped the mark when it came to voicing their opinion about the Empire and its military presence. As usual, it was Scarface who would always be the one to slap them back into line.

C-Unit arrived at an inconspicuous looking three-story building that sat at the end of the block. Looking like a common brick-rendered housing unit that could be found in any city on Earth, the entrance to the ANZAR labs served a dual function. Primarily used as guest residences, the building contained six fully-furnished apartments as well as meeting rooms, a function centre and a bar. From this site, ANZAR could host visiting guests without the need to allow them access to the more secure areas of the ANZAR wing which were located beneath the building on the outside of the station.

Ferine looked through a large reinforced window at what appeared to be the lobby of a decent, middle-range hotel. Plush, cushioned sofas and a long wooden bar filled the length of the room. A small reception desk sat unattended near the entrance to an open, but deserted, function room where row upon row of empty seats faced towards an empty podium.

"Looks like nobody's home," Sergeant Jackson said from beside him.

"They'll all be down in the station proper. If they're smart, they'll be hiding," one of the other troops said from the back of the crowd.

Scarface bent to the task of bypassing the steel security door which blocked their way into the ANZAR wing. Like the rest of his men, Ferine faced back towards the street with his weapon at the ready. Following routine, they searched vigilantly for a threat that they expected would not appear. News of their presence had spread, leaving the street all but deserted. The last of the tourists, either too brave or too stupid to have moved on with the others, gathered on the opposite side of the street to watch the impending action. They stood in a small group, swapping comments and opinions on what they thought the troops were up to and who they were after. Feeling secure in their detachment from the situation, they felt unthreatened by the weaponry that occasionally swept past their location. Although the Imperial Cavalry was notorious for the unrestrained discharging of weapons in the midst of a firefight, they rarely shot uninvolved parties without provocation. Not intentionally at least.

Explosives, on the other hand, were a different matter. The spectator's moods changed on seeing Scarface remove an explosive charge from his pack and place it on the door. Understanding the dangers associated with the indiscriminate nature of exploding objects, the onlookers swiftly departed via the nearest side street looking more than a little alarmed.

A smile played across Ferine's lips as he watched the last of the tourists disappear behind the nearest building.

"Watch how much of that stuff you use," Ferine said as he kept watch on the surrounding area. "We don't want to cause a hull breach and kill everyone on the station just to open a door."

Scarface responded without looking up. "Relax Cap. I've done this before. I'm using just enough to blow the locks. Trust me."

After another moment's work, Scarface rose to his feet and declared the job done. Ferine led the team around the corner of the building where they squeezed themselves against the wall.

Ferine felt an arm pass over his shoulder as he was handed a small remote control from someone behind him.

"Ready to go whenever you are, Cap."

Ferine looked down at the trigger for the explosives. He knew that once he pressed the button and breached the doors to the ANZAR facility, there would be no going back. Once a mission like this had begun, events tended to snowball until completion, regardless of the outcome. This was his last chance to call a stop to this whole thing, but knowing that the eyes of the world were on them, he knew he had no choice but to proceed.

"Okay, as soon as we blow the door, head in using the usual formation. I want a security sweep of all the rooms in the accommodation area completed before we move into the labs. Our orders are for these people to be taken alive, so that means all occupants are to be detained unharmed. Got it?'

They all nodded. A round of soft clicks issued from the group as they prepared their weapons for use by disengaging the safety controls. Gloved hands felt inside Jacket pockets and pouches as ammunition was tallied, radios tested, and the locations of essential equipment were verified as part of their routine equipment check.

Ferine watched the group as they performed their checks. When presented with a familiar task, they demonstrated a degree of competence that was at odds with their hard-arsed personas. Ferine always felt slightly surprised whenever this group of grunts showed signs of intelligence and discipline; he had decided that it was yet another testament to the thoroughness of military training.

Once satisfied that they were ready, Ferine took a final glance around the corner to ensure that the doorway was still clear. With the streets still deserted, he pressed himself against the wall with the rest of the team. After a three-second countdown, he pushed the button.

A deep bass rumble echoed throughout the enclosed confines of the station as a cloud of smoke and dust billowed around the corner. Before the last echo faded, the troops were on their feet and making their way to the newly created entrance to the ANZAR wing. In single file, they stepped over the collapsed door that lay in a twisted heap on the floor of the lobby. After no more than a few seconds, the surrounding street was once again deserted. They were in.

IMPERIAL CAVALRY BREACHES ANZAR WING, LIVE!

Alan Oldman, reporting from Newton Station.

"Well, I have to say that it's about time that the Empire got serious about this group of terrorists. As you can see from the images we are beaming back to Earth from the political free zone on Newton station; Imperial Cavalry troops have indeed breached the entrance to the ANZAR wing. This Police action happened just over five minutes ago when a small team of US Cavalry Manipulation Specialists expertly placed what appeared to be a ring of plastic explosives around the locking mechanism of the airlock. After hiding around a corner for a few minutes while they ensured the area was clear and that there was no danger to the public, they promptly detonated the explosives and made their way inside."

"Is there any damage to the station, Alan?"

"As far as I can tell from my vantage point up here in the zero-G section of the station, Mike; everything seems intact. There appears to be a bit of smoke issuing from the ANZAR entrance. We suspect that a few small fires may have broken out in the local vicinity of the explosion, although that's unconfirmed. We have a bird's eye view of the scene below us as you can see from this replay of the team's entry. The blast totally ripped that 120-kilogram door right out of its frame and littered the area with dust and debris. As far as we can tell, apart from the door to the ANZAR wing being demolished, there doesn't appear to have been any damage done to the outer hull of the station. That stands as an example of the professionalism and skill of our fighting men."

"So where are the Troops now? Has there been any movement in the area since?"

"Immediately after the blast, the Imperial troops moved inside the research facility where I can only assume they are in the process of detaining those whom we believe to be International terrorists. In answer to your second question, Mike, nobody has entered or left the facility since the troops went in. We expect it would take time for them to assure themselves that the area is secure before they bring anybody out."

"Are there any other ways in and out of this part of the station that you know of, Alan?"

"No, there isn't. You have to understand that until recently, ANZAR was a private research organisation that performed contract work for the governments of Australia and New Zealand. As such, they operated under very tight security which necessitated the need for one secure entrance to their facility. In short, this is the only way in or out. Sadly, for the scientists inside, their need for security has left them trapped inside a giant tin can with no way to escape. The far end is a sealed wall with only the vacuum of open space on the other side, at this end, lies freedom and about twenty freedom fighters that will kill anyone who tries to reach it."

"Be sure to keep our viewers and us updated if there are any developments up there, Alan."

"Oh, I'll do better than that, Mike. I'm going to follow them in."

23
Kids and Chips

Main Engineering bay – ANZAR labs. 6.00pm -

Sunday, August 16th, 2048

Karen stepped up to Craig and placed her luggage at his feet before she leant over and gave him a prolonged hug. He relished the feel and scent of her as she pressed her body against his and squeezed. He slowly ran his hands over the curves of her back and hips, enjoying her presence physically as well as emotionally. Craig felt deeply touched by her show of emotion and milked the moment for all it was worth.

Craig knew how much she longed to remove the kids from their virtual prison on the station. He shared her opinion that the children were the victims of circumstance and agreed that it was unfair for them to be kept locked away from the world, no matter how nurturing the environment they were kept in. He and Karen had often talked of the welfare of Jamie and Timothy; the two boys were like surrogate children to them both. The unplanned release of the kids was the only positive thing he could see coming out of this entire situation. Craig thought that he had made his feelings about the boys clear on many occasions; he thought she knew that he loved them almost as much as he loved her. In a small way, he felt hurt and appalled that she may have underestimated his feelings and thought him unwilling to help.

Leaving the station without her and the boys had never entered his mind.

Timothy and Jamie stood just inside the door to the engineering lab looking shy and nervous. They were uncomfortable with being confronted with the faces of so many people they had never met before. Searching for comfort in each other's presence, they unconsciously moved closer together and hugged themselves for reassurance.

Their size and shape were at odds with their demeanour. Although physically, they looked as if they should be afraid of nothing, their body language revealed they were not as intimidating as they first appeared. With large framed, muscular bodies reminiscent of professional weightlifters, the two boys stood at just under nine feet tall. Their short- cropped hair gently brushed against the high ceiling of the engineering bay as they looked around the room. Their childlike faces continually flashed through an array of emotions. Surprise, awe, curiosity, delight and fear repeatedly swapped places as they absorbed the strangeness of this new part of the station. After spotting the cockpits of the VAPER's poking through the floor, one of them spoke.

"Mummy, can we go on the spaceship now?" Timothy asked in a voice that was surprisingly soft for his size.

Releasing Craig from her grasp, Karen turned and looked up at the children. "In a minute, baby. The grown-ups need to talk about a few things before we can go."

The irony of the term 'grown-up' was not lost to anyone in the room as they looked at the two children who were already bigger than any of them ever would be.

A soft, almost fearful voice emerged from the group of scientists who stood staring at the two boys. "I don't suppose either of you is going to tell us what this is all about?" One of Doctor Tran's engineers asked.

Craig felt partly unnerved and amused at seeing the hesitant and wary reactions of these usually confident people. As men of science, with their expensive educations and firm groundings in reality, the children within them still seemed to fear the bogeyman as much as the next person. Craig could imagine childhood memories of evil giants from storybooks circling through the men's minds as the sight presented to them unsettled their sense of the conventional. He could almost hear the questions ticking over in their heads.

A junior lab engineer couldn't hide his surprise at seeing the two boys. "What are they?" he blurted.

Karen jumped to the children's defence. "What they are, are human beings, just like us." She glowered at the young engineer who had asked the question.

He looked abashed. "Sorry, I didn't mean anything by that. But they aren't exactly normal." He seemed to shrink under her menacing gaze. "I mean, what happened to them?"

"They were found in one of the rented labs just over four years ago. They were only a few days old when we found them. As far as we can tell they were part of a genetic engineering experiment carried out by an American Bio firm. It looks like they were trying to engineer some type of super soldiers for the Imperial military, presumably. All this muscle you can see on their bodies was genetically programmed before birth. This was not created through the use of any drugs or from the performance of exercise and weightlifting as you'd think. They were intentionally designed to look like this."

Although all the senior researchers knew about Jamie and Timothy, it was deemed necessary to keep their existence a secret from the more junior or casual members of staff. The last thing anyone at ANZAR wanted was news that they were hiding two genetically modified humans in their labs to become common knowledge. There would be dire consequences and harsh legal repercussions if they were discovered. Not to mention what would happen to Jamie and Timothy themselves.

"Wait a sec," another junior scientist stammered, looking a little confused. "Are you saying they're only four years old?"

Craig stepped over and took Jamie by the hand before answering. "Yes. We believe they were intentionally engineered for fast growth to test the viability of creating an assembly line of genetically engineered soldiers. When we found the kids, we had no idea what they were. We were at a loss to understand how a group of people could discard two perfectly normal looking children."

Craig looked back up into the faces of the two boys who gazed back at the strange little adults who stood staring at them. "You could say we were a little surprised when they grew up to their full size within two years. Apart from the moral issues associated with genetic modification and the abandonment of the kids, the scientists who created them did a pretty good job on them, physically at least. The only oversight they made was that their mental development outpaced their physical development."

"What does that mean?" someone asked.

"What it means, is that you can't genetically engineer maturity. You can engineer the body, but not the mind. Although they have the adult bodies of genetically modified nine-foot-tall super soldiers, they are still mentally and emotionally they're true age. They're essentially four-year-old toddlers trapped in bodies that were forced to mature faster than their minds could."

Luke looked up from the computer console he had been seated in front of since Craig had arrived in the lab. He turned to the group of people who stood talking in the centre of the room.

"Hey!" he yelled to get their attention. "You're going to have to cut your little chat short and get a move on. They're here. About 20 troops have just blown open the main entry door to our wing of the station and are in the process of tearing the accommodation area apart."

"My God!" Adam Fehrenbach gasped. "They used explosives? That doesn't make sense. Surely they know we would have let them in if they had asked."

Luke merely shrugged his shoulders in response and turned back to the computer he was seated at, the screen showed multiple views of Ferine and his troops as captured by the Nerve's myriad cameras. The high-quality colour images showed the Imperial forces ransacking the accommodation wing in their search for ANZAR staff. Ferine's men went from room to room kicking down doors and overturning furniture. Some of the more aggressive troops fired indiscriminately into each of the rooms before checking if they were occupied, hoping to score a few extra kill points without having to get their hands dirty.

"You really should be going, Craig," Luke said. "These guys are carrying some pretty heavy weaponry, and they've not been shy about using it so far."

"It's alright; we'll be out of here shortly. The quarantine door at the entrance to the labs should keep them out of our way long enough to do what we need," Craig said as he stepped away from the main group of ANZAR staff and made his way across the room. "We still don't exactly have much time, so we'll have to get the last of the gear into the VAPER straight away."

As Craig made his way over to the station's medical specialist, Doctor Anderson, he noticed that the extent of disarray that the engineering bay was being left. Boxes, packing containers and unwanted computer components littered the deck. Spare parts and puddles of oil had transformed the floor into a debris field reminiscent of the one that circled the Earth below. The American Empire had forced ANZAR into a position in which it was not only necessary to abandon their research but had left them no choice but to leave the station which they had worked so hard to build, in a shamble.

Stepping around a discarded engine cowling, Craig arrived at the room's central workbench where Doctor Anderson had managed to find a clear space amongst the mess to finish one last inventory. More pieces of equipment and files lay scattered over the work surface. At a glance, Craig could see that most of the stuff was of a standard variety that was freely available anywhere on Earth. Although still expensive, these medical instruments were easily replaceable and therefore dispensable.

"Peter," Craig said as he stepped to the doctor's side. "Sorry to interrupt, but we need to get those ModChip inserts done now. Everyone's here, and we need to get away as soon as possible."

Doctor Anderson turned towards the door where Karen and a few engineers were gathering up Jamie and Timothy's toys and luggage.

"It seems strange seeing them outside the crèche. Those two boys have lived their whole lives in three small rooms. It was a good idea for Karen to have let them have a look around the station before they leave. With the way things are going, I don't suppose it matters much that their secret is out," Doctor Anderson said in an almost reminiscent tone.

"Well, they're not safe yet." Craig stepped up to the doctor and placed a hand on his shoulder before whispering conspiratorially.

"We need to get Karen, Glen and the boys into the next room and have them fitted with ModChips straight away. We can't go anywhere until that's done."

The doctor turned and gave Craig a concerned look. "You're taking them with you?" he asked. "I'd have to advise against that. It would be much safer for you to let them evacuate with Professor Weekes and us after you're gone."

Craig shook his head. "Sorry, Peter. I can't do that."

"Look, having dealt with them on a regular basis while tending to their medical needs for the last three years, I've become as fond of those two as you have. But let me remind you, that despite their size, they are effectively toddlers in oversized bodies. Some of the research staff have an idea of what you're about to do and frankly, we applaud it. I applaud it. But with the dangers involved, I think taking Karen and the kids along may prove to be a costly distraction for you."

Craig looked back at the boys knowing that the Doctor was right, they definitely were a handful, but the alternative of placing them in harm's way by having them squeeze through the maintenance tunnel that led under the floor of the station with people they were unfamiliar with was something he couldn't bring himself to do. The boys had already been dumped at birth by selfish researchers who put their own careers before the welfare of the children; he wouldn't risk them being placed in that position again.

"Sorry, Peter. But I can't see any other alternative. I don't want them falling into the hands of the Imperials. They won't be able to sneak out and join a commercial flight back to the surface as easily as the rest of you will. They're too conspicuous." Craig waved a hand in their direction to make a point of how huge the boys were.

"Their scientists won't show them half the care and respect that we do. Besides, to them, Karen and I are their parents. We have a bond between us that goes further than being their carers." Craig shrugged. "Hell, they even call us mummy and daddy. Leaving them is not an option." Craig felt strongly about his feelings for the kids. His voice became thick with emotion.

"If you refuse to do this, you're condemning them to death… or worse."

"No pressure then? Hmm?" The doctor raised his eyebrows.

"Fine, fine." Understanding Craig's moral obligation to the children, Peter gave in without a fight. "Let's get them into the medical bay next door."

"Thank you," Craig sighed.

"I assume you want me to install the latest versions?" The doctor asked.

"Yeah, we'll need the full setup for these guys. Also, we'll need the same for Glen."

The doctor looked across the room at the pudgy Brit who stood gaping at the boys.

"You're taking the astronomer as well?" the doctor asked. "Good idea. The last thing you want is to get lost in the middle of nowhere."

"Yeah, literally." Craig gave a nervous laugh as both men turned and made their way back to the others.

"You know, I've been thinking about the fact that we don't know what the American troop's intentions are. I think it may be prudent to install chips in all the remaining staff as a precaution," the doctor said as they made their way back through the rubbish to the others.

Craig gave it a moment's thought before responding. "Yeah, you could be right. As long as we do the rest of the staff last, I can't see a problem with that."

With the VAPER now fully loaded and ready to leave, the ANZAR scientists allowed themselves a moment to become engaged in the midst of a deep discussion about the two oversized children. A small group of ANZAR researchers slowly circled the pair, scrutinising the anatomical differences between their super-sized Mister Universe bodies and their toddler-like faces the boys sat on the floor playing with a handful of toy cars that Karen had not forced them to place in the *Feynman*.

"Okay, guys," Craig said as he stepped up to the group. "We need to head to the medical bay next door and implant

ModChips in Karen, Glen and the boys. The doc and I think it would be a good idea if the rest of you get them installed as well."

"I don't see why we need to go through the discomfort of having those things installed. We are not laboratory animals who need to be monitored like a lost puppy. I see no need for the rest of the staff here to have one of those things shoved into the back of our necks," Henry Tran retorted.

Craig was a little taken aback by the attitude of Doctor Tran. The man was usually quite spoken and affable to everyone he met. Craig hoped it was merely the stress caused by their current situation that had put the Engineer out of sorts.

Luke spoke up from the computer terminal against the wall. "Uh, hello. Just a reminder, there are American soldiers in the accommodation wing! I wouldn't stand around chatting about it for too long guys." He gave the group a concerned look. "After watching these guys do their thing, I'd listen to Craig. I've been using The Perve to watch the troops and these guys are getting frustrated and beginning to shoot the shit out of everything."

Craig decided to use that to his advantage.

"Naturally, everyone is free to decline the offer of having a mod-chip installed," Craig addressed the group. "But I wouldn't advise against it. All of us have worked on the chips in one way or another, so we understand the benefits that arise from having one installed. Especially now that it looks like the Americans are going to do more than walk through the door and say *you're under arrest.*"

Craig was getting impatient and frustrated as he looked around the room at each of them in turn.

"Either way, we don't have much time. Karen, Glen and the boys definitely need to have a chip implanted for it to be possible for them to travel in the *Feynman*, so I'm sorry, but you four pretty much don't have any choice about this. The rest of you do though. If any of you decide that you want a little added security in case the Americans kick the door in while you're still here, then follow us into the next room."

Craig took a few steps over to Karen and took her by the hand. Looking up at the boys, he said. "Come on babe. We need to get these two ready to go."

Jamie and Timothy slowly rose to their feet, careful not to hit their heads on any protruding parts of the ceiling. With a few soft words, Karen and Craig led the boys into the medical bay next door for the quick but painful procedure of having their ModChips installed.

Doctor Anderson and Glen joined the small group before they were out the door.

The remaining ANZAR staff stood rooted to the spot as they exchanged concerned looks. Their uncertainty of what to do was evident on their faces.

As if reaching an unspoken consensus, the last of the ANZAR staff moved towards the exit of the engineering bay and followed the others out.

Adam Fehrenbach stopped before the open door and turned to Luke who had made no move to follow the others out of the room. He still sat at the computer terminal engrossed in the images displayed on the bank of monitors before him.

"Are you coming, mate?" Adam asked.

Luke looked up at his friend for a moment. "Nah, I'm already chipped. I had a ModChip installed a few weeks ago when the Professors and Craig had theirs done. I'll see you guys back here when you're finished." Luke pointed to an image showing Ferine and Sergeant Jackson kicking down the door of another cabin. "I'm gonna stay here and have some fun trying to slow these arseholes down."

"Who knows?" Luke said to himself after Adam had left the room. "Maybe I can even up the odds a bit by taking a few of them out."

24
Not for us to reason why...

Accommodation Corridor – ANZAR Wing, Newton Station.

6.02pm - Sunday, August 16th, 2048

Kyle Ferine entered the darkened room the moment Sergeant Jackson was clear of the door. He took a few fast steps over the threshold before he dropped to one knee and scanned the cabin, his rifle at the ready. It took him less than a second to examine the small space and appraise the situation. The room was in a shamble. A wall-mounted television silently displayed an old Peter Jackson film to the darkened cabin. The constantly changing light from the screen caused the shadows of discarded personal items to dance across the unmade bed. The starkness of the space and the scattering of personal effects told him everything he needed to know at a glance. This room was identical to the first twelve he had inspected. Empty.

"It looks like a crazy woman's underwear in here. There's shit all over the place," he called before getting to his feet and turning to his second in command.

"This is bullshit. The fucking President had to go on the Net and gloat about this mission, didn't he?" Ferine almost screamed as he stormed past Jackson into the brightly lit corridor of the accommodation wing. "I sometimes wonder how that man ever came to be the ruler of half the bloody world."

Being an ardent supporter of the Imperial regime, Sergeant Jackson appeared personally offended by Ferine's remarks. "I'm sure that the President had his reasons for announcing this initiative ahead of time. It's not for us to reason why…"

"Oh, give it a fucking rest will you, Jackson," Ferine cut him off before he could finish reciting the saying used by American ground troops for over a century. He wasn't in the mood to listen to one of the Sergeants speeches on blind devotion to the Empire.

To give himself a moment to calm down, Ferine dismissed the Sergeant with a wave of his hand. "Just go and round up the men and have them meet us at the quarantine airlock at the lab entrance, will you?"

Jackson looked as if about to say something more before a glance from Ferine helped him decide that it would be better if he made himself scarce.

As the echo of Jackson's footsteps faded down the corridor, Ferine began to walk toward the area that he felt would most likely provide him with a positive result, the labs.

Room after room stood empty with the doors ajar or off their hinges where his men had kicked them in. Each entry stood as a testament to the sheer number of people who had managed to vacate the station before their arrival. Every room stood empty, their occupants having fled to all parts of the world thanks to the head start supplied by the President's premature announcement.

Ferine turned a corner at the end of the corridor and almost bumped into a small group of his men who stood in a huddle. Their mission packs and general bulk blocked the hallway as they divvied up the contents of an abandoned jewellery box. High powered rifles lay slung over their shoulders, forgotten, as the men temporarily abandoned their search for the ANZAR staff and went on the hunt for gifts to give their girls when they got back home. They squabbled animatedly over necklaces, bracelets and chains as their large fingers prodded through the box, hunting down missing earrings that they needed to complete a pair. Ferine caught glimpses of gold chains and silver pendants as the goods disappeared into his men's pockets. Although officially illegal, looting on this scale was tolerated in the field as long as it didn't get out of hand or prove too distracting to the mission. Pillaging the goods of the enemy was seen as a perk of the job that was frowned upon but ignored by those in charge. As he had done in the past, Ferine decided to ignore it now as well.

"So how is the search progressing?" At the sound of his voice, the group spun around and snapped to attention with shocked looks on their faces.

"Nothing to report, Sir," Scarface replied in the usual clipped military tone.

Ferine eyed each man in turn and made a point of staring at the jewellery box that lay discarded at the men's feet, the last of its contents spilled on the floor. The group began to fidget slightly at the realisation that they had been caught stealing. They gave a mental sigh as it became apparent that Ferine was not going to make anything of it.

"So, you haven't come across anyone at all?" he asked.

"No Sir!" Private Dockrill answered. His face reddening with both the heat of his combat suit and his embarrassment at being caught looting.

"This place is emptier than a dog pound on Chinese New Year, Cap. We haven't seen a sole since we entered the wing," Scarface added.

"It certainly looks that way, doesn't it?" Ferine turned away from his men and stared at the floor for a moment as he considered what to do next.

"Are there any men forward of your group?" Ferine asked as he looked up into Scarface's eyes.

"No, Sir. We were on point duty with just a few rooms left to search before you caught up with us. A couple more bends, and we'll be at the airlock for the research wing."

"Well, it's safe to say that there's nobody here. This place is deader than an epileptic bomb maker." Ferine turned to make his way up the hall. "Come on; we can search these later. We're moving on to the labs."

Before he could take his first step, Ferine felt himself overcome by a sense of weight that he at first mistook for fatigue. He blinked his eyes to clear the fugue with little effect. His limbs grew heavier, and his back began to bow under the burden of his equipment pack as he felt himself being pulled towards the floor of the corridor as if by an unseen hand. With an effort, he turned himself around to face his men and was surprised to see that they appeared to be suffering from the same thing. Looks of fear and concern were plastered over the men's faces as they struggled to keep themselves upright against the growing weight of their bodies.

"Whaaa, fuck?" one of the men managed to slur in a near whisper.

The others groaned with the exertion of keeping their feet.

Ferine's knees started to bend, and his head was forced downwards by its weight. His helmet slid forward over his forehead leaving him a restricted view of his feet and the floor directly in front of him.

The sense of weight increased.

To steady himself, Ferine managed to reach out and grasp the handrail that ran the length of the corridor. The pressure on his body increased further as he was forced to one knee where he struggled to keep from falling flat on his face. He felt as if every individual atom in his body was pulled toward the floor where its weight would crush him.

Ferine began to feel as if he was experiencing a repeat of the symptoms that he – and the rest of the world - had suffered during the Blackout. The loss of energy and drowsiness were consistent with what he had experienced before. The only new factor was the sense of heaviness that had overcome him.

Maybe the President was right, he thought as he placed both of his hands on the floor to steady himself. *Perhaps these arseholes did cause the Blackout, and they're now turning whatever gadget that was responsible for it, on us.*

The yells of his troops echoed down the corridor. Cries of "What the hell's going on?" mixed with general murmurs and grunts of exertion as the men fought to remain standing. Although none of the troops panicked, a surge of fear pervaded their minds; one by one they lost the tug of war with their limbs and collapsed onto the deck.

Ferine became weaker by the second as the blood in his body was pulled towards the floor where it pooled around his lower extremities. A dark haze crept in from the edge of his vision. His head felt lighter, while his body grew heavier.

Realising that he could no longer fight the inevitable, Ferine used the last of his strength to reach up with one hand and unclip his equipment pack. It fell to the floor beside him with a thud that made the pack sound far heavier than it actually was. The sound echoed down the corridor to mingle with the moans from his troops as they struggled against unconsciousness.

No. This isn't like the Blackout, Ferine thought. *I can't feel the icy finger in my head. This is entirely physical. This is something else.*

Ferine's vision slowly darkened as he collapsed. He impacted the floor hard and just managed to roll himself onto his back before the added gravity made further movement impossible. He lay panting on the cold linoleum, fighting to draw in each breathe as his lungs were compressed by the increased weight of his own body. Ferine's back ached with the pressure being placed on his hips and shoulders as his body was pulled incessantly into the floor of the corridor. His internal organs shifted under pressure. His spine began to bend in a new direction that was entirely unnatural.

After a few seconds of extreme discomfort, an unfamiliar male voice broke the silence that had pervaded Ferine's mind. An Australian accent gave the speaker a familiar lilt that convinced Ferine he was remembering the voice of an old friend from somewhere in his past. It echoed through the haze of his mind, sounding both far away and very near at the same time.

So, this is what it's like to die, Ferine thought.

A sense of calm came over him. Ferine felt suddenly at peace with his situation and his life. The added pressure on his chest made it impossible to draw full breaths. Slowly, his brain was starved of oxygen.

This must be the part where my life flashes before my eyes. A tiny smile touched his lips as his mind began to wander. He almost looked forward to the flashbacks starting. At least through them, he would get to see the faces of his sons Sam and Max once again.

Right now, death didn't seem too bad.

25
Ultimatum

Accommodation Corridor – ANZAR Wing, Newton Station.

6.09pm - Sunday, August 16th, 2048

Ferine managed to concentrate his mind for a moment to catch a few words of what was being said. The young voice he could hear sounded friendly, even jovial as it spoke.

"Okay, let's ease up on the gravity. Looks like a few of you guys passed out on us for a bit."

The pressure on Ferine's body eased slightly. Although he still could not move, the release of pressure on his chest allowed him to draw in full breaths of air, his lungs wholly inflated for the first time in over a minute. The fresh, antiseptic tasting oxygen soothed his aching lungs and cleared his mind. As his stupor cleared, Ferine turned his attention to what the speaker was saying.

"Good evening, gentleman. And welcome aboard Newton Station. I'd like to take a moment to apologise to you all for the state of our facilities here in the ANZAR wing. As you can see, the place is quite a mess. With our staff having to leave in such a hurry, they seem to have forgotten to tidy up for you. As you gents may have noticed, we also seem to be suffering some kind of malfunction with our artificial gravity in this part of the station. I'd like to apologise for any inconvenience caused by the weight of this situation. But hey, it could be worse; the oxygen systems are still operating. At least you can still breathe."

So that's it, Ferine thought. *The bastards are doing this intentionally by fucking around with the artificial gravity.*

Luke Weekes, not wanting to wait idly by until the Imperial troops either captured or killed the remaining staff, continued to lecture the troops through the station's speakers.

"I'm sure we can end this disagreement peacefully, without resorting to mindless violence that will not benefit either party. All I have to do is turn the gravity control dial by a few more degrees, and I can wipe out your entire team by crushing them into the floor. But I don't want to do that. We're not the bad guys. We don't want any trouble here. Contrary to what you heard, ANZAR is a peaceful organisation that develops technologies that are designed to benefit humankind, not harm it. We never have and never will create weapons of mass destruction. You guys were lied to. You're being used in this game, just like we are. That's why I haven't killed you. And if you leave without a fuss, I won't need to."

"Bullshit!" Ferine managed to yell. "You haven't got it in you. If you were going to do us in you would have done it already. So, stop fucking around and let us up before you make this thing worse for yourselves."

"What the hell is an Aussie doing with these arseholes?" Luke answered with mild surprise at finding a fellow countryman amongst the Imperial troops. "Well, that was unexpected. Look, *mate*," he added with more than a hint of sarcasm. "I admit that I wouldn't find killing anyone enjoyable, even you guys. But the difference between us is that I would do it out of necessity and a sense of self-preservation, while the people you are with do it for money and the chance to gain the first choice at the goods they loot from their victims. I'm not an idiot, Captain; I saw what you guys were up to on the monitors."

There was a slight pause in which the only sounds were Ferine and his men struggling for breath in the high gravity environment they had unexpectedly found themselves in.

With a sigh, Luke finished speaking. "I know that I may have to kill some or all of you before this is finished."

"So, what do you want us to do then?" Ferine gasped from his place on the floor where he still lay pinned. "You can't reasonably expect us to walk away from this. We can't go back empty-handed from this one. We have orders to..."

"Yeah, I know, I know," Luke interrupted. "Your President made your intentions clear on the Netcasts he made; you're to arrest and detain all ANZAR personnel on the station as well as acquire any useful technologies that may benefit the Empire. Sound about right?"

Ferine lay on the floor without answering Luke. His anger grew stronger as he had his suspicions confirmed. ANZAR had effectively been forewarned by the President allowing them to evacuate and organise a resistance to the troops they knew were coming. Because of the vanity and stupidity of one man, he and his men would end up being the ones to suffer for that possibly fatal mistake. He realised that one thing was certain, he could achieve nothing laying here like this, he had to secure their release by whatever means possible. But under the current conditions, his options were limited.

"No answer, huh?" Luke continued after a moment's pause. "Look, all we need is a half hour to get our things organised, so we can be assured that none of our work is destroyed when your people start pulling this place apart. We have years' worth of research data stored here, this knowledge we have amassed is more valuable than either you or me, mate. Regardless of who ends up possessing it by the end of the day, we just want to ensure that it is not lost."

Silence.

No response.

"Well, I'll take your lack of protest as a sign of agreement. I'm going to lower the gravity back to normal levels slowly, so you can get on your feet again. All we need is thirty minutes to complete a data backup then I'll willingly open the entry door to the labs so that you can walk straight in unchallenged. From there you can help yourself to whatever you want."

Ferine felt a floating sensation as the pressure from the added gravity lifted from his body. His numbed limbs once again began to perceive physical sensations. A sense of dizziness overcame him as his brain flooded with oxygenated blood that his now unrestricted circulatory system began to pump more freely. His back, neck and shoulders ached with pins and needles as the blood flowed back into the areas that had been constricted by his weight. Numbness still pervaded his limbs and lower extremities as he struggled to his feet; he had to pull himself upright with the assistance of the hand railing that had proven useless earlier. With his legs wobbling, Ferine looked around at his men who stood unsteadily in a small group. With backs arched and grimaces of pain on their faces, they rubbed at the sore parts of their bodies in an attempt to ease their pain.

None of them looked happy.

"So, we have a deal, right?" Luke's voice broke in. "Thirty minutes. Feel free to grab yourselves some coffee from the common room back down the hall while you wait. I'll call you when we're ready to let you in."

With that, the intercom fell silent with a click.

26

20 - 14

Accommodation Corridor – ANZAR Wing, Newton Station.

6.18pm - Sunday, August 16th, 2048

"So, what now, Cap?" Private Dockrill asked as he rubbed the back of his neck.

"You aren't seriously considering letting this prick push us around like that are you, Cap?" Scarface added as he slung his rifle back over his shoulder.

The men stared at Kyle Ferine as they waited for a response. The circle of men tightened around their contemplative leader as each second passed. After a minutes thought, Ferine brought his wrist radio to his mouth and looked into the eyes of his men. Although not suicidal, this group had always shown a willingness to face danger in performing their duty. Their faces told him everything he needed to know about what they wanted to do. They wanted to continue, and so did he.

They had been embarrassed by these people. Ferine knew that whoever the guy on the intercom system was, he wasn't going to end up in custody after what he had done to them. He had humiliated an entire team of Imperial manipulation specialists by pinning them to the floor and making them feel helpless. He couldn't be expected to live through this. He would have to allow his men to reassert their control over the situation. For the sake of his team's morale, he would allow them this one kill at least.

He had to continue. If he didn't, there would be a mutiny.

He pressed a button on his communicator and spoke. "All groups move forward to the lab security doors on the double. Once on sight, we will perform an equipment check in preparation for going in. Regardless of what this guy says, we still have a job to do, so let's get to it."

With that, Ferine moved past his men who gave each other a quick pat on the backs as they grinned over the decision and the revenge they imagined themselves taking. They turned and began to follow Ferine as they continued their advance toward the ANZAR research wing. Their boots thudded loudly on the corridor floor as they once again made their way towards their objective.

From over the intercom system, Luke spoke once more. "Somehow I just knew you guys wouldn't walk away. This is for what you bastards did to my mother."

They had paused on hearing Luke's voice once more. A few of the men grabbed at the railings in anticipation of another gravity attack. A few seconds later the deafening noise of buckling metal exploded from around the corner behind them.

The group spun as one, and their weapons rose. Fearing a hull breach, a few of the men, including Ferine, struggled momentarily to release oxygen masks from their hips before realising that the air around them was not being sucked past them, there was no decompression and that they could still breathe. After a moment's pause, Ferine pointed back the way they had come, and they cautiously moved back along the corridor to investigate.

The troops made their way back to the stretch of corridor in which Ferine had found his men rummaging through the contents of a jewellery box they had found in one of the empty rooms. Their guns pointed into open doorways as they leapfrogged each other along the hall. The sounds of tearing, splitting and breaking from further down the corridor had merged with liquid noises that flowed with smaller snapping and popping sounds. Fearful of what they would find, Ferine and his men rounded a bend in the corridor where they were met with a scene of destruction.

"Holy shit, Cap!" Scarface growled from beside him as he pointed to the middle of the corridor. "Tell me that ain't our boys on the floor."

Ferine was shocked into silence. He had made a mistake in underestimating the bastard on the intercom system.

A big mistake.

The remains of half a dozen of Ferine's troops lay crushed in the middle of the self-destructing corridor. The men's equipment was the only thing recognisable about them as belonging to C-Unit. Mangled weapons, crumpled uniforms and twisted body armour lay strewn across the corridor in a fetid pool of human body fluids that ran from wall to wall. The liquefied mass writhed with the buckling floor to give a grotesque impression that the men were somehow still alive and struggling for their lives. Pieces of bone, skull and other body parts that were still recognisable attested to the fact that these men were most definitely dead.

Everywhere Ferine looked, there was blood. It had sprayed, splattered, burst and flowed onto every surface in the vicinity of his men's remains. The damaged corridor had been painted with it. No longer content to merely contain his men, the unknown voice on the intercom system had turned the artificial gravity up to its maximum setting, using it as a weapon to literally squeeze the life from six members of C- Unit.

A shower of sparks from above caught Ferine's attention and dragged his eyes away from the remains of his troops. He looked up to see that the ten-metre-long section of walkway before him was still in the process of collapsing in on itself. Ferine and those with him took a few steps back as the roof ahead of them buckled; the increased gravity twisted the metal sheeting of the false ceiling as it was pulled towards the floor. Ceiling panels fell away one by one as the weight of the foam insulation above became too heavy to support. Open cabin doors along the corridor bowed at the edges and were ripped from their hinges by their own weight. They landed in the pool of blood with deep wet thuds that made them sound more like slabs of lead rather than aluminium. As far back as they were, the splash from the impact sprayed the onlookers with gore.

Metal screamed, wood splintered, plastic split, glass shattered and finally, the light bulbs burst.

The scene ahead was hidden in darkness. One last shower of sparks fell across the hall, taunting the survivors with a final glimpse of their comrade's remains.

The hull of the station seemed to groan in appreciation as the gravity returned to normal.

With the strain released, Steel joints along the corridor relaxed. All became silent.

The men stared at the space ahead of them, lost in their thoughts over the lives lost, wondering who from their original team of twenty lay amongst them. They stayed that way for a while. Each man stood motionless as they contemplated the meaning, or pondered the repercussions that would follow the deaths of so many of their own. What each man shared was a common thread through what they were thinking. Each man thought dark thoughts. Each man contemplated revenge.

Shadows moved over the walls from the still lit section of the corridor beyond, catching Ferine's attention. He struggled to ascertain what it was that had caught his eye. He could make out little of the other end of the corridor through the forest of ceiling insulation, heating ducts and suspended wires that hung throughout the area of destruction. As he stared, human shapes began to form out of the gloom, recognisable shapes and forms reflected off the dull metal walls of the hall. The shapes of men were silhouetted from the lights beyond.

27
Not alone

Accommodation Corridor – ANZAR Wing, Newton Station.

6.24pm - Sunday, August 16th, 2048

Ferine and his group recognised the possible threat and reacted as their training demanded. They dropped to their knees and ducked around the corners of the intersecting corridors to conceal themselves. In just a few minutes the loss of six of their men had reversed C-Unit's position from that of confident invaders to defensive interlopers.

"Hold your fire until we can identify who they are," Ferine growled softly to his team. "We still have more of our own on the station."

With his weapon raised, Ferine called out a challenge.

"This is Kyle Ferine of the Imperial Cavalry!" he called. "You are to identify yourself immediately, or you will be fired upon."

An immediate response issued forth from the other end of the hall.

"Hold fire! Hold fire, Cap. It's me, Jackson," the familiar voice called out. "I just reached the guys at the rear when we heard the noise and came running. Are you okay?"

Ferine and his men gave an audible sigh of relief. They weren't alone.

"We're fine!" Ferine called back. "How many with you?" he asked.

A silence fell over the corridor as Sergeant Jackson took inventory.

"Seven of us," the answer came. After a moment, he added. "How many at your end?"

"Six and me. "

"Where's the rest of the team?" Jackson called.

Ferine made eye contact with the men around him before he replied. They all knew what had become of the rest of the team. Ferine knew it would be best if Jackson's group were left in the dark on that piece of information for the moment.

"How about you all come over so we can discuss this without having to scream at each other, okay?"

Ferine rose to his feet and stepped forward into the gloom to examine a damaged lighting fixture that hung just above his head. He cringed as the thud of his footsteps on the cold, dry linoleum floor was replaced by a thick squelching noise as his boots stepped into the carpet of blood and gore. He closed his mind off to the fact that he was treading on the still warm remains of his men. The coppery scent of blood invaded his senses, making it impossible for him to pretend he was walking through something less disturbing. He placed the back of his hand near the exposed cables from a destroyed lighting fixture without feeling any current. Apparently, this section of the corridor had lost all power and had fallen dead.

"As far as I can tell, the powers out, so it should be safe to cross over," he called to his men. "Watch your footing. The floors pretty wet with...with some sort of spill."

It took a few minutes for Sergeant Jackson and his group to inch their way over to Ferine. By the time the last man had arrived, the rest of the group had been informed of what had happened and had made the unanimous decision to continue. "Using the gravity in that way would cause a hell of a drain on the power, so we'll move out in single file with at least five metres space between each man. He can only amp up the gravity like that in one section at a time, so if he decides to pull that trick again, he'll only get one or two of us at most."

Ferine said to the huddle of men that surrounded him. "That's bloody reassuring," Scarface growled.

"Just keep cool heads till we get where we're going and don't let this guy spook you," Ferine said matter-of-factly. "Remember, this is just one man. He's probably just some nerd at a computer who got lucky and took us by surprise. He won't be doing that again. Got it?"

The group exchanged quick glances before grabbing their weapons and lining up for the move.

"Let's give this sum' bitch some payback, boys," Scarface snarled. "I say we set a score of one thousand points to whoever off's this pig. What do ya say, fellas?" He turned to the rest of the group who had fallen in line behind him.

A unified chorus of approval went up from the men as Ferine led the remaining members of C-Unit towards the entrance to the labs.

28
Cruel to be kind

Engineering Bay – ANZAR Wing, Newton Station.

6.27pm - Sunday, August 16th, 2048

Luke sat hunched over the computer console in the Engineering Bay. His now pale visage was reflected back at him on each monitor as he nervously watched the Imperial troops continue their advance. The ghost-like image he saw reflected on the screens appeared to Luke as an omen of his recent actions, a vision of his death.

Despite the coolness of the labs, a spray of sweat-soaked much of his skin. The slipperiness of his fingers combined with his shaking hands caused him to fumble at the controls as he switched between camera views on the displays. A vague concern that his body was going into shock over the confrontation lurked at the back of his mind. His entire body shook with the disbelief of what had just happened. He had done something that he had never dreamt he would; he had just killed six men. The finality and simplicity of the act weighed heavily on his mind. With the simple act of adjusting a few numbers on the computer before him, he had crushed the life out of another human being. The fact that those men had been sent to do the same to him, or at best arrest him, did little to alleviate his guilt. He tried to think of his mother who had been mercilessly killed along with hundreds of other people when members of the Imperial military had blown her plane out of the sky. Still, try as he might to justify his actions, Luke found this mental link between that incident and these men a bit too tenuous to accept.

Luke thought of the fourteen men who remained as he gingerly got to his feet and made his way to the medical bay next door. He was aware that he would only have a matter of minutes before he would be forced to decide on what course of action to pursue next. He knew that whatever he chose to do, whether to defend the station by continuing the assault or make a run for the maintenance tunnel, his actions would have repercussions for more than just the people now present on Newton. But before that decision could be made, he needed more information.

Luke heard the screams the moment the door opened. The impression of fear and panic coupled with the sheer volume of it snapped him out of his reverie.

The scene before him caused Luke to pause before he realised what was going on, what he saw quickly explained who had made the noise and why.

One of the kids, Timothy as far as he could tell, was being pinned to a surgical bed by what looked like most of the station's senior staff. Adam Fehrenbach, Doctor Tran and a few junior engineers wrestled with the terrified youth as Doctor Anderson sat straddled across the oversized child's back in an attempt to his use his weight to immobilise the boy. Craig stood beside Timothy whispering words of reassurance and placing soft kisses on his forehead. With his right hand and much of his forearm restrained in one of Timothy's giant hands, Craig awkwardly reached across with his left hand to gently stroke the boy's head. His cries subsided into soft whimpers as he slowly calmed.

Once Doctor Anderson felt Timothy was still enough, he raised a gun-like device and gently, but forcefully, pushed it into the back of Timothy's head. At feeling this sharp jab of pain, Timothy's arms and legs flailed as the process of inserting the ModChip onto the base of his skull continued. Usually, it was a twenty-second operation to install the device, a quick jab, the chip is positioned, and the wound quickly sealed. Timothy's fear and lack of co-operation was making the process last much longer than it should, thereby exacerbating the problem. It was a nightmarish scene which Luke would have found disturbing if he weren't aware of what was happening or the necessity of the operation.

Glen Hanson, the astronomer, stood off to the side of the room with a look of mild shock on his face. Luke could almost hear him wondering what the hell he'd gotten himself into.

Behind the stricken Astronomer, Luke noticed the still inert form of his father lying on a hospital bed. Tubes, wires and machines were connected to his unconscious body, keeping the Professor alive. A wave of emotion ran through Luke as he stared at his father. The famous Professor Weekes would be considered a valuable catch for the Imperial Military. Luke knew that if the troops made it through before he had a chance to put him on a trolley and wheel him out, his father would be arrested while still unconscious and be put to work as a slave in some secret lab the moment he woke up.

If he woke up, Luke thought.

It was likely that the Empire would find it too unprofitable to treat a comatose patient and would decide that it would be to everyone's benefit to perform an economic case of euthanasia on his father. Either way, Luke knew that his father's life would be over if the station were taken before everyone was safely away. He knew he had to hold off the troops long enough for Craig to get aboard the VAPER and for the rest of them to prep his father and make their way into the maintenance tunnel which led past the troops and out into the main body of the station.

More cries at the other side of the medical bay drew Luke's attention to where Karen stood cradling Jamie as best she could. The second child sat hunched on the floor, rocking slowly back and forth while holding the spot at the back of his neck where his chip had been inserted moments ago. The occasional whimper and sniffle was the only evidence that Jamie had taken the treatment as poorly as Timothy was now.

Dragging his thoughts away from the plight of his father, Luke quickly walked over to Karen to see how things were going.

"He okay?" Luke asked when he reached her.

Standing at her full height with her arms outstretched above her head, Karen found it a struggle to hug the boy, even with him sitting down. Her arms barely reached around the back of his neck as she clung on to the still rocking form.

"Not bad," she answered Luke." He took it about as well as we could have hoped. Luckily it was only a minor procedure as Craig put it."

Luke looked at her for a moment but could detect no animosity. She was obviously distressed by the whole situation but did not appear to be blaming anyone for this turn of events.

"How much longer do you guys need?" Luke asked as he looked back at the leading group in the middle of the room. His procedure complete, Timothy lay sobbing face down on the operating table. His arms and legs dangled down each side of the bed, resting on the floor.

Luke briefly made eye contact with Craig who seemed to shrug and gave him a look as if to say, *Suck's huh? But what can you do?*

Karen drew his attention back with her response.

"I don't know," she replied slowly. "The boys took so long that we still have to do the rest of the staff. There's about another five of us still to go."

Luke did a quick calculation and didn't like what he came up with. "That's too long."

He suddenly turned around and marched straight back out of the room. He knew he'd have to try and give the rest of the staff the time they needed to finish what they were doing. He stepped back into the engineering bay and approached the computer knowing that he had to do more to slow the Imperials down.

29

14·4

Outside the labs – ANZAR Wing, Newton Station.

6.32pm - Sunday, August 16th, 2048

Ferine and his men had arrived at the entrance to the ANZAR laboratory wing. A junction of corridors ended in what appeared to be a massive pressure sealed door set into the wall.

Around him, the troops turned their backs on the door and took up positions guarding the three corridors that ran back into the accommodation wing. The sealed door ahead of them created an artificial dead-end in which they had no escape route should anyone appear from behind. Weapons were unshouldered as the men crouched around corners looking back the way they had come, securing the only escape route available to them. Confident that anyone attempting to sneak up on them from behind would be spotted, Ferine and Jackson approached the lab's entrance to assess their options on getting inside.

It was bright to look at. The lighting of the corridor reflected off its polished chrome surface causing Ferine and Jackson almost to have to squint at it to make out the details of its design. The only notable feature on the facade was a large wheel that protruded from the centre of the door giving it the appearance of something that looked more at home on a submarine than a research station. To the right of the structure, Ferine noticed a security panel that hung at eye level. On it, he could see a range of dials, sensors and hand scanners set above the convex lens of a camera. For their security and as a simple act of defiance, Ferine rammed the butt of his rifle into the glass, shattering the lens.

Let the bastard see what we're up to now, he thought.

As he ran his eyes over the controls looking for an access port through which they could hack their way in, he noticed something that he had hoped for but never expected.

A thin sliver of light was visible along the right-hand side of the door.

It wasn't sealed. The door was ajar.

Ferine stared at the gap in the door as he considered what to do. Before leaving Earth, his mission brief had informed him that one of ANZAR's scientific team had been supplying information to the Empire in return for political favours. The source had promised to assist his men in gaining access to the labs covertly if circumstances allowed. Whether the door had been left open by a careless staff member who had been in a rush to evacuate the station, or if it had been left open intentionally, it didn't matter to Ferine. A way in had presented itself, and he had little choice but to take it.

With his left hand, he reached across and grabbed hold of the wheeled handle and gave a slight tug; the door swung outwards by a few inches. Beside him, Sergeant Jackson, who had been intently examining the security console, jumped back in surprise at seeing the massive door move.

Ferine pulled open the door to reveal a second, identical door, separated by a small decontamination chamber that now stood empty. He stepped inside and examined the inside of the airlock for anything that shouldn't be there. After the terrible start to the mission, he wasn't planning on taking any unnecessary chances. After a thorough look around, Ferine could see nothing out of place and noted that, at a squeeze, he could probably fit a half-dozen of his men in at one time.

He weighed his decision once more and could think of no other option but to proceed.

"Race, Warne, Chiapinni, Coleman, Phillipson and Sarno," Ferine called to his men as he stepped out of the airlock and back into the corridor. "Form up and get ready to move in. Everyone else, keep watch."

The six men he had called immediately rose to their feet and moved over to surround Ferine who stood facing the empty airlock.

"Hey, Cap," Scarface said over his shoulder as he kept watch down the right-most corridor. "How about letting me go in with the point group, huh?"

Ferine turned to face the enormous soldier who knelt on one knee on the floor beside him.

"Why?" he asked.

"I don't want to miss out on all the fun is all," Scarface said without any hint of humour on his scarred face.

Knowing what he was like; Ferine had no intention of letting that particular soldier loose where he wasn't around to keep an eye on him.

"Request denied," Ferine replied crisply. "I need you with me."

Scarface grimaced and shook his head in disgust at being held back. "Just save some for me," he said before turning his attention back to the empty corridor he had been watching.

"Alright, we've got access," Ferine began as he turned back to the six men that waited in front of the decontamination chamber's open doorway. "You six are on point and will enter the airlock and ready yourselves to secure the area on the other side. From what we've been told, you'll have to wait in the airlock while the system cycles through a quick decontamination procedure before the second door can open and allow you access to the labs. Once clear, you are to wait for the rest of the team to come through before proceeding. No matter what happens when you get through, you are to secure the immediate area on the other side of the airlock and are not to proceed any further into the station without us. Got it?"

The men answered with nods of their heads.

With a wave, he ordered them inside. They silently stepped into the small decontamination airlock; their equipment-laden bodies filled every inch of space in the room so that the men had to squeeze together with their weapons held tight against their chests, the barrels pointed safely at a smaller airlock hatch in the ceiling.

Ferine and Jackson pushed the door closed and stood back. The automated system took over as the manual release wheel turned itself to the lock position. A beep and a flashing green light on the control panel announced that the door was sealed and the chamber ready for decontamination.

The remainder of Ferine's team were now separated. Six of his men were now sealed in the decontamination airlock, eight more stood outside the door waiting for their chance to go through the process.

A sensation of warmth began to pulse outwards from the door. A small motor started to whine in the ceiling space above them, signifying that the decontamination process had begun. As the process continued, the corridor grew warmer. The sounds of rushing air could be heard through the adjoining wall. Lights blinked on and off as the stages of the decontamination cycle were completed, and new ones began. A few minutes after the door had been sealed it once again began to move.

A pungent cloud of steam billowed out of the gap as the door partly opened.

As soon as Ferine got his first whiff of the scent he knew something was wrong. His gag reflex recognised the origin of the odour before his mind had the chance to come to grips with what had just happened. He turned to one side and vomited on the concourse floor. His body doubled over as his stomach squeezed to empty itself of its contents. His first conscious thought was that he was being poisoned by a gas of some sort. The retching and gagging of the men behind him added weight to his theory. After a few more moments of dry retching, his stomach calmed, and his head began to clear. Through the acidic taste of his last meal, Ferine identified the odour that had caused him to be ill in the first place. The stench of burnt meat and melted plastic filled the air around him. He turned to look at the security door to see thick black smoke billow out of the opening and disappear into an air- conditioning intake vent in the ceiling.

As he watched, the air cleared. The smell didn't.

Sergeant Jackson moved quickly over to the door to see what had happened. Like a few of the other men, he had placed his emergency oxygen mask over his face to breathe in clean air and avoid the smell. His pace was slow and unsteady; Jackson seemed to sway as he crossed the floor to the partially open hatch. Whether his unsteadiness was from nausea or from the knowledge of what he would find when he looked inside, Ferine couldn't tell. Jackson grabbed the side of the partially opened door and pulled his hand back in pain.

"What! What is it?" Ferine called through the clear plastic of his oxygen mask as he placed it on his face and walked over. He had to step over two of his men that still lay on the floor gagging. Scarface and Private Dockrill had regained their feet, donned their oxygen masks and were now standing beside Jackson who was flapping his hand in the air.

"Damn thing's red hot!" Jackson replied.

Ferine grabbed the Sergeant's hand to see a line of blisters arise on the tips of the man's fingers.

"Stand back," Ferine said to his men who did as ordered.

With the butt of his rifle, Ferine pushed against the door until it clicked into the fully open position. Another cloud of smoke and moisture issued from the doorway. Luckily, the smell was lessened by the oxygen masks that most of the men now wore.

The four men who were standing stepped forward as one and peered into the airlock. At first glance, it appeared as if the small room was empty. The mist and fumes hid the truth from view. The scene was reminiscent of the corridor in the accommodation wing. A thick, gelatinous layer of debris littered the airlock floor. It bubbled and steamed in the heat of the room. Black crusts of burnt matter coated it in areas, the extreme temperatures in the place having boiled then charred the remains of what was unmistakably another six of Ferine's men.

A cry of rage built up in Ferine's chest. It had happened again. The crazy bastard in the labs had killed more of his troops in yet another obscene way. The fact of his men's deaths caused Ferine less anger than disgust at the way in which they had died.

From the briefing, he knew that the decontamination booth used low-level radiation and heat to decontaminate its occupants. That knowledge and the evidence before him strongly suggested that his men had been doused with high doses of radiation before being cooked and incinerated where they stood.

He wondered how long it would have taken. Was it quick or did they have time to writhe and scream as they burned?

The sound of metal screeching accompanied by a hiss of escaping air above his head caused him to look up. The locking wheel on the small access hatch embedded into the ceiling of the chamber was slowly turning. The station's intercom system began to scream with the sound of an automated alarm as Ferine realised what was about to happen.

"Grab something!" he called through his oxygen mask as he made a dive for the nearest railing. From the corner of his eye, he saw his men's training come into effect as they instantly reacted to his order. Ferine's tone and expression told them all that they needed to know. The situation had just gone from bad to worse.

His hand barely managed to get a grip on the waist-high railing in front of him when he felt his body grow light, all sense of up and down was lost.

The gravity was off.

Ferine's legs rose above his head in a jerking motion as the air around him rushed past as if in a hurry to leave. His uniform flapped rapidly in the artificial breeze as the rush of air turned into a torrent.

A loud pop inside his head caused Ferine almost to let go of the railing and throw his hands over his ears. A severe drop in air pressure had caused his ears to pop as the external airlock in the decontamination chamber came fully open, sucking the remains of the recently deceased troops out into open space. The only thing left of the six soldiers who had entered it minutes ago was a dark brown stain that covered the floor and lower wall.

With his grip on the railing secure, Ferine looked around to see the surviving members of his team holding onto the first solid objects they had managed to grab. To his left, Jackson, Scarface and Private Dockrill had taken his lead and had managed to reach a nearby railing which they had grasped with both hands.

Their bodies were buffeted by flying debris and personal belongings as they were carried past them by the wind.

Their grips looked tenuous but secure.

Ferine looked to his right just in time to see four more of his men die. In a rush to grab something solid two of them had anchored themselves on an open door that swayed back and forth in the rush of evacuating air. The combined weight of the two men proved too much for the door which twisted in its frame. Both soldiers lost their grip and were flung across the open space in front of the airlock. In a desperate attempt to save themselves, each man clawed at the flailing limbs of two other soldiers who had been struggling to hold onto the railing as they tumbled by. Rather than saving themselves, the two doomed Cavalry troopers only succeeded in loosening the grips of their fellow C-Unit members who joined them in their journey across the corridor and up towards the open airlock in the ceiling. A sickening crunch echoed around the hallway as the men's bodies slammed into the narrow opening and were bent and distorted into new and unusual shapes as they were sucked out of the station. Oxygen masks or not, they died instantly as they were snap- frozen in the vacuum of space.

The station grew colder as it emptied of air. Goosebumps erupted on Ferine's exposed skin. The steel bar of the railing began to ice over as moisture from the thinning air cooled and froze on its surface. A deep penetrating ache had pervaded his fingers as they rapidly grew colder. The desire to let go, to stretch his fingers, to rub his hands together for warmth, became an almost irresistible urge that Ferine had to consciously will himself not to give in to.

Books, clothing, papers and other objects continued to fly past the four remaining men as they struggled to keep their hold on the bar of steel that was the anchor for their lives. Time stood still as each man fought the suck of the vacuum, the pull of death. It could have been minutes or seconds later that the metallic thud of the hatch closing announced their survival of this latest assault. The air stilled, the scream of escaping oxygen died away.

The motion of the debris around the corridor slowed as they came to rest.

There was still no gravity.

The corridor stood silently with the four troops floating in midair, unmoving, their numbed hands wrapped around the railings, none of them dared to let go. Each man hoped that they had survived, that it was over, that they would not be subjected to another attack. They looked around the room at their companions, assessing who was left and who had been lost.

The only sound in the nearly deserted section of the station was that of their breathing as they slowly began to relax.

Without warning, the gravity returned. They fell to the floor and lay there stunned.

30
Disagreement

Engineering Bay – ANZAR Wing, Newton Station.

6.36pm - Sunday, August 16th, 2048

That was enough, Luke thought. *They'll leave now.*

He believed the troops would see the futility of trying to penetrate a controlled environment such as the ANZAR labs and, as a result, would do the sensible thing and leave. From the console he now occupied, Luke could make extreme – and deadly – adjustments to all of the environmental controls. Feeling confident that the invading soldiers now understood that any attack on the labs would prove impossible and give up, Luke stepped away from the monitors which showed the images of the remaining four troops gingerly getting to their feet.

They will leave now, Luke reassured himself again as he made his way across the engineering bay. *They'd be insane to try and access the airlock after what had happened to their mates. That's the only way in; they've got no other choice but to leave until they can get reinforcements.*

At least that's what he hoped.

During the time it had taken Luke to carry out his second assault on the troops and remove another eight men from Ferine's team, the other members of the staff had finished up in the infirmary and had returned to the engineering bay. They had walked through the door rubbing the backs of their necks and looking like they would prefer to forget everything that had happened in the last ten minutes.

If only we all could, Luke thought.

Craig was in the process of trying to fit one of the kids through the opening in the *Feynman*'s cockpit as Luke approached. The child's shoulders were too broad for him to fit on his own; it took the coaching of Karen and the shoving and pulling of half the staff to get the boy aboard the ship. Timothy's giant hands flayed around the VAPERS cockpit looking for something to grab hold of to help lever himself through the three-foot-wide opening. The sounds of laughter echoed off the diamond hull of the VAPER as Jamie yelled support to his brother from deeper within the ship.

"Your bum's too big to fit in the door!" Jamie laughed from below.

"No, your bum's too big you stupid head," Timothy yelled back as he came clear of the hatch with one last shove from those above. With a sigh of relief, Timothy looked up proudly at Karen as if to say *Look. I did it! Aren't I cool!* Before he quickly moved deeper within the vessel and found a place to sit next to his brother. As with most children after having undergone a medical procedure, the pain of having their chips implanted was now all but forgotten in their excitement to leave the station.

"How are our visitors doing?" Craig asked as Luke arrived on the opposite side of the VAPER's hatch.

"I think we've bought ourselves some more time. If they're smart, they'll be going home now."

Craig and everyone else in earshot paused to stare at look. He could see the fear and concern on their faces as they struggled to understand what he was talking about. Craig spat a question at Luke before he had the chance to explain what he had done.

"What do you mean?" Craig asked. His tone laced with dread. "What did you do?"

Luke looked at each face in turn as he made his response. "I just evened up the odds a bit," he replied confidently. His tone reeked of false modesty as he told the group what had occurred, he spoke in the manner of an athlete who was trying to talk about a recent victory without trying to sound like they were bragging... but failed.

"An hour ago, there were twenty men on the way here to kill us. You should have seen those guys; they were armed to the teeth. And big, man a few of them were huge. But now, anyway, now there are only four of them left, and I've got them all scared shitless to make a move on us. It's amazing what you can do to a person when you turn the artificial gravity up to maximum. I bet dad never expected it could be used as a weapon once the safeties were disabled."

"Are you joking? You turned the gravity up to maximum? You could have damaged the station... you could have ruptured the hull!" Adam Fehrenbach growled from beside Craig.

"Please tell me you didn't kill any of them," Craig sighed as he rested his face in his hands. He looked up at Luke questioningly. "Did you?"

"We had no choice," Luke began to say before he was cut off.

Craig groaned as he saw any chance they had left of surviving this crisis unscathed disappear out the window with Luke's misguided actions.

"Shit, man. You've just made things worse!" Craig yelled. "You've just made us the bad guys." He waved an arm to signify everyone in the room. "Any moral high ground we had to argue our way out of this mess has just disappeared. Until you did that, we would have just been detained until our government could have petitioned our release. The Empire had no proof of wrongdoing against us; in the eyes of the International community, we were innocent. The assault on our labs would have been an illegal move by them." Craig looked at the floor and rubbed his hands through his hair before continuing. "You should have checked with us first. You've just given them the excuse they needed to come in here en-masse and do as they please."

Craig could see that Luke was feeling sorry for what had happened. Whether he was upset that he had not been praised for his actions as he had expected, or if he was beginning to truly understand the error he had made, Craig couldn't say. For the sake of their friendship, he decided to change tact.

"Look mate. You know how the Americans work. They take any insult or threat to them - no matter how justified - and then they twist it around. They'll say that they were a group of security personnel who had simply come here to question us about our activities. They'll deny that any use of force was directed at us. In the public eye, they'll make us look guilty of whatever they want."

Luke began to point at Craig as he responded. The emotion of the situation and his friend's reaction to the help he had provided caused Luke a great deal of stress. Where he had thought he would be getting a pat on the back for his actions, he had found only criticism instead.

"Give me a break, will you?!" Luke spat back. "They'd already be in here by now if I hadn't done what I did. I see your point about how they'll twist this around, believe me, I know how they work. We both lost our mothers to those bastards, remember?" Luke knew that he had probably struck a low blow with that one; the moment for apologies would come later. "You would have had a gun shoved in your back while you were next door farting around having the kids chipped if it wasn't for me. I've just bought everyone in the room plenty of time to get away."

Doctor Anderson stepped between the two men to break up the argument. "What's done, is done," he said as he looked form one man to the other. "Regardless of what has happened we still have to get a move on so Craig can get the research and the children out of here. We don't have time to argue about something we can't change."

"What's the hurry?" Luke looked up at the Doctor. "Their commander has lost three-quarters of his men; he won't dare approach the labs now, not without reinforcements."

"Exactly!" Craig retorted. "That group of twenty men was just the advance party. They were just an assault team whose job it was to secure the labs. A second military plane with more troops and the scientific team that was to dismantle this place can only be a matter of hours behind them. All you've done is delay the inevitable and give them an excuse to be hostile."

Luke knew better than to continue the argument. His colleague's faces told him he was alone in his opinion that the situation had developed past the point of diplomacy. The others had based their views on incomplete information. Luke had seen the truth of the situation on the monitors. They were being hunted down in their station. None of them had seen the way the soldiers had shot up the empty cabins. No one but him had seen them move from room to room with murderous looks on their faces as they searched for someone, anyone, to hurt or kill. They didn't see the violence in the Americans actions or the cruelty in their eyes. The Imperial military already saw them as a hostile enemy. Somewhere, someone in the Imperial's higher branches of government had already tried, convicted and sentenced them to, at best imprisonment, at worse death. Luke knew he had done the right thing, regardless of whether the others agreed or not. He knew that he had saved the lives of many of those around him by holding off the troops until everyone had been chipped.

Knowing that it was useless to continue preaching to the ignorant, Luke held up a hand, shrugged his shoulders and shook his head as he turned and made his way back to the control console.

"I guess I'd better keep an eye out for those reinforcements that Craig is so sure are about to arrive," he said as he walked away.

Craig watched his friend walk across the room before he turned towards Adam Fehrenbach and the Doctor. "If those soldiers make it in here before you guys get a chance to use the emergency exit, then I think you should co-operate with them. You should be Okay. I can't see them gunning down Australian and New Zealand citizens when they arrive. We're not exactly from unfriendly countries, are we?"

Doctor Anderson placed a hand on Craig's shoulder and gave it a quick squeeze. "I tend to agree with you on that one, although I do think that Luke may have had a point. The more this situation progresses, the more I can't help but think that what he did may prove to benefit us in the long run. But, for now, we still have to get you out of here."

Adam Fehrenbach reached into his pocket and removed a small data cube which he handed to Craig.

"This contains all the information we were able to remove from the *Feynman* after it returned with Professor Weekes. It contains the coordinates for the six Conduit transits that the Professors made during the ten days they went missing." Adam looked from Craig to Doctor Anderson before finishing. "As you can understand, we haven't had time to find out where they lead, but... I guess we'll leave that up to you... if that's what you're intending."

Craig placed the cube in his Jacket pocket after giving it a quick glance. "I guess it's no secret anymore, is it? I obviously can't just fly down to Sydney and sit around while everything falls apart around us. I have to find out what happened to the Professors. Hopefully, I won't have to visit all six layers of the Multiverse they went to, but I'm hoping that we'll find some clue as to what happened to them after we visit the first few. Wherever they went and whatever happened while they were gone, their actions indirectly caused the death of one hundred million people. If we can find out where those spheres came from, maybe we can do something to stop all this. With a bit of luck, we can maybe even clear ANZAR's name as being the cause of this mess and find a way to fix the Earth's orbit."

"That's what we were afraid you were going to do," Doctor Anderson sighed. "What you're proposing does sound like it could save a lot of people and a lot of pain, but I have some very strong concerns that you're going into this unprepared."

"Yeah, it's a risk. I won't deny that, but I don't see that we have much choice. I can't just sit back and do nothing out of some selfish concern to protect myself when I could find a way to avoid the loss of all life on the planet."

Doctor Tran approached the group from behind and tapped Craig on the shoulder. He glanced down at a small tablet computer as he spoke, almost as if he was worried about making eye contact. "All systems are checked and cleared, and the *Feynman*'s reactor is running at full power. Everything's ready when you are."

Craig looked at the old engineer for a moment and wondered what was on the man's mind. He was about to ask but the urgent need to leave compelled him to postpone the question for another time.

"Thanks, Henry," Craig said as Doctor Tran handed him the computer with the *Feynman*'s status report. The two men looked at each other as if they were both about to speak. They held each other's gaze for a moment; their expressions said everything that needed to be said without either man uttering a word. With a final nod and a pat on Craig's shoulder, Doctor Tran turned and walked back to his engineering team who stood ready and waiting at one of the two engineering bay's computer terminals. At the other, Luke was looking for Ferine and his remaining three men.

As Luke stared at the screens, a smile spread across his face. He couldn't see them anywhere. None of the cameras showed any signs of the last of the invading Cavalry troops.

Luke chuckled slightly as he came to the conclusion that they must have left.

31
Alternate route

Outside the station – ANZAR Wing, Newton Station.

6.38pm - Sunday, August 16th, 2048

Kyle Ferine floated two hundred kilometres above the Earth and stared at the indented section of the space station. The tubular ANZAR wing looked compressed as if it had been squeezed by a giant hand, the extreme forces created from the increase in the artificial gravity had caused more damage than he could have imagined. Broken air ducts, piping and electrical cables poked through the station's external insulation in a jumbled mess. Ferine stared at the damage in amazement. He couldn't believe how the structure had managed to hold together. He couldn't fathom how it had withstood such intense forces without the hull breaching and spilling them all out into space.

Despite the destruction, he almost felt as if he was looking at a beautiful, contemporary work of art. He watched as a broken water pipe fired a fine spray of - what he could only assume was water - towards the moon. As the liquid came into contact with the cold vacuum of space, it was immediately transformed into small ice crystals that looked a hell of a lot like snow. The frozen spray spread outwards as it rose. A few hundred metres above the station it curved into a fan-like shape as it was pulled back towards the ANZAR wing by the station's gravity. Tiny particles of micrometeorite foam that had broken away from the station tumbled and turned through the orbiting snowstorm as they too were captured by the damaged section of the ANZAR wing. Around and around the particles floated in a slow ballet of movement that Ferine found mesmerising to watch.

Sunrise erupted on the far side of the station as the night- side of the Earth slowly retreated west beneath him. The strengthening beams of light from the rising sun played through the cloud of frozen water, backlighting the spectacle with blinding white light. With the rise in temperature, the particles of ice began to move more erratically; they began to vibrate, to shake, as if in angry at the change. As they began to melt and fade from view, each of the thousands of particles of ice appeared to bleed colour. As they shrunk out of existence, they gave birth to a billion tiny rainbows that danced across the outside of the station.

Ferine watched this natural wonder in amazement. *It's wrong for me to find beauty in the aftermath of something that took the lives of so many of my men, he thought. But still, my God it's beautiful.*

Movement below caught his eye and snapped him out of his contemplative mood. He looked down and saw Private Dockrill pull himself through the small service airlock embedded in the side of the station. Between him and Ferine, Jackson and Scarface had already clipped their safety lines onto the service ladder and were in the process of repositioning their rifles on their backs. The bulky, oversized life support packs made the task difficult, but essential. Although weapons were not standard spacewalk equipment and usually would not be brought into such an environment, Ferine had no choice but to bring them. They couldn't exactly re-enter the station without them.

Ferine repositioned his rifle which insisted on sliding off his shoulder and down his arm. He hooked the strap over a corner of the pack and turned to watch the other. "That's it Dockrill," Ferine said into the microphone located in his helmet. "Get your safety line hooked on before you start to climb. Take it slow and easy, and you'll be cool."

"Got it, Cap," the young soldier replied. "Man, I didn't think I'd be doing this shit when I got out of bed this morning."

"Me neither," Ferine whispered in reply.

He looked down to check his safety line. A thin steel thread of wire was the only thing anchoring him to the outside of the station. His heavily gloved right hand gripped the cable in an unconscious death grip as a means to reassure himself that he was still in contact with the island of safety that the station represented. Although having been trained in orbital emergency procedures, which included donning pressure suits and performing spacewalks, he felt ill at ease with his current situation. The sensation of hanging in the middle of nowhere with nothing above, below or beside him except for stars and the distant vista of the Earth left Ferine feeling disoriented and uneasy. He knew that one wrong move, safety cable or not, could send him floating off into space with no hope of recovery. He would spend eternity floating deeper into the void with the only possible ending to the scenario being his eventual suffocation when his oxygen runs out.

Ferine watched Private Dockrill pull himself up the side of the station. The stiffness of the pressure suits made movement awkward and the use of the occupant's legs almost impossible. The young soldier was forced to rely on his hands alone to lift himself up, and over the station, his legs floated out behind him, a useless mass of tissue which in the zero-g environment had become more of a hindrance than a means of locomotion. Ferine spoke words of encouragement over his helmet microphone, willing the boy to succeed. Out of all his men, Ferine cared most about what happened to this one. With his youth and comparative innocence, Private Dockrill had come to symbolise and to some extent replace, the relationships he had lost with his sons.

Ferine's head filled with thoughts of his two boys whom he had not seen in over five years. Sam and Max were only six years old when Marie stole his children from him in a petty act of revenge. He was almost, but not wholly, convinced that her leaving and taking the kids was Marie's way of demonstrating the loneliness and abandonment she had felt whenever he went away on assignment.

Well, whatever her reasoning, it had worked.

It had been a hard time for all of them when she had dragged the kids kicking and screaming out the front door and away to her mother's house. They hadn't wanted to go, Sam and Max idolised their father as all young boys did. They thought their dad was the coolest guy on Earth and were happy just to be in his company, following him around the house, trying to help in the garden, trying to be like him for the limited time that he was around. They didn't judge; they didn't present him with unrealistic expectations. True, they missed him when he was away, but unlike their mother, they somehow understood that their dad would rather be home with them and that he only left because he had to. It wasn't ideal, but the boys were happy for the time they could get with him.

Sadness always overwhelmed him when he thought of Sam and Max. He had his good days and bad. If not for Private Dockrill being on his team, he was sure he would have succumbed to the loss. Ferine knew that he was projecting his feelings for his estranged children onto the young soldier but was powerless to do anything about it. And frankly, he didn't know if he wanted to. He needed someone he could nurture and be kind to. He couldn't play the hard-ass all the time. Besides, the kid needed someone to watch out for him. Didn't everybody?

"Man, you should check out the view from up here, Cap!" Private Dockrill's voice echoed through Ferine's helmet. "This shit is so weird. It feels like I'm riding on the top of an aeroplane travelling at one hundred thousand feet. It's amazing."

All three surviving members of his team were now perched on top off the station, taking in the view of the Earth below. With a sigh, Ferine made his way up to join them.

"Okay, guys. Remember your training and take your time. They don't know we're coming so there's no rush to get in there. Now let's move out as we planned."

With that, the four soldiers began to inch their way across the top off the ANZAR wing. Hand over hand; they made their way towards the Engineering Bay airlock at the other end of the labs.

32
Into the *Feynman*

Engineering Bay – ANZAR Wing, Newton Station.

6.40pm - Sunday, August 16th, 2048

Craig shook hands all round and stepped over the edge of the dome that filled the centre of the engineering bay floor. Sitting on the edge of the opening, he swung his legs into the cockpit of the VAPER hidden beneath. He carefully felt around with his feet, trying not to hit any of the controls, until his toes found the soft base of the pilot's seat. With his weight partially supported, Craig allowed himself to drop down the last few inches to stand on the pilot's chair which he would soon occupy. With his head and shoulders still visible through the hatch, he turned to the remaining ANZAR staff that, apart from Luke and the engineering team, stood around the dome of the *Feynman*. He wasn't one for speeches, but under the circumstances, he felt that something needed to be said.

"I'm sorry everything worked out this way for us. I understand that my father and Professor Weekes wouldn't have recruited you all to work for them if they had any idea that this would happen. What's important now is everyone's safety. As soon as the *Feynman* is clear of the station I want everyone into that maintenance tunnel and on their way out, okay? I'm sure Professors Weekes and Turp wouldn't expect you to stay here and risk coming to harm for their work. Whatever happens, I'll see you all when this thing is over."

He looked around at the faces in the group that he had known for much of his life. Each met his gaze in turn; their strength gave him confidence that what they were about to do would succeed. Surprisingly for Craig, they all looked less afraid than he felt. With the ModChips installed in all of the staff, his optimism over the situation increased, slightly.

Craig turned and was about to step down inside the *Feynman* to take his seat when Doctor Anderson leant over and grabbed him by the shoulder.

"Here, take this," he said as he passed Craig what looked like a small hand-held tablet computer. At first glance, the device looked much like a mobile phone but without any buttons or controls. "It's a Remedial Regulator. Your father and I have been working on it for a while. It may come in handy to control the kids if you should get into trouble," he said sheepishly. "I know you may not want to use it. I know how much you and Karen love those boys and wouldn't want to put them through any trauma." Doctor Anderson paused. "But, well, it's there if you need it."

Craig looked at the device with a thinly veiled look of disgust.

"Has it been tested?" he asked the doctor.

"We were able to induce a state of hyperkinesis in both the kids. We only had it on for a moment, so we didn't get the chance to see if they became hyperdynamic though. Either way, once you activate them, you'll want to get out of their way. We only tried it once, it wasn't pleasant... but it did the job." Doctor Anderson looked away as if embarrassed. "Anyway, it's just for emergencies...you know... life or death." "Yeah, life or death," Craig muttered as he pocketed the device and lowered himself the rest of the way into the VAPER. Above him the heavy steel vacuum seal for the hatch slid closed, leaving them sealed off from the rest of the
station.

Light from the station's overhead fluorescent tubes shone through the six-inch-thick arched canopy of the *Feynman*, the manufactured diamond of the hull softened the harsh lighting and gave the interior of the small ship a cool, welcoming feel. The sharp steel edges of the controls, the decking and the exposed components appeared softer, less impersonal and mechanical. Craig examined the cockpit which was just large enough to seat three people without feeling overly cramped. Two passenger seats sat behind and to each side of the pilot's chair, one of which was occupied by the station's Astronomer,

Glen Hanson, who gave Craig a quick nod before resuming his study of the VAPER's interior.

From Craig's left, Karen and the boys stood watching him as if waiting for him to speak. Their heads and shoulders were all that was visible above the steel-plated flooring from the cargo level below. Karen sat cradled in Timothy's arms the way a mother would carry a child on her hip, the size of the children made this role reversal possible.

Karen smiled at him from the boy's arms. "I didn't take you for the speech making type."

"Well, circumstances called for something like that," he shrugged.

"Well, I'm impressed. You're usually a man of so few words," she smiled at him.

"So, we all set?" Craig tried to sound enthusiastic to reassure the kids. He was conscious of the fact that the boys were leaving the station for the first time in their lives. They were being forced to leave the familiarity of the only home they had ever known and flee into the unknown. Fortunately, the boys seemed fine about the trip they were about to take; they even appeared excited over the prospect of seeing some of the world. The light in their eyes and the smiles on their faces told Craig that he was the one who was probably the most nervous.

"Okay, boys. How about you both get comfortable down below so we can leave?" Craig instructed the kids.

"Before we go, I need you to come here for a sec," Karen said with a mischievous look on her face as she reached out to take one of Craig's hands in hers. Timothy sensed her intention and supported her weight as she leaned forward on the oversized child's hip and kissed Craig on the lips. It was a brief and intimate display of affection, a quick way to express what she was feeling at the time. Their lips separated as they moved away from each other, they both smiled at the reassuring contact their kiss had provided. Craig closed his eyes briefly and appreciated how lucky he was to be attached to someone as wonderful as Karen. His thoughts were interrupted with a second kiss on the lips.

This one was much wetter and firmer. And from Timothy.

The boy had grabbed Craig's head and pulled it towards his with enough force to drag him across the cockpit. With his face now covered in saliva, Craig was grabbed from the side and dragged towards Jamie who grinned from ear to ear.

"My turn now," the second boy said, just before muffling any objections Craig could make by covering half of his face with his lips.

With saliva dripping from his chin, Craig collapsed into the second passenger seat where he wiped at his face with his shirt sleeve. Beside him, Glen made small coughing noises as he tried not to laugh out loud. The astronomer's shoulders shook as he looked out the transparent dome of the *Feynman*'s cockpit and pretended to find the view of bare steel on the underside of the station interesting.

"Alright, the fun's over for now," Craig said. "Go and sit anywhere you want guys, the entire outer hull of this thing is transparent, so you'll be able to see everything no matter where you sit." He looked at Karen and the boys and smiled.

The kids nodded eagerly as they ducked beneath the floor of the cockpit. Their voices filled the vehicle with the sounds of their excitement as they began to chatter about the launch. The noise sounded deafening as their high-pitched voices reverberated off the diamond hull of the ship causing Craig to wince.

"Hey!" Karen called from below. "Inside voices please, it's too noisy in here."

"Inside voices!?" a reply came back. "It's not fair mummy. You always say inside voices when we talk. We're always inside. Now we're outside so we can talk properly.

Fair point, Karen thought. She couldn't blame them for their enthusiasm at being out of the crèche for the first time.

The boys continued to talk but managed to reduce the volume to a bearable level as they made their way through the cramped cabin. Due to the low ceiling height of the cargo area, Karen could stand and walk at her full height; the boys, on the other hand, were forced to crawl on hands and knees to make their way to the nose of the *Feynman*.

The two VAPERS that had been created by the ANZAR team were essentially small transport vehicles that consisted of only two compartments. A small, domed, three-seater cockpit sat atop the larger cargo area that formed the main hull of the ship. At twenty feet long, the *Feynman* was large enough to fit the boxes of research and prototypes while leaving enough room for Karen and the kids to stretch out.

"You know what that means Timothy? It's time for blast off!" Jamie cried.

"Cool. I bet we go faster than a laser bolt!" Timothy replied. "We're gonna zoom around really fast!"

Without a word, Craig rose from the passenger seat at the rear of the cockpit and eased himself into position in the pilot's chair in front of Glen. The soft, gelatinous seat covering shifted its form under his weight as it moulded itself to the contours of his body. Small sensors in the back of the chair measured Craig's body shape, weight and posture; the numbers were then compared against those of the ANZAR staff on file, identifying the occupant of the seat to be Craig Turp, an authorised user. With security checks complete and the pilot identified, the onboard quantum computer began the start-up procedure of the vehicle's systems and controls.

The control panel in front of Craig came to life, a series of glass-like touchscreens flickered to life in various shades of blue. Coloured rectangles, squares and swipe command areas were illuminated as the *Feynman*'s systems activated. Craig reached forward and moved his fingers deftly over the control panel that had been recently removed from a late model military jet and welded to the steel-plated floor. He swivelled in his chair and turned his attention to the gap in the ceiling he had recently entered through. With the soft slide of one finger across a control panel, the opening in the cockpit's canopy disappeared as if it had never existed. The clear dome of the VAPERs cockpit arched over his head in a smooth curve, once again free of any joins or seams.

A quick rush of air circulated the ship as the cabin was pressurised. Craig swallowed to relieve the pressure inside his ears. From the cargo bay below, he heard Timothy complain that his ears were hurting. Before he could call out to him, Craig heard Karen's soothing voice tell the distressed child to swallow, and the pain would go away. It evidently worked, Timothy immediately fell silent.

With the cabin sealed, Craig looked around the cockpit once again. It would take the technicians and 'ground crew' on the station at least a few minutes to make their way to the control room and set themselves up. He decided to use the time to perform his pre-flight check. He grabbed at the control stick that rose from the floor between his legs and moved it from side to side, a graphic depicting a three- dimensional model of the VAPER mirrored the moves Craig made on a small screen in front of him. As he moved the control stick from left to right, the tiny model of the ship tilted to one side and then back again, its left flank rising higher as its right side dipped. Craig then moved the stick forward and back, pushing it towards the control panel before pulling it back towards his chest, the little model VAPER on the screen first dipped its nose before raising it skyward once again.

So far so good, Craig thought.

Next, he tested the control pedals on which his feet were resting. As he pushed down on each foot alternately, the graphic of the VAPER once again responded to his movements, this time by turning its nose from left to right. Lastly, both controls were moved at the same time causing the miniature model of the VAPER on the screen to twist, turn and spin through all three dimensions. Satisfied, Craig turned his attention to what was the most important piece of technology that ANZAR had ever invented.

33
Talking technical

Aboard the *Feynman* – ANZAR Wing, Newton Station.

6.45pm - Sunday, August 16th, 2048

The Conduit control system's simplistic appearance belied its complexity. The visual interface of the system resembled the much larger version of the conduit display that hung on the wall in the control room. A circularly shaped screen sat fixed to the centre of the VAPER's control panel, on which a visual interface similar to that of an artist's colour wheel surrounded a 2D model of the VAPER. Blue, green, yellow and red bands of colour radiated out from the image of the small ship like spokes on a wheel, the colours mixed where they met to create an image reminiscent of a circular rainbow.

A small white dot that looked not too dissimilar to a radar blip flashed slowly on the screen, signifying the VAPER's location within the Multiverse. Craig reached out and touched the point gently with a finger, causing the computer to display a few lines of information relating to their current position. The date, universe address as well as x, y and z coordinates of their physical location in their current universe gave Craig all the information he needed. With this, he could ascertain his location and from that, plot and initiate a trip through the Conduit to any point in space and time he desired, providing he possessed the equivalent information for his destination point.

Glen leaned forward over Craig's shoulder to watch what he was doing more closely. He was aware of the principal of what Professor Turp's team had been working on from the fortnightly ANZAR group sessions. This was the first time that he had ever seen the finished product that he had indirectly helped create with his knowledge of astronomy.

"So, is that the thing that makes time travel possible?" he asked, pointing at the screen.

"Technically, no. It's the control panel that allows us to see where we are in space and time. The computer that searches out the wormholes and stabilises an opening for us to travel through is located directly below where you're sitting." Craig twisted in his seat to half face Glen as he answered. "What this does is simply tells us three major pieces of information which we can then manipulate to travel through space and time. You see the ring of colours located around the VAPER there on the screen?" he asked Glen as he pointed out the miniature rainbow.

"Yeah."

"Those colours represent the regions of the Multiverse that you probably heard us talk about in the meetings. Basically, the universe we live in is only one of many. There are thought to be an infinite number of universes jammed together and butting up against one another in what Quantum physicists have called the Multiverse. They believe that the Multiverse is spherical and that the infinite individual universes it is comprised of exist extremely close together and even overlap. The theory is that each universe is connected to and not dissimilar from, the other universes that surround it; each one is slightly different from the next by some small, seemingly insignificant variation. With the rules of Entropy and the natural order of things, we can safely assume that like universes would be grouped together, gradually changing characteristics as we travel around our colour wheel."

Glen interrupted Craig and pointed at the screen. "Yeah, I think I remember some of this. The blue area of the colour wheel is full of Universes that share similar characteristics to our own."

"Exactly," Craig nodded. "If we were to move around this theoretical colour wheel, we would travel through billions of universes before we would be able to distinguish any obvious differences between them. Statistically, we know that the Multiverse contains many universes that are near identical to the one we live in. Physicist's also believe that there are infinitely more universes out there that are as different and as alien to ours in ways in which we probably can't imagine. The solid bands of colour between the graduated areas signify a quadrant of the Multiverse that exhibits a distinct set of characteristics. The blue region, where we are here, is where the universes which share similarities to ours exist."

"What do you mean by similarities?" Glen asked.

"Well, it could be anything from the amount and locations of galaxies within a Universe to the type and composition of the stars and planets, to the possibility of whether they contain life or not. But these similarities aren't limited to physical characteristics either. Similar universes could share the fact that they both contain human life but differ in subtle ways including having different evolutionary histories or even have the same people within them performing different roles. I can guarantee you that there are other universes out there with other Glen Hanson's in them that grew up to be doctors or mechanics or even drug addicts on welfare. The range of possibilities is infinite."

"So, if we live in the blue area, what do all the other colours contain?"

"That we're not sure of as yet. The yellow quadrant which lies directly opposite our blue quadrant on the colour wheel is expected to contain universes with vastly different qualities than those in our blue area. Where universes in the blue area are full of life, including us humans, the yellow area should be the polar opposite, most likely empty and inhospitable. The other colour zones including the green and red zones we believe should contain a variety of universes that have either life, but not human, or no life but liveable worlds, or even a mixture of both. Or more likely, they may even be on a plane of existence that we can't even imagine or see. The colour wheel is a visual means of understanding where we are in the Multiverse and a vague idea of what conditions to expect."

"Sounds vague all right." Glen shook his head at the information. "How can you guys know this for a fact? Surely this is all theoretical."

"How can you know whether a planet that is a billion light-years away has water and oxygen on it just by looking at it through a telescope?" Craig shot back good-naturedly.

Adam Fehrenbach's voice suddenly erupted over the VAPER's communication system, startling the two chatting men. Craig spun back around in his seat and reached across the controls to turn down the volume.

"Hi Craig," they heard Adam say. "We're in the control room now, and you'll be delighted to hear that everyone has stayed to help. We're just getting the computers started up, so it will be another couple of minutes before you can leave. How's everything at your end?"

"Fine," Craig replied. "The kids are settled in below, and I was taking the time to explain to Glen how wormhole travel through the Multiverse works."

"Glen, you poor bastard, having to listen to him drone on," Adam joked. Craig was a little surprised at his seemingly light mood under the circumstances. "I'll let you know when we're all set."

The cockpit fell silent once more.

"So, you were saying?" Glen prompted Craig to answer his previous question.

"Oh yeah, right. Well, you are right about it being mostly theory. But we have sent probes into each of the major quadrants of the Multiverse to see what's out there. The information those probes sent back is what the Professors used to create this model of the Multiverse, so we do have a basic understanding of what we're on about."

"So where are we now on that thing?" Glen pointed at the Conduit's control screen.

Craig pointed at the flashing dot on the screen which he had touched earlier.

"See that dot? That spot marks our location in the Multiverse; right now, we are in our universe which is within the blue sector. The colour doesn't mean anything in particular; it was just chosen as a starting point to help us visualise something that is practically abstract. I think the Professors just called this section of the Multiverse the blue quadrant because it's where our Universe and Earth is." Craig shrugged. "You know, Earth being blue and all. Anyway, as it turns out that's more of an affectionate reason for naming it that way."

"Anyway, getting back to it. The dot on the screen shows us what region of the Multiverse we are in depending on what colour on the wheel we are in. If we want more detailed information, we can touch the icon, and the screen displays our location more exactly. Our position in time is also displayed on the colour wheel by the icons distance from the centre of the screen." Craig touched the black centre of the screen where the image of the VAPER sat. "This here in the middle is the big bang, the start of everything and as far back in time as we can go. As we move out from the centre of the screen, we travel forwards in time until we reach the present day where the icon is displayed now. Carry on farther out towards the edge of the screen past this point, and we move into the future and who knows how far that goes."

"And those numbers that look like a proxy code. What are they?" Glen indicated the small line of numerals that had appeared beside the dot.

"That represents our actual universes address. BL- 18:41.38-02.05.2049-186.235.889.742.221.2049. I've forgotten what all the numbers mean, but the BL stands for the blue sector, then we have the exact time, date and the rest stand for different points in multi-dimensional space. There is more information to this address, but the code is so long we abbreviate it down to these basic essentials for the display. To find any point in space and time within the Multiverse, you first have to locate the particular universe you want, then tell the computer what point in space and time you are going to. That's the all-important key to this thing. It took the professor's years to realise that the computer, as powerful as it is, had no hope of finding a given point in space unless it considered the date in which the point is located first. As you well know, everything in the universe is moving. As your research helped us figure out, the universe itself is expanding like a balloon taking everything inside with it.

Galaxies are moving away from the centre of the universe and getting farther apart as they travel. The galaxies themselves rotate as they move, so the solar systems within them are never in the same place from moment to moment. Our solar system revolves around the galactic core taking our sun Sol with it. Finally, the Earth rotates around the sun, so nothing is idle, nothing is static. Nothing is ever in the same place it was before or will be again."

"Yeah, being an Astronomer I am vaguely familiar with a lot of those concepts," Glen said half sarcastically. "So, I guess that's where all my research went, into making a computer program that can track and predict the Earth's location at any point in time."

Craig smiled at this remark. "That's only part of it. Your work allowed us to create a computer that can predict the location of every known body in our universe. That's the only way this thing can find any point in space you want to travel to, in our case, it's a tiny area in the Milky Way galaxy. That's the primary reason why this research is done in space. That's the only way you can do time travel. All the old movies where people hop in a machine and transport themselves through time from their basements are entirely inaccurate.

Popular culture had trained us all to ignore our true location in the universe and take for granted that the Earth is always under us. We've seen people pop in and out of time on TV and the movies where they disappear from one point in time and appear in another in the exact physical place they left from. It's total bullshit. Those time travellers' physical locations would remain static, and they'd find themselves floating in space wondering what the hell happened to the Earth. Like all things in the Universe, the Earth doesn't stay still, and it's never in the same place twice. That's why moving through time and ignoring your location in space is an instant death sentence to anyone dumb enough to try it."

"Of course. The Earth travels at 35,000 kilometres a second, so the further you travel in time the more the Earth would have travelled along its orbital path. Even if you travelled back in time by just a few minutes that would be enough to place you outside the Earth's atmosphere and kill you instantly. Man, I'd never thought of that. Or just as bad, you could end up within the Earth itself rather than on its surface. Woah, imagine finding yourself embedded in rock one thousand feet underground." Glen sighed as he pondered the thought of effectively being instantly buried alive with no hope of rescue and nobody even having a clue where you were. "There must be so many pieces of data for the computers to calculate to get this right."

"True. You can't accurately predict the locations of so many bodies with so many unknown variables affecting them. Even with our Quantum computers and the rest of the technology we have stashed on the VAPER, we can't be that accurate. We rely on getting ourselves close enough to the Earth's location in whatever time we travel to, so we can then make our way to the spot we want on the surface using more traditional means. The Professors only learnt this when we sent out the first probes. It was a good thing that they didn't do it like the scientists in the movies and go *haha, it's finished* and then jump right in and try it out. That would have been the end of them. That's why the VAPER is essential as a life support system and space vehicle of sorts. The vehicle itself isn't necessary to travel through time, but it is essential to survive the process."

A small beeping sound issued from the *Feynman*'s control panel to alert the ship's occupants that the warm-up process had been completed. Craig turned in his seat and grabbed at the controls, ready to depart.

34
Departure

Outside the labs – ANZAR Wing, Newton Station.

6.51pm - Sunday, August 16th, 2048

"We've uploaded the scans of everyone on board for the reconstruction process, and the VAPER has acknowledged that it has one pilot and four passengers." Adam Fehrenbach's voice came from a small speaker in the armrest of Craig's chair.

"I'm looking at the VAPER's stats, and everything looks good. So..." Adam gave a nervous sigh. "We're ready at this end whenever you are."

Craig could see through a gap between his feet that rested on the 'rudder pedals' below the VAPER's control console. The open cockpit gave him a clear view of Karen and the kids who had positioned themselves in the nose section of the VAPER. The boys sat cross-legged with their foreheads pressed up against the wall, giggling as they watched their breaths fog up the diamond hull. Karen sat nearby hugging her knees to her chest and looked very uncomfortable. She nervously studied the interior of the ship while half watching the boys.

"Okay, mate. We're all good to go. You can open the outer doors when you're ready," Craig replied.

"Got it. Doors opening now."

"Wait," Glen called from behind Craig. "Are we going right now?" he asked as he looked around his seat. "Hang on a sec. I can't find my bloody seatbelt."

Craig gave a small chuckle and smiled. "Don't worry about it; there aren't any. The VAPER uses a new propulsion system that we designed. The engine talks to the artificial gravity system to dampen any inertia felt within the ship. We could perform aerobatic maneuvers in this thing, and all you would do is rock in your seat."

Glen nodded his head and looked around the cockpit, seemingly unsure. He suddenly found himself missing the comfort and reassurance of being strapped into his seat. A lifetime's routine of buckling up when travelling in cars and conventional aircraft had conditioned his subconscious to rely on the restraints. He fidgeted in his seat as he found himself longing to feel the restrictive pressure of a tension belt across his chest.

He was about to speak again when a loud crack echoed through the small ship. The fluorescent light strips placed within the station's hull were extinguished, plunging the VAPER into darkness. The boys excited chattering mixed with the sounds of clanking metal and a strong electrical hum as unseen motors began to equalise the air pressure between the VAPER and the station. Air and power lines disconnected from the outer hull with a metallic snap. The VAPER's own life support system cycled up to full power to compensate for the loss of external support.

Everything around them grew brighter as the small ship was filled with the soft blue glow of reflected Earthlight. Below the VAPER, the outer hull of the research wing of Newton Station slowly slid aside to reveal the curve of the Earth. Everyone froze in place and stared at the sight of their homeworld that dominated the view. Small rainbows danced through the air, sparkling across every surface as the diamond hull of the VAPER refracted the Earth-light. It was a surreal scene that filled Craig with conflicting senses of fear and beauty. He took a moment to admire the view of the planet he hoped to save. The sight of the scarred and burning Earth below filled him with a determination to do everything he could to set things right. After all, he knew that he and everyone else on Newton who was involved in the Conduit research were indirectly responsible for this mess. If they had any chance of living out the rest of their lives beyond the next few months, he would have to find a way to repair the damage to the Earth's orbit. He'd have to find those that had pushed the human race onto the fast path to extinction and compel them to reverse the process. He was sure that the

Professors had gone somewhere in one of the six Conduit transfers they had performed and had attracted the attention of whoever - or whatever - was in those spheres. It was all the information he had. It was the only place to start.

With the turn of a handle beside his seat, Craig disconnected the VAPER from the underbelly of the station. There was no sense of movement, the only indication that anything had happened was the view outside the cockpit shifted slightly, and the bottom of the station seemed a few inches further away.

"Okay, here we go," Craig sighed as he pushed the throttle forward and aimed the VAPER's nose down. The curvature of the Earth rose above them as they silently floated down to meet the rising planet.

"I'm going to have to circle around the station so I can get us to the Conduit transit point," Craig said for the benefit of those listening in on the station. "I can't see any point in us hiding this thing any longer, so I'm going to take the direct route to save time. The quicker we get out of here, the sooner you guys can make your way to the airline terminal and get a plane out."

"Alright, Craig," Adam Fehrenbach replied. "Thanks to Luke, there's no great rush. We want to make sure you all get away safely. That's the priority right now, got it?"

Craig admired his friend for his loyalty and selflessness. It was a testament to his father's management skills that the staff had stayed on to help rather than run when things had turned bad.

"Copy that. There's not much anyone can do to us in this thing anyway." Craig looked up at the slowly retreating underside of the station as he spoke, he carefully got the VAPER clear of the steel and aluminium hull and came to a halt thirty feet below the outside of the ANZAR wing.

"Okay, boys and girls," he said to everyone within earshot, both on board the VAPER and with the ANZAR control room. "It's time to scare the shit out of some tourists."

With that, Craig fed power to the engines and pulled back on the control column, a deep hum issued from within the VAPER as the ship lurched forward with only a minimal sense of motion. The Earth below became a blur and disappeared behind them as they performed a high-speed loop around the tubular shape of the ANZAR wing.

35
The monitor

Engineering Bay – ANZAR Wing, Newton Station.

6.51pm · Sunday, August 16th, 2048

Luke sat at the control console in the now empty engineering lab wondering what to do next. There weren't too many options open to him at this point; he could either stay and wait to be arrested by the mass of soldiers that would eventually come, or he could head down to the control room and make himself useful until the same thing happened. Either way, the result would be the same, his life as he knew it was over no matter what he did.

Luke sat silently and stared at each of the security monitors in turn. Scenes from both inside the ANZAR wing and the outside of the station cycled through on the screens in front of him. Even with most of the staff gone, the Nerve kept its constant vigil on the empty halls and labs. All was still. Everything looked empty. Only three screens showed any signs of a human presence; he could see himself in one, viewed from behind as he sat motionlessly in the engineering bay. The second showed the medical bay next door where Doctor Anderson was busily getting his father ready for their escape through the maintenance tunnel. As Luke watched, the Doctor taped up wires and cords as the Professor lay unconscious in the only occupied hospital bed. In contrast, the third scene was a bustle of activity as those in the control room went about the business of preparing the Conduit for Craig's first wormhole transit. He knew he probably should be up there helping them. They were short staffed as it was.

Luke looked at the screens and thought; *I'll go up in a few more minutes. I'll just sit here for five more minutes. I need some time to think.*

246

The monitor on the top right of the bank of screens kept drawing his eye with the image of his father. Luke stared at the tubes, wires and life support machines that forced his father's lungs to keep breathing and his heart to continue beating. Luke was having a hard time coming to grips with the idea that his dad was probably lost to him forever. He struggled to make an emotional connection between the image of the man who lay dying on the hospital bed and the memories he held of his father. He knew it was the same man, but a part of him refused to accept that inside that human shell was the person who had loved and raised him his entire life. Fathers shouldn't leave their sons; they were supposed to stay with them forever. They were meant to be a constant source of love and support, guidance and advice. Luke needed his dad to be with him. He was all he had left. He had already lost his mother. If he lost him as well, he'd be utterly alone.

Luke touched a hand to the image on the screen, as much to make contact with his father as it was to hide his image from view. Although he could see his body and could still be near him physically, he would probably never get to talk with his dad again. The eminent Professor Brian Weekes was lost to him. Even though the old man's body was in the next room, he may as well have been cremated already for all the good Luke could see the machines doing. Luke was reluctant to go to the medical bay to be with him. That would make the situation all too real. At least like this, he could watch over his father with a certain level of detachment. It allowed a small measure of deniability. But Luke knew he wasn't responding to treatment. He felt he wasn't coming back.

Movement on another monitor pulled Luke's eyes away from the motionless form of his father. He moved his eyes to the screen below to see Adam Fehrenbach's team in the main control room. They were busily moving from console to console to get the Conduit's main system up and running with the skeleton crew they had onboard. The VAPER had launched just minutes before and was probably waiting nearby for the Conduits systems to be brought online. He once again debated whether to go up to the control room to help the others. He knew he was wasting time here, doing nothing, waiting for something to happen. He had brought the rest of his people more time with his unappreciated actions against the military, but now he was squandering that time. With the decision to act finally made, Luke rose to his feet and gave his father one last glance as he prepared to leave the room.

No change. Still motionless.

All of a sudden, another movement caught his eye. Not from his father, but from the screen directly beside his.

There were people outside!

They were only small on the screen, but he could clearly see four men in white pressure suits slowly making their way along the service ladder on the outside of the station. Part of him hoped that the Newton Control Sector had already sent a maintenance team out to inspect the damage he'd caused further along the ANZAR wing, but he somehow suspected that they wouldn't have reacted this fast. Luke grabbed at the controls and moved the camera to find out exactly where on the outside of the station the men were located. As the view on the screen widened, the plumes of frozen gas and air that still slowly leaked from the damaged section of the accommodation wing came into view behind the small white figures. As he suspected, they were heading away from the damaged area of the station. They were slowly making their way towards the far end of the ANZAR wing in which the labs were located.

Well, that settles that, Luke thought.

He knew they were not service engineers out on their routine patrol. The maintenance crews had already travelled the length of the station on their weekly inspection for micrometeorite damage; they had already checked all of the station's seals and connection points. As Luke watched their movements, he became confident of who they were. The real engineers were adept at the art of spacewalking. Their movements were graceful, efficient and clean. The exact opposite of what he was seeing from the group on the service ladder now. Their actions were slow and jerky, they lurched from rung to rung, their body language revealing the fear of the inept.

As the last man made it to the top of the station and they began to move forward, Luke noticed one small detail that confirmed his suspicions. All four men had large rifles slung over their shoulders. It was definitely the military.

Luke was impressed with their persistence; he'd figured that the rest of the troops would have pulled back after what he had put them through, but no such luck.

Luke sat back down in front of the control panel and prepared to go back to work. He'd reduced their number from twenty to four. He hoped these last few would be as easy to kill as the rest.

36
Sighting

Outside the station – ANZAR Wing, Newton Station.

6.53pm - Sunday, August 16th, 2048

The surviving members of C-Unit slowly inched their way along the outside of the station in single file. Their weightless bodies floated a foot above the external hull of the ANZAR wing as they used their arms to pull themselves along the ladder one rung at a time. Sergeant Jackson took the lead with Tony 'Scarface' Wilkes following closely behind. From his position just behind Scarface's feet, Ferine could see the shoulders and arms of the other man's suit rhythmically compress and expand as Scarface worked his muscles against the resistance of the fabric in his tight-fitting suit.

This is hard work, Ferine thought.

Claustrophobia and the exertion of pulling himself along the horizontal service ladder caused Ferine's body temperature to rise; the inside of his spacesuit soon became unbearably hot. One of the misconceptions about being weightless was the expectation that all movement in zero gravity would be effortless. As Ferine was finding out the hard way, that wasn't the case. Although a person no longer had a sense of weight, they still possessed their physical mass. It took as much energy to get that mass moving in zero gravity as it did on Earth. The muscles still had to work.

Sweat dripped down Ferine's forehead into his eyes, blurring his vision. Making his discomfort worse, Ferine's body sweated while his face felt irritatingly cold. A small air- conditioning vent in his helmet continually blew frigid air across his face in a failed attempt to keep him cool; its only effect was to chill the sweat on his face, making it itch. Occasionally, he would raise a hand to his face to scratch the itch or wipe away sweat, only to have it bump into the plastic of his visor. With no way to ease his discomfort, Ferine had no choice but to press on. He never imagined that this could be so hard or tiring, he felt hot, uncomfortable and scared.

All he could do was concentrate on getting to the airlock by pulling himself along using only his hands as his legs floated uselessly behind him. The service ladder ran the length of the ANZAR wing from the central sphere of the station to the tip of the cylindrical research wing. It was designed as a means for engineers and repair crews to move around the outside of the station in safety as they went about their work of inspecting the hull and replacing components when necessary. Each of the individual wings on Newton had at least three of them. Ferine felt glad that he had paid attention during the mission briefing that had mentioned them as a means to move through the station as a last resort. He never dreamed he would be in the position to utilise them though.

A rising sense of panic began to eat away at his self-confidence as he began to doubt his decision to continue their advance on the ANZAR labs by moving along the outside of the station. At the time, he had thought it was a good idea. Now, he wasn't so sure. Part of him acknowledged that he probably should have pulled C-Unit back and waited for reinforcements to arrive, he should have allowed his men time to recover. That would have been the sensible thing to do. The doubt continued to dominate his thoughts, to cause him to lose concentration. The more he thought about it, the more his sense of panic grew. He knew that if it got control of him, it would most likely result in his death.

You're just climbing a ladder in a zero-G exercise, that's all, he told himself. *It's just a test. Just move one hand in front of the other, and everything will be alright.*

Keeping his eyes facing forward, Ferine ran through the routine that he and his men had been undertaking for the last seventeen minutes.

Reach out with the left hand and grab a rung. Pull the safety line forward with the right hand, and move forward. Now reach out with the right hand and grab the next rung, pull the safety line with the left.

Good, keep focused, he thought. Just don't look to the right and you'll be okay.

A boot hit him in the helmet as he dragged himself forward in the weightless environment. The impact pushed his head to the right and startled him enough to cause his heart to skip a beat.

As he gripped onto the ladder with both hands, Ferine realised he could feel the station vibrate through his heavy gloves. The other members of C-Unit felt it too. The four men paused as the vibration increased.

Fuck! This is turning out to be one bitch of a day.

From below the ANZAR wing, a large crystalline object suddenly rose into view beside them. The large, arrowhead-shaped object slowly curved around the outside of the station. As it drew nearer, the frequency of the vibrations Ferine could feel through his spacesuit grew faster and stronger. As it made no sound in the vacuum of space, the object's sudden appearance had caught Ferine by surprise. The shock of seeing such a large - and alien looking - object moving in his direction caused him to jump involuntarily. His sweat soaked hands slipped inside his gloves, and his body twisted, causing him to fall free of the ladder. He tried to grab for the nearest rung as his feet swung over the side of the station, but it was too late, he was out of reach. Just as he thought he had somehow come loose and was going to begin the long freefall back down to the Earth, Ferine felt a sharp tug at his waist as his safety line drew taught and swung him against the roof of the station. The Earth arced above his head as his body twisted on the end of the thin line.

Thank Christ I've stopped, was the only thought he had time to register before panic seized him again. The momentum of his downward fall had turned into a sideways motion by the interference of his safety line. Stars pin-wheeled past his visor as he slid along the side of the station, the scene was soon replaced with the sight of an air-conditioning pipe as it rose up and slammed into his faceplate.

He finally came to rest.

"What the fuck is that?" the tinny voice of one of his team echoed within his helmet.

"Cap! What do we do?" another called.

Uninjured, but still scared witless. Ferine grabbed the edge of an air vent to steady himself and looked up at the thing that had caused him to fall. He had never seen anything like it in his life. He stared at the shape of the thing. It reminded him of a giant pumpkin seed, only transparent.

Well, that's different, he thought.

Familiar objects and shapes informed him of what he was looking at. He could see wires, cables, computer components and other machine parts beneath a glass-like hull.

It was a machine. A spaceship.

And a human-made one, by the looks of it.

As he stared at the vehicle, he realised he could see movement inside. Through the sweat that ran into his eyes, Ferine could make out the shapes of what looked like a couple of men and a woman. Ferine shook his head to clear his vision, causing tiny drops of sweat to fly off his face and stick to the inside of his helmet.

With his vision cleared, Ferine took another look at the strange ship that hovered above his head. As the craft slowly turned above him, the smiling faces of two immensely proportioned children came into view. At first glance, they looked like they were a couple of four or five-year-old boys, as the ship continued its turn, Ferine could see that something about them wasn't quite right.

They were massive, almost giants.

37
Space Men

Onboard the *Feynman* – ANZAR Wing, Newton Station.

6.53pm - Sunday, August 16th, 2048

Craig looked down at the four armed men on the service ladder. Despite the pressure suits they wore, he still recognised them for who they were. He wasn't too surprised to see that they were still trying to gain access to the ANZAR labs, even after the losses they had suffered.

They hadn't given up. He admired them for that.

Even so, he considered - just for a moment – doing something to stop them from reaching the labs. He could almost understand how Luke had brought himself to attack these men to protect the people he loved. Seeing them in the flesh and armed with intent, tempted him to join the fight.

But, no, Craig thought. *I won't go down that path.*

Craig was close enough to the soldiers to make eye contact. He could see the faces of the men that Luke had tried to kill. They were human. They were just doing their job. The sight of seeing one of them hanging helplessly from the side of the station reinforced the notion that to attack them would be wrong. He was determined not to become the bad guy in this scenario, whatever the world may already think.

Inside the VAPER, the voices of Timothy and Jamie could be heard as they called out in excitement at seeing the troops on the station. Being children, they didn't see them for what they truly were. They saw something more innocent.

"Spacemen, spacemen," they called out. "Mummy, daddy! We can see spacemen outside."

"That's nice baby," Karen said in response. Her tone showed that she did not share the excitement of seeing the spacemen that the boys did.

"Shit man," Glen said from the seat behind Craig. "Those dudes are armed!"

"Yeah, you noticed huh?"

"I don't suppose they can do us any damage if they decided to get trigger happy, Can they?" He turned towards Craig with a look of concern on his face.

"I doubt it, but I'm not going to wait around to find out." With that, Craig made a few adjustments to the controls, and they slowly began to move forward once more.

"Okay kids!" he called. "Say goodbye to the spacemen. We're leaving."

Ferine watched as the spacecraft began to move away. The two children he could see huddled inside the ship smiled and waved as it pulled away.

"Hey Cap. It looks like we've located what we were looking for. If I didn't know any better, I'd say that's probably one of the things people reported seeing before the Blackout," Sergeant Jackson called. "That thing pretty much proves their guilt. They've got ANZAR personnel on that thing." Sergeant Jackson pointed at the ship as he awkwardly turned to face Ferine. "The guy at the controls looked like Turp Junior to me."

Ferine hit a switch on the side of his helmet and changed radio frequencies so he could issue orders to their military transport on the other side of the station.

"Walters. You read? Over," Ferine called.

"Roger that, Sir," a voice in a thick American accent replied. "You have a bogey coming your way in about two minutes.

Get Ollafson to prep the *Penetrator* for an intercept," Ferine called. "And be quick about it."

"Copy that, Sir. What's our bogey's make?"

"Don't know," Ferine answered. "Unknown make. Unknown construction. But you'll know it when you see it. It looks like it's made of glass or something."

A momentary silence filled Ferine's helmet as the troops on the transport carried out his orders. Ferine watched the ANZAR spacecraft as it disappeared over the top of the main station.

"Sir, The *Penetrator* is being prepped now. What are our orders on this one?"

Ferine thought about it for a moment. The boys in Washington wanted him to arrest all ANZAR staff and capture as much of their technology as possible. He had just seen two objects on their most wanted list fly right by him. They had to be taken in one piece.

"Disable only. The object is a listed item. Only destroy if it becomes absolutely necessary to prevent its escape."

"Roger that. Disable only."

"Now get on the horn and notify HQ that they have possible incoming. I want somebody down there waiting for them in case they try and make a run for the surface."

"Got it. We'll keep you informed of the situation, Cap."

Ferine switched his com-link back to the local channel and addressed his men.

"Alright guys, the *Penetrator* will deal with that thing. We need to keep moving so we can get our job done. Scarface, get your arse over here and give us a hand, will you?"

A tugging sensation on Ferine's oxygen pack got him moving again, this time backwards. He slowly retreated from the edge of the station and the dizzying fall back to Earth that he was momentarily convinced would kill him.

"You alright Cap?" Scarface asked. "We felt the ladder vibrate then we looked around, and all I could see was your fucking legs poking up in the air."

Ferine could see the big man's face through his helmet as they both began to laugh.

"Yeah... yeah. That must have been a hell of a shock for you guys," Ferine joined in.

"Not as big as the one you got I bet." Sergeant Jackson was beginning to laugh as well. The tension of the incident was starting to drain away.

Good, Ferine thought. *Keep it up. I need this right now.*

"I think I'm gonna have to hose this suit out once we get back inside," Ferine laughed even harder. "I shit myself so much, I almost jet-propelled myself off the side of the station."

All four men fell into a fit of hysterics that lasted for no more than a minute. In the emptiness of space, they knew no one could hear them, so they laughed freely.

Once they had calmed down, Ferine spoke once again. "Alright guys, we better keep moving. I want to get the hell out of this suit ASAP. It smells like a Baghdad outhouse in here."

With one last chortle, the men rolled back onto their stomachs and continued to pull themselves along the ladder. Ferine's hands shook as he reached out to grab the first rung. The moment of levity had helped him regain his composure, but he was still less than confident about continuing along the ladder.

38
Game On

Onboard Imperial transport Jet – Docked at Newton Station.

6.58pm - Sunday, August 16th, 2048

Lieutenant Ollafson sat hunched over a keyboard in the dimly lit cargo hold of the Imperial military transport. A collection of monitors, not unlike the ones Luke sat in front of, filled the wall before him. Unlike Luke, Ollafson's choice of views was restricted to just six different angles of the same scene. He could look at the space in front, behind, above, below or to the sides of the *Penetrator* as it prepared to leave the launching pod.

What had begun life as a fighter-mounted M65 aircraft gun capable of firing 20mm shells at a rate of 6000 rounds per minute, had been transformed into a mobile, stand-alone weapon. The gun, now fitted with no fewer than 16 rocket engines, could be controlled remotely from hundreds of kilometres away. It was capable of speeds over Mach 3 in a vacuum and was highly maneuverable. The enemies of the Old United States had learned to fear these weapons in the early days of the Empire.

Ollafson sat forward at the controls as he moved an oversized joystick in his right hand from side to side. With his left, he pushed the throttle forward to give the *Penetrator* just enough speed to get it moving. The rocket engines on the craft moved the remote-controlled Gatling gun forward slowly as it slid itself out of the launch pod. Ollafson could feel the vibration of the engines through his chair as the thrust pushed against the transport's hull. His excitement grew as he began to maneuver the weapon away from the ship and towards the bulging centre of Newton Station. The stars on the screens before him spun out of view as the *Penetrator* made a ninety-degree turn. With another touch of the throttle, it began to move forwards once more.

This time, much faster.

After years of ongoing training, he was pretty chuffed about getting to be the first in his unit to use the *Penetrator* against this new enemy of the Empire. For the thousandth time in almost thirty years, this space-born relic of the Helium-3 wars was about to be put into use against a foreign force. The fact that they were unarmed civilians did nothing to curb Ollafson's enthusiasm. After all, he enjoyed his work. He had always loved playing video games as a kid and had found himself amazed at the fact that as an adult, he was being paid by the military to do just that. Usually, Ollafson was in control of ground-based combat drones known as Decimators. What were essentially remote-controlled tanks with a top-mounted turret containing more than a dozen computer-controlled machine guns, Decimators were frontline attack weapons that were sent into enemy territory programmed to kill anything that resembled a human being. Ollafson loved them for their simplicity and their ability to completely sanitise large areas in a short amount of time. Where the Decimator was an armoured, brute-force weapon that saturated the enemy with insane amounts of firepower, the *Penetrator* was a more elegant, but no less subtle, spaceborne alternative that required a great deal more patience and skill to operate.

Ollafson's mind was perfect for the role; it seemed incapable of connecting what he was doing with the violent reality of his actions. He didn't make the connection between the characters that fell dead on his screen and the bodies that filled the morgues later on. To him, they were two different things. His world existed solely on the screen in front of him where he was free to chase down and destroy the bad guys. The other world, the real world, the world of human emotion and consequence that he glimpsed only occasionally, was not his concern. To Ollafson it was someone else's problem, so he let someone else worry about it.

The stars on his screen twisted and blurred as he piloted the *Penetrator* through the protruding arms of Newton Station in search of his target. On one screen, the Earth spun around the edge of the display and disappeared from view as he curved the weapon towards the opposite side of the station.

A small glass like shape came into view, an easy target as it flashed and glowed in the unfiltered light of the sun. The object was still far off, but Ollafson recognised the distinct teardrop shape of the target as it had been described to him.

With the grin of a child that is about to play with his favourite toy, Ollafson aimed the barrels of the *Penetrator* at the *Feynman* and pushed the throttle forward as far as it would go. The scene in front of him jumped forward in a blur of stars as he took aim and prepared to fire.

39
Ghost in the Machine

Engineering Bay – ANZAR Wing, Newton Station.

6.58pm - Sunday, August 16th, 2048

Luke had listened to the men as they laughed on the outside of the station, unaware that they had only minutes left to live. They sounded almost human as they joked among themselves, a slight, fleeting pang of regret overcame Luke as he thought about what he must do to them, but it only lasted a moment. He wished Craig had used the opportunity that had just presented itself to use the VAPER as a battering ram and shove a few of them off the side of the station. Unlike the other ANZAR staff, he knew that they were in a situation where it was either kill or be killed. Apparently, Craig didn't get that. Luke had no misconceptions that these men would kill every last one of them if it meant getting what they had come for. It didn't mean he would enjoy what he was about to do, but in his eyes, it excused it.

Luke's hopes rose that he would have one less man to deal with when one of the troops had slipped and practically fallen off the outside of the station. He was disappointed to see the man's inevitable tumble into space halted by a safety line.

He thought about his options and knew that he'd have to act as soon as the group reached the next connection point on the safety ladder. They were now less than ten metres from the entrance to the nearest of the engineering bay's airlocks. They were just ten metres away from gaining access to the room in which Luke now occupied.

Just ahead of the troops, the last connection point on the station came into view on the monitors. Luke could see where the safety lines branched off in three separate directions to curve around the ANZAR wing and meet up on the opposite side. At this point, they would have to temporarily disconnect their safety lines to reconnect them to whichever of the three paths they decided to take. This was where Luke would mount his next assault. It was the best and last chance he would get.

The area was littered with small exhaust vents that regularly purged the station of waste gases. A mixture of carbon dioxide, steam and methane from the sanitation system was released in controlled high-pressure bursts. The ingenious system doubled as a means of waste removal as well as being a computer-controlled system to make minor adjustments to the station's orbital angle.

All he would have to do is wait a few moments more for the men to be in the right position. As they disconnected their safety lines, he would trigger the exhaust vents to fire and push the men off the station.

Simple, easy, no mess, no fuss.

The first soldier was approaching the connection point.

Luke's hands floated over the keyboard as we waited for the right moment. His breathing began to match that of the soldier's he could hear through his headset.

Just a little further, he thought. *C'mon, almost there.*

He was lowering his finger towards the button when a voice spoke through his headset.

"I'd rather you didn't do that, Luke."

For a moment, Luke thought that the soldiers outside had found out who he was and what he was planning. He was about to push the button anyway when the owner of the voice spoke again.

"I need you to trust me on this one, boy. You did the right thing by removing the rest of those so-called soldiers, but we need these last few to get into the station. Those four soldiers are very important men who have a key part to play in all of this." The voice paused for a moment as if thinking. With a deep sigh, it continued. "As much as I hate the idea, they need to be given access to the labs. They are important to everybody's survival and mustn't be harmed."

Luke couldn't believe what he was hearing. It must be some kind of a joke and a damn cruel one at that. He looked at the monitor on the uppermost right. His father was still unconscious. The machines were still keeping him alive. He wasn't moving.

Then how did I just hear him talking to me?

"Dad?" he whispered cautiously. "Is that you?"

A momentary pause ensued in which Luke began to think that maybe he had imagined the whole thing. *Perhaps the stress of losing my father and being forced to kill had...*

"Of course it's me, you dolt. Surely you recognise your own father's voice. Who else would it be?" Professor Weekes admonished him.

"Whoever this is, it's not funny!" Luke's voice echoed around the empty engineering bay as he yelled at the imposter. "You picked the wrong person to mess with Pal. If you were going to try and trick me, you should have done a better job at keeping up with current events." He paused for a moment before continuing. "My father's dead. I'm looking at his body as we speak... you can't be him."

"Oh, I'm not dead, Lukey. I just seemed to have misplaced my body." The Professor's voice took on a mournful tone as he spoke. "I'm lost, Lukey and I don't know how to get back."

Hearing what sounded like his father's voice call him by his childhood nickname caused Luke to pause, to start to believe. He wished desperately that it was his father but couldn't shake the suspicion, the *logical* doubt, that it was more likely that the voice was only one of the American's trying to distract his attention while the rest of the troops snuck aboard the station. He looked up at the monitors to see that the first of the space-suited soldiers was beginning to disconnect his safety line from the service ladder. He only had a few seconds to figure out what was going on before this opportunity was lost. He turned back to the image of his hospitalised father and asked a question.

"Okay then, Dad," he said sarcastically. "What were you last working on before you went away?"

"A test hey? Very well Luke, but make it quick, we're short on time," the Professor replied. "The last thing I worked on before I left with John Turp was the menu system for the ModChips."

Luke's headphones fell silent for a moment. "That seems like years ago now. In a strange way, it was." The voice laughed. "I do miss you so much, boy. It's been almost a year since I saw you last, from what I can see, you haven't changed a bit."

"Well, that proves you're a fake!" Luke bellowed. "My father only went missing thirteen days ago. You can't be him." Luke stood up and paced backwards and forwards behind his chair. Part of him satisfied that he had not been fooled by this deception, the other half of him heartbroken that it really wasn't his father.

"Sit down, my boy. Sit down and stop pacing. You're going to get yourself angry again. I can see that scar you got from the cricket bat on your forehead is already starting to turn red." Luke stopped and turned back towards the bank of monitors.

"You can see me?" he asked. "How...how do you know how I got my scar? It's barely visible."

"Unless you get angry." Luke could almost see his father smile as he said that. "As for how I can see you, well, I can see everything at the moment. It's like I have a thousand eyes and can see everywhere on the station all at once. I think I've somehow found my way into the station's computer system. Through the Nerve surveillance system, I can see and hear everything happening within the ANZAR wing, which at the moment doesn't appear to be very much."

"How did you end up in there?"

"I don't know really. I just found myself in here. All I can assume is that it seems as if I have become detached from my body somehow. Most likely in the last transit I made, the one in which I returned to the station. It's my fault. Do you remember how I asked you to slow down the cellular reconstruction phase of my return trip, so we could film the human body being reconstructed?"

"Yes, well...how did you know that?"

The speaker ignored the question and kept talking.

"Well, it seems like I may have made a mistake in doing that. You see, we didn't allow enough time for the brain and the nervous system to reform before my consciousness came through. I can remember floating inside the VAPER looking down at my body. As I watched my viscera snake its way through my abdomen, I thought, *this isn't quite right.* My mind passed through the Conduit's wormhole before my body was ready to receive it."

"Shit," Luke sighed. "We didn't think of that. We just assumed the entire process would slow down as a whole. We had no idea that altering the rate of reconstruction would throw the process out of sync."

"True. True. But like I said Lukey, I only have myself to blame. But now, we have other things to talk about. Firstly, I need you to let in the men who are floating outside the airlock door."

Luke looked to his left and saw four helmeted faces staring at him through the window of the outer airlock door. He had forgotten about the troops while he had been speaking to his father.

My father, Luke thought. *Dad's back.*

He consciously believed that the voice in the machine was his father. On a deeper level, he had believed it was him since the moment he had heard the voice. The conscious mind can be stubborn sometimes.

As any child would, Luke trusted that his father knew best.

He smiled as he stood up and walked across the room to open the airlock door, eager to make his father happy. Luke knew that his father loved him and wouldn't ask him to do anything that would put him in harm's way. From the way the professor had spoken, it sounded as if he were privy to information that filled Luke with confidence that he would not be harmed.

The four men outside watched him closely as he reached out and pushed the button to open the door.

40

The *Penetrator*

Onboard the *Feynman* – Low Earth Orbit.

7.03pm - Sunday, August 16th, 2048

Craig spotted the other craft the moment it rose into view over the top of the station. He could tell from the straight line it was cutting towards the *Feynman* that whatever the thing was, it was here for them. As it drew nearer, he could see it was relatively small and cylindrical with long steel-like rods that ran the length of its hull. As Craig watched, bright orange sparks of light appeared to flicker from its nose. At first, he thought this was a non-verbal attempt at communication, but he quickly changed his mind when he recognised the bright muzzle flashes for what they were.

"Hold on!" he called out to everyone on board. "We're being fired upon by some..."

His words were cut off by the deafening sound of red-hot bullets coming into contact with the *Feynman*'s shields. Blue flashes of light flowed across the surface of the ship in a rippling effect similar to that of rain on water. Sharp metallic cracks echoed throughout the ship as a few of the projectiles penetrated the shields and made contact with the diamond hull in a rapid barrage that rattled the skulls of everyone on board. Below, the children and Karen screamed in fright at this aural assault.

The concentration of firepower temporarily blocked Craig's view through the cockpit canopy. The usually invisible shield seemed to froth and bubble as it struggled to keep the incoming projectiles from striking the VAPER's hull. Flying blind, he turned the *Feynman* sharply to the right to avoid colliding with the station which was now hidden from view. The impacts from the *Penetrator*'s guns moved across the outside of the ship as he turned. The section of shield nearest the front of the cockpit once again turned transparent, clearing his vision. Although extremely strong, the synthetic diamond hull was not indestructible. To his left, a spattering of starburst cracks appeared in the hull as a few rounds of ammunition struck the edge of the canopy. Craig stared at the web-shaped fractures with concern and prayed that the VAPER would not shatter like a poorly cut diamond. The *Feynman* set about repairing the damage, and he breathed a sigh of relief as he watched the cracks fade from view.

"Oh, this is bullshit," Glen shouted from behind Craig. "Shoot back at him! Go on, blast the prick!"

"I can't. We don't have any weapons. This is a research vessel, not the *Millennium Falcon*," Craig grunted as he worked the controls in an attempt to maneuver the VAPER away from the *Penetrator*'s gun.

"You know, I'm not against the idea of running from a fight," Glen replied in a state of near panic. He had pulled himself low into his seat. His chin pressed against his chest as he tried to make himself as small a target as possible. "Feel free to fuck off to somewhere else if you think that will help."

"That's what I'm trying to do."

Craig pulled back on the control stick as he pushed down on the rudder pedals, putting the VAPER into a steep spinning climb. Outside the cockpit, everything began to blur as Newton station, and the Earth started to spin around the quickly rising VAPER. Stars streaked around them as they rose far above the orbital plane of the space station and dove deeper into space.

Despite the fact that the physical forces associated with the spinning were dampened, Glen felt his stomach begin to turn, and his head grow lighter as a wave of nausea crept over him. With the view of the spinning stars contradicting the milder forces that his body could feel, his brain began to become confused about which piece of information was accurate. Sensing what was going on, Glen closed his eyes to block out the nauseating view. As his stomach settled and his head cleared, he became aware of his butt slowly sliding across the base of the seat as the ship's muted G-forces gently tugged him to the right.

With his eyes closed, he found the sensation comparable to that of riding on a playground carousel moving at a sedate pace.

The reduced sensations of physical motion within the *Feynman* demonstrated how well the motion dampeners were working. The fact that the occupants of the VAPER were still alive was a testament to their effectiveness. Although the movement of the ship was still detectable, the motion dampeners were designed to reduce the possibly fatal effects of high speed, high G-force maneuvers. Without it, everyone inside the VAPER would have been pressed against the inside of the vehicle as it accelerated, their bodies would have been crushed to a pulp.

Temporarily clear of the *Penetrator*, the *Feynman* soared over the top of Newton station at a rapid speed as Craig attempted to make his way back towards the Earth. In the cargo area below, he could hear the boys sobbing as they struggled to get over the scare that the noise and motion had given them.

"Karen!" Craig called out without looking away from the controls in front of him. "Are you guys okay down there?"

"Could be better, but yeah, we're alright," she replied. "What was that thing?"

Craig looked at a small monitor on his control panel that showed what was behind the ship. In the distance, he could make out the silhouette of the *Penetrator* as it climbed above Newton to continue its pursuit.

"I'd say it's an old Helium-3 space gun by the look of it," Craig answered. "*Penetrators*, I think they were called."

"Sounds suggestive," Glen replied as he looked over his shoulder and squinted to see the craft behind them.

"It is. The Empire used them to penetrate the hulls of Helium-3 mining spacecraft from rival countries, hence the name. They used to fly them up alongside the mining transports, fire a few thousand rounds into it and watch as the hull opened up and sucked many of the crew into space. Those that managed to survive the rapid decompression were forced to abandon ship. The Americans would then dock alongside, weld a steel plate over the hull and hey presto, a new mining transport fully loaded

268

with Helium-3 was theirs. That nasty piece of equipment is one of the reasons they became the Empire they are now."

To know that the Empire was still using *Penetrators* made Craig furious. He was surprised and appalled at the lengths that the Empire was employing to steal their research. He had always known that his father's and Professor Weekes' work would eventually attract global attention, but he had never imagined himself in a scenario where people would be willing to kill him for it.

"Just to play it safe, I'm going to take us into the debris field where that thing can't follow us."

"Uhm, mate," Glen muttered from the back seat. "I hate to tell you this but going into the debris field isn't exactly a good idea. More than a few spacecraft have been destroyed in there. There's no way you can hope to navigate it."

"Trust me. With the shields and this diamond hull..." Craig tapped the canopy above him. "...we're practically indestructible. We'll pass straight through and out the other side."

Craig banked the VAPER to the right and lunged towards the Earth. He glanced at the monitors and saw that the *Penetrator* was still accelerating towards them. As confident as he was in the *Feynman*'s ability to deflect and repair damage, he didn't intend to let the *Penetrator* catch up. It was an immoral weapon from an insane age. He wanted to get as far away from it as possible.

41
Payback

Engineering Bay – ANZAR Wing, Newton Station.

7.03 - Sunday, August 16th, 2048

"Alright. Stand the fuck back!" Scarface screamed at Luke as the airlock door slid open.

The four surviving soldiers stepped into the hangar bay as soon as the opening was wide enough for them to squeeze through. They moved into the room at a fast walk and quickly divided into pairs. Two men headed straight for Luke while the others ran deeper into the engineering bay in what proved to be a futile search.

With two armed soldiers approaching him with their rifles aimed at his chest, Luke did the only sensible thing and raised his hands in surrender. He could see the faces of Jackson and Ferine as they cautiously moved closer, neither man looked pleased.

"Step away from the console!" Jackson said forcefully, his rifle jerked to the right to indicate the direction he wanted Luke to move.

Luke obligingly took a few careful steps to his left, distancing himself from the computer where he had been speaking to his father just a few moments before.

"Clear!" Scarface called form the other side of the room. "Clear!" Dockrill echoed.

"Where's everyone else?" Ferine asked. His voice was audible but muffled within the helmet of the space suit that he was itching to remove.

"Gone," Luke replied calmly. "Everybody left the moment they heard you guys were on the way."

"Bullshit!" Ferine barked as he spun his rifle around and slammed the butt of the weapon into Luke's forehead.

The younger man's head and shoulders flew back from the force of the blow. He took a few shuffling steps backwards and somehow managed to stay on his feet.

"I'll ask you again. Where are the rest of the ANZAR staff?"

Luke rubbed at his forehead for a moment and turned back towards Ferine with a look of defiance.

Despite Luke being unarmed and outnumbered four to one, what Ferine saw in this kid's eyes made him feel nervous.

"And I'll tell you again," Luke paused. "They're gone!" he snarled.

"Then if that's the case, you must be the one who attacked us on our way in."

Luke stared at the man and said nothing.

Ferine was suddenly sure that this was the person who was responsible for the attack on his troops. There was a look in the boy's eyes that he had seen many times before and had come to recognise as the gaze of the psychotic. The eyes told him that he and the other three surviving members of his team had been lucky to escape. He could see the anger and hate written all over this guy's face, and he knew that he would gladly kill Ferine right now if he could. Even though the kid knew that he was surrounded, even if making a move would mean his death, Ferine believed he might give it a go anyway.

Ferine would have to decide very quickly what to do with this one.

"Everyone, get changed," Ferine said to the others without breaking eye contact with Luke. "I'll keep this one covered while you get out of your E.V.A. suits."

Ferine and Luke stared at each other. Both wondered what the other was thinking, what the other's intentions were.

Around them, the other three troops began to pull themselves from their space suits, all the while keeping a close eye on the other two men in the room.

Luke and Ferine remained frozen in place for minutes as they stared into each other's eyes, squinting through the windows to their souls, looking for insights into what they should do next.

Ferine was trying to decide if he should kill Luke now and remove the potential threat the kid represented. It would save him a lot of time, but he would probably get hell for it later. Still, it would make him feel better, and he'd probably be doing the kid a favour in the long run.

Luke had already made his decision. He would gladly have killed all four of them if he could, but his father had forbidden it. As he stared into Ferine's eyes, Luke began to wonder if he had maybe made a mistake and if the voice in his headset wasn't his father's after all. Away from the console and away from the voice that had sounded so much like his dad, Luke began to have his doubts.

The staring match continued. Neither man moved.

Neither man blinked.

Ferine imagined the attack on his men from the other side. He sensed the lack of remorse that Luke had felt as he willingly crushed and destroyed sixteen men. He imagined the pride and relief that the other man had felt when he had seen the results on the screen.

Ferine grimaced at the images that filled his mind. He was disgusted by what the kid had done.

And angry.

Luke sensed the soldier was losing the staring battle the moment he saw the other man's face contort. Good, he was making the murdering hard-arse soldier feel uncomfortable. He smiled at this slight upper hand he had gained. He was glad for any pain or discomfort he could cause these invading bastards.

Ferine saw Luke's lips curl into a demented grin, mocking him and his inability to protect his men.

Yeah, I killed them. That look said. *And there's nothing you can do about it.*

"You're wrong about that, Sunshine," Ferine whispered. He fired his weapon twice.

Luke's eyes widened as the bullets struck him in the chest. His body flew backwards as it had when he was hit by the other end of the rifle.

This time, he didn't keep his feet. This time, he didn't get up.

42
Escape

Onboard the *Feynman* – Low Earth Orbit.

7.06pm - Sunday, August 16th, 2048

Craig eased the VAPER in amongst the wreckage of the debris field just as the *Penetrator* came within range. Ollafson didn't waste any time in closing the gap, the barrels of the gun started to turn and spit steel the moment it was in range of its target.

Sparks flashed as the bullets tore into the debris around the VAPER. The odd shot made it through to ring upon the hull and ripple the *Feynman*'s shields. The ageing remains of military spacecraft that had spent the better part of two decades stuck in orbit around the Earth were shredded and sent flying Earthward by the *Penetrator's* guns. Hull plating, discarded equipment and a myriad of other objects were reduced to molten metal around the VAPER as Craig struggled to find something large enough to hide behind. The shields rippled continuously as a mixture of hot metal and bullets struck the side of the ship.

Craig's movements were a blur as he tried to control the ship with one hand and program the onboard quantum computer with the other. His head jerked backwards and forwards from the view outside the cockpit to the small screen within it.

Between the bursts of gunfire, Craig recognised the sound of the boys whimpering as they grew more and more terrified of this strange, relentless, light show with each passing moment. Although he was sure they were ignorant to what was going on, the noise and violence of the explosions around them was an unpleasant assault on their senses and entirely at odds with the quiet, peaceful life they had lived on Newton. In a momentary pause in the shooting, when a high-pitched ringing in his ears replaced the noise of explosions, Craig heard Karen's soft, soothing voice as she tried to calm the two oversized, but distraught children.

Poor buggers, Craig thought. *Their first time off the station and they have to go through this.*

Craig continued to work the controls furiously, the task of entering a long string of code on the computer took his attention away from the viewport longer than he had intended, with the job complete, he looked up just in time to see the severed aft end of an old NASA shuttle coming into view. Recognising that they were seconds away from impact, he forgot about the computer for the moment, pulled on the control stick and moved the VAPER to the right. What would have been a direct hit was turned into a glancing blow as the *Feynman*'s shields sliced through the engine cowling of the shuttle. Everyone on the VAPER could hear the pop screech as the shuttle's engine was sliced open; the sharp diamond hull had cut through the ageing metal like a knife. Craig risked a quick look back to see a neat gash in the carbon-fibre and steel hull of the other ship.

Man, we built this thing stronger than we thought, he mused. "That was a little too close for comfort mate!" Glen yelled over the noise as the *Penetrator* once again found its target. "Why don't you take us down to the ground? Surely, it can't follow us through all this junk."

"I'm working on it. This thing's never entered the atmosphere before. I'm trying to reconfigure the shields, so we don't burn up on re-entry."

"Well hurry the fuck up, will you?" Glen called back. "I'm shiting my pants back here!"

"Alright, we're ready," Craig announced to everyone in the VAPER.

"You might want to close your eyes and hold on to something. I don't know how rough this is gonna get!"

Behind Craig, Glen grabbed the base of the seat to steady himself as he watched the moon travel across the left side of the viewport. His head twisted as he tried to keep the familiar object in view, desperate to get one last look at the thing that had inspired his choice of career. As an astronomer, it was the first thing he had ever looked at through a telescope, and so, it held special meaning for him. It gave Glen a sense of stability to be able to look up and see the moon overhead, always present, always the same.

He lost sight of it as it arced below the body of the ship. As it disappeared, a moment of sadness filled him. Almost, he realised, as if he had just seen an old friend for the last time. He closed his eyes and hoped that that wasn't the case.

The VAPER banked steeply to the right, pointing its nose toward the Earth below. Small pieces of debris continued to bounce off the shield in bright blue flashes of light as they rushed towards the waiting atmosphere of Earth.

As if someone had flicked a switch. The persistent crackling of the shields ceased. Silence fell upon those within the ship as they fell out of range of the *Penetrator's* guns. The only sound was the hum of the computers and the occasional soft thump of pieces of debris as they bounced off the ship's shields.

Through the silence, Karen's voice drifted up to Craig from the cargo area below. As he worked the controls, he strained to listen as she spoke to the boys. He couldn't make out the words, but he recognised the soft, soothing tone she always used whenever the kids became distraught.

Typical Karen, in times of stress and worry, she always put the well- being of others before her own, Craig thought.

He could almost picture her there, crouched on the floor in front of the two worry strewn faces, hands working softly and slowly as she wiped away their tears and whispered reassuring words. All the while smiling, constantly smiling.

God, I love her, he thought as his hand reached to the ring inside his pocket and touched it just to make sure it was still there.

The *Feynman* jumped as if it had been hit by something massive, shaking all romantic thoughts out of Craig's head. He tightened his grip on the controls to steady the VAPER's vibrations as they slammed nose first into the atmosphere. Like smoke in a strong wind, thin gusts of air blew past them, growing thicker by the second like. The VAPER bounced again as the atmosphere grew denser, buffeting the ship as friction began to bite. A jerking, rocking motion joined the bounce so that everyone on board was jostled in multiple directions at once.

The children cried out in alarm as the nose of the VAPER seemingly burst into flames.

"Shit!" Glen screamed as he bent forward in his seat and attempted to place his head between his legs. "Mate, we're on fire! The ships on fire!" he called out; his voice almost inaudible below the sound of the ship's vibrations, almost unintelligible from the muffling of his thighs which he had somehow managed to place his head between.

The violence of the re-entry caught everyone by surprise. The deep, bouncing vibration increased in strength the deeper they travelled towards the surface of the Earth. The rising heat and noise, coupled with the increasingly violent turbulence joined forces to assault the senses of everyone onboard. Tears ran down their faces as they tried to squeeze their eyes shut from the blinding glare.

"Craig!" Karen called out. "This doesn't seem right!" The tremor in her voice matched that of the vibration of the ship. He could tell by her tone that she was terrified.

"Hang on a sec," Craig called back. "This should make things a little more comfortable."

Craig squinted through the brightness at the controls; he frantically swiped at the screens, trying to find the control panel he was after. Tears streaked his face as he fought to focus on the small hand labels that stated each of the controls functions. His eyes stung from the intense light he was forced to stare through. Finally finding what he was after, Craig squeezed his eyes shut to block out the light. With one hand, he rubbed his face to alleviate the stinging, with the other he swiped his finger across a luminescent scrubber bar.

For a second or two, there was no change. The VAPER glowed with the light and the heat of flames which had now all but engulfed the ship. Craig flew by touch alone as he waited for the computer to redistribute power to the new device. Just as he became convinced that it wasn't working and was about to give the controls another swipe, a deep, almost inaudible throbbing sound reverberated around the ship. With the use of modulated sound waves, Craig had sent a series of vibrations through the hull which immediately set about realigning its atoms. Atoms turned and spun as the soundwaves forced them into a new configuration, realigning them in such a way as to transform the hull from transparent to opaque. As if someone were turning down the dimmer switch on a light, the inside of the VAPER grew darker. The blinding light of re-entry faded to tolerable levels as the walls around them turned black.

Craig opened his eyes and looked around in time to see the hull turn completely opaque. Where seconds earlier there had been an unbearable brightness, darkness had taken its place. As his eyes fought to adjust from one extremity to the other, a series of small lights blinked into life throughout the ship, pushing the darkness back just enough for the inside of the VAPER to become visible once more.

Sitting below the cockpit, the boys grew calmer as the events outside the VAPER became hidden from view. Karen could see the outlines of the kid's bodies as their heads moved from side to side as they struggled to take in the dramatic events that had transpired around them.

"Stars, Mummy," Timothy sighed as he looked up at the small cabin lights just inches above his head. "There are stars inside the spaceship."

"Yes, baby. Just like the ones on your bedroom ceiling, huh?"

"Yeah," Jamie joined in. "This is cool."

The process complete, the ship fell silent once more. The only sound was that of their breathing, and a steady vibration as the boxes and crates within the VAPER rattled against each other.

A small section of the cockpit canopy had been left transparent so that Craig could continue guiding the ship through the re-entry process. Although small and with a restricted view which showed only what was directly ahead of the *Feynman*, the window was both a curse and a blessing; it allowed Craig to see where he was going while also revealing the violent forces that were in the process of attacking his ship. His eyes squinted into slits to reduce the glare from the flames that leapt and danced across the front of the hull. Superheated plasma rippled and threw sparks into the thickening air around the VAPER as the shields struggled to keep the oncoming waves of intense heat back. Craig glanced down at the computer to see that the *Feynman*'s internal temperature had only risen by a few degrees Celsius.

That's one item I'm glad worked as promised. He smiled as the VAPER continued to fall into the atmosphere like a flaming, bubbling, shooting star.

43
Searching the labs

Medical Bay – ANZAR Wing, Newton Station.

7.08pm · Sunday, August 16th, 2048

Luke's still warm body slid smoothly across the polished linoleum floor as Kyle Ferine dragged it into the adjoining medical bay. The kid was only of average build, but the dead weight caused Ferine's muscles to ache after the exertion of the spacewalk. With his fingers wrapped around Luke's ankles, he pulled the body to the nearest hospital bed. They had no intention of giving medical aid to the boy; they could see no point in that.

"Hey Cap. Check this out," Jackson said excitedly from somewhere behind Ferine's back. "Look who we got here."

Ferine dropped Luke's legs and turned to see that one of the hospital beds was already occupied. An elderly man lay unconscious, arms folded across his chest as if taking an afternoon nap. He looked uninjured as far as Ferine could tell, but considering the fact he was in a hospital bed, he could have had anything or everything wrong with him.

"According to this, he's alive... barely," Sergeant Jackson said as he examined the life support equipment beside the bed.

"We'll have to make sure he stays that way." Ferine paused. "The research team will want to talk to him when they get here."

"It's Brian Weekes, isn't it?"

"Looks like it," Ferine sighed as he turned away from the old man's body to examine the one on the floor. He crouched beside Luke and turned his head to study his face.

"And this one must be Weekes Junior." Ferine crouched there in thought for a moment, not moving, just thinking.

"I don't think we're going to find anybody else onboard this station," he said. "I think this kid may have been telling the truth

279

when he said everyone had cleared out. I think he must have stayed behind to protect his dad."

Jackson stepped towards the body on the floor. "That explains why he risked attacking us then. The kid was probably grief-stricken over whatever happened to his father. He thought we were coming to take the old guy away from him."

"We were." Ferine stood up quickly and stared at Jackson, his face a mask of mixed emotions; anger, regret and pity.

"C'mon, help me get him on the bed," was all Ferine could say.

With a little effort, the two men managed to lift Luke onto the bed beside his father's. They laid him on his back and placed his arms in the same position as the old man beside him.

"Let's get the fuck out of here." Ferine turned and marched out of the room. Jackson followed.

The other two troops were waiting for them back in the Engineering Bay. Each man was in the process of fiddling with the abandoned scientific equipment that lay scattered across the room. Both men looked up as the door to the medical lab slid open when Ferine and Jackson returned.

"It looks like these guys left in a major hurry, Cap. Look at all this shit they left behind." Dockrill waved a hand at the room as he bent to pick up another interesting item. "Sorting this out should keep our research guys busy for a while." He spun back towards Ferine. "Hey, do you think we'll find the gizmos they used to make the Blackout?"

"I doubt it," Ferine answered as he strode straight past the other men and stopped beside the door.

"Let's go. We've got to make sure that this place is secure before we can bring the science boys aboard."

Ferine led his men out of the medical bay to begin their search of the labs. He knew that if his suspicions were correct, and he had killed the only remaining member of the terrorist group who wasn't currently in a coma, they would all be in deep shit. The failure to acquire the desired resources from the mission would make a lot of people angry, a lot of influential people who cared nothing for the human cost of their so-called war on terror. Results were all that mattered, and Ferine had the uneasy feeling that he might be going back to them empty-handed. The politicians would chalk this one up as a failed mission in which he would be attributed the blame. He would have to answer for the heavy loss of life, he would be accused of letting the terrorists of the Blackout escape, and he would be blamed for everything they felt like blaming him for. The brass in Washington wouldn't understand the reasons why he had killed the Weekes kid. He barely knew why himself. At the time, it had just seemed the right course of action. Either way, right or wrong, he would pay for the decision. He would be made the whipping boy of this whole affair, a sacrifice which would be given up to appease the citizenry.

Even though he was an atheist, Ferine prayed that they would find other ANZAR staff somewhere within the station.

44
Press pass

Accommodation Area – ANZAR Wing, Newton Station.

7.08pm - Sunday, August 16th, 2048

"So, what's the situation there, Alan?"

"Well, I've just entered the accommodation area of the ANZAR wing and boy, this place is a mess. The Cavalry has really turned this place upside down in their hunt for the Australian terrorists."

"Are there any signs of casualties as yet, Alan?"

"No, not yet. But as you can see from the live pictures I'm sending out, they did not discriminate about what they had been shooting at. If you look at the wall in front of me, you can see that it is riddled with bullet holes. I'd hate to speculate what happened in here, but the lack of blood in the room suggests that nobody was injured."

Alan Oldman stepped back into the main corridor of the ANZAR wing and turned his body to face down the long narrow walkway. The small hyper-definition camera in his hand beamed the images of the ruined station live around the world. Below him on the Earth, millions of people sat glued to their multimedia devices as they watched the historical images he was beaming back from the station.

Alan intentionally walked the length of the corridor as slowly as he could. He stepped slowly and carefully not only to ensure that the people back home got to see the smoothest image of this event but also as a means of instilling suspense into what even he had to admit was pretty undramatic footage. Besides, the longer it took him to walk the length of this corridor, the more viewers he would have by the end of it, and the more ratings hits the station would get.

And the bigger his pay would be.

As he walked, Alan's head was filled with the voices of the newscasters as they discussed the situation with a military expert who had joined them in the studio back on Earth. Words like extreme response, containment and damage control were bandied about as the news crew also attempted to draw out this event for as long as they could.

"Is there anything you can hear that we can't at the moment, Alan?"

"No, nothing of importance anyway, it's all quiet here. The only thing I can hear is something that sounds like rushing air, that's most likely the ventilation system."

Alan continued to move forward as they spoke, his eyes looking into every open door as he passed them, his arm bending and swaying to allow the camera to film inside. At each room, he made a small comment on the apparent disarray of the station. By the end of the corridor, he was running out of things to say and was beginning to hope that he would find something more interesting to film than just a hallway filled with empty, ransacked rooms.

Leaving the last door behind, Alan turned three hundred and sixty degrees and looked back the way he had come. Before he had completed the turn, the sound of a sharp intake of air erupted from within his headset.

"What was that?" Alan asked.

"Alan, we need you to point the camera back around the corner again. Trish thinks she saw something on the floor."

Alan stepped back around the corner and had a good look at what was in front of him for the first time. He debated covering the lens of the camera in case kids were watching this at home.

Fuck'em, he thought, *these images are being watched worldwide, chances are fifty percent of the viewing population of Earth and their children, would be in bed anyway.*

Alan stepped even more cautiously than before as he moved closer to the section of blood-slicked floor and continued filming. Finally, he was getting some good footage. This...whatever this was, would guarantee him a decent paycheck when he got home. In the back of his mind, he could hear the commotion in the studio as the two news anchors lost it. A cacophony of man-made noises echoed through his headset as the male news anchor screamed and the female one threw up.

"My god," somebody from the studio gasped. "What happened? Are those... are those our troops?"

Alan smiled at the drama of the whole scene.

This is how you make a great webcast, he thought.

45
Welcoming committee

Over the East coast of the Imperial Homeland.

7.14pm - Sunday, August 16th, 2048

Captain Gene Arton dipped his right wing in farewell as his squadron broke away from the carrier fleet. He pushed the throttle as far forward as it would go and sent his aircraft hurtling towards the United States mainland. With a quick glance over his shoulder, he saw the deep blue waters of the Atlantic falling further away into the distance. He could see the outline of the carrier as it sat surrounded by its escort of Navy frigates. As he watched, a myriad of jets swarmed around the carrier fleet in defensive maneuvers that, from this distance, resembled a swarm of hungry flies.

The five F-52 Rapier stealth fighters under his command had fallen into formation directly behind him. Despite the mystery surrounding the identity of their bogey, Captain Arton expected this to be a routine interception just like any other he had performed during his twenty-year career as a Navy pilot. As he turned back to his controls, Arton had no way of knowing that more than one of his aircraft was taking its final flight.

"Command, this is echo-zulu-niner, en-route to the interception point, estimate contact with the bogey in six minutes, over," he informed the ship.

"Roger that, Arton. Be reminded that the bogey is of unknown make and is to be considered hostile, over."

"Roger," Arton replied.

The six stealth fighters levelled out at 46,000 feet and fell into formation with their wingtips less than twenty feet apart. In the distance, a dark green line had appeared across the horizon as the F-52's neared the rapidly approaching coast. Seconds later, the semi-rural farming areas of Maine passed below them as they left the sea behind. Cattle fled, birds took flight and farmers jumped as the explosions from their sonic booms rumbled across the ground below.

As was always the way with these things, they were in a hurry.

Whatever it was they were after; it was expected to enter the atmosphere approximately three hundred miles from their current position. With only six minutes to reach the coordinates at which the bogey was expected to appear, the fighters climbed to their maximum operational altitude of sixty-five thousand feet to reduce wind resistance and increase speed.

Captain Arton knew next to nothing about the craft they had been sent to intercept. The minimal information he had been given described it as a significant security threat which had been detected approaching the atmosphere directly over the homeland of the Empire. For whatever reason, the guys at NORAD had deemed this bogey to be hostile and wanted it captured intact. Failing that, Arton's orders were to destroy it at the first move it made to escape. As he adjusted the controls, he couldn't help but wonder what the real story behind this situation was. He had become used to working under conditions in which he was supplied minimal information, the whole need to know credo he understood. What concerned him was the fact that the guys on the ground couldn't even give him a description of what type of aircraft he was after. It was almost as if they either didn't know what it was or were too concerned about eavesdroppers on the communication systems to risk broadcasting the bogey's make. Whatever the reason, Arton had a gut feeling that this wasn't going to be a regular day.

"Fleet, this is Rapier Patrol Echo-Zulu-Niner. We have reached the specified coordinates and will now begin our patrol. Will report in once we have the bogey sighted and initiated contact."

The response from the carrier group was drowned out by the loudest sound Arton had ever heard. A high, electronic squeal rapidly rose in volume and pitch from somewhere far above him. Despite being unsure of what the sound was, Arton was positive about one thing; it was coming towards him.

Fearing a collision, he rapidly swung his head from side to side as he desperately searched for movement beyond his small squadron of aircraft. The sky around him was crystal clear with only a few low clouds dotted along the far horizon.

As he looked, the sound became louder and harsher. As it grew nearer, he could define a rhythmic hum underlying the high-pitched, screaming tone. It was a sound unlike anything he had ever heard before, but one he still found to be somehow familiar.

As he continued to scan the sky looking for the object that he now instinctively sensed was on a collision course with his aircraft, Arton's mind flashed upon an almost forgotten memory of a Muse concert he had attended as a teenager. In the show, he had seen the lead guitarist of the band holding a high note on his instrument as he pushed his electric guitar towards the speakers. A high-pitched reverberating tone had filled the stadium, causing everyone except the most die-hard head-bangers to throw their hands over their ears. What Arton heard now made him want to do the same thing. The scream of the guitar at the Muse concert sounded almost identical to whatever it was that was coming his way.

The sound continued to grow louder as Arton frantically searched the sky for the source of the noise. His heart was beating rapidly, he knew something was headed directly towards him, but he couldn't tell from where.

"Anyone see anything?" he called to his men. "Negative."

"Negative, Sir."

"Sir, I've got it, coming in from nine-o-clock high, something has just entered the atmosphere right on top of us, and it's coming in hot."

Arton's headset erupted with the sound of a terrified scream that he knew had come from one of his pilots. Before he could react, a massive orange fireball bloomed directly beside him where the Rapier on his starboard side had been. His world filled with light, heat and noise as the impact of the compression waves slammed his aircraft sideward. As flames licked the outside of his canopy, Arton fought to steady his out of control jet.

He was too late. Arton's wing slammed into the cockpit of the Rapier immediately to his left, fracturing the fibreglass canopy of his wingman and knocking the pilot unconscious. The aircraft's computer, detecting the drop-in pressure within the cockpit, initiated an emergency evacuation procedure and immediately ejected the pilot out of the plane.

Arton stared through the smoke-charred canopy of his cockpit as his wingman's now pilotless eighty-six-million- dollar stealth fighter rolled over and turned its nose towards the ground.

"Plane down, plane down!" one of his men called. "Bitterman has been hit. Something just flew straight through him!"

"We've lost Rogers as well," Arton added. "We need to get a visual on whatever that thing was. Where the hell is it now?"

"We have a chute! Repeat, I have a visual on one chute!" another pilot's voice added.

"Make that two," Arton added as he saw his wingman's shoot open below him. As he watched the pilot float towards the ground, a long, arcing line of smoke caught his attention. At its head, he could make out a large dark object that was still partially covered in flames.

"Bogey sited at three-o-clock low. All fighters are to intercept using formation papa," he ordered.

In a practised procession, the four remaining fighters banked to the right and dove towards the fast-moving VAPER. As they neared, Arton could see the craft finally come into full view, the rush of fast-moving air had all but extinguished the flames on the outside of its hull. The black shape of the *Feynman* appeared, still trailing a column of slowly dissipating smoke behind it. To Arton, the shape of the vehicle looked as alien as the annoyingly loud noise it was making. With no resemblance to any aircraft that Arton had ever seen, he was reminded of the pumpkin seeds he and his brothers used to spit around the house at Halloween.

"What the hell is that thing, Sir?" one of the other pilots asked from their plane nearby.

"Looks like a giant pumpkin seed," another one answered.

That was my first impression as well, Arton thought. Images of pumpkin-headed aliens with deep, evil-looking Jack-o-lantern eyes immediately came to mind. Six months ago, he would have scoffed at the idea of an alien invasion, but with the events of The Blackout and the sightings of the strange spheres in the sky, he had come to believe that such a thing was not only possible but inevitable.

He knew they didn't have time to discuss the origin of this strange vehicle, that wasn't in their job description. He'd leave the analysing of this aircraft's design to the experts who were undoubtedly watching the live recordings the Rapiers were making from the safety of the ground. He could see now why they didn't want it shot down straight away.

They wanted to capture it and study it.

Well, that would be a big mistake that I'm not going to allow them to make, Arton thought.

Arton gave new orders to the pilots around him.

"All missiles armed. All guns off safety," he said as he brought his own weapons system online. "All craft are to fall in behind me so that I can make my first run at this thing. The rest of you will follow in call-sign order and initialise a CFS attack."

46
Heart of the Empire

Onboard the *Feynman* – Above Maine. 7.18pm -

Sunday, August 16th, 2048

The air inside the VAPER was warm. The air-conditioning unit gave off a continuous hum as it blasted jets of cold air into the cockpit to keep the ship cool. Sweat; created as much from the stress of the situation as it was from the heat of re-entry, dripped from Craig's brow as he levelled the vehicle at fifty-five thousand feet. He had a good idea of where he was and would rather remain undetected while he made the transit over the United States. He dared not go any lower where he would be at risk of being spotted by someone on the ground.

"What was that bump back there?" Glen Hanson pointed over his shoulder at the way they had come. "It almost felt like we hit something."

Craig gave the Astronomer a quick glance before returning his attention to the controls. A two-dimensional map of the globe filled a navigation screen to his left. With it, he was trying to find the quickest way out of Imperial airspace.

"I think you might be right about that," Craig eventually answered. "We definitely did come into contact with something on the way in. But I've got absolutely nothing showing on my radar. At the altitude we were at, at least we don't have to worry about it having been a commercial airliner or something. I wouldn't worry about it. It was most likely just a piece of debris that followed us into the atmosphere."

Karen's head came into view as she climbed the short ladder leading up from the cargo area. Her heavy-soled shoes clanked on each of the metal rungs as she climbed into the cockpit.

"How are we?" she asked as she sat in the vacant cockpit seat next to Glen.

Grabbing a handle near his waist, Craig spun his seat to face them both. "Fine, as best as I can tell. We don't appear to have been damaged at all in the descent. Everything seems to be working fine. No problems at all." He gave Karen a smile that looked a little strained.

"Did I hear you say something about us being over the USA?" Karen asked patiently. "I don't think that this is the best place we could be right now."

"No shit," Glen almost laughed.

Craig gave another smile, more relaxed than the first. "Don't worry about it. I've got the autopilot taking us towards the Pacific as fast as it can. We'll be out of Imperial airspace in less than thirty minutes."

"Is it night where we are?" Karen asked. "It's still so dark in here." Despite the heat, she hugged herself as if she were cold.

"That's easily fixed," Craig said and spun back towards the controls.

With the touch of a finger, the interior of the VAPER was bathed in bright sunlight as the hull once again became transparent. The children below laughed in awe as the world around them became bright again. Everyone on board turned their faces to the floor and squinted their eyes against the penetrating glare of the sun. After waiting a few seconds, Craig raised his head and took a look around. The world was a bright blur that grew clearer as the seconds passed. Blue sky came into view all around the domed cockpit canopy. It was a clear day over North America with barely a cloud in the sky.

Something moving outside the cockpit caught Craig's attention. With his tear-streaked vision blurring the details, he could still see enough to make out the outline of the Imperial fighters which had surrounded the ship.

"Ah, shit," he sighed. "You guys may want to hold on to something. They've found us already."

Just as he began to disengage the autopilot, the VAPER was consumed in a fireball of orange flames and black smoke. The impact rocked the small ship, pushing it sharply to one side.

Karen was thrown against Glen who struggled to stay in his seat. Both fell to the floor in a tangled heap.

Below them, the children began to scream.

47
Captured

ANZAR control room – Newton Station. 7.18pm -

Sunday, August 16th, 2048

Kyle Ferine stared out the window at the charred and damaged Earth. He gave a sigh of relief that his mission had not proven a total failure after all. Behind him, Jackson and Scarface were busy handcuffing the dozen ANZAR staff they had discovered in the control room. As each prisoner was cuffed, they were briskly shoved towards the floor where they were forced to sit against the far wall to worry and to wait.

The mystery of the glass-like vehicle that had passed them on the outside of the station filled Ferine's mind with questions. He knew it was important. He didn't have to know the details of what these scientists were up to understand that it was something they didn't want him getting his hands on. That vehicle, or spaceship, or whatever that floating bauble was. It was the key to everything that had happened and was yet to happen. Although he could immediately tell that the thing was not one of the sphere-shaped objects that had decimated the Earth, he still had a feeling that the two were somehow connected.

He glanced at the 'wall to his right where a sizeable hyper-definition screen displayed an interesting graphic. Although there was no text or any other descriptive markings on it, the act of staring at it gave him a clue as to what's its function might be. A large, round, wheel of colour shone silently on the screen. Within it, sat the unmistakable image of the vehicle he had seen outside. Although the meaning of the colours was lost to him, Ferine guessed they were in some way related to the vehicles main purpose; they were a means of monitoring its main function... whatever that was. He strongly believed that the next step in his mission would be to find out what this vehicle did, where it was going and hopefully, capture it. There was no doubt that its occupants were the ones he needed to make this mission a success. Until he had them and that odd vehicle, there was no way he could call this thing over.

Between Ferine and the prisoners, Private Dockrill stood hunched over one of the many computer terminals which filled the inside of the control room. His fingers moved over the keyboard with the swift familiarity and confidence of someone who had spent many hours bathing in the glow of a V-OLED display. The moment the control room was secured, Ferine had ordered the Private to one of the computer consoles to retrieve any information that would give them an insight into what these people were doing. Ferine wanted to know what was so important to them that they would stay behind and risk capture. He was sure that they were doing something that involved the other escapees in the spacecraft. All he had to do now was find out what that was and figure a way in which he could stop them.

Glancing back at the line of prisoners, he realised that he recognised a few of the scientists that had refused to evacuate the station. Luckily for him, the bigger fish in this pond seemed to be the ones who had stayed behind. Doctor Anderson - the chief physician, Adam Fehrenbach – operations manager, plus a handful of the others would go a long way in allowing his superiors to demonstrate that the perpetrators of the Blackout were being dealt with.

He turned back to the window feeling appreciative of this lucky break. Now all he had to do was decide which course of action to take from here.

Jackson stepped up beside Ferine and looked out the window. Both men stood in silence for a moment, taking in the view of the glowing blue Earth and the flickering, orange, spot fires that dotted the globe. Without counting, Jackson noticed that he could make out at least a dozen large fires within the small section of the Earth that was currently visible. Directly below them, the Indian Peninsula, one of the most densely populated areas of the planet, was burning.

The loss of life must be incredible. A small shudder ran through him as he imagined similar scenes of devastation spread across the entire surface of the globe.

"It's amazing that there's anything left down there," Ferine said without turning away from the view. "It's been three days since The Blackout and still parts of the world continue to burn."

He sighed. "What a fucking joke."

"At least we can console ourselves with the fact that we've managed to capture some of the ringleaders involved in causing this mess," Jackson answered without turning to face Ferine. He was having trouble taking his eyes away from the vista before him.

"You mean at least they all just threw their hands up and said *I surrender* when we walked through the door. We're lucky they didn't try to run or fight; otherwise, we could have ended up with nothing."

Ferine glanced at his second in command before returning to the view.

"Have you spoken to Washington yet?"

"That's what I was coming to see you about," Jackson replied. "HQ has received Intel that the Australian government has ordered a response to our mission. Apparently, there's a transport being prepared to leave Holsworthy base as we speak."

"How long have we got?"

"Not sure. We could have anywhere from one hour to three depending on how fast your guys act."

"My guys?" Ferine turned to face Jackson.

"Yeah. The Australians. You used to be based at Holsworthy didn't you?" Jackson asked.

Ferine nodded. That seemed like a long time ago now.

"Did HQ give us any orders on how to proceed?" Ferine asked after a moment's pause.

"They didn't give direct instructions, but they did specifically state that they don't want us to engage the Australian troops when they get here. They want us off the station with whatever technology or information we can gather between now and then. As far as what we do within those parameters is up to you, Cap,"

Ferine gave a nod and turned towards the back of the room where the ANZAR staff sat waiting. With their matching lab coats, Ferine thought they looked like a flock of large white birds that had been trapped, caged and were now doing their best to appear invisible. They squatted on the floor looking more than a little nervous as Scarface paced back and forth glowering at the tops of their heads. There was no denying that the large soldier was an intimidating presence, none of the prisoners dared move or risk making eye contact with him. The younger ones were too nervous, or too smart, even to raise their heads to look at him.

"Well, for starters. We should talk to a few of these guys while we have the chance," Ferine said to Jackson. "I want to know what that thing outside was and where it's going."

Ferine's eyes scanned the group as he assessed which one of them he would like to speak to first. Half of them looked like junior staff that, he assumed, would be able to tell him nothing of interest. Ferine's lack of knowledge about the openness of ANZAR's research and the fortnightly meetings in which everything was discussed openly, meant that he could easily have pulled any of these staff members from the lineup and received the same level of information. Being ignorant of that fact, he scanned the group looking for someone who appeared more senior, more in charge, therefore more privy to sensitive information.

As he studied the group, his gaze continually returned to one face in particular. A face he recognised from somewhere that he couldn't quite recall. A middle-aged Asian man wearing a lab coat stood defiantly at the edge of the group and returned Ferine's gaze. Obviously, with the getup he was wearing, Ferine correctly guessed that he was the eminent Doctor Tran, the most senior person left on the station.

"Jackson, bring Tran over here. I want to ask him a few questions."

"Yes, Sir" Jackson began to cross the room to where the prisoners waited.

"Oh, and Jackson."

The Sergeant stopped and turned to face the Captain. "Have Dockrill open that security door between the accommodation and research wings, will you? I don't want to have to leave here the same way we got in."

Jackson gave Ferine a quick smile before heading off. "I hear you, Cap."

48
News update

Alan Oldman continued to make his way through the demolished accommodation wing of Newton Station. He was forced to tread carefully; his shoes had been unceremoniously lubricated with the remains of his fellow countrymen that covered the corridor in a slick film. The squelching sound caused him to pause and look down at his feet; everything from the shins down had been painted a deep, dark, red. His shoes were rendered unrecognisable by the sheer volume of blood and gore that had become caked on them when he had to wade through the remains of the assault team.

I'm going to have to get some new shoes, he thought. *Who cares? I can buy a hundred pairs once I get paid for this job.*

The short walk he had taken through the blood-slicked floor of the accommodation area wasn't as big an ordeal for Alan as it would have been for most other reporters. His years spent in the Imperial Marines had hardened him to the sight of blood. He had seen and done a lot worse than what was lying back along the corridor. As gruesome as it was, those men would have suffered a relatively quick death compared to what he had been forced to dish out in the past. His tolerance for blood and gore was a key factor in his landing the job as a freelance military reporter with three of the major news sites. His military contacts had opened doors for him as a member of the press that his competitors usually had slammed in their faces. The now-famous Alan Oldman had made his name reporting from the front lines of most of the major military battles of recent years. His name had become synonymous with warfare. Viewers automatically associated seeing his face with the sounds and screams of military operations around the world. He was more than embedded; he was a part of the furniture. As far as the military was concerned, he was still one of them. He'd never left. In an arrangement that was beneficial to everybody, Oldman had managed to put himself in a position where he was routinely embedded with front-line forces in return for the freedom to publish unedited content. The government had learnt early on that he was a trustworthy citizen of the Empire. They knew he would never release sensitive or derogatory information that would either damage the Empire's military efforts or cast the regime in a bad light. In short, he was the perfect PR and propaganda tool.

And he knew it.

In fact, he banked on it.

The puddle of crushed Imperial troops would work perfectly for him and the Empire. The sight of the defiled bodies of the American men who had bravely volunteered to bring the perpetrators of the Blackout to justice would snap the general public out of their familiarity with death and violence. These men had not just simply been killed, that concept the American people understood, these men had had the sanctity of their bodies desecrated. The anger that would arise from this would be a valuable tool for the Imperial government in gaining public support for whatever action they decided to take next. Alan knew that he would benefit from being the one to give it to them.

A dramatic deep bass drum paired with the high-pitched fanfare of trumpets filled his headset as the webcast he was starring in came back from yet another commercial break. He imagined the websites revenue department laughing as they hurriedly sold ad space to desperate clients who wanted their brand names thrust between the images of this historic event. The station would be making a fortune from this footage; just as he hoped to, once the whole thing was over.

"Good morning, viewers and welcome to I-BLOG news, where the truth is just one touch away," the male newsreader's voice announced through Alan's headset and to the world.

"If you've just joined us, the hunt for the ANZAR terrorists has taken a new twist. We have received word from various sources in the military and air traffic sectors that one of the vehicles used in the Blackout is currently terrorising Imperial citizens over the Homeland. From what we can gather, this strange alien-like vehicle contains a small group of terrorists who fled their hideout on Newton station just before our peacekeepers arrived. Authorities have warned the public to seek shelter until the terrorist vehicle is either detained or destroyed. Tests are being conducted, but it is strongly believed that the craft is dispersing high doses of radiation via a strange, loud vibrating noise that can be heard for miles around. Authorities advise that anyone within earshot of this terrorist weapon seek medical advice at the earliest convenient opportunity, should your insurance allow it. We still have no word where the vehicle is going or what its final intentions are, but we understand that the military is currently in the act of trying to capture or destroy the terrorist craft. Until we have footage of this new development, we will cut back to the amazing images from Newton station where our roving military correspondent, Alan Oldman, has entered the ANZAR research wing to report on how the arrest of the remaining terrorists is proceeding. Alan, can you hear us?"

That's my cue, Alan thought as he went to work.

"Hi, Mike. There's been a bit of a development here on the ANZAR front. I've just reached the secure airlock that separates the ANZAR living quarters from the lab areas where we believe the technology which created the Blackout was developed."

The camera panned to the end of the corridor where the large steel door remained closed and impassable. Beside it, a smaller, unmarked door leading to a service closet hung by a single hinge. Its frame bent and marked with a strange looking set of scratches that Alan thought looked suspiciously like fingernail marks.

"I came across this door just a moment ago. As you can see from the damage, someone... or something, used a great deal of force to pull this door from the wall. There are..."

As they usually do, the news announcer cut him off. "That door looks pretty heavy. What would you say it's made of Alan?"

"Steel. Light-weight steel by the looks of it. It's not a security door or anything nearly as strong as the labs' security door to my right." The camera pans around to the security airlock that remains closed.

"What makes this thing interesting is the fact that this is a storeroom for the maintenance staff's space suits. Every wing of the station has them. And every storeroom has to have a regulation number of suits, which is six. As you can see from my images, this one only has two."

"So, what does that mean?" The announcer interrupted again. "Do you think some of the staff may have used them to evacuate?"

"No, they wouldn't have gotten far if that was the case. I'd say that our men probably used them to get around this security door beside me."

"We'd like to take this opportunity to remind our viewers that this is just an assumption on Mister Oldman's part," the announcer added.

"True, it is only an assumption, but it's what I would have done under the circumstances." Oldman casually replied. He wasn't going to let the wankers in the studio get one over him. What he'd found during his time as a reporter was that they all seemed to have an innate penchant for trying to make themselves look more knowledgeable than the reporters they were working with. So far, none of them had ever succeeded in that regard with Alan.

"But if the troops used those four space suits to continue their advance..." Mike continued. "Then, where are the rest of them? Surely, you're not suggesting that only four of the twenty Imperial Marines sent to arrest the terrorists survived that gruesome attack you informed us of earlier?"

"I'm not jumping to any conclusions as yet, Mike. But that's what I intend to find out," Alan answered.

An electronic hum accompanied by a soft hiss of rushing air sounded behind the reporter as he studied the inside of the supply closet. On hearing this new sound, he spun around to face the corridor behind him. His right hand automatically made its way to the inside of his Jacket where he removed his old service pistol that he kept holstered there.

There was nobody in the hall. Nobody was sneaking up on him. The area was empty.

But the large, vault-like security door leading to the ANZAR labs stood partly open.

On his headset, the news announcers back in the studio excitedly thrust questions at him about this latest development. What did he think this meant? What does he expect to find on the other side of the door? And a dozen other questions he chose to ignore.

Everything he'd learnt during his lifetime of military service came back to the forefront of Alan's mind. This unexpected development, finding himself in a possibly hostile situation without other troops around him for backup unsettled the reporter. His nerves were on edge as he stepped forward and approached the now still and silent door. With a gun in one hand and his camera in the other, Alan moved to within a few feet of the opening where he paused to answer a few more questions from the news anchors back on the ground. All the while he was watching and waiting, carefully controlling the timbre of his voice to hide his nervousness. As good a job as he felt he was doing in controlling himself, experience told Alan that the discomfort he felt would still be sensed by the viewers at home. Alan knew that those watching the broadcast would later say that they had heard the fear in his voice. That was to be expected. Different people interpreted emotions differently. What they called fear, Alan registered as more of a sense of disquiet or discomfort. He thought of it as more of a temporary lack of emotional security. Still, others would argue that that was exactly what fear was. He was confident of his abilities and would never admit to himself, or anyone else that he felt anything more than a slight case of nerves. Besides, let them think what they want, there was nothing he could do about that. It would work to his advantage by adding a sense of drama and danger to his report.

Alan stood motionless with both his camera and gun aimed at the silent and still opening to the ANZAR labs. He gave it until the count of twenty before he decided that nobody was coming through and slowly moved his camera around the edge of the door. The H-OLED screen on the Hyper- Definition camcorder displayed the scene that was hidden from him. He could see a long, well-lighted corridor that seemed to go for as far as the eye could see. Rectangles of yellow light illuminated the walls at random intervals along the corridor, indications of lab doors that had been left open in the scientists hurry to escape.

He saw no people. No movement.

Questions from the news crew on the ground trickled out and finally stopped as they got the point that he wasn't going to answer them. They sensed, as did Alan that he was about to get to the heart of this issue. That whatever questions they had would be answered in a matter of minutes. It became as still and quiet in his earpiece as it appeared to be in the corridor ahead of him.

With a deep breath and a racing heart, Alan Oldman stepped through the open airlock door and into the ANZAR labs.

49
Blackmail

ANZAR control room – Newton Station. 7.32pm -

Sunday, August 16th, 2048

Private Dockrill scanned the computer system for the personnel files that would allow him to identify the ANZAR staff sitting cuffed and silent along the wall behind him. He was amazed at the speed in which the search progressed. The terminal he was using operated far more efficiently than anything he had used before. On examining the system files, he was amazed to see that the power of the machine registered at an astonishing 60 xetabytes of RAM with an impressive 100 yottabytes of memory. He realised Impressive probably wasn't an adequate word to encompass what this thing could do. Inconceivable was more like it. As far as he knew, nothing in the world came close to this anywhere. As he pondered its significance, the most powerful computer known to man, the screen flashed with the results of his data search.

Nothing.

It was obvious that the researchers had been forewarned of their arrival. They had done a thorough job in clearing the computer systems of any evidence of their involvement in The Blackout. There were no staff files, no research papers, no incoming or outgoing telecommunications records. Hell, there weren't even any bookmarked folders in the web-search engine. The system had been totally wiped. Apart from a bundle of software that was in use by the staff and the basic station controls for life support, communications and security, this cupboard was bare.

A door slid open on the other side of the room from Dockrill's terminal. Ferine and the Asian scientist re-entered the control room after what Ferine had announced would be a 'private talk'.

Sensing that something was about to happen, Private Dockrill stepped away from the incredibly sophisticated, but otherwise useless computer console and faced the two men. The Asian scientist's face was a mask of emotion, showing no signs of fear or discomfort at the interrogation in which he would have just been subjected. Ferine's face, on the other hand, revealed a hint of pleasure that could only mean that the Captain had learnt something of value.

The imprisoned ANZAR staff noticed the look and had come to the same conclusion as the Private.

"What did you tell them?" Adam Fehrenbach almost snarled at Doctor Tran as the elder man walked towards the group. "What did you say, Henry?"

For the first time on re-entering the room, Doctor Tran looked a little uncomfortable. He looked at the faces of each of his colleagues, his expression pleading with each of them in turn for their understanding.

"I told them only what they would have found out anyway," Tran said defiantly. "What I said was in all of our best interests."

"God help me if you've ruined every..." Doctor Anderson fell silent when the muzzle of a rifle was pushed against his cheek.

"I recommend you all shut it, now!" Scarface said with a smile

"Scarface!" Ferine called as he strode across the room to Jackson who was still beside the large window. "Gather our gear together and make ready to move out. We're leaving the station."

"Yes, Sir," Scarface replied crisply as he continued to stare into the eyes of Doctor Anderson. The two men faced each other in a defiant battle of wills, neither willing to be the first man to break the other's stare. Both men were determined to win this minor battle, neither realising how immature and petty the contest was.

"Now, Tony!" Ferine called again.

Knowing that Ferine wouldn't bother to call to him a third time, Scarface turned with a disgruntled growl and stepped away from the prisoners. He knew he would have stared that dweeb into submission in a few more seconds. He could see it on the guys face; he was ready to crack, he'd had enough, he would have given in. Confident that his ego had survived intact, Scarface began to gather the troop's packs and communication equipment.

Over by the window, Ferine and Jackson stood together, both watching Scarface as he finally went about his work.

"God, that guy's a worry." Ferine shook his head at the immaturity of the man. "I can't help but feel that he's going to get us all in a lot of trouble one day."

Jackson simply nodded his head before turning back to Ferine.

"By the look on your face when you came out of that room, it seems like you managed to get the Doctor to talk."

"Oh, he was more than co-operative." Ferine grinned. "I have to admit that I don't agree with what the CIA has done to that guy or his family but in this case, blackmailing that poor son of a bitch has paid off for us big time. He told us everything we wanted to know and more."

"So, where are we going?" Jackson asked.

"We need to get our hands on that vehicle we saw outside. They call it a VAPER or something. Apparently, it's the pride of their research and is central to everything that they've got going on here. They've loaded it with every piece of research data and every prototype that their labs had ever worked on, including that government research that went missing a few years ago." Ferine began to look excited as he finished reporting what he had learnt. "But that's not the best thing. We were right about who we saw onboard. The damn thing is being piloted by Craig Turp. The son of one of the ANZAR head honchos."

"Sir!" Private Dockrill called from the computer console further back in the room. All eyes turned towards the young private, including those of the imprisoned ANZAR staff.

"I've just received a message from central command. The North Atlantic fleet has engaged that vehicle we saw outside."

"Shit!" Ferine turned on the spot and ran a dozen steps to Dockrill's console where the message was still on screen. "Respond to the message by telling them not to engage. Tell them they are not to destroy that vehicle. We need what it has onboard."

That would be typical, Ferine thought. *Our one chance of salvaging this fuckup of a mission will be ruined by a bunch of trigger-happy fighter jocks.*

Dockrill unrolled a keyboard in front of the monitor and began to relay Ferine's message. After a few moments of frantic typing and a few more moments of waiting, a response came.

"They report having lost two aircraft and have labelled the target as hostile. We're too late; they've already begun to fire upon the thing."

"Fuck!" Ferine screamed and turned away from the monitor.

50
The first transit

Onboard the *Feynman*.

7.34pm - Sunday, August 16th, 2048

Concussion waves rocked the *Feynman* as Craig desperately tried to lose his attackers. The ship was holding up well and appeared to have suffered no major damage despite the fact it had already taken several direct hits. The cockpit canopy around him erupted into intricate webs of cracked diamond as high-speed projectiles slammed into the craft. Bullets ricocheted off the hull with ear-splitting twangs that caused the hollow diamond they were in to vibrate at uncomfortably high frequencies. A firework display of crazed orange and red balls of light interfered with their vision as missiles exploded around the ship, turning the world outside into a kaleidoscope of crystalline shapes.

Craig looked at the hull around him as the VAPER struggled to repair the damage it was receiving. The ship's computers were managing to keep up with the Imperial Navy's constant bombardment... for the moment. The mass of data it needed to sort through and manipulate was beyond anything that the staff at ANZAR had envisioned it would ever need to cope with. The system was designed as a means of the orderly reconstruction of the vehicle and its occupants upon exiting a wormhole; it wasn't intended to be used in such a random and haphazard way. This kind of prolonged and continual use was not something that had been designed into the system. As appreciative as Craig was at this unexpected side-effect of the transit reconstruction system, he still had reservations about making it out of this situation alive.

Atoms were manipulated, super-strings had their vibrations altered, and matter was transformed into new, man-made shapes as the canopy around him was cracked and mended, cracked and mended over and over again. The computer was running at a rapid pace. The diagnostic screen to his right showed a constant stream of code as the Quantum computer continuously made calculations and adjustments. He had no idea how long the VAPER could continue to take this onslaught of abuse before a minor programming glitch or a simple miscalculation by the computer would result in a hull breach and their inevitable deaths.

He had to get out of the area at once, and there was only one way he could do that.

"Hold on! We're going back up!" he called over the cacophony of noise that permeated the ship.

No-one responded. Everyone was too intent on keeping their seats and controlling the urge to panic to form coherent sentences. The only sound Craig could hear from anyone else onboard was the high-pitched screams of Jamie and Timothy that echoed through the ship from the cargo hold. Craig felt sorry for the kids, for the first time in their lives they had been able to step outside the confines of their infirmed existence to experience new surroundings, only to find that the world outside was full of threats and danger. They had constantly been attacked since leaving the station. Craig worried what this chain of experiences would do to their emotional security and their view of the world.

Whatever it was, it wouldn't be good.

Pulling the control stick back, Craig pointed the nose of the VAPER towards the relative safety of space. The explosions died away as the pursuing Rapiers lost sight of their target. In the ensuing silence, Craig became distinctly aware of his passengers; the nasally sound of the boys crying in the lower compartment of the ship overlaid the softer, gentler sound of Karen trying to sooth them and Glen panting with fear in the seat behind him. He was hit with the sudden realisation that he was responsible for all of these lives. He had led them away from the station for a cause that, on the surface had seemed noble, but on closer examination was entirely self- serving. As much as he regretted the situation, he knew that all he could do now was try and keep them out of the hands of the Imperials. As for getting them all killed… well, that would take care of itself.

The *Feynman* rose higher into the atmosphere, gaining speed as it made its way through the steadily thinning air. Craig glanced behind him to see that the pursuing fighters had given up the chase. Having levelled out at their maximum altitude, they began to circle below the fleeing VAPER, no doubt reporting its position and their failure to capture it so that others branches of the Imperial military could continue the pursuit.

As the sky cleared and the stars came into view, a glint of light off to his left caused Craig to think of the *Penetrator*, and his heart jumped. He looked around the ship searching for any signs of the space mounted gun that he feared would be waiting in ambush for them, but with the debris field blocking his view in every direction but down, he found it to be an impossible task to identify anything amongst the tumbling, twisting junk. He searched the sky around them until he felt confident that all he had seen was the sun reflecting off a piece of free floating steel, or the external light from an abandoned Helium-3 transport whose reactors had still not run down.

"So where are we now?" Glen asked in a slow, sighing breath. Craig could tell without looking that the Astronomer was probably sitting there sweating and shaking after the events of the last half an hour.

Craig looked at the centre of his display. The image of the VAPER sat within the colour wheel, its positioning icon still located in the blue quadrant as it should be, beside it, their local position was displayed as being just three hundred kilometres from Newton Station itself.

"Oh, man. We're pretty much back where we started. We're only a few hundred kilometres from the station."

"Which means we're only a few hundred kilometres from that space gun of theirs. "Glen sat up alarmed. "Look, mate. This is a great little vehicle you guys have built and all, but as strong as it is I really think we better not push our luck by going anywhere back near that thing."

Glen was clearly and understandably agitated about the situation. Craig knew that he'd have to get them away from danger as soon as possible or risk a possible mutiny.

"Agreed," Craig replied.

Behind him, Karen slowly climbed back up the access ladder and once again took a seat in the cockpit next to Alan. She looked tired, stressed and strangely quiet. Beside her, Alan continued to talk.

"Good, we should steer clear of the station and try and find our way back to the surface. The Earth is a big place; surely, we can find somewhere else to go where there isn't somebody waiting to kill us. Somewhere not controlled by the Empire, preferably."

"Well that limits our choices a little, doesn't it?" Craig tried to joke.

"Tell me about it, mate," Glen sighed and ran his fingers through his hair before flopping back into his seat. He felt both emotionally and physically drained. It had been a hell of a week for him. What with having his parent's home bombarded by out-of-control passenger jets and falling unconscious in the Blackout, he now had to deal with the fact that the people he worked with had somehow been made the scapegoats for that monumental disaster, himself included. To top it all off, he had to go and be the one to figure out that the Blackout had changed the Earth's orbital path by a few degrees, thus placing it on a slightly wider orbit that would ensure the loss of all life on the planet it a matter of months. He wondered if maybe now might be a good time to calm down. After all, things couldn't get any worse.

The VAPER cleared the debris field and floated into clear space. As soon as the *Feynman*'s sensors were away from the cloud of interference that the debris field presented, Craig saw the one thing he didn't want to see on his radar, The *Penetrator*.

As soon as the *Penetrator* came into view, Craig knew that the American Empire would not give up and leave them alone. If he returned the *Feynman* to Sydney, sooner or later it would fall into the wrong hands, and he would lose the only thing in the world that was capable of finding his father. There was no way he could give up his only hope of ever seeing his father again. He had lost his mother when he was young. He refused to lose his father as well.

"All right, that decides it," he said to no-one in particular as he began hitting seemingly random buttons in rapid succession.

"Okay," he called out to everyone on board. "Make yourselves comfortable; we're going to make a jump to somewhere where these guys can't get their hands on us."

Behind him, Karen and Alan both turned and looked at the back of his head.

"What do you mean jump?" Karen asked.

"Yeah," was all Glen could manage to say. He looked almost as worried as he was confused by the discussion.

"Both VAPERs were designed as a means of travelling between universes. I'm going to use one of the pre-programmed addresses that the Professor's visited to jump us to another Universe where there won't be any Imperials waiting for us. From there we can work out what to do next and maybe get some clues as to what happened to my father while we're at it."

"Hang on a minute, mate," Glen stammered as he leaned forward in his seat. "How do we know that's safe? How do you know it even works? I mean, look what happened to your Dad."

"That was unrelated to the transit process. Whatever happened to him wasn't a problem with this ship or from the wormhole transit... it was something else entirely."

"What do you mean something else? You mean those spheres, don't you?" Karen asked.

"Sorry guys, no time to talk. That gun of theirs has spotted us and is on the way over," Craig replied as he continued to punch data into his flight control computer. "Just try not to freak out too much over what happens next."

With that, Craig hit one last button and leaned back into the padded gel cushion of the pilot's chair. A look of nervous determination painted his face. His knuckles turned white on the flight control stick where he had begun to squeeze it in fear and anticipation of what was to come.

A deep, bass hum began to vibrate its way through the ship's hull. The rhythmic sound rose and fell in volume as waves of body-shaking sound penetrated deep into the occupants of the VAPER. Craig was reminded of the last concert he attended a few years back with a few of his university friends in which the crush of the crowd had forced them to stand directly in front of one of the stadium's massive speakers. His body shook now as it did back then. Though this time, he knew it wasn't just sound waves that were impacting his body, he knew that the *Feynman's* systems were penetrating his flesh. The ship was scanning them, documenting the position of every atom in their bodies and clothing. Data scrolled down the screens as the computer double-checked the information against the scans they had each undergone before leaving the station. These two massive bodies of data would be stitched together for the ship to accurately separate the human occupants from the inert matter that made up the VAPER and its cargo. Once identified, each separate object, both living and dead, would be broken down into their smaller, component pieces for transport, making it possible to reproduce everything precisely as it was on the other side.

After what felt like minutes but was in truth only a few seconds, the ship fell silent. The breaths of everyone in the VAPER became the only sounds that could be heard after the deep invasive booms of the scanning process.

The silence didn't last long.

Pale blue flashes of light erupted from seemingly random points throughout the ship. Each flash of light was accompanied by a loud, sharp cracking report which Craig at first assumed to be the sounds of the ships components snapping. The sudden volume and rapidity of this new noise caused shocked gasps to escape the throats of the adults within the VAPER. Down below, Jamie and Timothy had begun to cry once again. Their muffled whimpering was barely audible over the near machine gun like staccato of the rapidly increasing pop-snapping sounds.

Craig was frozen in place with fear. The only part of him that moved were his eyes that rolled around inside his head as they followed the noises around the ship in a mad chase to keep up with the rapid changes that were occurring around him. He had always known the theory behind what the *Feynman's* computers accomplished to make the transit of humans through microscopic wormholes possible. Being in the position in which his body was about to go through the process first-hand, was a different and more uncomfortable experience than he had ever imagined. He held himself rigid in anticipation of the next step.

With each cracking sound, Craig observed a small, but identifiable part of the ship wink out of existence. As he watched, the engine seemingly fell apart and vanished one piece at a time. Wiring that was visible within the transparent diamond hull flashed blue and disappeared as if it were never there. The components they were connected to floated in space for a moment, disconnected from everything else around them until they too vanished from sight. Pieces of the hull, internal workings and even the controls that surrounded his lap winked out of existence in rapid succession.

The VAPER was in the act of sending itself through a series of microscopic wormholes to another universe, one piece at a time.

On a conscious level, he understood that the loud cracks he could hear were the sounds of the physical matter that comprised each object within the ship being separated, compressed and finally removed from this universe so that it could be recreated in another. He also understood that the popping sounds that accompanied each snap were the collision of air particles as the atmosphere within the VAPER rushed to fill the space that the disappearing components had left behind. The conscious awareness of this knowledge did little to calm his subconscious fears. All he could do to keep calm was think about his father and how he had somehow gone through this process half a dozen times without any significant problems... that he knew of.

With many of the computer screens and components gone from the VAPER's flight controls, Craig now had an unobstructed view of the cargo area below. Through the transparent diamond floor of the flight deck, he could see the kids curled up in each other's arms. They cried and held each other during what was a terrifying deal for all involved, let alone a pair of four-year-olds. Craig watched as his father's lifetime of work which had been sealed within secure shipping crates and ferried away from those who would steal it for their profit, disappeared one-by-one from around the two terrified children. As each box vanished, Craig remembered the hours and years spent in the development of their contents. He hoped that what he was doing would work out. He hoped he wasn't seeing his father's legacy disappear forever.

As each box vanished around them, the two boys flinched from the noise and the light. Craig's heart went out to them as the realisation of the enormity of what he was doing hit him. For the first time, he realised that everyone and everything inside this ship could be lost in what was a brave but stupid gamble on his part. Although he felt they had little choice, he wished he had been presented with another alternative to what he had planned. If it worked, everyone on the planet below would benefit. If it didn't, well... they'd simply just never be heard from again.

Behind him, Karen and Glen had obviously noticed what was happening, and both let out involuntary gasps of shock as pieces of the ship continued to disappear at an increasingly alarming rate. With the process nearly fifty percent completed in a matter of seconds, the VAPER's computer turned its attention to the ship's occupants.

A faint numbing, tingling sensation not unlike pins and needles overcame Craig's entire body. He was surprised to find that it was a rather pleasant sensation that made him feel strangely calm and relaxed despite his reservations about what was to come. With every nerve-ending in his body switched off, he felt as if he were floating in the middle of a glass bubble of flashing light.

Fresh screams filled the inside of the VAPER as Karen, Glen and the kids watched helplessly as lasers beamed pieces of their bodies through a hole in reality. From their reflection in the *Feynman's* domed canopy, Craig could see Karen and Glen each staring at their own raised hands in shock. Craig gasped as he saw Karen's skin disappear from her face and hands. Due to the numbing effect of the process, he knew she could feel no pain. The entire process was more of a psychological shock than a physical torment, though Craig was finding that his subconscious was having a hard time making that differentiation.

Beside her, Glen kept repeatedly swearing as he struggled to deal with the apparent injury his body was sustaining. Terror had reduced the world-renowned Astronomer's vocabulary to just one word.

"Shit, shit, shit, shit, shit," he repeated.

Staring at Karen's nightmarish reflection, Craig felt thankful that the woman he loved could not see her face as it looked right now with its skin gone and its cheekbones and muscle structure on show. He found it hard to make the emotional connection with the image of the thing that was currently sitting behind him and his mental image of the beautiful woman that he loved. He could no longer watch as his ship's computer dismantled his lover's body. With a great effort, he managed to avert his eyes from one gory scene and was faced with another.

Craig looked down to see that his clothes had already been sent onwards to their new destination. As had his skin. Pockets of fat and muscle glistened up at him as the computer dematerialised his body one part at a time.

He didn't want to watch the disassembling of his own body from the outside in but found he was incapable of looking away. He tried to close his eyes but found it impossible as he no longer had eyelids. The muscles of his chest and legs peeled away and disappeared one layer at a time. His usually full thighs grew narrower and seemed to atrophy before his eyes as they lost volume and shape. Thick blue and red veins, amazingly, still transporting blood, came into view and vanished. His penis and testicles disappeared from his lap leaving an ever-widening gap of disappearing muscle. His internal organs came into view and thankfully disappeared before he could increase his terror by being able to identify any of them.

A high-pitched whistle-like noise filled the inside of the *Feynman* during the last moments of the transit. As he looked down at the image of his still beating heart floating within his otherwise empty rib-cage, Craig wondered what could be the purpose of a screeching alarm that would alert them to anything useful this late in the transit.

As the sound peaked, the realisation hit him that it was not an alarm. It was coming from everyone inside the VAPER including himself. Despite having no lungs to issue it and no vocal chords to shape it, the sound he could hear was his own screams paired with those of his friends behind him as the last of their bodies broke down and disappeared.

Then, silence.

Five small, blue sparks of light floated in the space recently occupied by the passengers of the now non-existent VAPER. They hung in the vacuum of space for a fraction of a second before they too disappeared.

The *Feynman* and everything inside it were gone. Where it once sat, was now only empty space.

51
The next step

ANZAR control room – Newton Station. 7.39pm -

Sunday, August 16th, 2048

"So where did it go?" Ferine barked over Private Dockrill's shoulder as they stared at the computer monitor which now showed nothing but stars.

With a quick shrug and a shake of his head, Private Dockrill turned to face Ferine. "I'm not sure, Sir."

Both men reviewed the data that was now being displayed on the screen via a remote connection they had made by hacking into Newton station's flight control centre. Although technically illegal, this unauthorised use of flight control data was covered under Imperial law during times of war. It was seen as a necessary step in the war on terror that had been incessantly fought for the last fifty years. With the occurrence of the Blackout and the subsequent terrorist actions on Newton Station, Ferine's men were well within their legal, if not moral, rights to access the information

Just five minutes earlier, Ferine and his team had been relieved to see the ANZAR escape vehicle return to orbit after somehow escaping an attack from no less than six stealth fighters that had been sent to intercept them. Thankful that their position on the station had not been rendered redundant by the efforts of the Imperial Air Force's attempt at destroying the fleeing ship, the Private had tracked the VAPER to within three hundred kilometres of the station before losing its signal from the radar screen.

On seeing the ship heading back in their general direction, Ferine had begun to hope that the fleeing ANZAR staff had seen sense and were intent on returning to the relative safety of the station. For him, that would have been ideal. The return of the

Feynman would have solved all of Ferine's problems in a matter of minutes. He could have just sat back and waited for the terrorists and all the research onboard the runaway vessel to come to him.

In hindsight, that was a stupid assumption, Ferine thought.

Private Dockrill leaned in close enough to the screen for his breathe to fog the glass slightly. Amongst the multi-coloured radar signals that represented the routine traffic movements of incoming and outgoing sub-orbital flights to Newton Station, the Private stared at a now empty section of the screen that, until moments before, had shown a lone dot far off at the limit of the radar's range.

Ferine leaned further over the Private's shoulder and spoke quietly into his ear.

"Relax, kid. Whatever happened out there, I know it's not your fault. Just look at the data and give me your best interpretation of what you see."

"That's just it, Sir." Private Dockrill shrugged again. "There's nothing to see. Their radar signature simply faded out and disappeared. It just got smaller and smaller. It's almost like they shrank out of existence somehow."

"So, they simply just disappeared off the system? Could they have accelerated out of range?"

"Not possible, Sir. Although they were at the radar's sensor limits, they were still well within range to not be able to slip off the screen without leaving a trail. Their radar signature did a strange thing as it disappeared; it seemed to grow smaller, or less dense until it no longer registered."

The two men stared at each other, saying nothing. The Private took Ferine's silent stare for a look of disbelief. "Seriously, Sir. That's what the data is telling me happened. There's no other explanation for it."

"Okay," Ferine soothed the agitated troop as he stood and faced the rest of the room. "I believe you. After the Blackout, I wouldn't be surprised by what these guys can do. God knows what sorts of gadgets and gizmos they've got aboard that thing."

Ferine patted the Private on the shoulder as an act of reassurance before making his way over to the captive ANZAR staff that still lined the back wall of the control room.

"Doctor Tran!" Ferine called to the engineer who was now seated with his colleagues. "It looks like I owe you an apology. From what we've seen on screen, it appears as if you were telling me the truth after all." Ferine gestured for Tran to approach.

"We have nothing to gain from lying to you, Captain," Tran said as he pulled himself to his feet.

"I hope you haven't said anything that would compromise the safety of our friends, Henry?" Fehrenbach spat from his place on the floor.

"Don't worry, Adam," Henry Tran said over his shoulder as he continued to walk towards Ferine. "You know as well as I do that they can't follow without our help."

Adam Fehrenbach stared at Doctor Tran. "Somehow I get the feeling you're about to give it to them."

Scarface fell in behind Tran as he approached Ferine and Private Dockrill at the computer terminal. He stared at the back of the Engineer's head with a look that revealed he was hoping the man in front of him would do something stupid so he could give the engineer a good old pistol whipping.

"I think it's time we put your team to work by putting that idea you mentioned into effect," Ferine spoke calmly as he saw a direct plan of action unfold before him. "How long will it take for you to get the second one of those spaceships up and running for us?"

"Oh, not long," The doctor smiled. "The *Hawking* is in full working order. All I have to do is replace a few key components that I had removed and hidden before your arrival. I can have it ready by the time Doctor Anderson gets through with you."

"Well, we may as well get started then, hadn't we?" Ferine turned to Scarface who was watching this brief conversation with only a minimum of interest. "Scar, take the doctor to the Engineering bay and make sure he doesn't get up to anything he shouldn't."

The gouged flesh on Scarface's cheeks changed shape as he attempted his peculiar version of a smile. The look was less than light-hearted and far from genuine. "Don't worry, Sir. I'll make sure he doesn't get up to anything he shouldn't."

Scarface turned to Doctor Tran and motioned towards the door with his rifle. "Come on you, let's go."

Before they could take more than a few steps towards the door, Ferine called out. "Hang on a minute, Scar. I've changed my mind."

Scarface turned to Ferine with an impatient look. "Yes, Sir?" he snarled.

"On second thoughts, I think I'll get Jackson to escort the Doctor to the engineering bay." Ferine believed that the likelihood of the doctor having an 'accident' would be significantly reduced with Jackson watching over him. At this stage of the operation, the old engineer was far too valuable to risk with the likes of Scarface. Ferine nodded towards his second in command who immediately stepped forward to escort Doctor Tran from the room.

Turning back towards Scarface, Ferine gave the disgruntled troop new orders. "I want you and Dockrill to take the rest of these prisoners and lock them in that meeting room we searched earlier." Ferine patted the Private on the shoulder as he rose to his feet and grabbed his weapon.

"I want both of you to come straight back here once you're done. We've got a planeload of Australian troops on the way, and I don't want to be around when they arrive."

"So, you're letting us go?" Adam Fehrenbach asked from his place on the floor.

"Pretty much," Ferine replied as he turned away from the door to face the ANZAR staff. "I don't have the time or the inclination to bundle you lot aboard our transport and send you back to the surface. Besides, you aren't what I was sent here for anyway. What I need is with your friends that left the station on that spaceship."

"And you plan on going after it?" Doctor Anderson asked. "That's not your problem." Ferine waved the barrel of his rifle over the prisoner's heads with one hand while the other gestured for them to stand up.

"Come on, get up. These two gentlemen here will escort you to the meeting room down the hall where you can sip instant coffee and thank God for your change in luck until someone turns up to let you out."

As the ANZAR staff warily rose to their feet, Ferine stepped forward and gently grabbed Doctor Anderson by the forearm.

"Doctor Anderson. Before you can join the others, I'm going to need you to accompany us into the medical bay downstairs. We're in need of your... abilities."

"If you or any of your men need medical treatment I will do what I can to help," the doctor replied as he stepped away from the other ANZAR staff.

"From what I've heard of you I wouldn't be surprised," Ferine replied. "You seem to be quite fond of using your scalpel on your patients whether they require it or not."

Doctor Anderson said nothing. He just stared at Ferine, waiting for the other man to take this conversation where he feared it was going.

Sensing that he wasn't about to get a rise out of the Doctor, Ferine got straight to the point. "Doctor Tran tells me that to be able to travel in those vehicles your people have created. We need to have a full body scan and be implanted with a computer chip of some kind. Is that right?"

The idea of these people having the advantages of what this process would bring both chilled and excited the Doctor. He didn't know whether to be happy that this would see his work made public or to cry for all the destruction it would cause.

A slow nod was all the response he could give.

52
Everyone's a Terrorist

ANZAR meeting room – Newton Station.

¶7.44pm - Sunday, August 16th, 2048

Scarface was furious that Ferine intended to let the perpetrators of the Blackout go. With each step they took towards the meeting room, he grew more and more enraged that the bastards shuffling along behind him would get to walk away from the death and destruction they had caused.

Hell, sixteen members of C-Unit had died so we could get our hands on these pricks and now Ferine wants to let them go because it's too much trouble to ship 'em out? Scarface began to breathe deeper as his temper grew. Being at the front of the group, no one noticed his face twist and contort with rage as he became angrier and angrier.

No way, man. No way. This scum ain't gonna just walk. Not if I can do somethin' about it.

The door to the meeting room slid open as Scarface approached. The corridor and the people walking along it were bathed in the vibrant blue glow of Earthlight that shone through the meeting room's large window. Without entering, Scar stepped to one side of the door and glowered at the tops of each of the eleven ANZAR terrorist's heads as they entered the room.

Yeah, that's right. Bow your heads in shame you sick fuckers.

At the end of the queue, Private Dockrill stepped up to the door and stopped as he waited for Scarface to close and lock it in front of him. The young Private looked confused when, instead of sealing the room, Scarface spun on the spot and entered it. Not sure what was going on, Private Dockrill followed into what would become the most traumatic moment of his military career.

Unsure of what to do, the ANZAR scientists stood silently beside the table in the middle of the room. All eyes turned and stared at the large soldier that strode across the linoleum floor towards them.

Without saying a word, Scarface slid his sidearm from its holster, pushed it against Adam Fehrenbach's temple and pulled the trigger. A spray of blood and bone coated the face of the shocked ANZAR scientists as the side of Adam's head exploded.

Taken by surprise, Private Dockrill took a step backward and stared at the body as it crumpled to the floor with blood pumping from the gaping hole in its head. Crazy, confused thoughts flashed through the Private's mind as he struggled with what to do. This was entirely unexpected. They were just supposed to lock the prisoners in the room and head straight back to Ferine. This was beyond his range of experience. I mean, what do you do when a superior office goes nuts? What could he do? As crazy as Scarface was, he still outranked him.

A shrill scream broke out from one of the ANZAR scientists and snapped the Private out of his shock. He looked up in time to see Scarface turn his weapon on a young brunette with a bandage around her head and empty two shots into her face. Her head jerked backwards, and her body dropped to the floor beside Adam's.

Hesitantly, Dockrill took a step forward.

"Well, that's thirty points for me so far," Scarface said to no one in particular before placing the gun against the forehead of a junior lab technician and pulling the trigger.

"Make that forty."

"Stop, please! Why are you doing this?" one of Henry Tran's engineers pleaded as the group began to back away from the apparently insane soldier.

"Why am I doing this?" Scarface replied as he spread his arms and shrugged to show how obvious the answer to the question was. "Why do you think, Asshole?"

Scarface stepped forward and placed the muzzle of his pistol under the chin of the young engineer who had spoken and snarled into his face.

"You fuckers killed tens of millions of people when you made the Blackout happen. You're all just a bunch of stinking terrorists who deserve to die. I'm gonna do you all just like we did Bin Laden. You should all feel lucky that I'm in a hurry otherwise you wouldn't be getting done as quick as you are."

The young engineer shook as Scarface stared at him in disgust. The hot barrel of the man's pistol slowly burned a mark on the underside of the man's chin as he stood there waiting to die.

"Sir," Private Dockrill finally spoke up from behind Scarface. "We should be getting back, Sir."

The young soldier sounded almost frail and as terrified as the ANZAR scientists who stood in the middle of the room. He was just a young kid who had run away to join the military as a slightly less unappealing alternative to working the family farm for the rest of his life. He wasn't a killer. Hell, he'd only finished basic training three months ago and hadn't even had the chance to fire his weapon at a living target yet. He knew he wasn't capable of doing what he knew needed to be done. Especially not to a superior officer.

"Yeah, you're right, kid," Scarface snarled. He stared into the young engineer's eyes as they began to trickle tears.

"We should be getting a move on." Scarface leant in close to the young engineer who was now weeping openly and whispered in his ear. "After I'm through here, we're going to hunt down your friends who fucked off in that little bauble spaceship of yours and do the same thing to them that I'm about to do to you."

Scarface smiled and turned to the group who stood huddled against the back wall a few feet away. "The only good terrorist is a dead terrorist," he said gravely.

"We're not terrorists," was all the young engineer could manage to say through his tears.

Without looking back at him, Scarface squeezed the trigger and blew off the top of the young engineer's head.

"Fifty," he said as he raised the weapon in one swift movement and aimed it at the rest of the group.

"Everyone's a terrorist," he said before quickly taking aim at each of the nine remaining ANZAR staff and shooting them in the head. Most fell without a fight. A few tried to run but took no more than one or two steps before being shot down.

In a matter of seconds, the shooting was over. Scarface stared down at the crumpled bodies of the ANZAR staff and began to count on his fingers. After a moment's pause in which he stopped to stare at the blue glow of the Earth in the meeting room window, he turned to Private Dockrill who stared at the pile of corpses.

"One-sixty." Scarface smiled at the young Private who gave an involuntary jump on hearing his voice.

"Huh?" Dockrill stammered.

"One-sixty. I got one hundred and sixty points for that lot." He smiled, pleased with himself. "That puts me way ahead of anyone else in the competition. Looks like that nine hundred and fifty bucks is all mine."

Scarface looked at the Private and for the first time noticed the look on the kid's face. He took a few steps forward and lightly punched the Private in the shoulder.

"Hey, cheer up kid." He smiled as he slid his pistol back into its holster. "You're not out of the game yet. You can still catch up by bagging a few of the targets who fled in that spaceship thing. Hell, there are a couple of kids in that group, and they're worth one hundred points each. Bag them, and you'll have this thing wrapped up."

Private Dockrill stared at Scarface. A minor wave of relief washed over him as he realised the older soldier had mistaken his shock for disappointment at losing the points game.

Scarface patted the Private on the shoulder as he made his way towards the door. "C'mon kid. Let's go get the rest of these stinkin' terrorists."

With a whoosh, the door slid open, and Scarface left the room. Private Dockrill stared at the bodies as a tear ran down his cheek. He wiped it away and muttered two words to the dead ANZAR scientists whom he had failed to help.

"I'm sorry," he sighed and walked out of the room.

Continued in
EARTH TO EARTH
Many Deaths In The Multiverse:
Book Two

OUT NOW

www.manydeathsinthemultiverse.com